THE
INVENTORS

D0302271

Alexander Gordon Smith, 28, is a rubbish inventor. He can barely hammer in a nail without breaking a window, and probably a finger too. However, he isn't bad with a pen and paper, and has written a number of non-fiction books as well as contributing to several magazines. He also runs his own publishing company, Egg Box, which promotes talented new writers and poets. He lives in Norwich. *The Inventors* is his first children's book and was shortlisted for The Wow Factor competition. Gordon created the book with his brother, Jamie Webb, who is eleven and much better at inventing.

'It's a great story that moves at such an entertaining pace that it leaves the reader open-mouthed with excitement, rooting for the young characters and wishing you were just a little bit more like them yourself. In a novel like this, the story needs to fairly rattle along and this one rattles, rocks and rolls.' John Boyne, author of *The Boy in the Striped Pyjamas*

'*The Inventors* is a captivating story that should not be missed. It is refreshing, imaginative and thoroughly exciting – I only wish I had written this amazing book myself!' G. P. Taylor, author of *Shadowmancer*

'*The Inventors* is a thrilling read . . . There are moments of humour, adventure and sadness, but I kept on reading to see what would happen next. There are some unexpected twists in the tale that make the book even more exciting. I'll tell all my friends to buy a copy!' Robin Geddes, aged eleven, winner of 2005 Junior Mastermind

THE INVENTORS

ALEXANDER GORDON SMITH

AND JAMIE WEBB

First published in 2007
by Faber and Faber Limited
3 Queen Square London WC1N 3AU

Typeset by Faber and Faber Limited
Printed in England by Mackays of Chatham plc, Chatham, Kent

A CIP record for this book
is available from the British Library

ISBN 978-0-571-23310-6
ISBN 0-571-23310-4

2 4 6 8 10 9 7 5 3 1

For Lynsey and Lucy.
And for Mum, without whom, for so many reasons,
this book would never have been written.

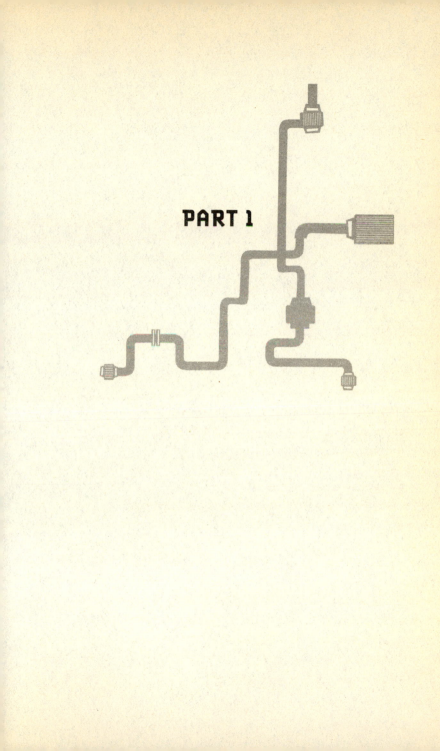

PART 1

1

A Very Bad Day Indeed

Nathan Wright was so excited that he couldn't lie still. Beams of light had started forcing their way through the cracks in his curtains ten minutes ago, revealing his duvet – crumpled after a sleepless night. Seven o' clock was only moments away, and then he'd know for sure if the weeks of hard work he'd devoted to his latest project were going to have been worth it.

His mother had made it very clear that he wasn't supposed to bring his inventions inside, especially when they involved the furniture. For that reason, he'd had to be extra careful. The wires he'd rigged to his bed, and to his wardrobe, were hidden inside special grooves carved into the walls (his father would murder him if he found out he'd ruined the plasterwork) and the springs beneath his bed were cleverly disguised as storage boxes. Robotic mechanisms inside the wardrobe had been harder to keep secret, but his mum had been so pleased when he'd offered to put away his own clothes every night that she hadn't ventured in there for quite some time.

The fat pigeon that always sat on the elm tree outside his window had started crooning, as it did every morning just before his alarm clock went off. It couldn't be long now, and he shuffled his body to the centre of the bed in preparation for the moment of truth.

Nate had seen this invention so many times in cartoons and never imagined he could actually make it work. But the maths was right, the scale model had been tested, and as far as he could tell everything would work perfectly.

The pigeon cooed extra loudly, hiccuped then went silent, and moments later Nate's alarm rang out. Behind the shrill whistle of his clock he heard the whirr of the gears beneath his mattress, and the whine of the wire as it tensed. The bed began to tremble – then, with a lurch that made Nate's stomach reel and his head spin, the top half sprang upwards like a catapult, sending him soaring across the room.

Time seemed to slow down, and as Nate saw the bedroom wall fly towards him he suddenly wished he'd spent more time making sure his calculations were right. He prepared for a painful impact, but at the last minute the timer in the wardrobe was activated and the door flew open.

When he'd tried this experiment with one of his mum's treasured china figurines in a model bedroom, it had flown into the specially padded door before the pre-programmed mechanical arms had removed a scruffy pair of pyjamas (which he'd sewn together from an old sock) and dressed it in a terrific three-piece suit and bowler hat. But as soon as Nate flew into the soft padding of the spare duvet taped to the wardrobe door he knew something was wrong.

The mechanical arms shot out from the top of the wardrobe in his direction, as planned, but instead of gripping Nate they missed him and grasped the frame of the upturned bed. Tensing, they pulled upwards as though removing a pyjama top, but the heavy bed refused to budge. A terrible groaning sound came from inside the wardrobe as the gears struggled with the weight.

The strain was too much for the wires behind his Wallace and Gromit wallpaper, and with a twang they flew outwards like metal whips, releasing a plume of plaster into the air. One swiped across the desk sending blueprints, papers and even his mum's well-dressed china doll on to the carpet. Nate threw himself to the floor to avoid a second wire that whistled past his ear and slashed a giant hole in the school jumper that hung from the door knob.

Looking up, he saw the wardrobe tilting towards him as the robotic arms continued to wrestle with the bed. Socks and T-shirts were sliding off the shelves and he barely managed to scrabble out from a pile of cotton before the wardrobe tumbled, crashing down on to the floor where he had been lying. Unaware of what was happening, the robotic arms that were still fixed to the top of the wardrobe groped around the floor helplessly in search of items of clothing.

In the silence that followed Nate heard the muffled sound of a door slamming down the hallway, followed by running foot-steps. His bedroom door crashed open to reveal two shocked faces gazing at the chaos in his room. It seemed as though minutes passed before his mum managed to speak.

'Nathan!' was all she could say. He could tell from her expression that she was flabbergasted. In fact, this was by far the most gasted her flabber had ever been. When she was annoyed she yelled at him endlessly, but he knew when she was truly angry because she barely said a word. She just stared at him, like she was doing now.

She took a step forward, waving her arms to clear the thick cloud of plaster dust that hung in the air, and scanned the small room, her eyes eventually settling on the pile of cracked china that had once been number three in her Women of the World collection. The head was the only thing that was recognisable, and it smiled up at them, still wearing a miniature black bowler hat.

'It's okay, Mum,' Nate said, his voice little more than a whisper. 'I'll clean it up.'

'My plasterwork!' his dad answered in a pitiful voice as he

 5

entered the room, dropping to his knees in front of the walls, two of which had enormous gashes along their length from the escaping wires. He looked as though he was about to cry.

Nate picked himself up off the floor and smoothed down his short black hair. He looked at his parents, trying to think of an excuse but knowing this time he wouldn't be able to explain himself. His mother turned to him, her mouth still wide open in shock.

'What have you –' she began, but before she could finish the wardrobe's robotic arms slammed a pair of tracksuit trousers over her head then dropped to the ground, limp and broken. From inside the trousers his mother's furious voice was little more than a muffled drone, which was just as well as Nate knew what she was saying wasn't pretty.

Hanging his head, he tried to work out what had gone wrong, but all he could think about was the fact that today was turning out to be a very bad day indeed.

The Wright family ate breakfast in stony silence. Peter Wright stared into his porridge with the look of a man who had just lost his winning lottery ticket. Nate couldn't make out what he was muttering about, but every now and again he caught the words 'plaster' and 'ruined'.

Wendy Wright sat at the opposite end of the table spreading butter on her toast so violently that the bread was coming to pieces in her hands. For a moment Nate thought there actually was steam shooting from her ears, before he realised it was the kettle behind her coming to boil. She hadn't said anything to him, hadn't even looked at him for that matter, since they'd stormed out of his bedroom.

Nathan had been an inventor for as long as he could remember. In fact, he'd started inventing things so young he *couldn't* remember them, and had to rely on stories from his parents about the self-recycling training pants or temperature-regulating milk bottles.

Some of his inventions worked, which went down well with his parents (his mum hadn't needed to do the dishes for three years since he'd come up with the Scrub-o-Matic 3000). But more often than not they ended in the same way as this morning. Or worse. Like the time he tried to make a weather machine, accidentally freezing his Aunt Betty for three days. When she'd come round in a hospital room full of equipment she had been convinced that aliens had stored her in ice and awoken her in the future. It had taken four years of counselling to convince her of the truth.

He always blamed his equipment, or lack of, for these disasters – because his mum and dad were so loath to provide him with supplies that might be used for inventing, he had to rely on anything and everything he found lying around the house. Hardly ideal conditions.

Despite this, inventing was what he loved more than anything else. When he put his brain into gear and started thinking about what new machines the world could really do with, and what new gadgets would help out his family and friends, there was no stopping him. It wasn't that he'd had any special training, or got it from his parents. He wasn't classed as a genius, and got fairly average marks at school. His mind just operated in a particular way – he could see how things were put together, how they worked. And a healthy obsession with scientific journals, textbooks and even instruction manuals for self-assembly furniture always came in handy.

He would disappear into his room, activate his inventing desk (neatly stored inside his walls to cause minimum clutter –

another sore point involving plasterwork) and spend hours drawing up blueprints, with his mum and dad hovering nervously outside the door to get a glimpse of whatever experiment he'd be involved in next.

His parents thought his love of inventing was unhealthy, and tried repeatedly to get him to go outside more.

'You're thirteen years old, Nathan. Why don't you play with your friends?'

It wasn't that he didn't have friends (although there were those at his school who thought his love of inventing made him a prime candidate for bullying). Actually, his best friend was an inventor as well. Sophie, who for reasons she never told anybody liked to be called Cat, had been inventing for almost as long as he had, and they had worked together on hundreds of projects. He'd known Cat since they were both newborn babies at the local hospital, and they'd been sharing spanners and wrenches since they were toddlers – which owed a great deal to the fact that Cat's dad had also been an inventor.

Nate's parents had wanted him to expand his social circle, as they put it, but with a friend like Cat he never saw the need – they were lucky enough to have found in each other their perfect inventing soulmate.

The thought of Cat ended his daydream and brought him back to the kitchen table. His parents were still frowning, but his mum seemed to have calmed down and now sat staring at her butchered toast, doing her best to work out how much it would cost to repair his room.

'I'd better go,' Nate said, glancing from his mum to his dad then back again. 'I'll be late for school.'

The seconds seemed to last for hours before his dad finally looked up at him. He had an extremely serious look on his face that would have been scary if it wasn't for the enormous dollop of porridge in his beard.

'Just remember that we can't go on paying for your mistakes, Nathan,' he said, his mouth full of half-chewed breakfast. 'Sooner or later this chaos has to stop, or we'll all end up on the streets!' He sighed, and the porridge on his face fell to the table with a splat. 'It has to stop, just remember that.'

2

Things Get Worse

But Nate had forgotten all about his Dad's warning as soon as the front door slammed shut behind him. His mind was on the experiment that he and Cat had tried out at school the previous day. It wasn't one of their most complicated tests to date, nor was it one of their kindest, but it was by far the most exciting.

It had been Cat's idea to use an experiment to get revenge on one of the most devious and horrible bullies in the country, Rachel Whitmore. Like many pupils at Heaton Middle School, Rachel hated the fact that Nate and Cat were cleverer than her. But while most were content to ignore the two inventors, she had spent every lunch break for the last three years jamming their heads into hedges, ruining literally hundreds of pairs of pants through violent wedgies and claiming a small fortune in dinner money as a protection fee (which, needless to say, never protected them from anything).

Rachel was one of the tallest kids in school, was built like a truck and had no perceivable weaknesses except for a love of the chocolate brownies they sold in the canteen at break time. Of course, this wasn't really a weakness at all but Cat saw it as the only way they were going to be able to get to her. Between them they had devised a chemical formula so powerful that even the most ferocious bully would fall foul of it. Bully Blow, Nate had wanted to call it, although Cat had insisted on the name Pergophosphaticus III, which didn't roll off the tongue quite as easily but sounded much more impressive.

As Nate rounded the corner of his road the sun emerged from the misty layer of clouds that hung above the town, illuminating the hordes of people fighting past each other to get to work on time. Not wanting to be jostled and barged by the morons in suits, Nate slung his bag over the crumbling brick wall that separated the road from the public park, then climbed over into the field beyond.

With the glorious heat of the sun on his face he strolled along the dewy grass in the direction of the school, trying to control his excitement as he pictured the various results of the experiment.

To the uneducated eye Pergophosphaticus III was simply a random bunch of kitchen ingredients thrown into a food processor and blended into a rather unattractive purée. But to those who knew about the secret properties of the select ingredients the lumpy blue mixture that sat burbling quietly at the bottom of the blender became a far more sinister substance.

Cat had selected over twenty products from her kitchen cupboards, including a frighteningly large amount of blue food dye, and thrown them in with a secret ingredient. After a little fine tuning (and a great deal of mess), the finished product was perfect for what they both had in mind.

'I'll bet you a brand-new welding iron that you're thinking what I'm thinking,' said a voice to Nate's left. He jumped, and swung his head around to see Cat, who was standing in the shade of a chestnut tree, watching him walk by.

'Actually, I was just thinking about what a *blue*-tiful day it is,' he answered as she pushed herself away from the trunk and strolled over, brushing a strand of short brown hair away from her eyes.

'I know, it's been too long since the wind *blue* like this,' she said after she'd bent down to give him a tiny peck on the cheek, and they both laughed as they cut across the park. 'Seriously, though,' she continued, 'do you think it worked?'

'It has to have worked,' Nate said, shifting his bag to his other shoulder so it wasn't pressing against the bruise he'd received that morning. 'It worked in your granddad's tea, remember?'

He thought back to Cat's poor grandfather, who spent all day every day staring at the telly in a care home on the other side of town. They'd sneaked a concentrated dose into his tea and he had changed colour in minutes. The nurse on duty had run around his room three times in an uncontrollable panic, and wedged her foot into a bedpan, before they managed to calm her down enough to explain his unnatural colour change.

'But maybe we didn't use enough on Rachel?' Cat continued, chewing her lip like she always did when she was worrying too much. 'Or perhaps it doesn't work the same way on children?'

'We definitely used enough,' said Nate. He could picture them using the turkey baster to inject the mixture into the brownie, bought at school earlier that day. They'd used so much that it had been oozing out of the sides resembling, thankfully, blueberry jam.

'But maybe she didn't eat it.'

Nate laughed out loud as they exited the park and crossed the road that led up to their school. Pupils of all ages were approaching the main gates but Nate couldn't see any bright blue faces. He realised that he also had a bruise on his other shoulder and took off his bag, dragging it behind him.

'Are you kidding?' he replied. 'Rachel would eat every brownie in the canteen if she could get her greedy mitts on them.'

He remembered the way they'd unwrapped the brownie right in front of her, in the section of the playground that double-backed around the side of the school, where there were no windows and no teachers. Her eyes had practically bulged out of their sockets and she'd started drooling like a starving dog before storming across the tarmac and snatching it out of Cat's hands, sending streamers of blue juice everywhere. She'd disappeared into a dark little hollow in the hedge to gnaw at her prize while Nate and Cat had walked off pretending to be upset.

'You're right,' she admitted as they entered the school grounds and headed for their form room. 'But I guess there's only one way to find out!'

Grinning at each other they quickened their pace, fighting through corridors full of shouting students and tired, pale-faced teachers. As they passed one group Nate heard the words 'completely blue' and he turned to Cat in amazement. She returned his wide-eyed gaze with one of her own and they broke into a run as they rounded the last corner before their class.

Bursting through the doors, they scanned the rows of faces in front of them desperate to find Rachel's, but when they did they were shocked to see it hadn't changed colour at all. Nobody's face seemed even remotely out of the ordinary.

In fact, the only unusual thing about the class was that everybody was sitting in complete silence, staring at Nate, Cat and at one other figure who stood silently in the shadows in the corner of the room.

'Oops,' Nate heard Cat whisper in his ear. The man began walking towards them, looking absolutely furious, and Nate's jaw dropped as he recognised the headmaster, whose face, hair and hands had all turned a rather remarkable shade of blue.

The rooms that made up the headmaster's office were on the top floor of the main building, lined with enormous windows overlooking the school field, and shelf after shelf of ancient books that he had collected over the years. He led Nate and Cat past his secretary, who did her best not to stare at his face, and slammed open the enormous wooden door that led to the Head Office.

They both shuffled in, Nate looking up from the floor only once to glance at the nameplate on the door that said Mr Green, and wondering if it would now have to be changed.

There were two chairs by the headmaster's desk and Nate and Cat both sat down, staring at their feet. Behind them they heard Mr Green close the door, then the unmistakable sound of it being locked.

Nate suddenly felt afraid. Were teachers still allowed to beat pupils with slippers and canes and old volumes of GCSE maths books? In fact, Mr Green could probably lock them both up for ever and just tell their parents they had run away. He tried to squeeze himself deeper into the leather chair, hoping that the headmaster would just forget he was there. But there was no chance of that. They had turned him blue, after all.

There was the sound of footsteps on the carpeted floor and Mr Green appeared in front of them, sitting himself down in the carved wooden throne on the other side of the desk. Nate didn't want to look at him, but after what seemed like an eternity of silence curiosity got the better of him and he glanced up.

The man in front of them was exactly the same colour as a Smurf. Even his hair had turned an identical shade of blue. In the purple suit he had chosen to wear that morning he resembled a massive blueberry with two white, angry eyes glaring out at them – with blue pupils, of course. He looked back and forth between Nate and Cat, occasionally opening his mouth as if to speak before closing it again, unable to think of what to say.

'First, how long does it last,' he spluttered eventually. Nate stared back down at his feet (noticing, under the desk, that Mr Green's ankles were also blue) and tried to think of a suitable answer, but Cat spoke first.

'Um . . .' she began, 'we're not sure yet. My granddad was still blue this morning, but we only tested it last night.'

'Granddad?' Mr Green asked, eyebrows and voice raised. 'You tested it on your granddad?!'

'It wasn't meant for you,' Nate interrupted.

'I know that,' Mr Green snapped back. 'I saw you give that brownie to Rachel. I – uh – confiscated it from her after you left.'

'You stole the brownie?' Cat asked.

Mr Green looked at her. 'No, I confiscated it.'

'That's the same thing!' Nate said, folding his arms across his chest.

'No, it's not. You'd gone, and it would have just been thrown away otherwise.' Mr Green had turned a little red with embarrassment, making him an odd shade of maroon. 'Anyway, that's not the point!' He got to his feet and began pacing back and forth behind the desk. 'I was at a very important dinner last night with the board of inspectors. I was due a pay rise! But midway through dessert my wife tells me I'm turning blue, and sure enough . . .'

He didn't need to finish the story; his face spoke for itself. Collapsing back into his chair he held out his podgy hands and looked at them sadly.

Nate and Cat sat in silence, both feeling extremely guilty. The only sound in the room was the slow ticking of the grandfather clock by the door, and Nate counted four minutes and twenty-two seconds before the headmaster spoke again.

'You two ought to know better,' he went on, his tone softer. 'I mean what if this stuff is dangerous? You especially, Sophie, should know what can happen when an invention goes wrong.'

The headmaster was referring to Cat's dad, Harold Gardner, who had been a legend in the inventing world until his untimely death six years ago. He had been working on a machine designed to generate water for drought-ridden countries, but had pushed himself too far and accidentally blown up the prototype that he'd been working on. He had perished alongside his invention.

Cat snapped her head up at the mention of her dad, unwilling to tolerate a bad word about him. But Mr Green's next words stopped her in her tracks.

'The school year has just started, and this sort of stunt is enough to get you both expelled,' he said. Nate felt his heart sink. Cat's expression had instantly turned from one of anger to one of desperation. She had tears in her eyes as she gazed at the floor. Mr Green looked at them and scratched his bulbous nose, which was a particularly striking colour. 'But I'm not going to ruin your futures by doing that.'

Both Nate and Cat looked at him, confused.

'You two are pretty much the brightest pupils we have here at Heaton,' he went on, leaning over the desk, 'at least you would be if you spent less time inventing and more time on your homework! And as much as I'd like to come into school one week and not have to face up to one of your ridiculous gadgets, there's no denying that you both have a real talent for ideas. I mean, people train for years to become inventors but you both seem to have a natural ability to see how things work. It's actually quite remarkable.'

Nate and Cat looked at each other, still confused.

'So listen,' Mr Green continued, 'instead of wasting these talents on teaching bullies a lesson, why not try and put them to better use?' He opened a drawer in his desk and pulled out a sheet of paper. 'Have either of you heard of Ebenezer Lucian Saint?'

Before Nate could even open his mouth to reply Cat had practically leapt from her chair.

'Saint?' she cried out. 'Of course I have. He's pretty much the most amazing inventor on the planet!'

Ebenezer Saint *was* the most amazing inventor on the planet. When only eighteen he had come up with the KleverKar, the small motor that ran on garden waste and caused no pollution, which had made him a multimillionaire. Now, aged only thirty-four, he was the head of Saint Solutions, the vast company that made practically everything from MegaMouse, the computer mouse that worked by the power of thought alone, to the Bubblematic, a suit with a built-in shower that had been adopted by almost every businessman and commuter on the planet. But the reason Cat was so excited was that he had also taken on Harold Gardner's invention after he died, making a working version and giving all the credit to Cat's father.

Saint was loved by some for his contributions to medicine, and feared by others who thought, quite rightly, that he was the most powerful man on the planet. Filthy rich and famous, he rarely appeared in public, but when he did there was always a stir.

'Good,' the headmaster continued. 'Well, you might be interested to know that he has arranged a competition for pupils in schools across the country. An inventing competition.'

Nate and Cat were on the edge of their seats. This was the last thing they had expected after being marched to the Head Office.

'What kind of inventing competition?' Nate asked.

'You have a month to come up with an idea so amazing, so stupendous, so utterly indispensable that Saint Solutions takes it on,' Mr Green read from the paper, drawing out his words to keep the suspense.

'So that's the prize?' asked Cat.

'No,' Mr Green went on. 'The prize for the twenty-five winners is a scholarship with Ebenezer himself at Saint Solutions, for a year.'

The room was deathly silent once again as Nate and Cat sat there, mouths agape, not daring to say a word.

'You get to work and study with Saint and, if you do a good enough job, he'll employ you when you've finished. You'd complete your academic education in conjunction with inventing work.'

'And all we have to do is invent something?' Cat asked, her voice barely audible.

'All you have to do is invent something that's better than the other few thousand entrants,' the blue headmaster answered.

'In a month?' Nate added weakly.

Mr Green leant even further over the desk, his arms splayed, his face so close to theirs that Nate could see all the little blue pores.

'I didn't enter you to start off with,' he said, 'because I thought it would interfere with your schoolwork. But after this,' he pointed to his blue face with a blue finger, 'I had second thoughts. The deadline is the tenth. You have less than a week.'

3

An Absence of Ideas

Mr Green unlocked the door and held it open for them, ushering them out with a chorus of 'it's all rights' and 'just don't let it happen agains'. Nate and Cat stood in the secretary's office unable to think of a single word to say to each other. To have moved so quickly from fears of expulsion to the opportunity of a lifetime had scrambled all logical thought.

'Um . . . classes have started, you two,' said Miss Jones the secretary. She was staring at them with a concerned expression as though they had just been given lobotomies by the headmaster.

'A week,' Nate whispered, ignoring her.

'Less than a week,' Cat replied in equally soft tones. 'Four days, to be precise.'

'Classes. Started. Now,' said the secretary, drumming her painted fingernails on the desk.

'Four days to impress Ebenezer Lucian Saint.'

'Four days to come up with something so amazing, so stupendous, so utterly indispensable that Saint Solutions takes it on.'

'Four days to make sure we don't waste our only chance to work with the master inventor for a whole year.'

Miss Jones was about to speak again when the intercom box on her table squawked loudly, causing all three people to jump.

'It will be four days' detention if you don't get to class,' barked Mr Green's crackled voice. 'Now hop it before I change my mind!'

The day seemed to plod by excruciatingly slowly. After racing from the headmaster's office Nate and Cat split up, Nate having to endure an hour of biology with Mr Cramp and a gruelling PE session of Murderball ('Rugby without the rules' as Bruce the student teacher would cheerfully call it), while Cat sat through double history with a tiny, short-sighted supply teacher who insisted that everybody's name was Dale.

Lunchtime was spent avoiding both Mr Green and Rachel, which proved extremely difficult because the headmaster and the bully were trying to avoid each other and that didn't leave much of the playground free.

By the afternoon Nate was tired and grumpy after such an exhausting morning, but thankfully he and Cat were in the same class until the end of the day. Religious education was usually a terrible bore but today Mrs Allen had a stomach ache and was content to sit them in front of a sequence of videos for two hours.

Taking a seat near the back, Nate and Cat huddled behind their desk as the room went dark and the first tape – 'Being Buddhist' – fizzled into action on the tiny screen. The volume was far too loud, giving the two inventors all the cover they needed to plan their invention.

'Any ideas?' Cat asked, glancing up at the teacher on the far side of the room, who sat with her head in her hands looking as though it was the end of the world.

'A couple,' Nate lied. He'd been thinking about it ever since that morning but in all the excitement he hadn't been able to get his brain into gear. 'What about you?'

Apparently Cat hadn't faced the same problem.

'I thought maybe a vehicle of some kind,' she whispered,

waiting for a quiet shot of a Tibetan village to end before continuing. 'Since that's what made Saint famous. What about a floating armchair that carries you around the house?'

'Four days, Cat,' was Nate's response.

'Okay, what about a rocket-propelled go-kart to get kids to school on time?' Nate held up four fingers and made a ticking sound.

'Fine, then why don't we start work on one of Dad's inventions – he had loads of ideas and nobody's done anything with them yet.'

'Cat, your dad was working on them all for years, and he still didn't crack them!' Nate said, shaking his head. 'Besides, it wouldn't be ours.'

'I know, I know. It has to be something new. How about an electronic book that lets you download any title in the world on to its pages.'

Nate slapped his forehead in frustration.

'Four days, yes I know.' Cat thought for a minute longer. 'What about a machine that prints money?'

'That's just illegal!' Nate answered, shocked.

'Oh, yeah. I forgot. Seemed like a good idea at the time.'

They were both silent for a moment as they watched the bespectacled Dalai Lama speak about Tibet.

'X-ray specs?' Nate ventured, regretting saying it immediately as Cat fixed him with a disappointed stare.

'Yes, Nate,' she answered sarcastically. 'Let's invent X-ray specs in four days.'

'Laser specs?'

'Nate.'

'Sorry.'

'I guess your dressing machine might be okay,' Cat whispered. 'You only started that a couple of weeks ago. How did it go, by the way?'

'Don't ask,' Nate replied, fingering his bruises. 'I didn't have any of the right materials so it was a complete disaster, and I'll need more than four days to fix it. Anyway, my folks won't want me playing with that idea any more.'

'Oh, parent problems again?'

'Worse than ever.'

'Guess we'll have to do this in my lab, then,' Cat said softly, meaning her bedroom. 'We could use one of our inventions and say it was new . . .'

'They'd find out, I'm sure,' Nate replied. 'We've brought all our best gadgets to school and the teachers would have to say something. And it just wouldn't feel right. I want to win this fair and square.'

'You're right,' Cat said, 'but that leaves us back at square one.'

'I'm sure we'll think of something.'

But no ideas had presented themselves by the end of RE and not even by the time they had left school and walked back towards Nate's along Main Street. In fact, as they entered the kitchen and slung their bags on the floor both Nate and Cat were extremely depressed.

'You two look miserable,' Nate's mum stated matter-of-factly as she strolled into the room, mug of tea in hand.

'Homework,' Nate answered, not wanting to talk about the incident with the headmaster so soon after that morning's disaster in the bedroom. 'Lots of it. Very hard.'

'Well you can't do it in your bedroom. Your father has locked himself in to fix your plasterwork and sealed the doors. You won't be allowed back for a few hours.'

'That's okay,' Nate answered, lifting an apple from the fruit bowl, looking at it for a few seconds then replacing it. 'I'm going to head over to Cat's. We've got a project.'

'Fine,' Wendy Wright muttered. Nate and Cat turned to leave but she called them back before they had reached the door.

'Oh, Nathan, I almost forgot. This came for you.' She rummaged around in her trouser pocket for a moment before pulling out a strip of paper. 'It was delivered by hand this morning.'

Nathan felt his heartbeat quicken. Who would deliver something to him by hand? Reaching over the counter he grabbed the paper from his mum and looked at it. His heartbeat quickened even further when he saw the simple, curved S of the Saint Solutions logo printed on it.

'Wow, that was quick,' said Cat, peering over his shoulder. 'Turn it over.'

'What was quick?' Wendy asked, but nobody was listening. Nate turned the paper over to reveal a photograph of Ebenezer Saint, with his trademark wild hair, dressed in shorts, shirt and a long coat, with his arm held out as if about to shake hands. There was nothing written on either side.

'That's odd,' said Cat. 'No instructions or anything.'

'What was quick, and what is odd?' Mrs Wright asked, her face suspicious.

'Oh it's just for this project,' Nate responded, ushering Cat out of the door and stuffing the paper into his pocket. 'Mr Green asked us to do it. It's perfectly legit!'

'Well as long as it doesn't involve any of your contraptions in my house I don't care,' she bellowed pointlessly as they slammed the front door behind them.

4

An Invitation

The walk to Cat's house usually took a little under ten minutes, but a year ago she had set up a handy aerial slide in the woods that ran along the back of her garden. This meant that if they took a slight detour down Queen Street and into the Bluebell Woods they could climb on to the seat, cleverly disguised by leaves and branches to stop unwanted travellers, then sit back and enjoy the ride which would carry them almost a kilometre to her back gate.

The great thing was that the seat was connected to a remarkably complex series of springs, cogs and levers. When activated, this mechanism could propel them through the woods at breakneck speed, slowing them to a gentle halt as they reached their destination. It was just as fast in the opposite direction, making it perfect for escaping domestic duties.

As they hurtled through the trees towards Cat's house, Nate took the time to finger the leaflet in his pocket. It was certainly odd that there was nothing written on it. Why would there just be a picture of Ebenezer Saint holding out his hand and nothing else? Where were the instructions, the terms and conditions, the rules and regulations, the details about prizes?

Perhaps it was simply a welcome card, a sign that you were in the competition, but then why didn't it say 'Welcome, you're in the competition'? He was desperate to have another look but he didn't dare let go of the rope – the last time he'd tried riding with no hands he'd ended up with severe whiplash after falling off.

Three minutes later the slide came to a halt by the back gate to Cat's house, a ramshackle green and yellow cottage surrounded by a veritable jungle of pot plants and flowers. Nate leapt off nimbly to tie the seat to the fencepost, putting the brake on to stop it shooting back through the woods without them. When it was secure, Cat eased herself off and skipped through the gate into her garden, making her way past the meandering chickens and the lone, wandering duck to the rear door. Taking a bunch of keys the size of a grapefruit from her bag, she sorted through them until she found the right one.

Nate hurried through the garden as quickly as possible, nervous of the chickens which had a habit of circling him ever since he'd once fed them cake. He dived in through the door, closing it behind him.

Cat had disappeared from the cluttered kitchen but he heard her rummaging around in the hallway. Unlike his stuffy parents, Cat's mum kept her house in a slightly more 'natural' state, meaning that the surfaces weren't always free of crumbs, footprints on the carpets were just part of the decoration, and the pot plants that seemed to be everywhere looked like wildflowers that had sprouted through the floor and walls.

It wasn't that she was untidy, but the family had always been more concerned with having fun than staying clean. Cat's dad had spent almost all of his time working in the capital, but when he found the time to come home he would play with his daughter all day – building toys, inventing gadgets and creating more mess than a herd of rampaging buffalo. When he died, Cat's mum decided to leave the house in a similar state of disarray – a constant reminder of his presence.

Coming here Nate always felt a huge sense of relief at not having to worry about mess. When Cat ruined her plasterwork her mum just smiled and slapped on some Polyfilla. Simple.

The sound of mail being pulled out of the letterbox came through from the hallway before Cat reappeared, triumphantly holding a familiar slip of paper in her hand along with a pile of official-looking bills and letters.

'It's the same as yours,' she said, throwing everything but the Saint flyer on to the counter. 'No words or anything, just the two pictures.'

'I'll bet a proper pack is in the post,' Nate said, taking his leaflet from his pocket and smoothing out the wrinkles that had occurred in transit. 'They have to send us something other than this.'

'Maybe Mr Green was supposed to give us more information,' Cat ventured, answering her own question before Nate could. 'But I guess he would have given us everything he had. He really does want us to win so we'll be out of his hair for a year.'

'His bright blue hair,' Nate commented, and they both burst out laughing, the tension of the day finally relieved. After a couple of minutes of uncontrollable giggling Nate realised he was dying for the toilet.

'Put the kettle on, Cat, I'll be back in a sec.'

Stuffing the leaflet back in his pocket he made a dash for the upstairs loo, taking the steps two at a time. He closed and locked the door, and was just lifting the toilet lid when he heard a voice behind him.

'What?' he shouted, thinking that it was Cat yelling something through the door. He would normally have ignored her, but last time he did that in her bathroom it turned out she was shouting to him that the toilet didn't work, which had left him in an extremely embarrassing situation that made him cringe even now, several years later.

There was no response for several seconds, then the voice

came again, causing Nate to jump in surprise.

'Nate, are you listening?' It was a man's voice, although it was quite high and playful, almost musical in tone, and it was coming from inside the bathroom.

'Yes,' he answered softly, the tremor in his voice a little more obvious than he would have liked. He wondered if the ghost of Cat's dad was still living in the house, and if so why he was only talking to him now after all these years and why he had picked such an inconvenient time.

'Good,' the voice continued. 'You don't know me, but my name is Ebenezer Lucian Saint.'

All of a sudden it clicked. Nate slammed down the toilet lid and wrenched the leaflet from his pocket. The image of Ebenezer Saint had not changed, but the paper was vibrating ever so slightly, as though something was alive inside it. Stunned, Nate sat down on the toilet and held the leaflet out in front of him.

'First,' the voice continued, 'let me say many thanks for entering my contest. I would have introduced myself sooner but I wanted to wait until you were alone – I know how competitive the business of inventing can be.'

Ebenezer's eyes seemed to look straight at Nate, and he felt for a moment as if they were boring into his brain, reading his mind.

'How does this work?' he asked, turning the paper over and over in his hands to try and work out where the speakers and the computer chips were located. It seemed impossible.

'I'm afraid that I can't answer your question, Nate,' the voice went on. 'This is a pre-recorded message, so I can't have a conversation with you just yet. Listen carefully, though, because I can tell you how the competition works.'

Nate shuffled on the uncomfortable toilet lid and prepared to take mental notes.

 27

'This contest is a one-off, a once-in-a-lifetime chance for the country's brightest young minds to work with me. It isn't just about inventing, it's about making the world a better place. There are two rounds: the first is to invent something so amazing, so stupendous, so utterly indispensable that Saint Solutions takes it on as a product. You only have one month to make this work, although in your case, Nate, you only have four days.'

Nate raised an eyebrow in surprise.

'But I have every faith you won't disappoint me. The winners of this first round – and there will only be fifty of you – will each earn a place in the final, which will take place at the Saint Solutions complex. Here, I will pick the twenty-five most promising young inventors in the country and offer them a year's scholarship with me.'

Nathan realised he was holding his breath, and let out a deep sigh as he waited for the voice to continue.

'The rules are simple. Inventions must have been thought of in the month leading up to the deadline, and they must be fully made. No bundles of sketches and blueprints, thank you! They must be handed in to your headmaster or headmistress on the day of the deadline ready for testing here at Saint Solutions. The good news is that we're pretty quick over here, and the fifty hopefuls will be announced a week later. Not long to spend chewing your nails, eh?'

Below him Nate heard the kettle come to a boil, and he strained to see if he could detect any voices from the kitchen. But Saint began again.

'Inventions can be anything, Nate, anything you dream is possible, although we do like those things that do good in this world. Weapons will be frowned on, although I know that won't stop some people from entering them into this competition. Not you, though, Nate – I sense great things from you.'

Nate felt his cheeks redden. It occurred to him that only his closest friends called him Nate. In fact, none of his teachers even knew he went by that name. How had Saint found that out?

'So, if you really want to enter, press your thumb against my palm.'

Nate shifted his thumb over the image of Ebenezer Saint's hand. There seemed to be something barely perceptible under the surface, something warm.

'But only do it if you really want to enter, if you really want to be part of something big. Once you've shaken my hand, Nate, there is no going back.'

He paused for a moment, suddenly nervous. It was just a competition, he thought. If he decided he didn't want to enter, he just wouldn't invent anything. But then, why wouldn't he want to enter?

'Stop being such a wuss,' he said out loud, moving his thumb over Saint's palm again. Taking a deep breath he pressed down on the warm patch.

The leaflet seemed to quiver for a second and Nate felt something soft move over the surface of his thumb. Lifting it off, he saw the faint trace of his fingerprint on the surface, set over the image of Saint's hand. As he watched, the whorls and lines of his print seemed to disappear into the paper, radiating an odd green light for a split second before vanishing completely.

'Thank you, Nate,' said Saint's voice. 'It's an honour to have you on board. Now, let's waste no more time and get inventing!'

And with that the vibrations inside the leaflet stopped. Nate sat still for a moment, unable to take in what had just happened. Perhaps he'd fallen off the aerial slide on the way here and was now dreaming all of this on the way to the hospital. That certainly seemed to be a more believable scenario than a talking, fingerprint-reading scrap of paper.

He turned the leaflet over in his hands again, trying to work out its secrets, holding it up to the light streaming in through the window to see if he could make out the mechanisms inside. But there was nothing. It was just a scrap of paper.

Unlocking the door, Nate bolted down the stairs, crashing into the kitchen and narrowly missing a spider plant by the door. He careered to a halt beside Cat who was standing by the counter staring at her leaflet in shock, her face pale and covered with beads of sweat. She slowly turned to look at him and he knew that she had just received the same message from Ebenezer Saint.

'This is serious,' she said. 'This really is our chance to work with Saint.'

Nate nodded, and opened his mouth to reply. But before he got the chance he realised that he was still absolutely bursting, and sprinted back upstairs to the bathroom as fast as his wobbly legs would carry him.

5

What a Spectacle!

After the excitement of a personalised message from Ebenezer Saint, both Nate and Cat were in desperate need of a cuppa. Cat especially. She sat on one of the tall stools in the kitchen slurping milky tea from a Harry Potter mug and gazing dreamily at the picture of the famous inventor, which she had pinned to the notice board above the breadbin.

'He's very good-looking, isn't he?' she said, dropping her head into her hands and sighing gently. Nate put down the packet of Ebenezer's Teasers he was munching on – the gear-shaped jelly sweets with the motto 'Don't Play With Your Food, Make Something With It!'. He looked at the image of Saint, then at Cat, then back at Saint.

'He has stupid hair,' was all he could think of to say. He wasn't quite sure why but he suddenly felt quite angry that Cat was drooling over Ebenezer. It wasn't that he wanted her to be his girlfriend – far from it, he had always turned his nose up at the idea. But at the same time he didn't want her to be anybody else's girlfriend either. Especially not somebody rich, famous and, yes, very good-looking.

'I wonder if we'll actually be working with him, or just his staff,' Cat said, frowning as if deep in thought.

'Probably just his staff. I can't imagine he'd have much time to work with twenty-five students all at once.'

'Well, I hope he does teach us personally. I'd love to meet him.'

'I bet you would,' Nate muttered beneath his breath, taking a big sip of tea. Cat didn't catch what he said but she understood the tone, and she sat up and turned to face him, smiling.

'Stop being such a jealous baby,' she said, poking him in the ribs with a finger. 'I know you want to meet him too.'

Nate brushed her hand away but smiled back. He actually really did want to meet Saint. He had done ever since, as a kid, he'd seen him on television when he was awarded the Nobel Prize. Saint had arrived somewhat dramatically, riding a contraption that looked like a cross between a helicopter and a unicycle, landing with a bump on the grass outside the building then cycling rather unsteadily to the ceremonial hall. He had stayed on the unicycle throughout the awards, even when he was presented with his prize, and then taken off after a brief interview with the press. He was, without doubt, a fascinating character.

And Nate knew that Cat's infatuation with Saint had nothing to do with his good looks. Cat and her dad had spent all their time together inventing and building, and when he had died the seven-year-old girl, blaming his occupation, had vowed never to touch a hammer or spanner again.

All this changed three years later, on the day that a white-suited man, riding in a ridiculously long limousine, had delivered a letter to Cat and her mum. Furnished with an elaborate seal, and written out in beautiful golden calligraphy, the letter was from Saint. It told them how Harold Gardner's Miracle Machine had been completed, and how it was going to save hundreds of thousands of lives. When Cat read the part about what an amazing man Saint thought her father had been, she instantly dived back into her toolbox and had never looked back.

'He still has stupid hair, though,' Nate joked when he stopped reminiscing.

'Fine,' Cat said, giving up the argument. 'He does have ridiculous hair.'

After finishing their tea they headed upstairs to Cat's bedroom to begin work. Her room was larger than Nate's and its complete opposite in almost every way. Where Nate had to keep clothes in the wardrobe, books on the shelves, CDs in the rack, pens in the pot, underwear in the drawer, toys in the cupboard and the bedding on the bed, Cat was free to arrange her living space any way she wanted, meaning that it was a glorious confusion of clutter. Apart from the underwear, that is – even Cat had some standards.

Piles of books, papers and CDs lay everywhere, one enormous stack of school manuals half hidden by the crumpled, misplaced purple duvet. Clothes were strewn here, there and everywhere, covering the unusual assortment of dolls, toys and scientific equipment that lay abandoned on the floor. As they tiptoed carefully around the mess Nate realised that he had never seen Cat's bedroom carpet.

Reaching her desk, Cat brushed off a sheaf of notes and sketches and pressed a button hidden beneath the bottom-most drawer. With a low, buzzing sound a panel set into the desktop slid away and a small laptop rose to the surface to sit next to the framed photograph of her dad. The lid opened automatically and a series of codes flashed across the screen.

At the same time, the drawers on the left-hand side of the desk slid out together, revealing a hidden compartment of scientific and mechanical equipment, including a colourful array of bubbling potions and mixtures left over from previous experiments.

While Cat logged in on her laptop Nate pinned his leaflet on the wall behind them, the image of Saint facing outwards as inspiration, then glanced upwards at the shelves that lined the wall opposite the door. They were full of the gadgets, gizmos and other wondrous machines that Cat had put together ever since she had picked up her first spanner. Literally hundreds of inventions were crammed on to the narrow wooden planks, all covered with a couple of centimetres of dust and what looked like an ancient spider city of cobwebs and dead flies.

His eyes fell on the bunch of wind-up toys that huddled together near the wall. There was a little drummer boy, which Cat had made up from a kit her dad had bought her one Christmas. She had become obsessed with them, working out what they were made of and how they moved and then building them herself from bits and pieces she found in the garage.

That was another big difference between Cat and himself. While Nate had always built useful things (or at least things that were designed to be useful), Cat enjoyed making beautiful things – inventions designed to do no more than look and sound pretty.

'Have a play,' he heard Cat say. She had followed his gaze to the toys and was smiling. 'They could do with a good dusting.'

He was tempted – he'd had many good times with those toys when he was younger and even now if he'd had a particularly bad argument with his parents or been given a terrible mark at school he'd pop over to Cat's and pluck one from the shelf, winding it up and losing himself in the tinny tune for a few minutes until he was feeling less angry and less stressed. It always worked. But he was too excited at the moment to be angry or stressed, and turned from the toys to look at the computer screen.

'No time,' he said to Cat, who was loading up her favourite graphics program. 'We've got some inventing to do.'

The rest of the afternoon was spent in typical inventing fashion. The process was always more or less the same. Cat would take charge of the computer, sketching out ideas with the stylus and turning them into 3-D models on screen, while Nate would use an old-fashioned pen and paper to rough out blueprints and make lists of pros and cons. As they worked they threw ideas back and forth at each other, brainstorming suggestions and improving designs until they had the ultimate invention.

'Right,' Cat said when her program had booted up. 'Pick an idea.'

Nate, who had fished out his drawing pad from one of the numerous hidden compartments in Cat's desk, tapped his pen against it for a few moments and pulled what he thought was an expression of intense concentration.

'And try not to stick your tongue out like that.' Cat frowned at him. 'It makes you look like a dog.'

Nate adopted his normal face. For some reason his mind kept wandering back to the Dalai Lama from the video earlier that day.

'I still think we can do something with glasses,' he said quietly, ignoring Cat's glare. 'There's so much potential there and most people ignore it.'

'That's because most people know X-ray specs and laser specs aren't sensible inventions,' Cat replied.

'Okay,' Nate persevered, 'but other types of glasses are. Bear with me.'

He began to sketch out a pair of glasses on a clean page of his pad, talking as he drew.

'How about a set of glasses that can be used to identify people around you, like spy glasses?'

'Nate –' Cat began, but he ignored her, drawing what looked like a tiny camera on the side of one of the lenses, and a wire stretching back to a device on the back of the frame, behind the ear.

'Think about it. There's a tiny camera mounted on the glasses, which looks wherever the wearer looks,' he went on, pointing at the camera with his pen. 'The camera scans the scene and sends the information back to this computer behind the ear.'

'Right,' Cat said, drawing the word out as she raised an eyebrow.

'The computer is designed to pick out any faces within a picture and compare them against a list of people stored inside the computer. If the glasses spot anybody they recognise they report it to the wearer using a tiny earpiece.' He added the microscopic speaker on to his sketch. 'And the spy, or policeman, or whoever is wearing the glasses, can identify a suspect without having to wave a load of photographs around suspiciously.'

Nate whirled the pad around and presented Cat with the sketch. She stared at it for a moment, chewing her bottom lip and making interested 'hmmmmmm' sounds. Eventually she glanced up at him and smiled.

'I think you may be on to something,' she said. Turning to the computer, she began to plot in a pair of spectacles that looked a little bit like those worn by Dame Edna Everage. 'We could run the wires through the frame to make them invisible, and maybe disguise the camera as a tiny screw.'

'I've still got some mini optical-fibre cameras from that spy kit I won last year,' Nate added. 'They're really small.'

'Excellent,' said Cat, using the mouse pen to sketch an exact replica of a tiny camera into the frame, 'and I'll put together a little computer from my mum's palmtop.'

'But doesn't your mum use her palmtop?' Nate asked, remembering how many times he'd seen Mrs Gardner roaming around the house typing important dates and telephone numbers into the notepad-sized computer.

'She'll understand,' Cat replied, not taking her eyes off the screen. 'I'll take it to pieces and just keep the bits we need. I bet we can shrink it down to the size of a box of matches.'

'Too big,' Nate said. 'It's got to be invisible.'

Cat thought hard for a moment.

'Well, I'm pretty sure I can make it the size of a business card if I really try.' She changed the drawing of the computer from what looked like a bulky matchbox to a slim card. 'And you can write the computer program to identify the faces.'

'Great,' Nate said, feeling more excited than ever. 'Now there's just the earpiece.'

'Well,' said Cat after a brief pause, 'does your gran really need her hearing aid?'

'Nah,' replied Nate, 'we never really talk to her anyway.'

They both laughed as Cat finished the 3-D model of the glasses and sat back in her chair. Behind them, unnoticed by either inventor, the printed eyes of Ebenezer Saint seemed to glow for an instant before fading.

6

Undercover Missions

By dinner time the desk was hidden beneath a sea of blueprints and printouts from Cat's laserjet, while hundreds of sketches and doodles lay discarded on top of the mess that already covered the floor.

At one point during the evening there had been a persistent rustling from underneath one particularly large pile of schematics, but the inventors had been too busy to notice it. It was only when a tiny black paw poked up between the papers, accompanied by a forlorn meow, that Nate pulled the family cat, Grub, to safety. It flashed them an evil look before trotting out of the door, still gasping for breath.

'Wow,' said Cat when the final plan had emerged from the humming printer, oblivious to her pet's near death. She laid it on the desk for them both to see. 'I think we've actually done it!'

'Well, planned it at least. Putting it together is going to be the hard part.'

'Nate,' Cat said, turning to him, 'we always have this argument. Inventing is ninety-nine per cent inspiration and one per cent perspiration, remember?'

They did always have this argument. For Nate, putting the idea together and coming up with the plans was the easy bit because it was all about using your imagination and know-how. For Cat, however, getting things down on paper, or on

 38

the computer screen, was tricky, and the fun bit was getting out the tools and making things.

'Well, we'd better get perspiring,' Nate replied, standing and stretching to get rid of the crick in his back. 'I'm going to head over to my gran's to do a bit of pilfering. When is your mum home?'

'It's late-night shopping,' said Cat, doing her best to tidy up the loose sheets of paper on the desk. 'She won't be home until nine.'

'In that case,' answered Nate as he walked towards the door, 'get the palmtop tonight and I'll get the earpiece. We'll start work tomorrow, straight after school.'

Nate's grandmother lived in a tiny flat a few roads over from his house, on a street that seemed to be absolutely full of people over seventy. His parents had often taken him to visit her when he was a little kid, and he had been terrified of the legions of shaking, dribbling wrinklies that always tottered along the pavement all around him, advancing like zombies to stroke his hair and tell his mum what a lovely young man he was.

It was getting late, and Nate knew his gran didn't stay up much after eight, but it was also getting dark, and he decided against the aerial slide just in case he bumped into one of the odd characters who seemed to be drawn to the Bluebell Woods at night. Instead, he left Cat's house through the front door and headed off the long way round.

As he walked he thought about the glasses they had just invented. It was an amazingly simple idea, but if it worked it would be so useful. Cops could go on stakeouts without carrying round their mug-books with them, security guards at football matches could identify troublemakers before they could make trouble. Paparazzi photographers could pick out celebrities even if they were in disguise. Okay, so all the uses weren't actually useful, but he was sure the spy specs would win them the competition.

Reaching his gran's street, Nate peered around the corner to make sure the coast was clear. One particularly ancient old man was shuffling round in circles by the telephone box halfway down the road while on the other side a cluster of four or five tiny old ladies, who were apparently joined together by their enormous handbags, was moving away from him at approximately the same speed as a drunk tortoise with two legs. He guessed the old man would be no trouble, but he recognised one of the old ladies and knew that if she saw him she'd keep him talking all night.

Realising that time was short, he swallowed his fear and dived over the hedge into the first garden he came to, dashing across the grass and almost tripping over a sleeping poodle before reaching the next fence.

His gran lived on this side of the road, six flats down, and Nate managed to make it there by vaulting over the fences and hedges, all the time keeping his eyes on the bobbing blue-rinses that he could make out on the pavement beyond. He reached the front door just as the old ladies drew level with his gran's flat, and turned the handle at the moment they saw him, disappearing into the cool, dark hallway as they began to cross the street cooing like pigeons.

He slammed the door shut, casting a suspicious eye through the window to make sure the old ladies were retreating down the pavement once again. He was on the verge of shouting hello to his gran when he had an idea. Tiptoeing through to the living room, he saw the tiny old lady sitting by the window, knitting. Thankfully the television and radio were off.

'Oh,' she said, a little startled to see Nate strolling in. 'I didn't hear you come in, Nathan.' She bent down slowly to put her knitting on the floor and started to get up. 'It's so lovely to see you.'

Nathan paused for a second, unsure whether he had it in him to try and con his gran out of her hearing aid. But his thoughts soon turned to Ebenezer Saint and the competition and he realised he didn't have any choice. Taking a deep breath he waited for her to look up before mouthing the words 'hello gran'.

'What's that, dear?' she asked, frowning and slumping back down in her chair. At eighty-four she looked frail but Nate knew she still had a lot of fire in her. If she found out what he was up to she would still be able to give him a painful belt round the ear. Feigning confusion, Nate began mouthing words again, this time randomly. His grandmother looked at him for a second as if he was mad, then began to prod her left ear where the hearing aid was nestled.

'Hold on, son,' she muttered. 'Think me hearing aid's gone off on me.'

Nate did his best to stop a grin spreading across his face and moved closer to his gran, taking a seat on the pouffe opposite her. When he had caught her eye he started silently mouthing more words, this time as though he was shouting. After a couple of random sentences involving the phrases 'bald monkeys squashing angry coconuts' and 'Mr Humphreys belched on the ridiculous bottom crunchers', his gran held up a hand, still poking herself in the ear.

'It's no use, Nathan, I can't hear a word you're saying. This bloody thing's not working.'

With a pair of shaking fingers she pulled the hearing aid from her ear. Outside, a car horn sounded and Nate scowled at it through the window.

'That's odd,' his gran continued, holding the tiny, pink aid in her palm. It looked like a glob of chewing gum. 'It was okay this morning.'

Nate took a piece of paper and a pen from his pocket and began to scrawl something on it. When he'd finished he handed it to his gran.

'You'll take it and get it fixed?' she read hesitantly. 'Well, that's very kind of you, if you have the time. I mean, one of the girls around here is bound to know what's wrong with it, it will save you the bother.'

Nate took back the piece of paper and wrote two more words.

'Well,' said his gran, holding out the hearing aid, 'if you insist, Nathan. And I do appreciate it.'

She dropped the earpiece into Nate's palm. He tried to ignore the sensation of warm earwax on his skin. 'It will take four days or so, Gran, I'll take it in right now,' he wrote, handing the paper to her then getting to his feet.

'Are you sure you don't want to stay for a cuppa?' his gran asked, but Nate waved away the offer and made for the front door, blowing a kiss in her direction and feeling a pang of guilt as her final words came after him. 'Aren't you an angel!'

More than happy with the way their plan was going, Nate headed straight home and, after saying a brief hello to his parents, retreated to his room (which was now immaculately plastered from floor to ceiling and tidier than he had ever seen it). He dropped the hearing aid into the secret safe hidden in his desk and then crawled into bed, exhausted after the day's excitement.

His sleep was plagued by seemingly endless dreams about

being assaulted by legions of old ladies all pawing and drooling over him to try and get back their hearing aids, but he woke to the sound of the pigeon hiccuping outside his window, feeling bright, fresh and ready for anything.

This was just as well, because pretty much the first face he encountered on entering the school gates was that of the headmaster. Fortunately, it seemed to have returned to its ordinary shade of ruddy pink. All except for the nose, that is, which hadn't changed at all and now stuck out like a giant purple plum. Nate wondered if this was worse than being completely blue, but he didn't get a chance to ask as the irritated Mr Green ushered him through the main entrance to class.

Inside their form room students were milling around waiting for the bell, and Nate made his way over to Cat, who was sitting in the corner looking extremely miserable. He sat down on the desk in front of her and prodded her squarely in the forehead.

'You look like somebody's died,' he said when she looked up at him. 'You're not worried about Mr Green's nose, are you?'

The question brought a smile to her face for an instant before it reverted to a look of pure unhappiness.

'I managed to get Mum's palmtop,' she muttered, staring at the desk, 'but she caught me taking it to pieces. She was so mad she broke a tooth.'

'Oh,' Nate wasn't quite sure what to say. 'She actually broke a tooth?'

'She was gnashing so much it just cracked, and she was so busy shouting at me she didn't notice, and spat it on to the desk. When she saw what she'd done she got really mad.'

'Really mad?'

'She ran out into the garden and started screaming at the chickens, then she slipped over on some mud and landed on one!'

'Is she all right?' asked Nate in disbelief.

'Yeah, she's fine – we just picked her up and put her in the coop. She'd forgotten about it by this morning.'

'No, is *your mum* all right?'

'Oh, no, she's not all right, not at all.' Cat paused and switched her gaze to the window. 'She's threatened to take away all my inventing stuff.'

'She won't,' Nate said uncertainly. 'That's all your dad's equipment and she'd never want you to stop using it. Anyway, did you tell her about the competition?'

'Of course, I told her everything. She even threatened to stop me entering it!'

'Whoa,' Nate shouted, holding up his hands. 'She's probably just upset that you've ruined her expensive toy. She'll calm down eventually. She's your mum – she lets you get away with everything!'

'She usually does. But this feels different. I've never seen her this mad.'

The sound of the bell echoed through the corridors making them both jump. Nate ruffled Cat's hair and made some comforting sounds before sitting down on the chair next to her.

'So,' he asked as their form teacher walked in, 'with all the kerfuffle did you manage to put together the computer?'

Cat shot him an evil glance.

'What do you think?' She hissed, the frown changing to a smile. 'Of course I did.'

7

Disaster Strikes

Impossibly, classes seemed to drag on more slowly than usual that day. Even woodwork, which both Nate and Cat thoroughly enjoyed under the tutelage of the portly Mr Pervis, plodded by at an excruciating speed.

During lunch break Nate told Cat the story of how he stole his grandmother's hearing aid (adding a few impressive but imaginary details such as combat rolls over two-metre-high fences). Unfortunately one of the dinner ladies was listening in on their conversation and gave Nate a lengthy lecture on respect for the elderly.

They moved swiftly outside afterwards, only to be confronted by Rachel. She looked furious, but was too nervous about mysterious colour changes to demand any food from them. After half-heartedly threatening to beat them senseless, she waddled off.

Afternoon lessons seemed to last for an eternity, especially because they were in different classes. Nate had completely forgotten about a maths test that had been scheduled weeks beforehand, and painfully struggled through a series of twenty questions on trigonometry. His mind kept straying to their invention, and to the possibilities that lay ahead with this competition, and by the time the bell rang for the end of the school day he realised that he hadn't even finished the test. Handing in his paper, he escaped from the room before his teacher noticed the unanswered questions and headed to the gates to wait for Cat.

It was a good ten minutes after hometime that she finally appeared, her face and arms covered with mud and bruises. Nate stared at her open-mouthed.

'PE,' she said as an explanation.

'What were you doing?' Nate asked. 'Playing rugby with the All Blacks?'

'Worse,' she answered as they both walked from the school. 'Hockey with Year 11. One of the older girls made some crack about my inventions and I just snapped. After last night I was about ready to blow up at somebody and it just happened to be her.' Cat laughed as they crossed into the park. 'Poor girl never knew what hit her.'

Nate laughed nervously. Most people saw Cat as a quiet, sensible young lady with the patience of a saint but he knew better than anybody that she had one hell of a temper. If there was something on her mind or something bothering her she wouldn't try and get it off her chest in the normal fashion, by having a calm and logical conversation. She'd wait and stew and brood over whatever it was for hours, days or maybe even weeks, then, when you were sure it had all blown over and things were okay, she'd explode like a furious, terrifying volcano.

He'd been with Cat on a number of occasions like this, and had even developed techniques for avoiding flying scientific equipment and tantrum spittle.

'Our hockey match turned into a bit of a riot. Poor old Cheesebreath didn't know what to do.'

'Well,' Nate said as they made their way across the grass, 'at least you've got it out of your system.'

Cat turned and scowled.

'That's what you think,' she said, and despite the fact that she smiled at him, Nate suddenly felt very nervous.

Given what had happened the previous night, they decided to try and build their invention at Nate's house. They made a brief detour to Cat's pad to pick up the modified computer, Nate waiting outside just in case her mother was still there and looking for someone to take her anger out on.

The chickens milled around him in their usual fashion in the hope he'd brought some cake – all except one, that is, which stayed in the shadowy doorway of the roost scanning the garden with its beady eyes and clucking nervously.

Thankfully Mrs Gardner was out, but she had left a note for Cat, pinned directly over her Ebenezer Saint flyer, saying that there would be no more pocket money/equipment/ days out/food until the palmtop was paid off. Cat emerged with a sour look on her face but she soon cheered up as they whizzed through the Bluebell Woods on the aerial slide, talking about the Spy Specs.

There was nobody in at Nate's house either, which was a nice relief. Nate put the kettle on and prepared two cups of tea – trying not to look at the china doll on the table, which had been badly stuck back together with superglue – while Cat went upstairs with the final set of blueprints and laid them out on the bed.

By the time Nate had struggled to the top of the stairs and entered his room, practically spilling a river of tea on the landing, she had already activated his inventing desk and accessed his hidden safe, and was now pawing the hearing aid with a revolted expression.

'Hey,' he muttered, plonking the tea down on the desk. 'How did you find that?'

'Are you kidding?' Cat answered, looking up at him. 'You're about as predictable as my cat. I've always known what your password is for the safe. Only you would actually use the word *Password*.'

Nate laughed, taking a sip of hot tea.

'Well at least I don't use the password *Ebenezer*, eh?' he teased. Cat blushed and looked away, picking up her mug and uttering a rather disgruntled sound. After taking a couple of swigs she set the tea down and began rooting around in her school bag, eventually pulling out what looked like a small, black business card.

'Ta daaa,' she said, handing it to Nate with a flourish. 'Here it is!'

Nate turned the contraption over in his hands. Cat had basically stripped away everything except for the palmtop's processor, coating it in a fresh case of black plastic and leaving a USB port in one side for access and a small audio socket to connect it to the earpiece. It was an incredibly professional-looking piece of craftsmanship, and Nate was extremely chuffed, although a little jealous.

'I was so angry last night I stayed up until two putting it together,' Cat explained, taking the microcomputer from Nate and looking at it with a proud expression. 'All Mum's data is still on here so she can have it back as soon as we're done with it. I'm pretty sure I can repair it. As soon as you've written the computer program we can input it, and with any luck we'll have our Optical Detection Device.'

'You mean our Spy Specs?'

'No, Nathan.' Cat frowned in Nate's direction. 'Our ODD.'

Nate was too excited to argue. He tapped a small button on his chair and his laptop slid out of its compartment in the wall, unfolding in one smooth action to land on the desk, open and activated.

'It's impressive,' he said to Cat as he waited for the computer to boot up.

'Actually, it's *extremely* impressive,' she replied with a grin.

While Nate began work on the computer program, scanning in pictures from various class photographs and family albums, Cat sat herself at the workbench beside Nate's desk and began to fiddle about with the earpiece.

Not content with almost giving her mum an apoplectic fit of rage by dismantling her palmtop, she had also stolen her spare pair of glasses and now sat carefully inspecting them to see how they could be converted. Rooting around in Nate's inventor's kit, she pulled out a tiny optical-fibre camera and began taking careful measurements.

For the next few hours they both worked in relative silence, breaking it only to utter cries of success after completing a difficult task or to curse repeatedly if they failed to do what they were trying to.

After Nate had scanned in around thirty faces from various photo albums, he started work on the actual program itself. He carefully typed in a series of codes using his knowledge of programming languages (and a stack of electronics journals, which he consulted whenever Cat left the room), gradually putting together a crafty recognition system. Information fed to the program from the camera would be analysed, and any faces would be compared with those on the database using key features such as head, nose and mouth size, eye and hair colour, and ear-sticky-outedness. If there was a match, the computer voice, which he based on his own, would read the name out through the earpiece.

Meanwhile, Cat had used the smallest drill piece she could find to file out a microscopic tunnel inside the frame of the glasses, removing a screw and replacing it with the optical fibre camera, and using superglue to hold the frames together. She ran the fibre, which was little thicker than a paper clip, through the tunnel to the curve at the back that ran around the ear and stuck it there with tape until the computer was ready.

After this she modified the hearing aid (first cleaning it rigorously on Nate's jumper) by fitting a tiny radio receiver to it and designing an equally microscopic transmitter for the computer. After three hours and forty-five minutes she was done.

'Hurry up,' she shouted at Nate, sitting back in her chair and looking at him smugly. 'Haven't you finished yet?'

Nate pulled a face and peered in closer to his computer screen, trying to ignore her.

'Come on,' she teased, leaning forward and poking him in the ribs. 'You only had to design a teeny-weeny little computer program. I've practically made the glasses already.'

'Puh,' he spat dismissively, typing in a couple of lines of code and scanning the text on screen to make sure it all looked okay.

'Good comeback,' she answered sarcastically. Nate looked at her and tapped the Enter key, causing the code on screen to begin to filter into a fully working program. In under two minutes the computer made a sound like a bleating goat.

'Done,' said Nate. He plucked a blue USB memory stick from the back of his computer and plugged it into the modified palmtop, copying the computer program across to the tiny black device. Cat began wiggling her fingers impatiently.

'Gimme gimme gimme gimme,' she said, snatching the microcomputer from his hands as soon as the transfer had finished. He watched as she delicately fitted the optical-fibre cable to the computer using a pair of tweezers, then soldered the black plastic case on to the glasses frames using the little iron that came as part of Nate's junior mechanics kit. Finally she plugged in the radio transmitter to the back of the computer and held the glasses up in the air.

'Ebenezer Saint, here I come,' she said, changing the 'I' to 'we' when Nate gave her an irritated look. 'Would you like to do the honours?'

'By all means,' Nate answered, happy to be the one to try out the glasses. He took them from her and ceremoniously placed them on his face, slotting the pink hearing aid into his left ear. Taking a deep breath, he looked at Cat and waited to see what happened.

The glasses gave out an almost imperceptible whirr as the optical-fibre camera focused, then a slight whine as the computer spun into motion. Seconds later he heard the quietest of clicks in his ear as the hearing aid began to pick up the signal from the computer. Then, to Nate's delight, it spoke to him.

'Subject identified,' it said in his own voice. Nate felt his heart pounding and wished the device would hurry up. Milliseconds later it spoke again, but not quite what Nate was expecting to hear.

'Maurice MacHiggenbottom III,' the earpiece said, 'Earl of Berkshire.'

Nate was about to tell Cat they had a problem when the computer whined extra loudly then popped, giving Nate an electric shock so powerful that three things happened simultaneously: his hair stood on end, he yelped like a chihuahua, and he flew backwards off his chair to land painfully on the floor.

8

A Stitch in Time

It took Cat some time to pick Nate up off the floor. The electric shock had stunned him badly, and for around ten minutes as he lay on the carpet, his hair smoking, all he could do was talk absolute nonsense.

'Good evening, Maurice MacHigginbottom III,' he muttered to Cat as she carefully removed the glasses and tried to pick him up. 'It's nice to meet you, your earlship.'

'Nate,' she said, straining to hoist his body upwards. He wasn't big, but he was surprisingly heavy, and after several attempts she gave up, letting him crash back to the floor with a thud.

'I must be *Mrs* MacHigginbottom,' he went on in an unsteady falsetto, not making any sense at all. Cat thought that if this was a cartoon he'd have little birds and stars circling his head right now. The thought almost made her laugh except for the sad truth that their invention hadn't worked. In fact, it had been a complete disaster.

'Nate!' she shouted at the boy on the floor, who was pouting like a woman and wiggling his hips, and muttering something about how lovely it is to be married to an earl. She grabbed the back of his pants and pulled them as hard as she could, thinking that a wedgie would be enough to snap him out of his trance. It didn't work, so she took a run-up and kicked him hard in the ribs. That did the trick.

'Ooooow!' he screamed, his sense returning instantly. 'What did you do that for?'

'I'm sorry, your ladyship,' Cat replied sarcastically, offering Nate a hand and helping him to his feet. He was rubbing his side tenderly, cringing when he poked a sore rib. 'But there's no time to be unconscious or in a trance – we've got some serious work to do.'

'Ladyship?' Nate said, clueless about the events of the last few minutes. 'Have we tried out the glasses yet?'

'Yes,' Cat said, picking them up off the bed and looking at them. 'And with shocking results.'

She picked a screwdriver from Nate's toolbox and began tightening the framework and checking the seals between the connections. Nate looked around in confusion, gradually remembering what had happened and fingering his hair, which had stopped smoking now but which was still standing on end at an alarming angle.

'Have you got any electrical tape?' she asked. 'The stuff that protects you from electric shocks?'

'Bit late for that now, eh?' Nate grumbled, rooting through his odds and ends drawer and pulling out a reel of thick black tape. Cat took it and began winding it around the portable computer and its battery case until the entire thing was covered. When she was finished she threw the tape back into the drawer and held the glasses up.

'Right,' she said. 'That should have solved the problem of the electricity overspill. I think it was just a glitch, the first time the computer's been used in its new compact shape. It should be fine now that it's had a chance to settle.'

'Well, there's only one way to find out,' said Nate, taking a couple of steps away from Cat. 'And it's your turn.'

'Fine,' said Cat with a feigned expression of bravery. She placed the glasses on her face and popped the earpiece into her ear, using the duvet to wipe a rather large dollop of Nate's ear-wax from it first. Giving the computer a tap to make sure it was still working, she looked at Nate and braced herself for a painful shock.

To her surprise, however, the computer simply whined ever so slightly, then the earpiece whispered into her ear. When it had finished she took the glasses off and placed them in her lap, chewing her lip.

'And?' demanded Nate, desperate to know if the specs were a success. 'What did it say?'

'Well,' she answered, 'we've fixed the problem of the electric shock.'

'But . . .'

'According to our amazing Optical Detection Device your name is Baron von Dingaling.'

Although it was getting late Nate and Cat spent the next two hours racing around trying to find people to test their invention on, just in case Nate's new name was another fixable glitch.

Unfortunately, it seemed that the glasses were completely incapable of recognising anybody on their database. Nate's Mum, shocked at seeing her son in glasses, was christened Helga Pooplegrutt, while Nate's dad, when he returned from work, was diagnosed by the earpiece as being a certain Mr Brad Summerbum.

Even the next-door neighbour, who popped around as he did every week to try and talk the Wright family into voting Conservative, was renamed – although Nate couldn't bring himself to repeat the title, even to Cat, and as soon as the filthy words had entered his ears he pulled off the glasses and threw them on to the sofa in disgust.

'Well, that's it then,' he said, collapsing into a heap next to the failed invention, and covering the glasses with a pillow so as not to be reminded of what had gone wrong.

'No scholarship for us,' Cat finished. She walked over to the window, and wiped away the condensation to reveal the world outside, shrouded in darkness and drenched from the rain that had begun to fall. She stood there for a minute in silence, resting her head against the cold glass and sighing loudly. The only sound was the shrill ring of the phone in the kitchen, followed by the drone of Nate's mum as she answered.

'I wish Dad was here,' Cat said quietly. 'He'd have helped us.'

Nate didn't reply. He knew that when Cat talked about her dad like this it was always best to stay quiet, and leave her to it. She sighed loudly, then seemed to perk up, turning to Nate and smiling at him.

'But if he was here,' she continued, 'he'd say that it wasn't too late.'

She sat down next to Nate on the sofa and rescued the glasses from under the cushion. 'We've got two days, we can still make them work. All we need is a tighter program, and to make sure there are no loose connections. It's a doddle. We've managed to get out of worse situations. All we need is time.'

'All we need is time,' Nate repeated unenthusiastically, turning to look at her. He hated to be the pessimist, but he couldn't bring himself to echo Cat's enthusiasm. 'Tonight and tomorrow, Cat, that's all we've got. That's thirty-six hours at most, including sleep.'

'Make that twenty-four,' said a voice from the corner of the room. They both turned to see Nate's mum, who was standing in the doorway holding the cordless phone. 'I don't know what

 55

you two are plotting but your mother wants you home for supper, Cat, right now.'

Cat opened her mouth to argue but Mrs Wright wasn't about to let her speak.

'She asked me to remind you about last night. You're treading on thin ice, was what she said. I'm not one to make a fuss, but she sounded quite clear on the matter. It's home now or no home at all.'

Nate turned to look at Cat, raising an eyebrow at the thought of Mrs Gardner throwing her out of the house. But Cat's expression stopped him dead. Barely able to keep the tears from her eyes, and her bottom lip from quivering, she pushed herself off the sofa and walked solemnly from the room without so much as a goodbye. Nate called her name, and stood to chase after her, but before he could reach the hallway he heard the front door slam shut and the sound of footsteps on the gravel outside. Reaching for the handle, he heard a voice behind him.

'And don't think you're off the hook after yesterday morning, young man,' said his mother, who had followed him into the hall. 'You can sort things out with Sophie tomorrow, but right now it's dinner, homework, then straight to bed. It's almost nine.'

He turned to argue, but he knew from the way his mum was tapping the soft carpet with her slippers that he wouldn't be able to talk her round. *All we need is time*, he said to himself in his head, echoing Cat's words. But time was the one thing they didn't have.

9

Feelin' Blue

The rain continued through the night, and it was so overcast the following morning that even the hiccuping pigeon seemed to have slept in. Nate had to double-check his alarm clock to make sure it wasn't still the middle of the night, but it was seven-thirty and time to start the day, with nothing but the prospect of school and an angry Cat to look forward to.

It took his sleepy head a few moments to remember the night before, and the disastrous results of their Spy Specs, and when it came flooding back all he wanted to do was bury himself beneath the duvet and go back to sleep. But he knew he couldn't leave Cat to struggle through the day by herself, and after showering and dressing he trudged downstairs for some breakfast.

His parents did nothing to cheer him up, attempting to force-feed him burnt toast and rubbery scrambled eggs while simultaneously lecturing him on the importance of finding hobbies that took place outside the house. His dad even had the nerve to recommend taking up rugby, adding that the captain of the local team – the Mudrats – was a friend of his at work.

Nate simply scowled at him and walked out of the door, preparing himself for what he imagined would be the worst day of his life. As he clambered over the wall into the park – accidentally throwing his bag into the biggest puddle he had ever seen – he tried to think of something to make Cat feel better, but he was so miserable that he couldn't come up with a single thing.

As it turned out, it didn't matter anyway. When he entered their form room Cat was nowhere to be seen. He popped his head out of the window to search for her among the milling crowds in the playground but she wasn't there either. Before he could go and search for her around the toilets, their form tutor had entered and instructed them all, in her usual timid voice, to sit down immediately.

Ten minutes later, when everybody finally did sit down, Cat's was the only chair in the room still to remain empty.

Mrs Truelove (which, as Nate's classmates often pointed out, was an amusing name as the little old lady had never married and lived with her cats) began calling out the names on the register. She raised her head when there was no response to Sophie's and looked at Nate.

'Sophie won't be in today, Nathan,' she muttered, encouraging a round of wolf whistles from the classroom directed at Nate's reddening cheeks. 'Her mother rang this morning to tell me, and to pass on a message to you that the piece of work you're doing together will have to wait.'

Nate frowned. Why would Cat's mum say all that on the phone?

'She also said that her dog, Saint, might not be dead after all, whatever that means.'

'I thought you were Cat's dog,' whispered Allan, the mean, spotty boy who sat in front of Nate's desk. But Nate didn't answer. The message was a code from Cat. Her mum hadn't rung at all. Cat had obviously decided to take the day off school.

That meant only one thing: she had a plan.

Form period seemed to stretch on for ever, and Nate was tapping his fingers so frantically on the desk as he waited for it to finish that he practically drummed a hole in the ancient wood.

When the bell finally rang he sprang to his feet and sprinted out of the door, turning left and heading towards the room where his morning English lesson was due to take place. When he thought there was nobody watching him, however, he doubled back up the Year 7 corridor and along past the gym towards the back door.

The staff room was almost always empty at this time of day, but Nate made sure he ducked down under the window as he made his way past in case any stray teachers saw him.

Unfortunately, Mr Cramp the biology teacher was leaving just as Nate shuffled by on all fours, and although Nate managed to convince him that he had dropped his contact lens on the floor, it led to an enormous delay as several passing students and staff dropped down to help him find it. Fifteen minutes and no contact lens later Nate jumped to his feet, claimed in a shaky voice that he had actually forgotten to put his lenses in that morning and bolted down the hallway, leaving the confused crowd behind him.

By the time a further quarter of an hour had elapsed Nate had made his way through the woods and was entering Cat's scruffy garden. Shooing away the chickens, he ran up to the back door and knocked three times. There was no sound from inside the house, so he tried again.

Several frantic knocks later, and with sore knuckles, Nate began to wonder if he had completely misread Cat's message, or indeed if there had been a secret code at all. Maybe Cat was ill, in bed, and did have a poorly dog called Saint that, for some inexplicable reason, he had never seen in the thirteen years they had been friends.

Slinging his bag over his shoulder he turned around to leave,

 59

and was walking back to the gate when he heard a quiet sobbing from inside the chicken coop.

Confused, and half fearing an ambush by the cake-loving birds, he poked his head through the small door to see his best friend sitting on a bundle of hay with her head in her hands. Clasped in her fingers, as though it was the most important thing on the planet, was the Ebenezer Saint flyer. Trying to ignore the smell of chicken poo, Nate dropped his bag and scrambled inside.

'Er . . . Cat?' He whispered, hovering around the doorway just in case she was in one of her more explosive moods. 'What on earth are you doing?'

Cat didn't reply, but simply pushed her head further into her hands, drawing her knees up so she resembled a tortoise in soggy red clothes. Nate didn't quite know what to do. He'd never seen her this upset before. Sad, disappointed and with tears in her eyes, yes – he could remember when she had been told the news about her father's death, how furious and upset she'd been, and how she used to hide in her room for hours sobbing. But that had been different. There had always been a fire in her eyes then, a determination not to let things get to her even if they were really bad. They had been tears of sadness, but also tears of anger, a sign that she was about to fight back.

Now, Cat looked as if she had given up, as if she had resigned herself to failure and could spend the rest of her days curled up in the chicken coop because of one broken dream. That thought scared Nate more than any of Cat's violent mood swings. Taking a deep breath, he shuffled over and put his arm around her shoulders.

'Hey,' he whispered, ignoring her half-hearted shrug. 'It isn't that bad, is it?'

Cat began to talk, but through the tears and snot and layers of fabric pressed against her head Nate couldn't hear a word.

After a good thirty seconds of mumbling he put a finger under her chin and gently pulled her head up. Her face was a mess, all hair and drool, and her red eyes were about as sad as he had ever seen anybody's.

'I was just so looking forward to it,' she said, her words barely a whisper. 'We're just about the best inventors I know. I can't believe we couldn't even invent something for this competition. We'd have won, Nate, if only we'd had a little more time.'

Nate couldn't think of anything to say, and in the silence that followed they both stared forlornly at the image of Saint looking up at them from the crumpled leaflet. Seeing Cat like this made Nate realise just how much he'd been looking forward to it as well, how much he'd have liked the opportunity to work with the master inventor, how much of a life-changing experience it could have been.

'And I wanted to do it for my dad,' she went on, bursting into tears again. 'It's just what he would have wanted for me. He'd have been so disappointed to see us give up, to see that we'd run out of time.'

She stopped talking as she blew her nose on her sleeve. Nate thought about the times he'd been around Cat's dad, the enthusiasm that Harold had always shown towards even the smallest of projects. Even if it had been coming up for midnight, and the children were barely able to keep their eyes open, he'd claim that there was still time to finish. And they always had. The thought brought a lump to his throat, and he turned to look outside. The chickens were huddling together in the rain looking miffed that their house had been invaded.

'I thought you'd phoned the school and left that message because you'd had another idea,' he said eventually, playing absentmindedly with a piece of straw from the floor. 'I thought maybe you'd save the day, like you always do.'

Cat wiped her nose with the back of her hand, paused for a second and started sobbing again.

'I thought you might have had one,' she answered, her words barely audible through the tears. 'I couldn't face going in to school so I decided to stay at home. Then I managed to lock myself out when I was fetching the milk and this was the only place I could stay dry.' She looked up at him hopefully. 'I don't suppose you fixed the glasses?'

'Nope,' he answered, picturing the faulty specs lying in his waste-paper basket at home, minus the earpiece and the remains of the palmtop.

'Or that you've had any more ideas?'

'Nope,' he repeated. Another moment of silence followed, during which Nate realised that the straw he was playing with was actually a stringy piece of dried chicken poo. Chucking it away in disgust he wiped his fingers on his trousers and turned to Cat.

'Don't be so down, Cat, don't be so blue,' he said, giving her a squeeze and a playful punch on the arm with his other hand. 'We'll get another chance. Your dad will never be disappointed.'

'"This competition is a one-off, a once-in-a-lifetime chance to work with me,"' Cat quoted. 'We're not going to get another shot at this.'

But Nate wasn't listening. A strange thought was nagging him, fluttering in the shadows at the back of his head.

'It's all over,' she continued. 'I'm going to end up working in a burger joint for ever and ever.'

It was something to do with what he'd just said, something about his words to Cat. He desperately tried to pin the thought down, to work out what it was.

'And ever and ever and ever.'

He retraced his words, looking for inspiration, ignoring

Cat's droning voice, fighting to grasp the idea before it disappeared altogether.

'And ever and ever and for ever.'

Don't be so down. Don't be so –

'Blue! I've got it,' he shouted, jumping to his feet so quickly that he cracked his head on the coop's wooden roof. The chickens that had been gathering around the doorway squawked and flapped to safety, deciding they'd be better off living in the trees. Ignoring the pain, he turned to Cat and grabbed her by the shoulders, shaking her enthusiastically.

'Nate, what have you got?' she asked, looking at him as though he had lost his mind.

'Blue,' he answered, grinning. 'Don't be so blue.'

'Blue?' Cat looked confused, and was eyeing the exit to the coop just in case Nate really had gone insane.

'Blue,' he shouted, barely able to string his words together in his excitement. 'Cat, we can use the Bully Blow, we can use the Pergophosphaticus III, we can still win the competition.'

Cat's expression began to lift as she realised what he was saying.

'It's unique,' she said.

'And we've invented it in the last month.'

'And it's pretty amazing.'

'And stupendous.'

There was a moment's pause.

'But utterly indispensable?' she said, frowning. Nate smiled.

'That is what we have twelve hours to get right.'

10

Making a Mess

A frantic dash for Nate's house followed, with the two young inventors practically crawling over each other to get out of the chicken coop. They leapt aboard the aerial slide – Cat pulling the lever before Nate could climb on properly, forcing him to cling on for dear life as the springs propelled it through the glistening trees – then ran the short distance from the Bluebell Woods to Nate's front door.

After scouting the house to make sure his parents weren't home (if they caught him taking a day off school like this he would be shipped out to a boarding school quicker than it would take his mum to clip him round the ear), Nate opened the front door and they sprinted upstairs to the lab.

'It can't just be a revenge thing,' Cat said, dropping down on to Nate's bed in order to catch her breath. 'We can't encourage people to turn their enemies bright blue just because they feel like it.'

Nate fell to his knees and opened his mouth to speak but was so exhausted after running up the road, and the stairs, that he couldn't get a word out. Maybe his dad was right, and he should start playing sports.

'So we have to find a use for it, maybe a party trick, fancy dress, or a festival thing. It would look great at Notting Hill, and much safer than body paints.'

Nate could still only produce a faint wheezing sound, so he

let Cat carry on.

'Or perhaps it could be a school thing – naughty pupils could spend two days walking around as a funny colour, so everyone knows what they've done. We just need one good use for it, one thing that makes it indispensable. Are you planning on joining in this conversation?' She sat up on the bed and looked at Nate, who was still panting. 'Nathan Wright,' she exclaimed, 'just how unfit are you? You've gone bright red. I can barely see you against that carpet!'

Before she had even finished the sentence they looked at each other and grinned.

'That's it,' Nate finally managed, staggering to his feet. 'You've done it!'

'Camouflage,' she continued, 'for the army. It's perfect!'

Nate looked at his watch. It was coming up for midday.

'You get started on the mixture,' he said, pulling out his chair and pushing the button to activate his desk. 'I've got an idea that will make this the best invention since sliced bread.'

Serenaded by the sound of food processors, microwave timers, hand-held blenders and an assortment of crashes, cheers and curses from the kitchen, Nate sat at his computer and planned out an addition to the formula that would make it ideal for soldiers in a battle.

Fishing the faulty glasses from the bin, he stripped out the camera and the optical fibres and strapped them to a bowler hat that he found in his parents' wardrobe. His dad had been given the hat as a leaving present by colleagues at his old job, mainly (although they had never admitted this) because he looked like the Fat Controller from *Thomas the Tank Engine*. It was his pride and joy whenever he and his wife went out for dinner, but it was also the closest thing that Nate could find to a soldier's helmet, so he had to ignore the thought of his dad's anger as he drilled a hole in the side to feed the cables through.

Once he'd finished with the hat, he set to work on the processor, connecting it to the computer via a USB cable and changing the program from the previous facial-recognition software to a much simpler colour-recognition one.

When he was midway through writing, Cat stomped upstairs absolutely covered in blue gunk, and deposited a batch of Pergophosphaticus III on the desk. It looked even more disgusting than before, and was bubbling slightly – each pop releasing the sickly smell of blueberries – but Cat claimed it was exactly the same mix, and would have exactly the same effect.

'Trust me, Nate,' she said. 'Try some if you're not sure.'

Nate thought about Mr Green's violet nose and declined the offer.

'It's hard work, though,' Cat moaned. 'Just don't ask me to make any more.'

Nate turned to her and rubbed his chin thoughtfully, wondering how she'd react to his suggestion that they make several more batches, each a different colour. Underneath the globs of colourful gunk that were plastered over her face, Cat was wearing a big smile, so he decided to push his luck.

'We need five more lots, Cat,' he said, ignoring her scowl. 'Red, green, yellow, white and black. Mum's food dyes are all in the same place, above the bread bin. I think she's got most of those but you might need to use flour for the white one.'

Cat bounced off the bed and dashed across the room as though to punch him.

'Think of Ebenezer,' he blurted out, covering his eyes, but instead of the familiar discomfort of a dead arm he was greeted with a kiss on the forehead followed by the furious patter of feet as Cat hurtled down the stairs back to the kitchen.

His heart racing, Nate returned to the computer and added the finishing touches to the program, then began scrabbling around in his odds-and-ends box for some plastic test tubes. Pulling six up from beneath a pile of rusty rivets, he bolted them to the inside of the hat, where they would hold the different colours of Bully Blow. Next he rigged up a small mixing machine, which would be connected to the test tubes with some plastic piping and which was where the different colours were blended to produce the desired shade. Lastly he ran a long, thin straw down from the mixing machine so that it would stick out in front of the mouth. By the time he had finished it was mid-afternoon, and he turned to see Cat lying on the bed watching him.

'So you've finally finished,' she said playfully.

'Yeah, how long have you been there?' Nate answered, placing the hat on top of his head and adjusting the mouthpiece so it sat right in front of his lips.

'About half an hour. You were engrossed so I didn't want to disturb you.' She got to her feet and walked over, pulling the bowler hat down over Nate's eyes. 'You look ridiculous, by the way.'

'But imagine it's a soldier's helmet,' Nate said, pushing the hat up with one finger in what he thought was a Fred Astaire kind of move. 'You're out on the battlefield, you find yourself in thick jungle, you can be seen for miles around. You activate your Camo Craze and bingo, you blend in immediately.'

Nate noticed the six small cartons of coloured ooze sitting on his bedside table and picked up the red and yellow ones.

'Or you're dropped off in the middle of the desert, and you are being hunted by the enemy. The hat scans your surroundings, mixes the right amounts of red and yellow to create orange and

 67

you'll be invisible against the sand for as long as you need to be!'

He dipped his finger into the pot of red goo and pulled out a long thin trail that looked like toxic toffee. Cat strolled over and looked at the computer program, scrolling through the code and nodding approvingly.

'So the camera detects what colour the surroundings are, the mixing machine blends the right shade and you suck it up through the straw,' she said, speaking to herself. 'Then the soldiers can swallow it without having to stop doing whatever they're doing.' She looked up to see Nate pouring the different colours of Pergophosphaticus III into the test tubes, doing his best to avoid spilling any on the pristine red carpet.

'And a smaller dose should mean the soldier only stays that colour for a few hours,' Nate muttered, not taking his eyes off the string of tar-like black liquid as it dripped into the plastic test tube. 'Not like Mr Green.'

Cat began downloading the program to the palmtop's processor, and perched herself on the desk as Nate finished up. When the computer made the sound of a bleating goat she unplugged the credit-card-sized black box and pulled the hat from Nate's hands, fitting the tiny computer into the pocket he'd sewn into the lining and plugging in the cables that connected it to both the camera and the mixing machine.

'Well,' she said when everything was firmly in place.

'Well,' Nate echoed, feeling an immense sense of relief that they'd been able to put such a complex invention together in a few hours.

'There's only one thing left to do,' Cat went on, 'and that's test it.'

Silence followed as they both looked at the bowler hat and its odd attachment.

'It's either you or me.'

'Paper, scissors, stone?' Nate suggested, placing the hat on the floor to free up his hands.

'Or slaps?' Cat added, referring to her favourite game, which was won by whoever could slap their opponent's hand fast enough. And hard enough.

'I'd rather something less violent,' Nate muttered, but he knew from experience that Cat would settle for nothing less. Sighing, he put his hands together as if about to pray then stretched them out towards Cat, who was grinning. Touching fingertips, there was a moment of tense stillness before she lashed out and slapped him around the back of the palm. Nate drew his hands back, feeling his skin throb.

'Best of three,' he shouted. Putting their hands together again he lashed out with what he thought was a lightning quick motion only to find that Cat had already moved her hands. As soon as their fingertips made contact again, however, he felt the familiar slap of flesh on flesh and realised that he'd lost.

Huffing, Nate picked up the hat and slammed it down on his head, flicking the switch to activate the camera.

'Fine,' he hissed, annoyed at Cat's smug smile. 'But let's go into the bathroom. It's orange in there.'

For reasons known only to her, Nate's mum had decided to paint the bathroom a shade of orange that bordered on being radioactive. Not only was it so bright that it hurt your eyes if you were standing in the shower, but Nate was convinced that if you stayed in the small room for long enough you'd actually get a tan. It was the perfect place to try out the new invention on desert setting.

Closing the door behind them, Nate activated the processor and waited, looking at Cat for support. A slight whining sound informed them that the camera was taking in the surroundings, then the gears that connected the mixing machine to the hel-met began to turn, and Nate heard the sound of the Bully Blow gargling out of the test tubes. Before he could object, a disgusting globule of liquid was pushed forward into his mouth like a rancid bogie. Coughing in surprise, Nate made a noisy swallowing sound as the snotty lump disappeared down his throat, then he glanced up at Cat.

'I hope you didn't put anything nasty in that,' he said, clutching his throat.

'Of course not,' she laughed. 'Only a bit of spit.'

'Cat!' Nate shouted, screwing up his face in disgust. The mixture tasted like oranges, but beneath it was the most repulsive aftertaste he had ever experienced in his life – a mix of sweaty socks, public toilets and the stink bombs that Allan used to let off in his bag after PE. 'You have to do something about the taste.'

But Cat wasn't listening. Her expression had turned to one of amazement.

'Oh my God, Nate,' she whispered, not taking her eyes from his face. 'You're turning orange.'

Nate could feel the skin on his face tingling – not an unpleasant sensation – and a warm feeling radiating up his arms and neck. Looking down he saw that his palms had begun to turn a strange shade of orange, and that the colour was stretching along his fingers and up to his elbows.

'You did it!' he exclaimed, laughing at the speed at which his skin was turning the same colour as the bathroom. 'You really did it!'

'We both did it,' she answered, grabbing his mandarin-coloured fingers and shaking them wildly. 'We're back in the competition!'

Brushing past Cat to look in the mirror, Nate was astonished to see that his face had turned the same colour as his hands. Gradually, as he watched, it was blending into the bathroom walls, making it look as though the bowler hat was sitting in mid-air above a pair of ghostly white eyes – with orange irises, of course. He was about to comment on how fast the mixture was taking effect when he heard the sound of a car pulling up on the gravel drive outside.

'Mum!' he exclaimed, turning to look at Cat, whose expression of horror mirrored his own.

'The kitchen!' was all she could think of to say. Stumbling out of the bathroom, they ran downstairs.

It was as if a bomb had been detonated in the vicinity of the sink. The counters were covered in food dye – mixed with chemicals that reeked of blocked drains – and glasses, bowls, vials and Petri dishes filled with a dazzling assortment of fizzing, bubbling concoctions. Broken crockery littered the floor, along with almost an entire set of cutlery and at least a hundred footprints all with the distinctive pattern of Cat's trainers. The cupboard handles were covered in dripping blue goo, the oven was still on and smoking, and even the windows were so drenched with grease that you couldn't make out the garden.

'Cat,' Nate said, astonished, 'what were you doing? Having a food fight with yourself?'

'It's an art form,' she replied. 'I can't help it if I make a little mess.'

'A *little* mess . . .' Nate replied, trying to take in the destruction. But it was too late. Behind him he heard the front door open and his mum's cheerful rendition of 'The Way to Amarillo'. Six footsteps later and she appeared at the kitchen door, the song frozen, her expression one of disbelief. It was a good few minutes before she could think of anything to say.

'Blue,' was the only word to leave her mouth.

Slowly, she turned to look at Cat, who ran her finger sheepishly along the counter and didn't take her eyes away from the filthy floor. Then she glanced at Nate, her eyes widening even further as she saw the colour of his face.

'Orange,' was all she could think of to say. Then she collapsed in a heap on the kitchen floor.

 71

11

A Narrow Escape

Some quick thinking saved the day. While his mum was unconscious, Nate dragged her through to the living room and lifted her on to the sofa. She wasn't a big woman, but he strained so much to lift her that his orange face was soon spattered with odd red patches, making him look a little like an Oompa Loompa with the plague.

When he'd finished, he ran back through to the kitchen to help Cat tidy up – scrubbing the grease off the windows and using a toothbrush (his dad's) to try and clean the multicoloured goo from pretty much every surface in the room. After less than half an hour they'd managed to get the kitchen back to its normal state of impeccable tidiness, and Nate sent Cat to the bathroom to clean up.

'Just sling on some of my old clothes,' he said, ignoring the face she pulled at the thought of wearing one of his tatty, unfashionable T-shirts. 'And make sure you get all of that Bully Blow off your face – it might stain.'

'Speaking of which . . .' she hinted, pointing at Nate's bright orange features. 'You only took a tiny amount, so it should start wearing off any time now.'

'I hope so,' Nate replied. 'This plan, and my life, depends on it!'

Cat scampered upstairs while Nate put the kettle on, glancing at his reflection in the window every thirty seconds to see if the colour was fading. Fortunately, as the water came to the boil, he noticed that his fingers were a slightly less toxic shade of orange, and by the time he'd soaked a towel in hot water and made three strong cups of tea his mirror image was as pink and fresh as the day he was born.

Relieved, he carried one of the cups through to the living room, where he laid the towel on his mum's forehead. Groaning, she opened one beady eye and looked at Nate, then opened the other, scanning the room for anything unusual.

'Nate,' she whispered, 'what's going on?'

'I think you must be coming down with something, Mum,' he replied tenderly, handing her the cup of tea. 'You came back from work looking feverish, and then sat down in here and fell asleep. You were muttering something about blue and orange. I think it was the Rainbow Song.'

Raising an eyebrow suspiciously, Mrs Wright grabbed Nate's chin and pulled his face closer, searching for any sign of unusual colour.

'You were orange,' she said. 'I swear it. And my surfaces . . .'

Getting to her feet and holding the towel to her forehead, she staggered through to the kitchen. After a moment of silence in which Nate tried desperately to remember if they'd managed to tidy up everything she returned and sat back down, this time on an armchair.

'You do have a bit of a temperature,' Nate said. 'I put that cold towel on your forehead and look how warm it is now.'

Confused, she peeled the towel away and laid the back of her hand against her temples.

'Well, how strange,' she said. 'I haven't been ill for months.'

'There's lots going around at the moment,' Nate replied. 'Kids are dropping like flies at school.'

'You're right. Sue at work had to go home early yesterday because of flu. Oh dear, I hope that's not what I've got.' She took a sip of her tea, then looked at Nate and smiled. 'Thanks for the tea, Nathan. You're an angel.'

After so narrowly avoiding a lifetime in a detention centre for unruly children, Nate headed upstairs where Cat was putting together the blueprints, plans and formulas to submit with their invention the following day. They worked together in relieved silence for an hour, putting the finishing touches to the hat – Cat sewed on some camouflage using a pair of green and brown pants she found in a drawer while Nate topped up the test tubes to replace the Bully Blow he'd swallowed earlier.

They'd barely got everything done before Cat looked fearfully at her watch and declared she had to head home to start on the chores her mother had left her.

'If I don't get back in her good books there will be no scholarship even if Saint himself comes round and begs her on his knees,' she said as she headed out of the door. 'I'll leave all this with you – just don't forget it in the morning. Nine o'clock deadline, Nate. Don't be late.'

But a fitful night's sleep and another dingy, overcast morning with no sign of the pigeon meant that Nate did sleep in, and a knock on his door from his father at ten to eight sent him flying out of his bed and straight into his uniform.

He was so panicked that he put his trousers on back to front then managed to tear them by accidentally ramming both feet into the same trouser leg at once. Cursing, and telling himself to calm down, he hopped down the stairs three at a time and flew into the kitchen.

'Your mum's not well, Nathan,' said his dad as he stood

waiting for his toast to pop up. 'Although I can't see a thing wrong with her.'

'It's flu,' Nate replied, digging around in the carrier bag drawer for something to carry the invention to school in. 'Nasty bug, everybody's got it. I've got to run. Early start today.'

Nate heard his dad muttering some kind of approval as he sprinted back upstairs, carefully placing the camouflaged hat into the bag and covering it with the blueprints and printed sheets of data just in case his curious father wanted to see what was inside. As it turned out, when Nate rushed back down the stairs and out through the hallway his dad was busy trying to fish out his smoking toast with a wooden spoon. Shouting good-bye, Nate opened the front door and stepped out into the rain.

By half past eight he was standing, dripping wet, in the hall-way leading up to the Head Office, waiting for Cat. With ten minutes to go until the deadline Cat stumbled in looking as if she had almost drowned. Shaking her hair like a dog, she skipped up to Nate and took the bag from him, peering inside.

'So it's all here, then,' she said, dripping giant drops of rain-water on to the blueprints.

'No,' Nate answered sarcastically. 'I decided to leave all the important stuff at home.'

'Well then,' she said, punching him on the arm, 'let's get our entry in.'

They walked up the hall and the secretary nodded for them to go straight into Mr Green's office. He looked up at them from a pile of papers on his desk and they were relieved to see that his face had returned to its normal shade of ruddy pink.

'Ah,' he said as they made their way over to the leather chairs, 'the Terrible Twosome. Mrs Truelove told me that you both managed to miss your classes yesterday, and I'd be having strict words with your parents now except for the fact that I'm curious to see what godforsaken contraption you spent your time on. How did you get on?'

'Fine, thanks,' answered Nate, placing the bag on the desk and taking out the wad of papers. 'Here are all the working documents, blueprints and recipes.' He pulled out the hat and placed it on top of the form the headmaster was filling out. 'And here's the invention.'

Curious, Mr Green picked up the hat and began turning it over in his hands, poking the mixing machine and the test tubes full of bubbling colour.

'It's just a prototype,' Cat said, leaning over the desk and flicking the switch on the hat to boot up the processor. 'The real one will be in an army helmet.'

'An army helmet,' said the headmaster placing the hat over his head and moving the straw so it sat right in front of his mouth. 'Dare I ask what it is, or is it top secret?'

Nate and Cat looked at each other for a moment then back at Mr Green, who was pretending to fire an invisible machine gun out of the window while muttering phrases such as 'Alpha Bravo move in' through the straw.

'Well, actually you already know what it is,' said Nate cautiously. Mr Green stopped what he was doing and looked at the two young inventors.

'Tell me it isn't related to whatever was in that chocolate brownie,' he said. When Nate and Cat started nodding he snatched the helmet off his head and held it at arm's length, as though it was a poisonous snake.

'It's for camouflage,' Cat said, taking the invention and putting it back in the bag. 'For the army, so people can turn the same colour as their surroundings.'

'It makes them invisible,' Nate added.

'I wish you two were invisible,' the headmaster said, still looking suspiciously at the hat, but then he smiled. 'Well done, though. That's quite remarkable for four days. I'll make sure it gets sent off to Saint Solutions today, and with any luck you'll be on your way to the final in no time at all. Now, until then, haven't you got classes to go to?'

Grinning at each other, Nate and Cat got up off their seats and left the office, and even the thought of double maths with smelly Mrs Glute couldn't dampen their mood.

12

The Results are Announced

Needless to say, the following week dragged on as though time itself had slowed down. The seconds ticked by like giant, plodding footsteps and the minutes felt long enough to take a weekend break in.

Absolutely nothing of interest happened at school, except for one field trip to the Broads during which the short-sighted minibus driver managed to back the two rear wheels of the bus out over the water and on to a boat. The AA spent three hours trying to recover the vehicle from the small yacht while a horrified businessman and his guests sat fuming on the riverbank.

The remaining days were spent trying to concentrate on schoolwork, although it was a pointless exercise as neither Nate nor Cat could take their minds off the competition, the results of which were due to be announced at the end of the week.

At home, Cat managed to cheer up her mum a little by inventing a special contraption that brought in eggs from the chicken coop every morning. She spent three nights working solidly on the project, creating a special claw that hoisted the surprised chickens from their roosts and a vacuum attachment that sucked up the eggs from beneath them, before plopping the birds back down on the hay.

After a couple of disastrous early attempts – during which one unfortunate chicken was sucked halfway down the Hoover pipe and remained there for forty-five minutes – Cat managed to get the mechanism just right, and even engineered a nifty model train to carry the eggs to the kitchen, via the cat flap. Her mum was delighted, but still didn't forget about the palmtop.

Nate, meanwhile, spent his evenings trying to avoid his parents. His mum still claimed to be terribly ill, and after she had been off work for five days his dad was getting increasingly annoyed. Both seemed to think that Nate was the cause of the phantom flu, which had no symptoms and didn't seem to be contagious at all, but neither could find any evidence, or think of any reason, why their son would do such a thing.

Nate's dad seemed to think he was going senile, as he couldn't for the life of him find his toothbrush or his bowler hat, both of which he had needed rather urgently for a meeting with his boss later in the week. Nate had told him it was simply stress, and that he should calm down, at which his father gave him a stern glare and implied that it was his fault these things were missing. Again, though, he couldn't prove a thing.

After a week of denying constant accusations of foul play, Nate was relieved when it was Friday. He met Cat outside the main gates before the morning bell and they ran straight to Mr Green's office, desperate to hear the results of the competition.

'This is it,' Cat said as they shuffled nervously outside the enormous wooden door.

'The moment of truth,' Nate added.

'The most important piece of information we'll ever hear.'

'Ever.'

'The news that will decide what we do with our lives, what we'll become.'

'And how much money we'll make,' Nate finished, earning a scowl from Cat.

'And whether we'll meet Ebenezer,' she offered. 'It's not about money, Nate.'

 79

But when Mr Green finally did usher them into his office he had a blank expression and no news. The results were due today, he told them, but nothing had been reported to the school. Softening his tone, he sat on the edge of his desk and stared at the two forlorn expressions before him, telling them not to get their hopes up, and that they might not have made it.

'You only had four days, after all,' he said as they made their way back out into the hallway. 'It's not the end of the world.'

But to both inventors it was exactly that. They sat in their classes staring at the walls like zombies, trying not to think about the competition. Of course, there might be something waiting for them at home – a letter of congratulation, a phone call – but surely they would have been informed through the school if they had been successful. Cat kept looking at the date on her watch, hoping it was wrong, but it was confirmed on the school calendar: today was the day, and there was nothing.

When the last bell rang out at three fifteen, both Nate and Cat made their way slowly to the front gates. Mr Green was on home duty and he shrugged at them as they passed to inform them that he'd still heard nothing. Cat could barely keep the tears from her eyes, but they were the old, angry tears, not the ones that had been falling in the chicken coop a week ago. Not wanting his best friend to go home to an empty house in such a furious mood, Nate followed her up the road and into the woods, murmuring words of comfort.

It did little good. As soon as they were out of sight of the pupils and passers-by Cat exploded, passing up on the aerial slide to storm through the trees, ripping up bushes, snapping branches, kicking molehills, punching leaves and cursing Ebenezer Saint with every foul word she knew. By the time they had reached Cat's house it looked as though a hurricane had hit the Bluebell Woods, but Cat was exhausted and much calmer.

Inside, the answering machine's light was blinking, and Cat practically leapt on the play button only to be greeted by the sound of her mum telling her she'd be late home because she was having a manicure. Even the information that there was lasagne in the freezer and iced buns in the bread bin didn't cheer her up as she listened expressionlessly to the beeps that signalled there were no more messages.

The post proved to be just as fruitless, with three bills and a flyer for plumbing services. Cat stomped up to her room, returning seconds later with the picture of Ebenezer Saint that they'd received the previous week.

'Well, so much for this loser,' she said, collapsing on to the sofa and staring at the image of the man who used to be her hero. 'Who wants to be an inventor anyway?'

'Cat!' snapped Nate, sick to the back teeth with her sulky moods. He walked over to the television and switched it on, flicking through the Sky channels until he found an episode of *Star Trek*. Walking to the sofa, he sat down next to Cat and looked at the image of Ebenezer. 'It's not over,' he continued. 'We don't know if we've won or lost yet, so don't get too mad.'

Still furious, Cat moved to rip the leaflet in two but faltered, unable to bring herself to tear up the smiling, enigmatic face.

'It is over, Nate,' she said, then fell silent, dropping the leaflet to her lap.

They both turned to stare at the television, neither knowing what to say next. On screen, Captain Picard was on the bridge claiming that they couldn't attack because it was against regulations. Nate suddenly remembered how much Cat hated *Star Trek*, how she always wanted them to 'kick some alien butt' instead of finding a peaceful, and boring, way out of it.

'Nate,' she said, 'turn it over.'

'Allow me,' came a voice from nowhere. Nate felt his heart stop for a fraction of a second as adrenalin flooded his veins. He looked around, half expecting a burglar to appear from the hallway, one kind enough to offer to change the channel before making off with their valuables. But there was nobody to be seen.

'What's going on?' Cat asked, perched on the edge of the sofa staring at the screen.

'Someone's here,' Nate answered, but before he could get to his feet Cat had taken hold of his arm with a grip of steel and was pointing with her other hand to the television.

'It came from the box,' she said.

'It surely did,' came the voice again, clearer this time. They both recognised the musical lilt of Ebenezer Saint. The picture of Picard was beginning to morph, contorting into a series of circles and whorls. These bubbles of colour began to rise to the top of the telly where they popped noisily, gradually revealing another image behind them. When they realised that this second image was Saint himself, they scrabbled forward over the carpet and knelt in front of the telly, noses practically touching the glass.

'Ah, now that's better,' said the white-suited Saint, popping the last bubble of colour with his finger so that he was the only thing on screen. He was sitting at an enormous ivory desk which was covered with wind-up monkeys, all beating cymbals together and toppling over the edge. He redirected one that was about to fall into his lap and sent it waddling off towards the camera.

Running his hand through his untidy mop of blond hair, Saint straightened his golden tie and bent forward as if straining to see the two eager faces before him.

'I can't actually see you,' he went on, sitting back and folding his arms across his chest. 'But I can hear you thanks to the microphone in that flyer. And I know you can see me, so hi!' He waved his fingers without moving his hands. 'Bet you've been wondering when you'd hear, thinking you hadn't quite made it, raiding the post, listening to the answering machine. Well, I'm very sorry to have kept you in the dark. It's most unfair.'

'Oh my God, Nate,' Cat whispered in awe. 'You were right, it's not over yet.'

'Not on your nelly, Cat,' said Saint. 'It's never over until the fat lady sings, and I can't see any fat ladies round here. Unless your mum's back?' The last of the wind-up monkeys shivered to a halt on Saint's desk and the master inventor looked down at it with a frown. 'It took me ages to wind all those up,' he said, then with a motion that caused both Nate and Cat to jump he swept a long, muscular arm across the surface of the desk, sending the tiny toys flying across the room. 'Anyway, where was I? Oh yes, apologies again, but it took us a long time to get back to everybody who didn't get through. There have been a lot of entries, you know.'

'And us?' asked Nate, holding his breath. 'Did we?'

There was a moment of silence as Saint slowly leant forwards towards the camera. Only when his face was inches away, appearing huge on the television screen, did he speak again.

'Of course you did!' he yelled, tapping on the camera and causing it to shake. 'Your invention was fantastic, stupendous, amazing. I haven't laughed so much in years – we had one of our testers try it and he turned bright green. We put him out into the garden and spent an hour trying to track him down. He was sitting at the top of a tree completely naked and we only found him when he turned back to his normal colour. Hilarious! I myself went for the blue option, like your headmaster. I don't know what he was complaining about – it felt great to be so colourful! Bravo to the pair of you.'

He sat back in his chair and beamed at them.

'Of course, I wouldn't have expected any less from the daughter of Harold Gardner. I never had the honour of meeting your pop, Cat, but he was a great man and he took enormous strides towards making this world a better place. I know he'd be proud of you following in his footsteps.'

Cat's cheeks reddened and she turned to Nate, tears filling her eyes. He smiled at her as she brushed them away, and they both returned their attention to the television.

'Thanks,' said Cat in a whisper. 'So what comes next?'

'Goodness, aren't we keen!' he commented, raising his eyebrow and stroking his chin thoughtfully. 'Well, you'll be going head to head with forty-eight other inventors right here at Saint Solutions, and you'll have a day – just one day, nine till nine, no overtime, no excuses – to invent, plan and build something that will knock my socks off.' He raised his leg and pulled up his spotless white trousers to reveal a huge bare foot. 'And I don't even wear socks, so it's going to have to be pretty impressive!'

Nate laughed.

'I'm glad you found that funny, Nate, I've been planning it all morning,' Saint put his foot down and reached inside his jacket, pulling out a strip of paper which he held up to the camera. It had another picture of himself but this time it was surrounded by text. Both Nate and Cat strained to read it, ignoring the sound of the letterbox snapping shut in the hallway.

'This,' he said, waving the piece of paper in front of them, 'is the sheet of instructions you'll need to follow to be eligible for the next round. Read them carefully because you've only got one shot at this.'

The two young inventors moved even closer to the telly to try and make sense of the text that was being waved in front of it.

'It's probably easier if you read the leaflet that's just come through the letterbox,' Saint said, snatching the paper away

 84

and throwing it over his shoulder. Cat got to her feet to run through to the hall but Saint raised a hand to stop her.

'Hold your horses,' he said. 'I just want to say, in all serious-ness, many congratulations for making the grade. You're one of an elite handful, but you're not out of the woods yet. The com-petition is tight, and you'll find yourself facing some pretty impressive rivals.' He gestured to the camera with his long, bony fingers. 'I mean, this amazing contraption I'm talking to you with now was one of the entries!'

Nate's mouth fell open in surprise when he realised what they were up against. He glanced at Cat, who was watching the screen with a similar expression.

'So, get yourselves ready and warm up your brains, and I'll see you right here in a week.'

'A week?!' shouted Cat.

'A week!' Saint answered enthusiastically, then the screen went black.

13

Big Changes Ahead

Both Nate and Cat stared at their dark, twisted reflections in the black screen for a moment, unsure of what to say. Gradually the image of the Starship *Enterprise* appeared, prompting Nate to reach up and switch the telly off. By the time he had got to his feet Cat had returned from the hallway brandishing two copies of the leaflet that Saint had been holding.

'I told you we'd be okay,' said Nate, taking hold of the copy she passed to him. The picture of Saint was identical to the previous one, only instead of holding out his hand to be shaken he was sticking up his thumb in congratulations. Nate ran his finger over the printed digit to see if anything happened, but the leaflet remained still – it was just paper this time.

'I knew we would, too,' Cat answered, scanning the text. She had apparently forgotten the destruction she had wrought less than an hour ago as they walked home. But Nate could still picture the terrified expression of one squirrel that had been catapulted through the trees by a rebounding branch.

'Listen to this,' she went on. '*Each of the competitors must arrive at the Saint Solutions compound on the morning of the 24th, bringing everything they need to reside there for a year.*'

'*If you are chosen as one of the twenty-five finalists,*' Nate continued, '*you will start your scholarship straight away, moving immediately into quarters in the Saint complex and remaining*

 86

there for a year – *we can't have you taking home our secrets at the end of each working day! Of course, you can head home for a week-long Christmas break if you really must – even I wouldn't want to get in Santa's bad books – and there will be another short holiday at Easter so I don't have the Easter Bunny on my case.'*

Cat took over: *'Spanning one hundred and seventeen acres, the facility has everything necessary to keep you happy and busy for the time you will spend here, including cinemas, parks, sports facilities and libraries. You'll be able to talk to your loved ones whenever you like via state of the art videophones.'*

'And, of course, you'll all have free rein to work with me and my technicians to create the most marvellous inventions you can imagine.'

'If you're not one of the finalists,' Cat went on, *'you'll be asked to leave after the day is over. But don't be disheartened, as you'll still be considered one of the finest young inventors in the country.'*

'The competition itself involves a day's work,' Nate finished off. *'We provide everything you need so long as you provide the ideas. It's a cinch!'*

'That's it?' asked Cat.

'These are just instructions on how to get there,' Nate said, turning the leaflet over to reveal a map and a route planner. 'It doesn't say anything else about the competition.'

Realising that their legs were shaking, Nate and Cat sat down on the sofa, both clutching the leaflets as though they were made of gold.

'We've got to start thinking of ideas,' Nate said.

'Especially given who we're up against,' Cat replied. 'I mean who on earth could have invented a destination-specific television transmitter to announce the results on? I wouldn't know where to start with that kind of technology.'

'Well, they had a month, remember,' said Nate defensively. 'I'm sure we could have worked it out.'

'We're going to need a miracle,' said Cat after a moment's silence, but Nate was feeling curiously optimistic. Standing up, he walked through to the kitchen, shouting back over his shoulder:

'Cat, we are miracles. All we really need is some tea.'

Nate was still at Cat's house when her mum returned later that evening, her nails immaculately shaped and polished. Cat was so excited that she blurted out the details of the competition straight away, without warning, mentioning for the first time that the winners would be away from home for a year.

Her mum burst into tears and gave Cat such a powerful hug that her fingers went blue. Five minutes later, when the crying and the bear hug and the comments about how she couldn't face losing a daughter as well as a husband still hadn't ended, Nate awkwardly waved goodbye to Cat – who was trying to worm her way out of the iron grip – and sneaked out of the back door to make his way home.

He was dreading the same response from his parents, but when he got back he found that their Bully Blow invention had been dropped off outside the front door. His dad sat in the kitchen fuming while trying to unstitch the camouflage from his favourite hat. For some reason he was using the same wooden spoon that he had rescued his toast with earlier, making it practically impossible for him to undo any of Cat's tight stitches. He gave Nate a look of barely contained fury that sent him scurrying up to his room without a backwards glance.

Later that evening, when Nate heard his mum return, he made his way back downstairs and told them the news. His dad was sitting in his favourite chair wearing the hat, which now looked like a half-chewed boot with a giant hole cut in the side.

Beneath the drooping brim his face broke into a grin when Nate mentioned the length of the scholarship.

'You mean you'll be working there for a year?' he yelled, almost jumping to his feet before trying to mask his happiness.

'Peter!' his mum snapped, walking over to Nate and holding his hand tenderly. 'If you're sure this is what you want to do, you know you have our support.'

'Well, I don't even know if I'll win yet,' Nate replied.

'Of course you will, son,' said his dad. 'You're a genius, you and Cat both. You're bound to be one of the finalists.'

'Peter!' his mum repeated. 'We'll miss him if he's away for a year.'

'He'll be back for Christmas!' his dad exclaimed.

But later that night as he lay in bed, after a series of hugs from his mum and dad, Nate heard the sound of glasses being taken from the cabinet containing all the expensive kitchen-ware, followed by the pop of a champagne cork and a series of cheers.

He laughed to himself and pulled the duvet around his shoulders. They had good reason to celebrate – a year with no ruined plasterwork, no hunting around for missing items of clothing and equipment, no strange chemical concoctions blowing up accidentally in the bath or bizarre homemade machines chasing the milkman down the street. They wouldn't know what to do with themselves!

Neither Nate nor Cat could get excited about the few remaining days of school. Fortunately they were excused from several of their classes for meetings with the headmaster and their parents, along with representatives from Saint Solutions, to discuss how their schooling would be affected by the scholarship, if indeed they won.

The two teachers from Saint Solutions were young, attractive and extremely enthusiastic. All of the adults in the room seemed very impressed when they said that each one of the twenty-five winners would have their own tutors who would not only carry on their formal education, but would teach them all of the skills necessary to become a fully fledged inventor.

Even more lessons were missed because of publicity meetings with members of the press. Mr Green, knowing that the two overexcited inventors would only be a distraction in class, agreed to let the papers, radio and TV come and interview them before they set off for the final.

Nate was more than happy to talk to the friendly man from the local *Heaton Gazette*, but when the sharp-suited national reporters and the ferocious television presenters appeared, jostling past each other to get a good shot, he suddenly felt extremely nervous and barely uttered a word.

Cat, on the other hand, couldn't stop talking, and gave the press all they needed for the features that emerged over the following days. She was so keen to talk, in fact, that by the end of the day most of the reporters had disappeared, leaving only one little old lady from the *Inventor's Chronicle* – who was far too polite to walk out – sitting listening to Cat's endless chatter.

With only two days remaining before the final, Nate and Cat were local celebrities and pictures of them both were plastered over their houses, the school, the community centre and even some lampposts in town. The same photo was used everywhere – showing Cat beaming at the camera and Nate cowering in her shadow, pulling a nervous expression that looked like he'd just noticed a giant lump of dog poo on his shoe.

With all the activity, Nate and Cat barely had any time to themselves, and it was only on the afternoon before the competition, as they left school for what could be the last time in a year, that they managed to escape the crowds. Cat had agreed to pop over to Nate's house to help him organise his suitcase, but as they turned out of the park on to the high street she abruptly changed direction, heading out of town and dragging Nate after her by his sleeve.

'I just want to call in on Dad,' she told him without looking back. Nate pulled her fingers from his jumper and squeezed her hand, and together they entered the woods that provided a handy shortcut to Heaton Cemetery.

Less than ten minutes later they were standing in silence over the grave of Harold Gardner. The modest headstone, inscribed with his name, age and the words 'You gave us everything', stood in a secluded section of the cemetery. It was situated at the top of a hill, overlooking stunning views of the town, embedded in a green and golden quilt of countryside. On the other side stood a bank of silver birch trees which filtered the orange afternoon sun through their leaves, creating playful shadows that swayed and circled across the moist grass.

'Hi, Dad,' Cat whispered. Nate wondered if he should give her some time alone, but she wrapped her fingers tightly around his sleeve again as she continued. 'I guess you probably know what's going on, but I thought Nate and I would come up and say hi before the big day.'

'Hi, Mr Gardner,' said Nate, waving awkwardly at the grave.

'I know you'll be there with us tomorrow,' Cat went on, 'and I'll be counting on you to help out. I just hope that some of your genius finds its way into us.'

'It already has,' Nate said when she had stood in silence for a few seconds. She didn't look up, but nervously chewed her lip as she stared at the writing on the headstone.

'This is all on the level, isn't it?' she said eventually. It took Nate a while to realise that she was talking to him. 'I mean, spending a year with a stranger doesn't exactly seem risk free.'

'Come on, Cat,' he replied, 'it's Saint. He's about the most famous man on the planet and I should think legions of lawyers, guardians and security personnel will be following our progress to make sure everything goes smoothly. And anyway, you know he's got a good heart – he finished your dad's invention and gave him all the credit. We'll be fine. It's just going to be a bunch of us working in one of Saint's labs building toys and gadgets. How bad can it be?'

Cat turned and gave him a smile as he continued.

'And your dad always said that the risk was worth it if you were building something to make the world a better place.'

Cat nodded as she rested her hand on the cold headstone for a second. She bent down and whispered something that Nate couldn't make out, then she stood and they walked back down the hill to the cemetery gates. It was only as they entered the woods again and started walking towards Nate's house that the silence was broken.

'I'm exhausted,' said Nate through an almighty yawn. 'And I can't believe I haven't even started packing yet.'

'I'm too excited to be tired,' Cat replied, picking up a stick, arching back then throwing it with all her strength down the path. It clattered through a few branches then fell to the dusty soil. 'I can't believe this is happening.'

'Me neither.' Nate picked up another stick, realised he probably couldn't throw it as far as Cat and let it slip discreetly from his fingers. 'It feels like a dream.'

'A good dream, though,' Cat said, turning to look at him. She was smiling, but he sensed the question in her voice.

'I think so. This is what you want, isn't it?'

Somewhere off the path, to their left, a tree groaned in the faint breeze. They reached the point where Cat's stick had fallen and she picked it up again, but this time she simply stroked the rough bark, lost in thought.

'I think so,' she echoed. 'It's a bit overwhelming, though. A year is a long time, even if we do get to come home for Christmas and Easter. I'm going to miss my mum.'

'I'm not,' he joked, but it was a lie. He was going to miss his parents more than he could imagine. And his gran, even his house. Free from the hectic bustle of school, it suddenly struck him just what a huge change winning this competition would mean, and he suddenly felt choked with a strange kind of sadness. Cat, always sensitive to his moods, slipped her warm hand into his and clenched it. The contact instantly turned his mood to one of joy, and he squeezed back.

'We'll be fine,' she said, pulling her hand away, a little embarrassed. 'We'll just stick together. You and me against the rest of them.'

'You and me against the world,' Nate added. 'And if we don't like it we can always leave, right?'

'Right,' she answered, smiling at him. 'Anyway, enough of this. It's getting late. Why don't you go sort your stuff out and I'll head back to mine and start packing.'

'Yeah, you're right.' Nate stopped walking and did an abrupt about-turn while Cat carried on up the path. 'I'll see you bright and early.'

'Not if I see you first.'

14

A Last Night at Home

Nate arrived back at home to find his mum, dad and gran all sitting around the kitchen table, the smell of macaroni and cheese wafting from the oven and bacon sizzling in the pan – his favourite combination. When he entered the room his mum stood up and walked over to him, kissing him on the cheek and taking his hand. Even his dad was smiling.

'Blimey, am I in the right house?' Nate asked, raising an eyebrow. His mum gave him a harmless clip round the ear and walked over to the oven.

'We just thought it would be good to have everybody over,' she said, 'since it might be your last night here for a while.'

'See you off in style,' added his dad, opening a fresh bottle of champagne. 'Bit of bubbly?'

'Thanks, Dad,' Nate said, dropping his bag, kicking off his shoes and pulling out a chair. He was about to sit down when he realised his gran was sitting staring into space, unaware of anything that was being said around her. Excusing himself, he ran upstairs and emptied his waste-paper bin on to the floor, rummaging around until he found the repulsive hearing aid. Cleaning it with his shirt, he bolted back to the kitchen and handed it to his gran.

'Oh Nate, thank you, dear,' she said, slipping it into her ear with a wrinkled finger. 'That's much better.'

Nate's mum eyed him suspiciously as she pulled a steaming

dish of macaroni from the oven, kicking the door shut behind her, but she didn't say anything.

'We're all very proud of you,' his gran continued, taking his hand in hers and shaking it up and down excitedly. 'Nobody in the family has achieved anything like this before.'

Nate saw his dad turn and glare at the old lady before starting to pour the champagne. He obviously wasn't used to the job, as it bubbled out of each glass to form a large puddle on the colourful tablecloth.

'We are proud of you, though,' said his dad, staring at the overflowing glasses as though embarrassed to have said the words.

'And we'll miss you,' added his mum. 'The people from Saint Solutions came round today and we've signed all the forms. It actually feels real now.'

Nate looked at them both and felt tears beginning to well at the thought of being away from them for so long. Thankfully an enormous plate of macaroni cheese soon materialised in front of him and his appetite took over.

'I'm going to miss you guys too,' he said, scooping up a forkful and raising it to his lips. 'I'm going to miss you a lot.'

Dinner turned out to be fantastic. He sank his first glass of champagne, and although he wasn't allowed any more he stole his gran's when nobody was looking, so by the time the main course was finished and the ice cream emerged he was feeling extremely happy and relaxed.

He hadn't spoken to his parents so freely for many years, and he talked openly about the competition, how he'd miss being at home and how he was nervous about meeting new people.

They in turn told him how much they admired his skill at inventing (something he'd never heard before) and how they hoped it would work out for him tomorrow.

After helping to clear up, he made his way to his room and dug out the giant suitcase that he kept under the bed. When he had emptied out all of the inventing equipment from inside, he began rummaging through his wardrobe, throwing in a few pairs of jeans and his favourite T-shirts, plus jumpers, underwear, socks and even a vast brown cardigan that his gran had knitted him for Christmas a couple of years ago.

There was still plenty of room left, so he wrapped up a few of his favourite tools – his soldering iron and his spanner set – and picked a couple of books from his shelf just in case he got bored. Not that there was any chance of that.

Changing into his pyjamas, he made his way downstairs where his mum was sitting watching *EastEnders*.

'I'm going to hit the sack,' he said. His mum turned and blew him a kiss.

'Well, sleep well, love,' she said. 'Your dad's just nipped up the road with your nan, but he said we'll be setting off about seven tomorrow morning. I'll give you a shout.'

'I'll probably be okay,' Nate replied, walking back towards the stairs. 'I don't think I'm going to sleep a wink.'

Closing his bedroom door behind him, he took one last look around his room – the posters of elemental tables and star charts, the postcard-sized picture of Lara Croft that Cat always tried to take off the wall, the racks of scientific equipment that he had been collecting since he was three. With a lump in his throat at the thought of leaving it all behind, he climbed into his bed and pulled the duvet completely over his head so that he was lost in the comforting dark warmth.

'I'm not going to sleep a wink,' he repeated to himself under his breath. But the excitement and exhaustion of the previous week soon caused his eyelids to droop and his breathing to slow, and before he knew it he had drifted into unconsciousness.

Things were decidedly less pleasant the following morning. Nate was woken by an impatient hammering on his door – obviously his dad, from the muttered curses that floated in through the thin wood – and looked at his alarm clock to see that it was six o'clock. He had a headache, although he didn't know why, and grumbling to himself he struggled from the tangled duvet and made his way out of the door.

Outside, both his parents were stumbling around in the hall-way as if they'd had lobotomies. His dad was dressed, and trying to put on a sock while walking at the same time – something that is physically impossible – while his mum was watching her husband's graceless performance with an unimpressed scowl.

'Damn these stupid socks,' his dad cursed, almost falling down the stairs. He looked at Nate and scratched his head. 'Sorry, son,' he said before traipsing down to the front door.

'He's just tired,' his mum said, 'and he drank too much champagne. Now go and get ready. We should leave in an hour.'

Forty-five minutes later, and Nate was still sitting on the edge of his bed staring absentmindedly at his suitcase. He had picked out his best clothes to wear that day – a pair of dark blue jeans and a clean black T-shirt – and had even combed his hair, but he still wasn't sure if he was taking the right things.

He wondered what Cat would have packed. Probably an assortment of survival gear – pocketknife, water purifiers, flares – plus a tent and a kitchen sink, but he didn't own any of those (apart from the kitchen sink, and he didn't fancy having to explain the mess to his mother).

Walking downstairs, he found his dad drinking his third cup of coffee and rubbing his temples, while his mum was cooking up another feast of eggs and leftover bacon.

'Do you think you'll need a packed lunch?' she asked, spooning a heap of fried food on to a slice of toast and handing it to Nate. He took one look at it and felt his stomach shrink. Placing it in front of his dad, he picked an apple from the bowl and began nibbling on it.

'It's a multibillion pound centre for innovation and excellence, Mum. I think they'll probably have food there,' he said between mouthfuls. 'And I really don't feel like a fry-up, thanks.'

She was about to reply when the sound of footsteps on the gravel outside signalled the arrival of Cat and her mum. Nate unlocked the door and let them in, noticing from the dark bags under their eyes that both had been crying.

'Hiya,' said Cat, stepping in and throwing her suitcase down on the floor.

'Howdy,' Nate replied. 'Hi, Mrs Gardner.'

'Hello, Nathan. Are you ready?'

'Just about,' he said, then, after a moment's thought. 'Well, not really.'

'I don't think any of us are, to be honest,' she went on, wiping her feet then walking through to the kitchen to say hi to Nate's parents. Cat was standing in the hallway staring at her feet. She didn't look herself at all.

'How're you doing?' Nate asked.

'Not sure,' she muttered, almost inaudibly. 'Nearly stayed in bed this morning.'

'Yeah, me too. Would have regretted it though.'

From the kitchen came the sound of Peter Wright pushing back his chair and jingling his car keys, a sign that it was time to leave.

'Here goes nothing,' Nate and Cat said together.

15

Saint Solutions

The Saint Solutions headquarters was in the capital, a good hour's drive away from Heaton, provided the traffic was okay. The Wrights and the Gardners had all decided to pile into Nate's family car because it was a bulky, if ancient, Volvo estate, and Cat hated driving with her mother in her clapped-out VW Beetle.

Somehow, Nate found himself in the most uncomfortable seat in the vehicle, wedged in the back between Cat and her mum and with his seatbelt clasp sticking firmly into his left buttock no matter which way he shuffled.

They had only been driving for seven minutes before his mum and dad started arguing about best routes. Peter ignored Wendy's advice and took the motorway, only to find out halfway that she hadn't been making up the warnings of road works bringing traffic to a halt.

After thirty minutes of crawling along at the speed of a con-cussed sloth, they passed the last set of speed restrictions and bombed up the fast lane until they saw the signs to the city. Several wrong turns, dead ends and shouting matches later, they found the first of the signs bearing Saint's grinning face, and followed them without further incident to the miracle of architecture that was Saint Solutions.

As soon as Saint had made his first billion he had begun buying up property in the riverside area of the city, eventually purchasing nearly a hundred hectares of prime land. Within days a vast, white wall of marble had sprung up, and although nobody was allowed to see exactly what was going on inside, the sheer cacophony of explosions, bangs and crashes let everybody know what the master inventor was up to.

People had complained about one man owning so much land in the centre of the capital – even the Prime Minister, who claimed that it was a security risk. But Saint got his way, as always, and within a month he had transformed the area into the most advanced research facility on the face of the planet.

Saint Solutions was so enormous that even when the car had reached the wall it took a good ten minutes of speedy driving – and endless moaning about uncomfortable seats and sore bums – to make it all the way to the main gate. But as soon as the front of the complex came into view everybody in the car fell silent – even Nate's parents, who needed a very good reason to stop arguing.

Through the left-hand window the vast, curved, glass-fronted gatehouse – as big as a tower block in its own right – rose from the veritable jungle of foliage that lined the side of the road, glistening in the morning sun. A set of enormous lasers mounted on the roof moved in sync to generate a vast, three-dimensional image of Saint performing a bizarre tap dance above the road, which faded every now and again to be replaced by the names of the competition finalists.

Everybody in the car leant to the left to get a better view of the awesome sight, including Nate's dad, whose curiosity almost sent them careening into the vehicle in front.

'He certainly likes his own face, doesn't he,' Peter said, returning his attention to the wheel.

'Who wouldn't with a face like that?' added Nate's mum dreamily, misting up the window with her words. Cat and her mum gave approving murmurs, while Nate and his dad tutted in mock annoyance.

Curious onlookers had lined the streets to watch the fleet of arriving cars as they passed through the enormous gates, which stood open in welcome. Nate and Cat waved at them, but froze as soon as the interior of the Saint Solutions complex became visible.

Compared to the bustle of people and traffic outside, the world beyond the gates was heavenly. It seemed as though the entire estate was covered in soft, downy grass. A series of green rolling hills, like something from *The Hobbit* only much larger, stretched out in every direction as far as the eye could see. As Nate strained to get a better look he saw that each of the hills had rows of discreet, tinted windows set into them at regular intervals.

'That must be where all the technicians work,' he blurted out, pointing to the surreal landscape.

'That's all very well,' muttered Nate's dad, 'but how the bloody hell am I supposed to know where to park?'

Five jaws in the car dropped simultaneously as the answer became evident. To their right, and so large that nobody had seen it through the car's small windows, was a robotic Ebenezer Saint. Standing a hundred metres tall, the metallic figure was an exact replica of the master inventor except that instead of arms it had at least twenty vast claws that spun around towards the cars driving through the gates.

'That's impossible,' Peter whispered, his voice a strange mixture of awe and fear that Nate had never heard before.

'This is Saint's world,' Cat explained, gazing up at the enormous robotic figure.

With a deafening hiss and the scream of pneumatics, the robot extended its claw towards the car directly in front. A tiny probe emerged from the tip and scanned the interior – checking the identity of the stunned passengers – before the claw lifted the vehicle effortlessly from the ground and swept it off away from the gates. Before the occupants of Peter Wright's estate could object, they saw an identical probe peering through their window, then felt the gut-wrenching, roller-coaster sensation of being pulled up from the ground.

The experience was too much for the adults in the car – both Mrs Gardner and Mrs Wright had turned such a violent shade of green that Nate thought they had accidentally swallowed some Bully Blow, while Peter tried desperately to turn the steering wheel left and right as if it would change the direction of the airborne car. But Nate and Cat both whooped with excitement, peering out of the windows as the ground below flew past revealing the Saint Solutions empire in all its glory.

'That must be Saint's headquarters.' Nate followed Cat's finger to a stretch of the compound that he hadn't even noticed, and for a moment thought she was seeing things, as there was nothing there except for a vast stretch of grass and the cloudless sky.

As the car moved round, however, the angle of the sunlight caught the apparently empty space and as if by magic a towering building made up of glass panels appeared, shimmering in the blinding light like a desert mirage. The panicked noise in the car gradually faded as the robotic arm carried them closer to the building, which grew ever more enormous and impressive as they neared.

'That has to be at least three hundred metres high,' whispered Nate's dad as the arm began to descend, gently placing the car down on a grassy slope facing the tower block. The building was so awe-inspiring that it took the shocked passengers a minute to realise that there was a crowd of people outside the car – competitors, parents, staff and giddy onlookers all cheering fanatically.

When Nate and Cat's stomachs had settled they turned their attention back to Saint's headquarters, noticing that the building sat in the middle of an immense pit in the ground – like the flag in a hole on a golf course. A single bridge spanned the abyss between the grass of the complex and the tower's main entrance – a pair of ridiculously high gleaming gold gates that were shut fast against the outside world. Every now and again a ring of electric-blue light would radiate from deep inside the hole, travelling up the building and gradually fading as it neared the top.

'I've seen this place on the telly,' Nate said, thinking about the various news reports he had seen about the tower. Conspiracy theorists claimed that the building didn't just appear to vanish because of the glass – but that it actually moved. It was a ludicrous idea, though – the tower was enormous. 'I never thought it would look like this, not really.' He switched his gaze from the tower itself to the crowd that was gathered beneath it, next to the bridge.

'If they think I'm leaving my car here . . .' Peter Wright started, but he didn't have time to finish as the doors of the station wagon opened automatically. As soon as they did, Nate heard cheering and glanced out to see that the crowd was actually much larger than he had first thought.

He waited for Cat to clamber out, then stepped into the sunlight to see an endless throng of people standing behind red velvet ropes on either side of a path that led to the bridge. He recognised some of the reporters who had interviewed him and Cat that week, and waved nervously at them. None returned the gesture – they were too busy trying to film rare footage of the interior of the Saint Solutions complex.

There were a group of people standing on the inside of the ropes, all dressed in white overalls with golden gloves – with the instantly recognisable image of Ebenezer's face stitched on to their chests. Nate watched as two of the smiling Saint employees walked to the occupants of the car that had been in front – a skinny, freckled girl, who looked the same age as Nate and Cat, standing between two equally thin parents, all looking terrified. They took them by the hand, leading them off towards the tower. Two more began to walk towards Nate and Cat, and the inventors looked at each other nervously.

'Well, here goes,' said Cat, brushing a strand of hair from her eyes. 'You and me, remember.'

'You and me, Cat,' Nate replied, then turned to greet the two young white-suited members of staff.

'Nathan Wright,' said the young man, looking at Nate.

'And Sophie Gardner,' added the other, a young woman, reaching out and taking Cat's hand. 'Welcome to Saint Solutions. If you'd like to come with us we'll show you to the competition room.'

'Please feel free to follow,' said the man to the trio of parents who were standing awkwardly watching the next family being ushered out of their car. 'You will have the opportunity to watch the competition and say goodbye to your children. Then, of course, you will be returned to your car.'

'Better be,' Nate heard his dad mumble as they followed the two guides down the soft grass path, waving to the people who had gathered to watch their arrival. Some were obviously employees, judging by their overalls, but others looked like ordinary families who had turned out to get a glimpse of the children who had wowed the wealthiest and most enigmatic man in the country. As they walked, the two guides spoke softly.

'This is Saint Tower,' said the woman, who was still holding Cat's hand. 'It contains over a million tonnes of glass and is five hundred and fifty metres tall.'

'Five hundred and fifty?' exclaimed Nate's dad. 'That's impossible.'

'Only part of that is above ground,' said the man, turning to look at Peter and smiling gently. His smile was perfect, Nate noticed, just like his teeth. The flawless expression made him feel a little uneasy, although he couldn't explain why. 'One third of the tower lies underground.' He pointed to the vast abyss between the crowd and the tower: 'That's where the most important and secret research takes place.'

'The rolling hills that you see all around you,' continued the woman, 'are staff quarters and smaller research labs, as well as leisure facilities such as gyms, libraries, cinemas and restaurants.'

'And what about Saint?' asked Cat. 'When will we be meeting him?'

'Soon enough,' said the two guides in unison, in tones that were almost perfectly harmonised. Nate raised an eyebrow and turned to look at Cat, but she was too excited at the thought of meeting her hero to return his gaze.

Ahead, at the foot of the bridge that led to the golden gates, a small collection of children and adults was milling around talking to a seemingly endless parade of guides, and Nate and Cat were ushered into the centre of the group.

Looking around, they saw what must have been close to fifty children all standing with parents, grandparents, brothers, sisters and guardians, some kids in groups of two or three, others standing alone and overwhelmed, clinging to coat sleeves and staring at the surrounding sights in awe. Some were in tears, and being consoled by the guides, others were laughing amongst themselves and grinning with delight. Nate wasn't sure whether he was about to imitate the criers or the laughers.

'These are your fellow finalists,' said the young woman, who had let go of Cat's hand in order to raise her arms in the direction of the crowd around her. 'As you can see, we're almost ready to go in. Only a few families have yet to arrive.'

Nate felt a hand grasp his own and turned to face his mum, who was looking at him with wide eyes.

'Are you okay?' she asked, not waiting for a reply before continuing. 'I had no idea there would be all these people, or that this place would be so huge, or that there would be so many cameras here.' She flashed a grin at a photographer who was shouting at them from behind the rope. 'If I'd known I'd have put a nicer dress on.'

'You look fine, Mum,' he replied, squeezing her hand briefly then letting go, not wanting to appear child-like in front of all his potential rivals. She ruffled his hair then resigned herself to giving her husband a hug. Not wanting to be left out, Cat's mum wrapped her arms around Peter Wright from the other side, and between them the two women squeezed him hard enough to make him wheeze. Shaking himself free, he glanced around in embarrassment and took a step backwards, making both Nate and Cat laugh out loud.

Cat opened her mouth to make a comment, but before she could speak the ground started to vibrate, softly at first then with more force, sending a tingle through Nate's feet and up his leg bones. The murmur of the crowd died down as the vibration continued to grow in strength, until another of the giant rings of crackling electricity shot up from the hole in the ground, circling the tower and rising upwards with incredible speed until it vanished near the upper storeys. Lost for words, Nate stood with his mouth agape.

'That's the building's primary power source,' said the female guide, whispering into Nate's ear as though it were some incredible secret. 'It's generated deep underground, even deeper than the lowest floor of the Saint Tower, and feeds every single piece of electronic equipment in the complex.'

'But don't tell a soul,' the first guide added, tapping his nose. 'It's all classified.'

This time, Cat did return Nate's look of concern. Behind them they heard a car door slam shut, and looked to see another family standing in awe. Almost as soon as they had been greeted by the last of the guides in white, a gentle chime sounded from the direction of the golden gates. Turning to look, Nate and Cat saw the vast, ornate doors begin to open, not making the slightest of sounds despite their immense size.

Before they had opened fully, four holographic projectors slid out from the bridge, angling upwards. Then, with a sound that resembled a light-sabre igniting, lasers blasted upwards from the projectors, flickering for an instant before creating a three-dimensional image of Ebenezer Saint's face in front of the building.

'It's time,' said the two guides together, looking at Nate and Cat. 'Let's go inside.'

As the group of finalists and their families walked forwards, cheered on by the crowds behind them, the image of the master inventor grew more solid, expanding so that his transparent, smiling mouth covered the golden gates. Nate realised that in entering the tower they would have to walk through Saint's open lips.

'You have to be kidding me,' said Nate's dad, evidently noticing the same thing. 'What an egomaniac!'

They walked on to the bridge, which was much larger than Nate first thought, stretching over a hundred metres to the giant gates. Both Nate and Cat risked peeking over the edge.

Beneath them spanned the bottom half of the tower, the complete opposite of the section that stretched gloriously skyward. It was crafted from what looked like a solid block of obsidian, a giant black stake with no windows.

The tower was secured to the sides of the wall by several giant struts, and as Nate's eyes adjusted to the dark he saw why. The hole in which Saint Tower sat seemed to stretch on for ever. Bolts of liquid blue electricity could be seen racing up from the very depths of the earth, snaking their way up the dark walls and striking the building with alarming regularity. The shimmering, dancing blue light was reflected in the metallic sides of the tower, creating a sight that, while beautiful, was undeniably terrifying.

He thought once again about reports of the building disappearing, and felt his stomach flip. The hole looked like a giant tunnel, or the throat of some gargantuan beast. The image made him want to throw up there and then, and walking away from the side of the bridge he focused on the gates ahead. His heart was racing; everywhere he looked there were things that he couldn't explain, that he never even knew existed.

As if reading his mind, the male guide turned to him and offered the same perfect smile.

'It's a lot to take in,' he said. 'We were all a little overwhelmed when we first arrived.'

Cat walked up to Nate and threaded her arm through his, clutching him with all the strength she could muster. Pulling her closer and gripping her with the same force, Nate led her slowly into the giant, grinning mouth, and together they entered Saint Tower.

16

Saint Makes an Appearance

If the outside of the tower had seemed slightly sinister, the inside was worse. Beyond the vast gates stretched a ludicrously big reception area, easily half the size of a football pitch and painted entirely in white. In the middle of the room, a good thirty seconds' walk away, was a tiny white desk manned by another young woman in overalls – barely visible because the immaculate room was so uniform in colour.

As soon as the last of the group had entered, the golden doors began to close, their enormous bulk sliding effortlessly across the polished floor and meeting with a gentle click.

With nothing more than a farewell wave the guides all filtered to the outskirts of the room, disappearing through several white doors that were invisible against the smooth walls. Like wildebeest on the plains of the Serengeti fearing an attack by a pride of lions, the visitors clustered together and shuffled fearfully towards the reception desk. When they eventually arrived the receptionist looked up and smiled at them.

'Welcome to Saint Tower,' she said, scanning the group with friendly blue eyes. 'Mr Saint knows you are here and will be with you very shortly. He apologises for the delay, and asks for your patience.'

With that, she lowered her gaze to the computer screen that was set into the white plastic desk and began to run her fingers across the glass, obviously entering data of some kind.

The room remained deathly silent for what seemed like an eternity – but even Nate's dad, who once complained after being made to wait four seconds for a Big Mac, didn't utter so much as a disapproving breath. Eventually, a white light began to blink on the desk and the receptionist picked up a small phone, replacing it seconds later without a word.

'Mr Saint is on his way down,' she said.

A murmur of excitement began to brew as the pupils and parents awaited the arrival of Ebenezer Saint. Even those who had no interest in inventing knew the man and his legend – they had all seen his grand entry during the Nobel ceremony, heard about his love of adventure, his wacky, virtually insane sense of humour, his eccentric behaviour – and of course they all knew his face almost as well as their own.

Everybody in the group waited with bated breath to see how he'd greet the winning children, the ones who had passed the first heat of his unprecedented test. Would it be by a helicopter hat? Rocket-powered boots? Maybe even teleportation?

After a short wait a soft chime sounded from the other end of the reception hall, and a set of lift doors opened. The group moved around the desk to get a better look, squinting to try and make out the tiny shape emerging from the distant doors. The figure seemed to pause for a minute, stagger to one side and right itself, then started to move forwards. It wasn't walking, however, but seemed to be bouncing, on what looked like a giant red ball.

The shape gradually got closer and closer to the reception desk, and the form of a tall, thin man in a white suit with long, messy blond hair began to materialise. It also became clear that Ebenezer Saint's grand entry was actually taking place on a space hopper, and that the master inventor had apparently never, ever used one before.

He would bounce a couple of times, fall to one side and stick out a lanky leg to try and right himself. Then he would spin round in a panic to catch his balance. Once he even fell backwards and presented the stunned crowd with the image of two long legs poking up in the air from behind a giant red bubble, waving frantically to try and make contact with the ground again.

After five minutes of clumsy acrobatics, accompanied by the squeak of rubber on marble that seemed deafening in the shocked silence, Saint finally reached the crowd. His face was red with effort, and no small amount of embarrassment, and with a nervous smile he pulled a small cord on the side of the bulging red hopper. It began to deflate like a balloon, filling the reception hall with an immense, thundering raspberry.

When all the air had been released the hopper folded itself up and disappeared into the tails of Saint's coat with a painful-sounding slap. Wincing, he performed an awkward flourish and stared at the crowd as though waiting for a round of applause.

'It's a work in progress,' he said, his deep, lyrical voice filling the entire hall. 'Although we've obviously progressed less than I thought.'

He was greeted with around a hundred and fifty open mouths, all gaping at him in amazement, surprise or just plain shock.

'Well, if I ever need to catch flies I'll know where to look,' he said, laughing. 'You can close your mouths whenever you like – I'm not terribly happy about finding puddles of drool on my reception floor.'

This time his remarks drew a quiet laugh from several members of the crowd, including Nate and Cat. Saint glanced at them, and in the eerie white light of the room his eyes looked almost golden.

'That's better,' he said, 'you *are* all alive.' He spun round on a pair of white, pointed boots and started walking back towards the lift, the deflated red space hopper flapping against his bottom like a loose pair of pants.

'If you'd all like to follow me,' he said over his shoulder, prompting the group to begin walking slowly forward. After no more than three steps, however, he whirled round again, causing the confused crowd to stop dead in their tracks. 'The kids, that is,' he went on, 'not the parents. If the wrinklies here would like to watch these young inventors at work then there is a viewing hall upstairs, somewhere. I'll have somebody show you the way.'

There was a groan from some of the parents, including Nate's dad, and Saint frowned. 'Of course for those of you who would rather have your nostril hairs plucked out by an angry monkey, there's plenty here to keep you occupied for the day.' This piece of news practically brought a cheer from the older members of the group, followed by some disapproving clucks from the kids.

'Right,' said Saint, turning and walking again, 'it's getting late. Time please.'

Several members of the group reached for their watches but before anybody could answer him the glowing numbers and hands of a giant clock face materialised on the wall above the reception desk (it might have been the ceiling – because everything was the same colour it was difficult to see where one ended and the other began). It was five minutes to nine. Saint flashed a look over his shoulder as they walked.

'Good, isn't it,' he said, nodding at the clock, which was fading back into the white surface. 'Try it.'

Hesitantly, some of the children in the crowd started to mutter 'time please', each attempt causing the glowing Roman numerals to appear. Some of the adults began joining in, and before long the clock face was flickering on and off like a strobe light. Saint stopped walking, spun round again, and with a stern expression said, 'Not too much – you'll break it!'

There was a bashful silence as Saint set off across the reception, tutting loudly, the children hesitantly following, and waving goodbye to their parents, who were left standing awkwardly in the giant room. As Saint walked, he talked.

'I'd meant to do all of this earlier,' he said, 'but you know what these things are like – they take longer to plan than you think, then you spill coffee on your best suit in the morning and spend half an hour trying to remember the password to get into your walk-in closet.'

As they approached the lift the doors slid open, revealing an enormous white interior. Saint ushered the finalists inside, then stepped in himself. 'And no, before you ask, this elevator cannot take us to every room in the tower. It only goes up and down. I am *not* Willy Wonka.'

Some of the occupants of the lift laughed gently as Saint waved his hand in front of the immaculate white wall beside the door. A set of glowing numbers, projected like a hologram, appeared from nowhere, and Saint pressed one firmly with his gloved hand.

'Going up,' he said, turning to the fifty faces before him. 'Wow, so many of you,' he continued, 'that's good. Now, I was planning to say all of this upstairs but as we're short of time I'll go through it now. In a minute or so you'll be thrown out of this elevator into the conference room, which has been decorated with fifty workbenches, each with pretty much every tool and raw material I can possibly think of, minus those that can be used to make nuclear weapons.' He studied the faces to see if anybody looked overly disappointed.

'You can work as you like, either alone, or in groups. It's up to you, but remember that if you team up you need to be able to trust who you're working with, because if they let you down you're both out.' Nate and Cat looked at each other and smiled.

 113

'You'll have twelve hours. There's food and drink provided, take as many breaks as you like, and good luck.'

As soon as the last word had left his lips the lift came to a halt and the doors opened to reveal another enormous chamber, this one appearing to take up one whole floor of the tower. The giant round room was surrounded by a single wall of glass panels, each thirty metres tall, and the ornate ceiling, decorated with Renaissance-style paintings of Saint, tapered upwards like a circus tent. Set into the marble floor were dozens of oak-panelled benches, arranged in concentric circles and each surrounded by racks of tools, equipment and parts.

'Go go go!' shouted Saint, shaking the fifty competitors out of their stunned trance. 'Find a desk, explore your brains, get started.' He began hopping up and down on one foot, his face twisted into an expression of nervous anticipation. 'Time's running out! It's running out!'

The panic in Saint's voice was contagious, and the occupants of the lift began to file out rapidly, running across the echoing chamber to claim a workspace. Nate and Cat bolted to the left and sprinted to the outer ring of desks, with Cat taking the lead and actually shoving a short, plump boy out of the way before leaping on to the green leather surface of a desk. Nate apologised to the out-of-breath teen before joining the grinning Cat.

'Where's your competitive spirit?' she asked, letting loose a howling laugh that sent a chill up Nate's spine. At least she was back to normal, he thought.

Cat pushed herself off the desk and jogged over to the impressive window, placing her hands on the glass and staring out at the view. Nate walked over and joined her, making sure to leave his coat on the desk to show that it had been claimed.

The lift ride hadn't taken long, but as he approached the transparent wall he saw that they were at least halfway up the tower, with an unrestricted view across the entire complex. The green hills did actually stretch for miles, rolling all the way to the white marble wall that encircled the complex, and which resembled a distant, coiled serpent. To one side lay a vast lake that had been hidden before behind the uneven ground. Barely visible in the flickering light that reflected from its surface was a flotilla of colourful sails making its way gently towards a stretch of golden beach.

'Nate,' whispered Cat, not taking her eyes from the view, 'we have to win this competition.'

'Then we'd better get to work.'

It was a good minute before either of them could peel themselves away from the stunning view, but as soon as they did they made their way back to the desk and started to plan their day. In the chaotic activity of the previous week they hadn't had any time to think of ideas, and although both had several suggestions (including a meal in a pill from Nate and Cat's idea of an extra pair of legs for people in a hurry), none was even remotely possible within such a short time frame.

Nobody else in the room seemed to be having the same trouble. In every direction, on every desk, frantic fingers and furrowed brows made it clear that some furious inventing was taking place.

On the desk to their right a large, red-faced boy wearing a three-piece suit (complete with bow tie) was welding rods of steel together to make what looked like a small harness. Nate had overheard him ask for canisters of liquid oxygen and liquid hydrogen, which could mean only one thing – rocket fuel.

Some distance to the left sat a quiet, handsome, blond-haired boy who was rigging up a series of giant batteries beneath his desk. Immediately ahead of him a cluster of three girls looked like they were experimenting with a food processor, although one which every now and again gave out blinding flashes of light before producing cups of smoking, grey gunk. The boy Cat had shoved out of the way was smearing what looked like manure all over his desk and planting a number of seeds.

Two rows down and three desks across, a tall, curly-haired lad was busy wrapping himself in white bandages, like a mummy, while directly opposite him a girl was fumbling with what looked like a shotgun. Nate swallowed nervously, glad that he wasn't anywhere near her, and suddenly wondered if Saint had thought to include any kind of safety precautions for the competition.

Glancing to his right he saw two canisters of fuel being deposited by the large boy's desk, each with 'Warning: Highly Explosive' written on its shiny metal sides and each being showered in sparks from his welding iron.

'Oh God,' he muttered. Cat also looked concerned, but after a few seconds she pushed herself off the desk and began pacing up and down, staring at the floor, her mind back on the job.

'We've got to think of something amazing,' she said, not taking her eyes off the polished marble. 'It can't just be another jet pack.' She said this loud enough for the kid with the bow tie to hear, but he ignored her. 'Or a propeller hat or a watch powered by human sweat or a vacuum cleaner that lives on dead insects. It's got to be mind-blowing, it's got to be good enough to win outright.' She stopped pacing in front of Nate and turned to him, grabbing him by his T-shirt and giving him a shake. 'We're going to build a robot.'

Nate looked Cat in the eye. She had a strange, haunted expression that made her look very slightly loony, and it scared him. He placed his hands gently over hers and tried to smile, although it turned out to be more of a grimace.

'Cat,' he began, about to point out their obvious time constraints.

'I don't want to hear it,' she interrupted. 'I know we can do this, Nate. I know we've got what it takes to win.' She began to shake him more energetically. 'Let's do it. There's a computer – write a program. I'll make the frame and the mechanics. Dad's watching over us. We *can* do this.'

Nate paused for a second, considering what she was saying. It was ludicrous to think they could build a robot in eleven and a half hours. Even more ridiculous to think that he could possibly write an entire computer program to operate one. But something about Cat's tone, something about the desperate way she looked at him, made him nod his head. She might be crazy, but there was no way on earth he would let her down.

'You and me,' he said in what was fast becoming their catchphrase.

'Against the world.'

And so it began.

17

Building a Robot

Not wasting another second, Nate pulled out the chair beneath the desk and booted up the computer. Opening up the standard code-development software, he began typing in the core directives, setting out the parameters needed to make the robot operate as it should.

As he typed, Cat set to work on the internal mechanics of the invention, submitting a lengthy list of required ingredients to an eager assistant who dropped them off on the desk within ten minutes. Using her small, dextrous fingers, she shaped strands of strong but flexible plastic into a lightweight framework, attaching them to a series of gears, cogs and rotors with tiny jabs of the welding iron. Nate fired off questions to her as she worked.

'So, what is the robot for?' he asked quietly, tapping the table as he waited for an answer. Cat paused until she had attached a fiddly chain link.

'I don't know,' she said, looking up at the assistants who were scurrying around the hall. 'How about to help around the house? To show guests to their rooms – to fetch stuff, like these guys?'

'Whoa, whoa,' said Nate, typing a series of mathematical strings for a neural network into the laptop. 'One thing at a time. So, helping us out.' He began to program the layout of the room in which they were working into the machine, setting out geographical landmarks like benches and tool racks. Cat carried on with her welding until the soft sound of keys being hammered fell quiet.

'And fetching stuff,' she repeated. 'Kitchen equipment, inventing tools, you know. I'm giving it four arms to help it pick things up.'

'Four arms?!' Nate groaned. 'That's twice as much work for me to do! How am I going to stop it tying itself in knots?'

'You'll cope, lad,' she said, echoing the northern accent of their lovable woodwork teacher. Nate laughed and deleted the section of code he had been writing for two arms, typing frantically to make up for the lost time.

So engrossed were they both that neither Nate nor Cat paid any attention to the other people in the hall, and they soon forgot that they were in a competition at all. For a while it seemed almost as if they were back at home, in their bedrooms, trying to put together another ridiculous invention from odds and ends, with bedtime the only deadline left to meet.

Freed from the stress of the day, they worked smoothly and quickly, breaking up the silence with jokes, comments about Ebenezer Saint's ridiculous entry and even once having a short fight with various plastic nuts and bolts, which caused half the hall to turn round and watch with amusement.

It was only when a deafening explosion rang out from the far end of the room that they were pulled from their private world. As they turned to stare at the smoke rising to the decorated ceiling, the reality of the situation came flooding back.

'Crikey,' said Cat, watching as the white-suited assistants ran over to the flaming desk, spraying it with fire extinguishers until the blaze had been quenched. 'What time is it?'

Nate looked down at his watch and almost choked.

'It's half past bloody two!' he snapped, looking up to see the assistants loading the stunned finalist on to a stretcher. The boy looked as if he was in shock, and not surprisingly – his skin was completely covered in soot and smoke from the blast, and he still held a steaming test tube in his left hand.

'Well, the good news is that there are only forty-nine candidates now,' Cat said dryly as the poor boy was carted from the room. The entire hall watched him go in silence, but it wasn't long before the clatter of activity began once again. Nate stretched and saved his progress on the computer.

'I've pretty much established the robot's primary code,' he said proudly. 'He's not going to be building any cars but he's certainly designed to look after his owners, protect himself from danger and obey any commands that he understands. He can also learn, so any glitches he should be able to fix himself. He's voice-activated, although it might take him a while to learn to recognise us, and I've stolen the dictionary from Saint's word-processing program so he should know more words than both of us put together. Does he have a voice box yet?'

'That's a job for this afternoon,' Cat answered. 'And what makes you think that our robot is a he?'

Nate was about to answer that he'd programmed its brain so he got to decide, when Cat held up the body she had been making. Built from welded sheets of beaten steel, made flexible by a number of hinges, it was a female figure about the size of a pint glass with a large metal skirt and what looked like clogs.

'Oh,' said Nate. 'Well all I can say is that it's going to be a very confused robot.'

They both laughed, and Nate took the opportunity to call over one of the assistants, ordering a can of Saint's Strawberry Slurp and a cheese sandwich, with a packet of Ebenezer's Teasers for afters. Cat put down the robot's frame and sat thoughtfully for a moment before ordering a filet mignon steak, rare, with sautéed potatoes and cabbage cooked in red wine, and a strawberry bombe for dessert. Nate looked at her with his eyebrow raised, but to his amazement the assistant nodded and left.

'Think big,' was all she said.

They worked through their lunch, although Nate spent most of his time staring enviously at Cat's enormous plateful of glorious food while munching regretfully on his rather dull sandwich.

As soon as he turned his attention back to the computer, however, he forgot all about his stomach, and began poring through the dense lines of seemingly impenetrable code in search of any possible errors. When he was sure he had ironed out all of the problems, he requested a microprocessor and began downloading the information on to it. As an after-thought, he gave the robot the manliest name he could think of, Clint, and programmed in a few extras that would help rein-force its gender, including a variety of farts and belches.

Meanwhile, Cat adjusted the framework, adding in a small voice synthesiser that she ordered from a young man in white overalls, and which took a good half an hour to arrive, and a pair of optical sensors that she welded into the eye sockets in the frame. Lastly she added a microphone, and turned to Nate with her hands outstretched, flicking her fingers impatiently for the main ingredient.

'And bingo,' Nate said, waiting for the last of the code to transfer then holding out the little silver box to Cat. She grinned and took it, carefully fitting it into the metallic skeletal framework, fixing it inside the chest next to a battery and weld-ing it so that it remained securely in place. Shooing Nate out of his chair, she began running wires from the processor to each of the robot's many limbs, all of which were connected by a del-icate series of artificial joints.

It took a good thirty minutes for her to run the red and black wires to the right ports, during which time Nate continually glanced at his watch to see the little hand move closer and closer to the nine. He was distracted by a loud sigh from Cat, and looked up to see her staring back at him.

'Well, here goes,' she said, slipping the feminine steel outer body over the frame and twisting a number of screws to keep it in place.

'Fingers crossed,' he replied.

Lifting one of the steel plates and reaching into the robot's ribcage, Cat flicked the tiny switch on the microprocessor and drummed her fingers impatiently as it booted up. Whining, it seemed to pause for a moment before fading, and both Nate and Cat leant forward tentatively, fearing that nothing was going to happen.

After a moment's hesitation, however, the processor kicked in and the entire framework began to vibrate. The first thing to move was the robot's left leg, which seemed to wobble for a minute before poking out to one side and shaking wildly like a dog's. Then one of the four long arms did the same thing. The tiny robot shook each one of its limbs in order, then did the same with its head, before starting to walk hesitantly across the desk.

It was like watching a baby take its first steps. Nate and Cat clung on to one another like proud parents as it stumbled along the green leather desktop, spinning every now and again to get its balance. At one point it fell backwards, with all limbs scrabbling desperately in the air for purchase, but Nate simply lifted the pint-size machine up and placed it back on its feet.

'Thank you,' it said in a mechanical whisper, batting its long eyelashes at Nate before continuing to make its way around the desk in circles.

'You taught it manners!' Cat said, impressed. Nate was about to proudly agree with her when the robot bent over in a rather awkward manner, and with great bravado announced, 'I am Clint' before unleashing a deafening belch from its vocal synthesiser. The noise was so loud, and went on for so long, that everybody within a twenty-metre radius turned to look at Nate and Cat in horror, some giggling and others uttering tuts of disapproval.

'Nate!' Cat shouted, giving him a slap around the back of his head that actually hurt. 'How could you?!' She bent down to pick up the robot but before she could it had caught sight of its reflection in a leftover piece of polished steel on the desk.

'I'm female!' it exclaimed in its rasping electronic tones. 'How odd, I feel just like a male.'

Panicked, it started running around in circles waving all four arms in the air, uttering strange noises and whistling. Cat made a lunge for it but it leapt gracelessly from the table, clattering to a heap on the floor and struggling to get to its feet, reminding them both of a beetle trapped on its back.

'Get it!' shouted Nate. 'It's gone doolally!'

Clint managed to flip himself over seconds before Cat made a flying leap for him. She landed painfully on her shoulder as the robot scuttled over her legs and made a run for the next desk.

'Clint, behave!' Nate shouted, but the robot wasn't listening. It had darted beneath the chair of the boy to their right, who was now wearing his newly constructed jetpack on his back. The three-piece-suited lad was one of the largest competitors in the room, but he lifted his legs up in shock, in much the same way Nate had seen his mum do when there was a spider in the room.

By now, the entire hall was again looking in their direction, transfixed by the miniature robot that was starting to climb up the boy's chair. Every time he raised his little robotic leg to push himself higher, he made the sound of breaking wind. Cat shot Nate a look that nearly killed him before jogging over to try and recover their invention.

Something told Nate that chaos was about to ensue. He wanted to help Cat but he felt paralysed as he watched Clint climb on to the boy's lap, still muttering nonsense about being a girl. The terrified competitor was desperately trying to push the robot off, but one of his haphazard slaps accidentally brushed against the ignition switch for the jetpack.

For a moment, there was absolute silence as the boy stared at Nate, realising what he'd done. Then the liquid fuel combined, and with the sound of thunder the jetpack soared upwards, its trail of blue fire instantly incinerating the desk and the chair. Squeaking in alarm, Cat dived to the ground, covering her head and managing to stay clear of the flames.

But Clint wasn't so lucky. The upward acceleration of the jetpack forced him to loosen his grip, even with twenty fingers, and he toppled to the ground in the direct path of the booster flame.

Having not yet fitted the stabilisers, the poor kid with the jetpack flew halfway to the ceiling before the boosters sent him earthwards, blasting him to and fro between the desks of terrified, screaming competitors then round and round in an impossibly fast corkscrew. Ignoring the threat to their own safety, the assistants clambered on to the desks and over inventions, leaping for the boy when he passed but never managing to hang on to him for long.

Eventually the spluttering rockets gave out, and he glided unsteadily into one of the reinforced windows like a giant fly, falling to the ground with a noise halfway between a crunch and a splat. He was instantly surrounded by a dozen assistants, who stripped away the jetpack, doused his shoes with fire extinguishers and helped him to his feet. The boy had gone a strange shade of green, but despite only being able to walk in uneasy circles, he waved away their help and slowly returned to what remained of his desk.

'I am *so* sorry,' said Nate as he passed, but the large, swaying boy simply rested a hand on Nate's shoulder and paused for breath.

'No worries, old chap,' he said, his voice a tremor. 'That was damn good fun. Besides, I think I'm the one who should be apologising.'

They both turned to see Cat kneeling on the floor in the charred ashes of the desk, trying to pick up a glowing red lump that had once been Clint.

18

Disaster Strikes!

As always, Saint's assistants were quick to the scene, one approaching with a fire extinguisher and spraying a ridiculous amount of foam over the smouldering shape, cooling the metal and allowing Cat to pick up the deformed robot. Distraught, she held it out for inspection.

'Well, so much for that,' she said. She pulled back her arm as if to hurl the metal shape across the hall, but the jetpack boy ran over and stopped her, prising the tiny robot from her fingers and bringing it back to the desk.

'Don't be in such a hurry,' he said, pulling out a small hacksaw from their tool rack and setting to work on the smoking metal. 'I've been using this same steel for my jetpack casing. It's pretty strong stuff, and I'll wager that your circuit boards and mechanics are all right inside.'

Curious, Cat walked over to the desk to get a better view of what was happening. The boy carefully cut away the outer layers of steel and fished out the frame, complete with the processor, from inside. Laying it on the table, they all peered over to see what the damage was.

Incredibly, after a couple of seconds, Clint's left eyelid opened and the optical sensor inside began scanning the three faces above him. Very slowly, his four arms began feeling up and down his body as if checking for injury, and when he was certain he felt okay the robot struggled upright and stood there unsteadily.

When the robot finally spoke, all he could manage was, 'Good lord, I'm naked.'

Laughing in relief, Nate and Cat hugged each other, then turned to the boy, who was standing looking dejectedly at his charred desk.

'Thank you so much,' said Cat. 'You've saved us.'

'It's no problem,' he replied, not turning around. 'He's a lovely little fellow and well worthy of the prize. Alas, I think my entry may not make it.'

The jetpack still lay in a sad little heap where it had fallen, drenched in foam. Nate felt terrible, but looking at his watch he saw there was less than an hour until nine, and he doubted that even Saint himself could have fixed the flying machine on time.

'I'm David, by the way,' the boy said, turning around and shaking Nate's hand, then Cat's. 'David Barley.'

They both introduced themselves, and while Cat chatted to David about past inventions, Nate set to work on providing Clint with a new outer casing to replace the ruined dress. There was no time left for another steel-clad uniform, so instead he turned his attention to the only thing nearby that could possibly serve as a decent coverall, his Saint's Strawberry Slurp can. With Clint sitting on the edge of the desk swinging his feet and watching his every move, Nate opened up a large slit in the side of the can and cut off the bottom end.

'You must be joking,' said Clint, watching him carefully, but Nate ignored him, picking up the robot and dropping him into the modified can. A couple of careful welds later, along with some holes for his limbs, and Clint once more had his modesty preserved.

'There, you're the best dressed robot in the room,' said Nate, trying to suppress a grin as he watched Clint prance around on the desktop, once again looking at his reflection in the polished steel.

'I'm the only robot in the room,' was the response.

For the next forty minutes Nate and Cat sat at the desk making minor adjustments to Clint's programming, deleting the flatulence and tightening up his rotary movement mechanism to try and make him walk less like a penguin. Terrified that the little robot would run off again and cause havoc somewhere in Saint Solutions, Nate put together a tiny radio wave transmitter that would act like a homing beacon, fixing it directly on to the little robot's central processor.

'This won't stop you getting away again,' he whispered menacingly into Clint's ear. He carefully fitted a receiver into his watch, waiting until it had picked up the signal before carrying on. 'But it will help us track you down and squash you if you try another stunt like that!'

Unable to even pick out his notes from the charred rubble that was once his workstation, David Barley sat on the edge of the desk offering his advice on the extra bits and pieces of code that Nate was typing in to the laptop. Around them the activity in the room had become desperate as the competitors all fought to get their machines, potions and vehicles ready on time.

At five minutes to nine, the assistants began to move to the outskirts of the room, standing by the windows with their hands clasped behind their backs, all wearing the same identical smile. Shortly afterwards, with only seconds left to go, the lift doors opened, releasing a cloud of white smoke. Everybody in the room fell silent, stopped what they were doing and looked into the swirling mist that filled the interior of the lift.

For a second, nothing happened, then with a whoop and a holler Saint blasted into the room on a steam-powered flying machine. A pair of giant wings beat lazily against the heavy air while a large chimney located just behind the pilot's seat churned smoke towards the ceiling. Grinning maniacally, Saint sat alone on the strange contraption, which looked like something that belonged in Victorian times.

He guided the wobbly vehicle into the centre of the room, the parchment-thin wings blowing gale-force winds every time they swooshed downwards, creating a blizzard of paper around the desks.

'Now that's more like it,' he said as he landed gently on the marble floor. Coughing and wheezing, he climbed off his seat and placed a cap on the chimney to stop the smoke. He stood proudly for a second, then began to stroll forwards.

'Well done!' he shouted so that the whole room could hear. 'We've been watching you all and you've done some amazing things. Truly amazing.' He cut through one of the rows of desks, continuing to talk as he walked, occasionally picking up an object and looking at it with fascination before setting it down.

'You'll be delighted to know that the – er – little accidents we had earlier have all been sorted, and there are no serious injuries or deaths. In fact, I'm remarkably pleased and surprised that none of you managed to horribly hurt yourselves.' He seemed to look straight at David when he said this, making the boy blush. 'Well done, again.'

With the speed of a cat, he hopped effortlessly on to the desk of a startled girl, who had to pull a vial of colourful potions out of his way to stop them being trampled on.

'But now comes the hard part. As much as I'd like to keep you all here, some of you have to go. I'm going to call out some names, and if you hear yours I'd like you to make your way to the elevator. I'm not going to tell you who's in and who's out until the groups have been separated, just in case there's a riot.'

The girl with the vials placed them on the floor and tugged at Saint's trousers. Squatting down on the desk, he leant forward and Nate saw her whisper something into his ear. Laughing, he stood up again.

'Oh yes,' he sang out. 'We've already seen your inventions. This room has eyes, you know, and ears, and even fingers, though we don't tend to use those. Me and my most favourite technicians have spent the last twelve hours watching you all like hawks. No sense in parading round and umming and ahing like this was a bake-off – we know exactly who we want to keep.'

The competitors in the room all looked at each other, some disappointed that they would not be given the chance to show off their inventions, and others relieved for the same reason. Saint pulled a roll of paper from his pocket, unfurled it to reveal a sheet of parchment as tall as he was, and began reading from it.

The names were in no particular order, and Nate forgot them as soon as they had been read out, eager to find out his and Cat's fate. One by one the competitors left their desks – the three girls with the food processor, the guy with the bandages, who had managed to tie them too tightly around his feet and had to shuffle across the room painfully slowly, a girl who, for some inexplicable reason, had lost all the hair from the top of her head but who had grown a metre-long beard, and a boy whose entire body was glowing as though he'd swallowed a gallon of luminous paint. The seconds ticked excruciatingly by until only twenty-five people, plus Ebenezer and his assistants, were left in the room. They all watched as their fellow inventors vanished behind the closing doors.

Nate was nervous. Some of the people who had left had produced some impressive pieces of equipment, making him think that they were the ones who had been selected for the scholarship. On the other hand, people like bandage boy didn't seem to have made anything other than a terrible mess.

Of course, David Barley still sat perched on the end of their desk, fiddling with his bow tie, and he hadn't been able to present anything at all other than a broken jetpack and a lot of ashes. Nate looked at Cat, who was chewing her lip as though she hadn't eaten in a month, and knew she was making the same nervous calculations in her head.

Saint seemed to be getting a little too much pleasure from the suspense, and hopped athletically from desk to desk barely able to contain his excitement. When he realised that all eyes were on him, waiting for an end to their agony, he stopped and coughed apologetically.

'Do excuse me,' he said. 'I got carried away. I guess you're all dying to hear the verdict, then.'

You could just about cut the tension in the room with a knife. Saint spoke the next few words excruciatingly slowly.

'You . . .' Nate placed his thumb in his mouth and chewed so hard it hurt.

'Lot . . .' Cat was just about pulling her hair out.

'Are . . .' David Barley yanked so hard on his elastic bow tie that it flew off and sailed across the room, pinging a girl on the ear.

'Losers.'

19

A Pleasant Surprise

Nobody moved. Nobody spoke. For what seemed like a minute, nobody even breathed, and Saint stood on the desk surveying the crowd with a blank expression waiting for some kind of reaction. Nate felt his heart sink, and saw Cat's head droop to the floor. He heard David mutter something along the lines of 'oh well' as he hopped off the desk to retrieve his bow tie. Someone in the room had started sobbing.

Saint seemed frozen to the spot. After several seconds had ticked past he straightened himself and ran a hand through his tangled hair, looking slightly awkward.

'I mean winners,' he said, almost apologetically. The room still remained silent, and both Nate and Cat looked up at him, confused. He jumped off the desk and landed nimbly on the floor, spinning round and ramming his hands into his trouser pockets. 'I'm sorry, I couldn't help it. I was joking. You lot are the winners. You've won. You're champions. You're here to stay. Well done.'

The silence in the room still remained unbroken, except for the sobbing, which only grew in volume.

'Oh, for pity's sake,' Saint muttered, removing a hand and scratching his nose. 'I'm serious this time. Those guys,' he gestured to the elevator, 'were the losers. They're gone. You guys have won – you are now my guests, my employees, here at Saint Solutions. No kidding.'

This time, the room erupted. Cat ran up to Nate and wrapped her arms around him, kissing him on the cheek then jumping up and down frantically. Unable to believe his ears, Nate hugged her back and began jumping too, bouncing around the desk whooping at the top of his voice.

'We did it, Cat!' he shouted, feeling so emotional that he thought he would burst out crying at any moment. Cat had already started – tears of joy ran down her cheeks and dropped on Nate's shirt.

'I knew we would,' she whispered, letting go of him and performing a ridiculous solo dance involving star jumps and a clumsy moonwalk that went forwards rather than backwards. Nate glanced to one side to see David performing a waltz with Clint the robot, holding him out in front of his face as he side-stepped his way through the ashes of his desk. Everywhere he looked, Nate saw children cheering and hugging and dancing and crying with happiness, and for a moment the sensation was so overwhelming that he grew faint, and had to sit down before he passed out.

'How could you even have doubted yourselves?' he heard Saint shout, and turned to see him strolling around the desks. The master inventor walked up to a boy and a girl who were standing beside an odd device that looked like an ancient record player with a microphone attached. Saint leant towards it and began speaking in French, and a crystal–clear voice sounded from the speakers: 'You've built a fully operational translation device.'

He whirled away and ran across the room to the desk that was covered in manure. Several strange orange flowers had grown on the surface, and when Saint approached them they swooned towards him, their petals opening like mouths and nibbling gently at his hands. Saint patted one on the head then turned to the short boy who had grown them.

'You've created flowers that think,' he exclaimed, then leapt

133

over a chair with his spindly legs and slid on to another desk, picking up a small, round object the size of a gobstopper and holding it to his eye. The girl standing next to him held out her hand and muttered something that sounded like a warning, but Saint ignored her and threw the object at the floor with all his strength. It bounced straight up and hit the curved ceiling, shooting off at an angle and speeding through the air with remarkable velocity. It rebounded off a window and headed back into the crowd, knocking over a test tube holder before hitting the underside of a desk and doing an impersonation of a pinball stuck between two pegs.

The girl made a dive for it and managed to smother the ball in the folds of her jumper. 'A ball that will bounce for ever,' Saint went on, running even further around the room and performing a bizarre pirouette.

He spotted the charred remains of David's desk and charged over, dancing around the soot so as not to dirty his shoes. He grabbed the boy and shook him wildly.

'And I saw your joyride,' he said, loud enough for everybody to hear. 'What a hoot! You went as green as a cactus, I thought you were going to go straight through that window. Good job I didn't try and save money on the glass! But what a great attempt – anyone who can mix oxygen and hydrogen in their liquid forms as elegantly as you've done is okay in my book.'

He let go of David but snatched up Clint, holding him in front of his eyes and turning him around. The little robot looked shocked to be investigated with such relish, but thankfully didn't say anything.

'And a robot! I mean what on earth were you thinking? How did you dream you were going to pull it off? This is truly remarkable, you guys, I'm lost for words, I can't think of a single thing to say, I haven't been this quiet for months, truly and utterly remarkable.'

 134

Nate and Cat glanced at each other then scrambled to catch the robot, which Saint threw gently at them before dashing off to a desk in the next row. It was the one used by the blond, handsome lad who had remained fixed to his workbench all day. He'd erected plates of steel around the green leather so that it was impossible see what he was building, although every now and again flashes of purple light from behind the metal screens had lit up the entire hall with such strength that everybody had turned to look.

Saint stood on his tiptoes and peered over the steel, before pulling a screen out completely and throwing it to the floor. The boy didn't react, but stood back to let Saint have a closer look.

'In fact, the only thing we don't know about is this,' Saint said, stroking his chin as he looked at the bundle of wires and metal on the desk.

Everybody in the room crowded round to get a better look, and Cat set down Clint who scrabbled over the desk and on to the floor on a self-appointed reconnaissance mission. Nate took the opportunity to test the tracking device, looking at the numbers on his watch that showed how far away the robot was and in which direction.

'But then Travis Heart here was the brains behind the transmitting device we used to contact you last week, so there was no way he was leaving early.'

Saint pulled up a chair and sat down, crossing his legs and resting his chin on his hand as if concentrating on a lecture. 'Travis, tell us what you've made.'

Still expressionless, Travis lifted a long, thin object the size and shape of a postal tube from the desk. Obviously struggling with the weight, he tucked it into his chest and pressed a small red button on the side.

Instantly the underside of the object lit up, rays of oranges, reds, yellows and purples pulsating up and down the length of the tube. At the same time, the sound of a small generator powering up filled the room. Nate noticed that the tube was plugged into a row of ten enormous batteries, and began to suspect the worst. His thoughts were confirmed when Travis adjusted the position of the tube so that he was holding it like a rifle. The people closest to him began to step away uneasily, and even Saint sat back in his chair, disconcerted.

'It's a light-amplified particle disrupter,' said Travis in little more than a whisper. The light from the gun was reflected on his face, throwing him into shadow in the same way as a torch held under the chin does at Halloween. Gradually all the colours were darkening into purples. 'It has a range of three hundred metres and is powerful enough to stop a small armoured vehicle at that distance, provided the weather is right.' The last of the yellows and oranges gradually disappeared to leave a glowing purple tube. 'At close range, it is lethal.'

Travis scanned the room, stopping when he saw the shape of Clint perched on the desk directly ahead of him. He won't, thought Nate, he can't. But without so much as a pause the boy hoisted the tube up to his shoulder and pressed the button again. The tube began to rumble, and he was obviously fighting hard to keep it steady. The clouds of purple colour inside were becoming more and more agitated, swirling around with great speed. All of a sudden they seemed to stop, then with a terrifying motion they were propelled to the tip of the weapon.

Ebenezer Saint, seeing what was about to happen, leapt to his feet, grabbed the leg of his chair and swung it in an upward arc with the precision and speed of a black belt in karate. It made contact with the tube just as a blinding ray of purple light exploded from the end, and deflected the shot. Instead of striking Clint at point-blank range it shot off skywards, hitting a section of the glass wall where it met the ceiling.

With an almighty crash, which drowned out the screams inside the room, one of the giant glass panes erupted into a million splinters that sprayed outwards. At the same time, a chunk of decorated concrete split from the ceiling and crashed to the floor, leaving a crater in the marble inches from one of the assistants, who had turned as white as his overalls. With the glass broken, the sound of the wind outside was deafening.

'Benjamin J. Franklin on a hoverbike!' exclaimed Saint, snatching the tube from Travis and depositing it unceremoniously on the floor. Everybody in the room was cowering, including Nate, and all eyes were on Travis, who seemed unmoved by the incident. Saint scratched his head and stood still for a moment before clutching the expressionless boy's shoulder. 'Great stuff,' he said, surprising the crowd of terrified inventors. 'A laser gun. Smashing. Just be careful with that one, okay?'

Then, as if nothing had happened, Saint motioned towards the elevator and began ushering people inside.

'It's getting late and your parents are bored stiff,' he said. 'Let's see them on their way and get you settled.' With a holler, he dived in through the sliding doors and waited for everybody to join him.

Feeling as if he was in some kind of crazy dream, Nate waited for Cat to crawl out from beneath the desk then jogged to where Clint was cowering behind a laptop screen. As he picked him up he met the pale blue eyes of Travis Heart. The quiet young inventor simply stared at him, without the slightest hint of a smile or a scowl. Looking away, Nate walked over to the elevator, but he could feel Travis's glare boring into the back of his neck, and the sensation chilled him to the bone.

20

Saying Goodbye

As it turned out, Saint was lying yet again. Their parents weren't bored at all, they were having the best time of their lives. The elevator took the finalists back down to the reception hall where the adults were brought in to mingle with them. Both Cat's and Nate's mothers appeared at exactly the same time, looking absolutely radiant.

'We've had a wonderful day,' said Wendy Wright, kissing Nate on the cheek. She smoothed down her hair, which had been trimmed, dyed and styled into a jet-black bob. 'Hair cuts, massages, saunas, makeovers, free food and wine, and even a show!'

'And we got these outfits, too,' said Mrs Gardner, spinning around in a sequined ball gown that was totally inappropriate for anything other than a royal wedding. 'That Mr Saint sure is generous.'

'But well done, you two,' Nate's mum continued. 'We heard the news, and we're delighted.'

'Yes, delighted. Your father would be so proud of you,' blurted out Cat's mum, but as soon as she had spoken she burst into tears and clutched her daughter. It was clear that she'd had more than a drop of wine. Clint, who was still nestled in Nate's grip, leapt on to Cat when he saw she was upset and began hugging her arm. Nate left them to it.

'Where's Dad?' he asked.

Before his mum had time to answer, one of the doors in the reception opened and Peter Wright appeared. He wore a napkin around his neck and was holding a chicken leg in one hand and a glass of Scotch in the other. Two white-suited assistants were standing in the doorway, looking red-faced and nervous, and it soon became clear why. Taking a bite of the chicken leg, Peter charged towards them like a bull at a matador. He bumped into the assistants and they all vanished through the door, before reappearing seconds later with reinforcements.

'I haven't finished eating!' Nate heard his father shout as he was bundled to the ground by six fresh members of staff. Like some famished Incredible Hulk, he threw them off and stood up, straightening his shirt and downing the Scotch, which miraculously had remained in the glass. 'Saint said we could eat as much as we liked, and I'm not full.' For a second it looked as though he was about to bolt for the door again, but he obviously thought better of it and skulked over to the crowd.

'"All we can eat" my hairy backside,' he muttered, before grasping Nate's hand and shaking it furiously. 'We knew you'd do it, boy,' he said, pulling him close and giving him a hug. 'Well done.'

'How do you feel?' asked his mum. He could tell from her expression that she was holding back tears. Once again he found himself thinking about how long a year was, and how far away Christmas seemed.

'Okay, I think,' he said, but in truth he didn't know how he felt. He was utterly exhausted, and the whole experience felt so surreal that he barely knew what to make of it. 'I'll be okay. Me and Cat will stick together.'

Cat had managed to free herself from her mum's iron grip, and walked to Nate's side, with Clint perched on her shoulder. Mrs Gardner joined Nate's parents and there was a rare moment of stillness as they all took stock of the massive change that was about to occur. Around the enormous hall the finalists were saying goodbye to their parents, siblings and other loved ones in a scene that must have resembled the evacuation of children from London during the Second World War.

'This is ridiculous,' said Nate's dad, looking around. 'We'll see you on the videophone, whatever that is, and you'll be back home at Christmas. Besides, I'm sure Ebenezer Fruitcake will let you out to see us any time you want.'

'Yeah,' said Cat, looking unsure. 'We'll see you plenty.'

In all the commotion, nobody had seen Ebenezer Saint vanish, but the chime of the elevator doors announced his reappearance. Turning around, the emotional crowd saw the charismatic inventor stride from the lift followed by what looked like an army of dogs, all yelping.

Shocked, some of the parents and children jumped backwards, and Clint almost fell from his perch, grabbing Cat's hair to stop himself tumbling. As the squabbling flock of black canines got nearer, however, it became clear that they were actually small toys, about the size of a terrier. They filtered through the crowd, each picking a set of parents and nudging them with their noses. The cries of distress turned to moans of delight as mums and dads alike bent down to stroke the lifelike machines.

'These are your videoscreens,' Saint said over the noise of contented panting, which came from the dogs, not the people. 'Use them to stay in touch with your children.' He bent down to the dog that had stayed by his side and stoked its muzzle. 'Lie down, boy,' he said, and the robotic dog obeyed. 'When you get a call, the monitor will slide up automatically and the robot will bark.' The dog rolled on its side, yelping softly, and a small, flat television screen emerged from its torso. As it blinked into life, a picture of Saint appeared on the screen and continued to address the group.

'It's just like being there,' it said, 'and you can talk back to this camera mounted on the screen. Like this: Hello, Ebenezer, you're looking good.'

'Likewise, Ebenezer,' replied the real Saint to his on-screen image. 'I love your hair.'

'Why, thank you, I must say yours looks rather dashing too.'

The exchange continued for almost a minute until Saint remembered he had an audience. Coughing, he slid the screen back into the dog and stood up. The dog rose as well and began running around Saint's legs with excitement.

'It's just a little gift from me that will hopefully remind you of your children and help ease the pain of their absence,' he went on. 'You don't need to feed, water or charge it, and if you'd rather just use the telephone or, God forbid, a pen and paper, then just throw it in the cupboard and forget about it. Oh, but they do also make very handy clothes horses, should you ever need to dry your washing.' As if on command, the dog's legs began to grow, raising it to a good two metres in height.

'Now that will be handy,' Nate heard his mum comment.

Saint patted the dog on the head and it shrank back down to its original size. Strolling forwards, he raised his arms and whispered 'time please', causing the glowing white clock to emerge from the wall above the reception desk. Without looking, Saint announced the correct time, which was half past nine on the dot.

'I'm afraid it's time for fond farewells,' he said, addressing the parents. 'Gracious goodbyes, sad sayonaras, awful au revoirs, even cheesy ciaos if that's your cup of tea. I know this is hard, I know you must all have your doubts, but ignore your maternal and paternal instincts and believe me when I say this will be the best experience of your offsprings' lives.'

Turning, he made his way back to the elevator. 'Children,

when you're done, meet me in the lift and we'll carry you to your destiny!'

And with that he was gone. Nate turned to his parents and smiled. He was looking forward to heading straight to bed, and was curious about where his quarters would be, and what kind of luxuries he'd find in his room. After the stories his parents had been telling him about massages and all-you-can-eat meals, he was fairly confident that he'd be spending the next year in the lap of luxury. Not that he wanted to tempt fate. His mother was crouching to play with the artificial dog, which had rolled on to its back and was letting her tickle its smooth metal belly.

'Well, this will certainly help brighten things up around the house now that you're not going to be there,' she said, giggling as a smooth pink tongue shot out of the creature's toothless mouth and lapped at her hand.

'And it will do less damage to the walls,' added Peter. Nate could tell by the way his dad's bottom lip was quivering that he was upset. 'You just look after yourself, Nathan,' he said, placing his hand on Nate's shoulder and squeezing gently. 'And remember to call us whenever you need to, or whenever you want to.'

'And never less than three times a week,' his mum added. 'Preferably never less than ten times a week, actually.'

'I'll do my best,' Nate replied, giving his mum and dad a hug before turning to look at Cat. She had given her mum one last squeeze and was watching tearfully as she made her way towards the golden gates. Nate's parents waved goodbye and turned to follow, the two black dogs trotting close behind and snapping playfully at one another. Nate and Cat watched them go, watched all the parents go, and before long found themselves standing in the giant reception space with twenty-three other stunned, silent kids.

'I hope we've done the right thing,' he said.

'We have,' came Cat's reply. 'Just think, we're about to spend a year with Ebenezer Saint, in Saint Solutions. We've got free rein to make just about anything we can dream of. This is heaven, Nate, heaven.'

'Heaven!' exclaimed Clint from Cat's shoulder.

Nate wanted to agree, but as he watched the golden gates slide effortlessly shut he felt suddenly uneasy. The click of the lock slamming into place filled the entire room, echoing off the walls with a sound that made him think of nails being driven into a coffin lid. He walked to the elevator alongside Cat and the rest of the winners, where Saint greeted them with a look of sympathy.

'I know it's hard,' he said. 'I know you must all be feeling pretty upset about leaving your folks. I do know what it's like. I do know what you're going through. But we're all about to experience some big changes, and they're changes for the bet-ter – changes that will make us better people, give us better times, amazing times, changes that will make us happy, changes that will improve the planet.' He leant forward and looked every person in the lift dead in the eye before continuing. 'Trust me.'

He waved his hand in front of the wall and the holographic panel appeared again. He jabbed at a button.

'Going up,' he repeated. But the way that Nate's stomach tightened when the lift started moving felt strange, as if they were moving deeper, not higher. Nobody else seemed to have noticed – even Cat, who got travel sick at even the most subtle change in movement, smiled at him and mouthed the word 'heaven'.

It was only when Nate's ears popped from the change in pressure that he knew for sure they were on their way down, and he couldn't help but wonder why, if this was heaven, it felt so much like he was on the fast track to hell.

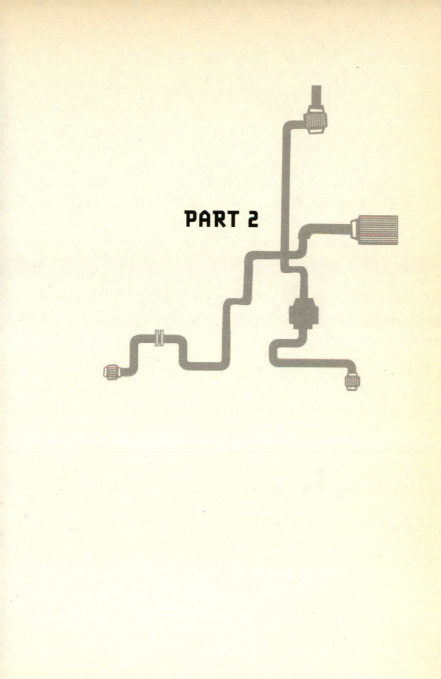

PART 2

21

Feeling at Home

It didn't take long for Nate's sense of unease to pass. In fact by the time the lift stopped moving and the doors opened to reveal the orange rays of a beautiful autumn sunset, he felt decidedly silly for thinking that he was being sucked down into a terrifying underworld.

The group of tired but excited winners followed an equally tired but excited Ebenezer Saint out into a stunning indoor paradise. The enormous tropical space was filled with a veritable jungle of palm trees, bushes and bubbling, clear blue pools, and ringed by glass windows as large as those in the conference room.

The master inventor gave them a very quick tour of what he called the communal garden, which was for the exclusive use of the competition winners, then led them down a sandstone path towards a cluster of bizarre chalets that lay in beautifully manicured gardens. The buildings were identical in every way, with terracotta walls, large windows and flat roofs equipped with sunloungers. Roses grew around the doors, and the small gardens were immaculately designed with green lawns and flowerbeds. Best of all, each of the chalets was set at an angle that gave it a perfect view over the sun-drenched wonderland outside while concealing it from the other abodes around it.

'We've worked out that this temperature is optimum for happiness and productivity,' he explained as they reached the first of the chalets. The balmy warmth and cool breeze reminded

Nate of his local leisure centre, and he found himself smiling. 'Now, let me show you how these work.' Saint stared at the building and read out the name carved above the door: 'Lucy White, come here, my dear.'

A pretty girl Nate hadn't seen during the competition stepped forward tentatively and walked up to Saint, who had manoeuvred himself to the chalet's front door. He smiled warmly at her before spinning her around, lifting up her right hand and waving it furiously in front of the handle. A holographic panel, like that in the lift, sprang up in front of the girl's surprised face, and Saint slapped her thumb against it. There was a slight pause, then the panel faded and the door unlocked with a quiet beep.

Nate wondered how he had managed to get hold of their fingerprints, then remembered the entry form, and shaking Saint's hand with his thumb, and the thin green lines that had been absorbed into the paper.

'Easy as pie!' Saint said, giving Lucy a shove so that she fell through the door into the chalet's interior, landing on her face. Saint didn't seem to notice, and stepped forward towards the gaggle of spectators. 'You've all got one of these,' he went on, 'and as far as I know you've all got thumbs. Everything you need should be inside. If it isn't, then you only need to call and one of my assistants will be right there. They've all been trained as scientists, assistants, teachers, technicians, chefs, DIY experts, doctors, gardeners and even agony aunts, so any one of them will be able to help you with pretty much anything you have a problem with. You may not be able to spot them, but trust me, they are everywhere.'

He gestured to the side of the path and Nate was shocked to see that tucked into the foliage, barely visible in the shade, were several white-suited assistants standing absolutely motionless, still smiling.

'Now, if you'll excuse me,' Saint said, stepping back on to the path, 'I have to get my beauty sleep, or I'll end up looking like some of your parents.' He seemed to shudder at the thought, before flashing them one last smile and bounding up the path on his long legs. His voice faded as he disappeared round the corner towards the lift. 'Well done again. Sleep well. Alarms set for seven!'

Left alone, the winners milled around for a few minutes, muttering to each other about how nice it was here, and how pleased they were to have won. Nate felt elated to be among kids his age who didn't want to tease him, punch him or give him wedgies because of his love of inventing. Gradually, either alone or in groups of two or three, they began filtering off to find their chalets. Nate and Cat did the same, following the meandering path around the substantial homes, until they discovered theirs. The two chalets were side by side, thankfully, and to their immense surprise the doors were joined by a short aerial slide.

'Wow,' said Cat, impressed. 'He has done his research.'

Nate looked at her with an expression that was part smile, part frown.

'Don't you find that a bit weird?' he said. 'It's like he's been spying on us. I mean how would he know we travelled between houses by aerial slide?'

But they were both so exhausted that neither could bring themselves to think about it. Opening his front door with his thumbprint, Nate invited Cat in for a cup of tea. She accepted, placing Clint on the floor and watching as he scampered off to explore. Following the robot into the large front room, both inventors gasped as they discovered a luxury apartment, complete with 42-inch plasma television, DVD and Playstation 4, with surround sound and two reclining, massaging leather lazyboys with attached stereo headphones. Various other pieces of sleek, stylish electrical equipment dotted the room, each with the word 'prototype' stencilled across it in red letters.

'These must be Saint's newest inventions,' said Nate, walking up to one that looked like a black egg carton on the floor. Pressing it gently with his foot, he found himself face to face with a life-size, three-dimensional figure of King Kong.

Screaming in a falsetto that was worthy of an opera singer, he fell backwards, tripping over his feet and landing painfully on his rear end. Cat burst out laughing, slapping her thigh with delight before clicking off the holographic projector and hauling him back up.

'Real brave,' she said, still giggling. 'My hero.'

'That wasn't a scream,' he replied, blushing. 'It was a battle cry.'

'Of course, and that was a ninja karate roll you demonstrated so effectively there.'

This time Nate laughed as well, and they both set off to explore the chalet's remaining rooms. Behind the main lounge was a small corridor with four doors, one of which led to a workspace complete with desks and tools, one to a kitchen stocked with what looked like a million packets of Ebenezer's Teasers and another to a marble-clad bathroom with a power shower and a whirlpool bath, in which Clint had managed to get stuck like a spider. Nate was delighted to see that there was a water fountain next to the toilet, and was about to take a drink before Cat pointed out that it was actually a bidet.

'It's for cleaning your bum,' she whispered.

The final door led into a spacious bedroom, with a double bed and another plasma screen set into the wall. Sitting on the duvet was Nate's suitcase, although it had been unpacked, and the crumpled assortment of clothes ironed, folded and neatly arranged on the shelves beside his bed.

Returning to the sitting room, Nate and Cat sat down in the comfortable chairs and enjoyed a moment of silence, Clint scrambling up on to Cat's lap. Nate felt his eyelids drooping after such a long, hard day and switched on the chair's vibro-function in the hope it would wake him up a little.

'What a day,' he said, the chair vibrating with such strength that his voice shook and his teeth chattered. 'I can't believe we're here.'

'Me neither,' Cat replied. Stretching, she yawned so hard that her jaw popped. 'What do you think of Saint, now we've met him in person?'

'He's an absolute nutjob,' Nate replied without hesitation. 'Completely and utterly off his head. I mean, look at this place. This tower is like something from *Star Wars*, with its electric power rings and ginormous rooms. And what was that entrance on a space hopper all about?'

They both started laughing, recalling Saint's skinny legs waving around in the air as he tried to right himself on the giant red ball.

'You're right,' Cat said eventually. 'He is loopy.' She paused, chewing her lip and gazing into space.

'It's going to be fine, Cat,' Nate whispered, reading her thoughts. 'He may be mad but he does want the best for us. If we get homesick he's bound to let us out for a weekend or so, or invite our folks round for tea. I mean, his staff must go out for their groceries and they don't spill Saint's secrets.'

'I know,' she replied, her tired eyes brightening. 'And it's only three months until Christmas. I bet we get extra presents this year because they'll have missed us so much.'

For a while, the only sound in the room was the soft hum of the chair and the staccato of Nate's teeth. Looking over, he saw that Cat's eyes were closed, and that her head was sliding ever so slowly towards her left shoulder. Clint was lying on her stomach, snoring quietly. Switching off his lazyboy, Nate walked over to Cat and shook her gently.

'Cat,' he whispered, smiling as she opened her eyes. 'Go to bed.'

She yawned again and stood up, lifting the little robot and nodding. Giving Nate a hug, she made her way to the front door, which was still open. She turned as she left the chalet.

'Thanks, Nate,' she said.

'For what?'

But she left the question unanswered, closing the door behind her. As Nate walked through to the bedroom he heard the familiar sound of the aerial slide as Cat crossed to her own chalet, and it made him think of happy times in the Bluebell Woods. He collapsed on to the bed, and before he could even climb under the sheets he was fast asleep, and dreaming of home.

Nate woke once during the night, and only because he sensed that something was wrong. The room was pitch black apart from a flashing red light on the plasma screen, and it was deathly quiet.

All except for a slight grinding sound, a rumbling, like distant thunder. It was so soft that at first he thought he was imagining it, but then it came again, accompanied by a soft vibration that shook the bed. Nothing dramatic, just the kind of gentle shake caused by a truck driving past the window. The noise and the motion rose and fell, came and went like waves at the beach, and after a while Nate forgot about it, letting the undulating sound lull him back to sleep.

But not before hearing one extra loud rumble during which

he felt his stomach tighten, almost as if the room was moving. It was the same sensation he had felt in the lift, that of dropping, of descending.

'Don't be ridiculous,' he muttered to himself, but even when the noise stopped, and the room once again fell quiet, Nate couldn't help but feel there was something very important that Saint wasn't telling them.

22

Let the Games Begin!

Hours later, he was woken by the softest of whispers in his ear.

'Nate,' it said, stirring him from a dream in which he was meeting Beyoncé. For a moment he thought it was her talking, but when the whisper sounded again, louder this time, the fantasy slipped away and he opened his eyes to see the grinning face of Ebenezer Saint practically pressed up against his own.

'Bloody Nora,' he exclaimed, rolling over so fast that he flew out of the far side of the bed, banging his head on the carpet. Crawling back on to the blankets, Nate rubbed his eyes and took a closer look at the figure standing before him, realising that it wasn't Saint at all, but a holographic representation of him.

'And here's me thinking I'd be a little less scary than King Kong,' the figure said, pouting. Nate poked it in the face, watching as his hand slid right through the coloured light. It was being emitted from the black egg carton that had somehow made its way through from the sitting room.

'Ow!' joked Saint. 'Do you mind?' Leaning back, the hologram looked at a bare wrist as though reading the time. 'Seven a.m.,' it said. 'Time to rise and shine. We've got some inventing to do, m'boy! See you at the elevator in half an hour.'

And with that, he was gone. Nate struggled off the bed. His head felt like it was full of cotton wool, and he tried to shake it to wake himself up but succeeded only in making it ache. He blinked and scanned the room. Saint must have a camera in each chalet, he thought, otherwise how would he have known what Nate was doing? Eventually he spotted it – a tiny black dot embedded in the joint between the wall and the ceiling – and he waved at it hesitantly. It was a little weird to think he was being spied on, but then he guessed it was for his own safety.

Walking over to the plasma screen mounted on the wall, he noticed that the little red light in the bottom left-hand corner was still flashing. Pressing it, he was greeted with the image of his parents. Or their legs, anyway. They were squabbling, by the sounds of things.

'Hi, Nathan,' he heard his mum say. 'We've just got back and we thought we'd send –'

'It's not on yet, woman,' his dad shouted. His large black shoe was prodding the screen, making the camera rock. 'I'm telling you, it's not recording.'

'Peter, leave it be,' said his mum again. 'I don't know if you'll get this or not, Nathan, but we just wanted to say well done again, and we'll be in touch soon. Goodnight, son.'

'Wendy, listen to me,' said his dad. 'He won't get this, I'm the exper –'

And with that the screen went dead. Nate couldn't help but laugh at the thought of his parents trying to get the high-tech black pooch to work, and he was still giggling as he made his way out of the shower ten minutes later and dressed in a pair of white overalls that he found hung over a rack in the sitting room. They fitted like a glove and, beaming, he made his way outside.

The miniature village was bathed in glorious sunshine from the enormous windows. The dazzling light created dancing diamonds on the surface of the trickling pools and reflected upwards on the walls of the chalets and the soft brown wood of the palm trees to create the illusion that the entire room was shimmering. Something flew past Nate's ear and he realised that the giant space was full of colourful canaries that dashed and darted between the trees.

The competitors were gradually making their way out of their chalets, all stretching and yawning and admiring their identical white overalls. Nate waved at those he recognised from the previous day, then jumped on to the aerial slide and slid the short distance to Cat's chalet, hopping off and knocking on her door. Seconds later she answered, her eyes heavy and her hair a mess.

'Too early,' was all she said as she fastened the last couple of buttons on her overalls and stepped out on to the sandstone path, shielding her eyes. 'And too bright.'

Together they walked over to where the cluster of winners were gathering. Nate spotted David and called out to him, and the tall, portly inventor cantered over. He was wearing his overalls, but for some reason he had decided to keep on his bow tie. He caught both Nate and Cat looking at it, and frowned.

'It's my lucky dicky bow,' he said, fiddling with it uncertainly. 'Keeps the muse with me.'

'Fair enough,' said Cat. 'How did you both sleep?'

'Like a log,' Nate answered, not wanting to mention the odd noises he had experienced in the dead of night. David made a murmuring sound and looked around secretively.

'I'm next door to that funny fellow who made the raygun,' he whispered. 'And he kept me up all night with his rattling around and his hammering. He's making something in there, you know. He doesn't sleep. He's a robot, I tell you. And I swear I saw flashing purple lights through my curtains.'

'It's probably just his nightlight,' Cat said, but Nate felt very nervous at the thought of facing Travis Heart again, especially if he'd made himself another weapon. He changed the subject as the late risers finally joined the group and they all set off towards the lift.

'Speaking of robots,' he said to Cat, 'what happened to Clint?'

'I took him to bed with me last night,' she said, 'but he spent the whole night running round fetching pencils and trying to stick them up my nose. Kept me awake for ages so I had to switch him off. If we have any free time we'll try and sort out the bugs in his program.'

Nate laughed. They hadn't been bugs. He'd secretly inputted a subtle piece of code that made Clint think Cat's nose was a pencil pot.

As they rounded the corner, passing a cluster of particularly tall palms, the group noticed the vast windows and made a short detour to get a better view. Hopping across a bubbling brook, Nate and Cat jogged to the glass and pressed their noses against it, gazing out at the Saint Solutions complex beyond. The windows were tilted outwards slightly, providing a terrifying view down the length of the tower towards the gaping black abyss below.

'We're much higher than we were yesterday,' Cat said unnecessarily, glancing at the rolling hills that seemed minuscule from their current position. 'We must be pretty close to the top.'

'We must be *at* the top,' said David, who had joined them. 'By my calculations, we would only be able to see the complex from this angle if we were, say, one or two storeys from the penthouse.'

'I'll bet Saint lives at the very top,' said Nate.

'Well, I hope he gives us a tour,' Cat added. 'I'll bet his pad is amazing.'

Nate threw Cat a knowing look before turning away and walking back in the direction of the lift. She jogged after him, asking 'What?' as if she didn't know what he was thinking.

When they were back on the path they turned to see that David was still standing at the window, scratching his head and looking confused.

'David,' Cat called. 'Come on, we'll be late.'

He waited a moment longer, then turned, stepping gingerly over the flowing water and rejoining them.

'Sorry,' he said, still looking baffled. 'Just trying to work something out. My calculations must be wrong – must still be tired after yesterday, eh?'

Unsure what on earth he was talking about, Nate and Cat watched him trot down the path and round the last corner. They joined him and the rest of the group moments later to see the lift doors open and waiting.

Although Saint didn't meet them in the lift, it had obviously been pre-programmed to carry them down several floors. When it stopped, the doors slid open to reveal a laboratory. But not just an average laboratory – this room was vast, easily as large as the conference room but three times as tall. It was circular in shape, with the lift shaft in the centre and hundreds of platforms fixed to the towering walls, which stretched as high as the stunned competition winners could see.

Each of these workstations was the size of a small room and was kitted out with screens and control panels. Hundreds of Saint's assistants, all dressed in white suits, manned the platforms, working frenetically at various experiments and seemingly oblivious to the fact that they were so high above the ground.

Stunned, everybody bundled clumsily out of the lift into a chamber of chrome and light, mouths agape – even Travis

Heart, who Nate had so far seen wearing only the most expressionless of faces, stared at the scene with eyes as large as pickled eggs.

Giant glass tubes ran between the workstations, pumping clouds of coloured gases and flickering tongues of electricity to every part of the room, while super-size screens replaced the windows, displaying rows and rows of statistics and images such as rockets blasting skywards, astronauts floating in zero gravity and what looked, for a fraction of a second, like a two-headed goat.

Most incredible of all were the flocks of small, black vehicles resembling Zimmer frames which hovered effortlessly between the various wall-mounted platforms, some carrying files and equipment, others ridden with delight by the staff. As the group stood and watched, one of the hovering contraptions descended towards them from a workstation near the top of the room, cutting down through the busy traffic and coming to a sudden halt just above their heads. It was Ebenezer Saint, and he looked delighted.

'Kids!' he shouted, manoeuvring the craft in gentle circles around the outside of the group. The bottom of the black frame pulsated with a glowing blue light, each throb lifting the vehicle up slightly before letting it dip as it faded. 'I'm glad you could make it. This,' he yelled as he shot up and spun around, so excited that he almost fell off, 'is my lab!'

He whizzed back down to ground level and continued to talk.

'Well, one of them. The main one. It's pretty decent, you know – all high-tech and jam-packed with gadgets. Most of them I invented myself. Some I didn't. Like the light bulbs, that damned Edison got there first. I'd have done it quicker, though.' He performed another dainty circle in mid-air. 'There are other labs, but I don't use them. This one's much more fun and you get to ride these little beauties! Now, if you'll follow me I'll give you a guided tour.'

Without waiting, Saint flew off at high speed around a corner, disappearing behind a bank of computer monitors. Some members of the group started running after him, but stopped when they realised they'd never be able to catch up. Nate scratched his chin and looked at Cat, one eyebrow raised.

After a minute or so, the figure of Saint reappeared again and he flew up to them, landing with a bump and hopping off his craft.

'It's probably better if we walk,' he said, then ran off in the same direction as before, only this time chased by twenty-five bemused children.

23

Exploring the Lab

The tour of the lab was one of the most surreal experiences of Nate's life. Saint stopped running after a while and slowed down to show them some of the experiments that his company was working on. He was terrifically excited, and got carried away on several occasions, grabbing papers and throwing them into the air. Once he even spun an assistant round on his chair so many times that the poor man fell off, his face the same shade of green as the plants he was dissecting.

At each workbench some new wonder was revealed – things that would make the scientific community wet its pants if they were to find out; things that would change the world if they were released on to the market.

At one, manned by a bunch of smiling, white-suited members of staff, a small screen in the desk showed a microscopic enlargement of virus cells; at another, yet more scientists were leaning over a large incubation chamber watching a giant Venus flytrap swallow a dead sheep whole.

In the centre of the room, several benches and consoles were arranged around another holographic projector, showing a life-like model of a rocket taking off. Saint paused to watch the craft as it arced smoothly up and over the curve of the earth, entering the darkness of space as its boosters dropped away.

'Be with you shortly,' he said to the young inventors, who were watching the rocket's progress in amazement. 'We've just sent a shuttle into space. We're building a station up there but it's hard work because we don't want anyone to know about it.'

The last of the rocket's external tanks fell away, allowing the thin silver shuttle to drift silently upwards, only using the occasional blast from its small directional boosters to guide it. 'But anyway, you shouldn't really know about that.' Saint turned and gave them a look that was deadly serious. 'I might have to kill you.'

Leaping away from the command centre, he performed an impromptu cartwheel and dashed off towards the far side of the lab, pointing out other remarkable scientific breakthroughs on the way – some biologists dressed in biohazard suits in a glass-walled booth who had just uncovered the cure for the common cold, and even the two-headed goat, which sat in a cage butting itself continuously.

'Of course not all our inventions have any practical use,' he said, staring forlornly at the goat. Then he broke into a smile. 'But they sure are fun – look at that fellah go! Wallop, wallop!'

Nate felt slightly sick at the sight of the poor, confused goat, but said nothing as the group continued to make its way around the seemingly endless chamber. After what felt like miles, Saint led them into a small hangar where they saw a fleet of the remarkable hovering platforms. Walking down a row of them, he slapped his palm on a large red button on the centre of each frame he passed, and by the time he rejoined the group they could barely hear him over the sound of humming engines – a sound not unlike the noise that would have been made by an orchestra of kazoos.

'These are our Antigravs. Now who fancies a ride?' Saint shouted, earning an immediate gaggle of replies from almost everyone in the room. David, who must have still been bruised from his near-fatal jetpack flight the previous day, barged past the people in front of him to be first in line. 'Great stuff,' said

Saint, stepping back to let the excited boy clamber on board the frame, following it up with, 'Nice bow tie.'

'Thanks,' David replied, blushing. As soon as he had put his weight on the platform it rose slowly and hovered a metre or so above the polished chrome floor.

Saint hopped on to the Antigrav to the right of David's, then instructed everybody to climb on board one of their own. There was a moment of chaos as the group all tried to find a free machine, and Nate found himself bundled out of the way by the more eager young inventors. Walking to the last row, he stepped on board an Antigrav and gripped hold of the bars so hard that his knuckles turned white. Looking to his right he saw that Cat had done the same, and that she looked seasick already even though hers hadn't left the ground.

Slowly and gently the machine rose upwards, tilting shakily every time Nate made the slightest move. Ahead of him Ainsley Stumps, the short kid who had been working with the manure the previous day, had managed to back his Antigrav into the person behind, creating a domino effect of wobbly, reversing hover-frames.

'Hold on, hold on,' he heard Saint cry out. 'Don't try and fly the bloody things just yet.' He swooped up and around so that he was hovering over the group. 'Just press the white button on the dashboard and say my name, and your Antigravs will follow mine.'

The inventors obeyed, and almost instantly the first of the contraptions – David's – lifted effortlessly off the ground with a flash of blue light and moved round to float behind Saint's. One by one the other machines followed, until an impressive conga line of floating frames had assembled. Saint looked mischievously over his shoulder, flashing David a wink.

'Now, hold on,' he said, and before anybody could argue he fired his Antigrav forwards, accelerating with stomach-churning speed out of the hangar and into the lab. The rest of the machines shot off at exactly the same velocity, causing a cacophony of screams, yelps, cries and prayers.

Nate clutched hold of the rubber bar for dear life, planting his feet firmly on the small base and trying not to look down. Saint looked like he was heading directly for a desk piled high with scientific glassware, but at the last minute he pulled the frame towards him and shot straight up, the young inventors like a dragon's tail behind him as he accelerated towards the lab's ceiling. His voice, automatically fed to each Antigrav's radio, was barely audible over the howling of the air as they wheeled around the room.

'Ain't this fun?' he shouted, adding a lengthy 'Wheeeeeeeeeeeeee' as he pulled sharply away from the ceiling and did a 180-degree turn, plummeting back down towards the chrome floor a hundred metres below. Nate felt his stomach turning unpleasantly, and offered thanks that he hadn't eaten any breakfast.

Risking a backward glance at Cat, he saw that she was flying blind, her eyes clamped shut and her head held low beside the handlebars. He knew she hadn't eaten either, but she looked as though she was about to throw up anyway.

Saint waited until the last minute before breaking his kamikaze plunge towards the ground, almost forgetting to pull up altogether and causing the rear end of his Antigrav to hit the floor and bounce. As a result, everybody else's did the same as they followed the master inventor's path, and Nate saw two of his fellow competition winners fly from their machines. One girl he didn't recognise careened into a group of scientists, who managed to stop her fall with their arms, but Ainsley crashed into the cage with the giant Venus flytrap.

Before Nate could see what happened to him, Saint had accelerated again and was weaving in and out of the scientists on the ground, causing them to leap out of his way in fear of their lives.

'Sorry,' he yelled to the white-suited assistants. 'Sorry, sorry, sorry,' he said over his shoulder to the terrified inventors. 'Very sorry,' he yelled to Ainsley, who might or might not have been eaten by the monster plant. 'Not long to go now,' he added.

But for Cat it was too long already, and as Saint once again pulled up, Nate heard her retch, and turned to see a stream of liquid sick fly from her mouth, arcing downwards to the lab below. Someone was in for a nasty shock, he thought, but he didn't have time to see who as the floating convoy reached its destination and came to an abrupt halt. He realised that his heart was pumping, and that he was drenched in sweat.

Saint had taken them to a large opening in the circular wall, located a good fifty metres above the ground. Disengaging the homing mechanism, he manoeuvred his Antigrav in front of the giant portal, which, up close, looked like a tunnel. It was large enough to fit three enormous buses down at once, but curved in such a way that you couldn't see what lay at the far end.

Saint adopted his most serious expression before addressing the twenty-three remaining inventors.

'Now that was fun,' he said, 'but what I'm about to say isn't. It isn't fun at all. In fact it's most grave.'

Nate did his best to focus on what Saint was saying, but looking down he saw the white-suited scientists below scurrying around like ants. He couldn't take his mind off the fact that there was nothing between him and them except a prototype hover-frame that worked using physics he had never heard of.

'Most grave,' Saint repeated, drawing the words out in a husky, intimidating voice. 'You are my guests here,' he went on, returning to his normal lyrical lilt. 'You are my friends, and hopefully by the end of the year you will be my family. *Mi casa es su casa*, as they say somewhere or other. You can go wherever you like in this entire building, anywhere you like, absolutely anywhere at all.' He gestured behind him. 'Except through here.'

If Saint had been trying to put people off the enigmatic tunnel, he had done a terrible job. Almost immediately everybody in the group started craning their necks to get a better look inside, including Nate. The size and shape of the lab was such that the tunnel couldn't lead anywhere except out of the building, but Nate couldn't recall seeing any kind of annexe or extension on the exterior of the tower. Maybe it was a test of loyalty – anyone who flew through the opening would end up outside the tower and be unable to get back in.

'No, no, no!' Saint went on, watching them all stretch. 'You don't want to know what goes on in there.' He paused. 'You will all find out, however, in good time. Every one of you will get to see what takes place on the other side of this wall, but only my most trusted scientists and inventors can make that trip, because there is no going back.'

All eyes returned to Saint, curious, but he said no more about the tunnel, and what lay beyond.

'Time for breakfast. If you don't put fuel in the oven, you don't get fire in the brain. No, that's not right, if you don't set fire to the stove . . . Wait, it's on the tip of my tongue . . .' Everybody watched as Saint struggled, but eventually he gave up and re-activated the homing mechanism on his Antigrav. Slowly, everybody else filed into line, fearing another puke-inducing ride back to the hangar. But taking pity on them, Saint dropped gently to the ground below.

'I must dash,' he said as he hopped off. 'But you'll see me later. Enjoy your morning, my little champs.'

And with a whirl of his coat flaps he was gone.

24

Breakfast

The competition winners were guided out of the lab by a handful of assistants and into the lift, which took them back up to their Oz-like living area. Here, they were led to a previously hidden terrace tucked away behind a bunch of particularly dense palm trees. The terrace was set out like a restaurant, with large tables, booths and even floating chairs in one of the many pools that ran alongside it.

'This place never ceases to amaze me,' said David, who had walked up behind Nate and Cat. 'It's like a paradise on earth.'

'Speak for yourself,' Cat replied. She was still shaky from the ride, and had needed to lean on Nate all the way from the lab in order to prevent herself from falling over. Making a bee-line for the nearest seat she collapsed and put her head in her hands, her muffled voice barely audible as she cursed Saint and his flying machines.

'I thoroughly enjoyed it,' David went on as he and Nate sat down beside Cat. 'Those Antigravs must be rigged into the power source that controls this entire building. I'd make a guess that they run on some kind of reverse-ion polarisation, like a magnet only much stronger, but I really don't know how he managed to control it. Scientists have been trying to harness that kind of power for decades.'

Nate nodded, remembering from one of his numerous science journals just how much governments around the world were willing to pay in order to get the kind of free, reusable and safe propulsion that they had seen being used like toys in the lab.

'That guy is remarkable,' he said.

'He's off his rocker,' Cat answered, lifting her head from her hands. 'That kid Ainsley nearly got eaten, and Saint almost killed us all as well.'

Nate smiled, happy that Cat seemed to have lost her crush on the master inventor. She saw his smug expression and stuck her tongue out, quashing Nate's mood by saying: 'But I guess that just adds to his appeal.'

When everybody was seated, assistants began taking orders for food. There was no menu, so Nate, Cat and David suggested the most obscure dietary combinations they could think of to see what they would get away with.

Incredibly, ten minutes later the white-suited staff reappeared with three plates full of toast and crackling covered with sautéed squid and blackberry jam, an omelette made with seventeen different cheeses and served in an old shoe, and a small castle made entirely of marmite. The three inventors took one look at the meals and immediately regretted their game, wishing they'd ordered something sensible. There was no time, however, so Cat simply shared out a packet of Ebenezer's Teasers between them.

As soon as the group had finished eating they were whisked back down into the enormous laboratory, where they were guided through a door in one wall to a smaller lab beyond. It was decked out with pristine desks and brand-new equipment, and above each workspace was stencilled a name in large black letters. The desks were arranged in such a way that they were all concealed from the rest of the room by the racks of tools and materials beside them, allowing for privacy, but still faced outwards into the centre of the room so that they didn't feel cramped.

Unlike the main laboratory next door, their lab had been given a set of large windows that started halfway up the wall. Too high to look out of – 'Don't want you gazing dreamily at the world when you could be working,' explained Saint – but enough to ensure the room was drenched in sunlight. It was, all in all, a masterpiece of design.

'You'll find everything you need here,' Saint said, spinning across the room and hopping on to one of the desks as if he was going to break into song. 'And if you don't, then all you have to do is give a little whistle,' he whistled cheerfully, 'and help will come.'

And it did, almost immediately, in the form of two smiling assistants who sailed through from the main lab. They walked up to Saint and he placed his hands on their shoulders, using them to leap back down on to the ground.

'You're dismissed,' he told them, and they flashed each other a look before walking off, still wearing the same sickly beam. Saint turned back to the group and continued. 'Try it,' he said. 'It's fun.'

Hesitantly, they all put their lips together and whistled, except for David, who could produce nothing more than a bubbly farting sound. For a moment nothing happened, then the sound of approaching footsteps began to emerge from the hallway that joined the two labs, and seconds later the room was filled with white-suited, grinning lab technicians.

They milled through the group of inventors, all talking at once, asking them what they needed in the high-pitched, patronising tones normally reserved for infants. The noise was deafening, and Nate found himself panicking – there were too many people in the room, and not enough air, and he felt that he couldn't breathe.

It was almost as if they could sense his discomfort, and those assistants nearest to him turned slowly round to face him, asking him in unison if he was okay. He backed away, trying to find space to draw breath, but hit a desk immediately behind him. The white-suited staff began to close in, offering hands of support and words of comfort, but it was too much. Their faces – all young, all beautiful – swam before his eyes and he felt himself growing faint.

'You're dismissed,' he heard a voice shout from beside him. 'You're all dismissed.'

Turning, he saw Cat standing next to him, waving away the assistants. They obeyed her instantly, filing out of the room, and Nate took a deep breath, savouring the oxygen as it flooded his lungs.

'Thanks,' he said to her, and she smiled sympathetically. He watched the members of staff walk out of the lab door. They turned to look at Nate as they left, all still wearing that same smile, and in the half-light of the corner of the room Nate could swear that their eyes were golden.

Later that afternoon, when everybody had taken time to get used to the new working conditions, Saint led them back to the main lab, and to the horror of some members of the group – including Cat – to the Antigrav hangar.

'Now you really do need to get the hang of these,' he said. 'Some labs and workrooms can only be accessed by flying, they're so high up the damn walls. I was going to put stairs in, but I talked myself out of it. I mean, how old-fashioned is that?'

Nobody replied, so Saint clambered on board an Antigrav and fired it up. Rising to hover inches above the ground, he continued to address the group.

'They really are dead simple,' he said, moving effortlessly

upwards and round. 'It's like riding a Segway that can go up and down as well as forwards and back. All you have to do is push or pull the handlebar in the direction you want to move in.'

He demonstrated with a few simple moves, then asked the group to find an Antigrav of their own. Nate and Cat walked right to the back of the room and climbed on board two of the lightweight plastic frames. Cat didn't even have time to press the red ignition button before she hopped off, ran to the corner and threw up again, much to the amusement of Saint and the rest of the group.

'Stick with it, luvvie,' he called out as Cat got back on the machine, looking as pale as a ghost. 'You'll get used to it.'

'You won't get used to my foot up your backside, though,' Nate heard her mutter in Saint's direction as she fired up and began to rise. Nate did the same, enjoying the feeling of being weightless.

'Now, just have a play,' Saint said. 'Work the bar gently and you'll see how easy it is. It will all be fine.'

But it wasn't fine, not at all. While Nate found that he could make his machine go slowly forwards, it seemed to be unable to go in a straight line, and he found himself going round and round in a giant circle for a good ten minutes, repeatedly colliding with other members of the group who appeared to be having similar problems. It reminded him of geriatrics trying to ride the dodgems.

David seemed to be the only person capable of making the Antigravs go up, and he earned a round of applause from Saint as he elevated himself to the level of the hangar's low ceiling. Then, in a moment of madness, he decided to clap himself – a move that resulted in the Antigrav flying off to the side and sent David crashing painfully to the floor.

Other disasters were quick to follow. Ainsley, still in shock after his close encounter with the Venus flytrap, managed to climb to a height of six metres or so before falling off, clinging on to the handlebar in a way that made the machine spin round as fast as a tumble dryer. It wasn't long before he had to let go, and sailed out of the hangar doors into the lab beyond, causing Saint to grimace. Fortunately, he was carried back in minutes later by two white-suited assistants, dazed but okay.

The worst injury by far came when a girl named Lynsey Smith, who hadn't been able to make her Antigrav move an inch, sneezed violently and fell into the handlebar, forcing it all the way forwards. In the blink of an eye the machine had accelerated to a ridiculous speed, sending her hurtling into the hangar wall. Despite a bloody nose and a murderous expression directed at Saint, she climbed back on to try again.

Fifteen minutes later, and the room looked like a war zone. A pile of broken Antigravs lay in the centre of the hangar and a collection of bruised and fuming young inventors had begun to accumulate near the door. The good news, however, was that most of the group seemed to have got the hang of things.

Both Nate and Cat had taken a couple of gentle trips around the large hangar and, finding they liked it, were now engaged in a game of tag with the delighted David, who had so far written off three machines and was now riding his fourth with careless abandon. As other people gained their confidence, the game spread until it had spilled out into the lab beyond. Even Saint joined in, unable to control his enthusiasm as he sailed around the room chasing the inventors and trying to tap them on the shoulder.

Before long Nate felt like he'd been riding an Antigrav all his life, and started performing death-defying manoeuvres to dodge whoever was 'it'. Even Cat seemed to conquer her travel-sickness to try a couple of loop the loops.

They were enjoying it so much that when Saint finally called them all together, they didn't want to stop. Activating the homing mechanism and leading them back to the hangar, Saint spoke over the disappointed moans and complaints to tell them it was time to start work. Nursing their bruises, and trying to calm the furious beating of their hearts, they all filtered through to the lab to begin their scholarships.

25

Success!

It took Nate much less time than he thought to settle into the Saint Solutions way of life. After the first day it was always the same: up at seven, breakfast at half past, work in their smaller lab at eight right through till five-ish, with as many breaks as they needed to stay fresh and alert. In between inventing sessions they would have short classes with the white-suited assistants on school subjects, but they were all so excited about getting back to their projects that none of the winners could concentrate on things like the water cycle and differential equations.

Saint made it clear that they could leave the lab whenever they liked, and either take their inventions back to the living area to look at over dinner, investigate the countless leisure activities on offer in the tower, or simply retire to their chalets alone or with friends and watch films, listen to music or occasionally even sleep.

Nate spent almost all of his time with Cat. They adopted their usual pattern of working: Nate coming up with the ideas, developing them together, then Cat getting her fingers dirty with the manual labour. On most days Clint would sit on their desks, dangling his legs playfully over the side as he watched them work, or running around the equipment as though it was an obstacle course. Every now and then he would disappear on what he called a 'secret mission', scrambling around the lab before returning with a piece of equipment, a test tube or even just somebody's lunch.

The best thing about being there was that they didn't have to rely on faulty equipment and materials dragged from the rubbish. All the scientific tools and gizmos known to humankind, and some that weren't, were available to them. Cat had tried out just about every one of them, taking her time and getting to know the best ways to use them. When not inventing with Nate, she built wind-up toys, much to the amusement of the other members of the group. These started off small, but after two and a half weeks she had started constructing enormous critter-like contraptions from the seemingly endless supply of raw materials handed to them by Saint's assistants.

Now, it was rare not to start work without being assaulted by a two-metre-high metal dinosaur that lunged like Frankenstein's monster at your chair, or tripped up by a fifty-legged beetle scuttling across the smooth floor powered by nothing more than a tightly wound rubber band.

In fact, Cat almost brought about the early death of Saint himself one day when he strode in for his usual morning walkabout and was blindsided by a metallic flying squirrel that Cat had just wound up and let loose. Kept up by a series of rotor blades, the rodent had actually clipped off some of Saint's hair as it knocked him to the ground, before spinning around noisily then dive-bombing the stunned inventor in the stomach. The entire room had gone quiet, but Saint simply hobbled to his feet, picked up the squirrel and congratulated Cat on making such a wonderful toy.

Nate and Cat soon became firm friends with several other competition winners. Lucy White would often spend time with them in the morning before disappearing behind a desk full of gears, pistons and metal plates. She claimed to be building a suit that could make even the most uncoordinated person dance like a professional, but it was clear she had a long way to go. Almost every afternoon they saw her strutting her way across the lab, her hips wiggling uncontrollably as she fought to turn the metal harness off.

Adam Watson also took a keen interest in what Nate and Cat were doing, although it was hard to take the boy seriously as he was working on ways to breathe underwater and always had his head stuck in a contraption resembling a goldfish bowl.

One of the nicest girls there was Lynsey Smith, but she was obsessed with tidiness. The invention that she was working on at present was a tennis-ball-sized bomb that killed any kind of germ within a ten-metre radius. She was a great laugh, but every time she came over she would spend several minutes tidying Nate's and Cat's desks, which soon became annoying.

Many of the other competition winners were friendly enough, but kept themselves to themselves. The girl who had designed the ball that would bounce for ever, with the tongue-twisting name Marie Mary Morley, never said much to anybody. Instead she spent most of her time inside a human-sized rubber ball which, she claimed, would act as a safety capsule that could be ejected from planes in an emergency. The boy and girl who had built the translation machine, Bella King and Dominic Drake, were both painfully shy, and avoided interacting with everyone else by speaking to each other in French.

Of course, some of the young inventors were a downright pain in the butt. In the first week the short, dumpy, bespectacled Ainsley Stumps took a shine to Cat and spent all his time either staring at her from the other side of the lab or muttering incomprehensible phrases to her as they passed in the corridor. His speciality – genetically enhanced manure and flower-growing – meant that practically every day he would run up to Cat and present her with a bunch of colourful blooms. Cat, oblivious to his feelings, usually just commented that he smelled like a cowpat before dumping the flowers on the floor and returning to work.

It seemed harsh, but there were far more important things to be getting on with. With free rein to invent anything they liked, Nate and Cat set about trying to create the most ridiculous invention they could think of. After taking turns to dream up impossible things such as an ejector seat for a helicopter and a chocolate teapot, Cat suggested trying to build a cloud of steam that could be used as a video camera.

'Just imagine what people could do with it,' she said. Nate frowned – he was thinking, but only bad things came to mind.

'We'd never be free of our parents again,' he said, imagining a world where little clouds of steam followed children down the road every time they skipped school, or where, God forbid, they hung in the corner of the bedroom keeping an ever-watchful eye on their every move.

'No, silly,' she said. 'It could be used to track murderers on the run without them knowing, or to investigate a hostage situation and work out where the baddies are so they can be sniped.' She imitated the action of somebody firing a rifle. 'It could be ace.'

So they set to work, planning, experimenting, boiling endless kettles to try and work out a way of keeping a cloud of steam in a reasonably solid shape. The more time they spent on it, the more determined they were to see it work, and their passion became contagious, with Saint making a beeline for them every time he appeared in the morning and sitting down for at least an hour to check on their progress and suggest improvements.

Although he was undoubtedly a genius, Saint seemed genuinely impressed with what they were doing, and was forever making comments like 'That's a great idea' and 'Blimey, I'd never have thought of that'. One thing he repeated again and again was 'That's why I brought you here, you little bundles of brain matter', which always brought a smile to Nate's face.

Saint's enthusiasm reminded Nate of Cat's dad, and the way that he had helped them with their inventions all those years ago. Just like Harold Gardner, Saint bounced up and down with excitement when they overcame a particular obstacle, and would muss their hair and punch them gently on the arm when they hit upon a solution to a problem. He never pushed them, but just let the two inventors work at their own speed with their own methods. It was clear from the way that Cat gazed at Saint when he was working with them, and hugged him when he made a useful suggestion, that she too saw elements of her father in the master inventor.

Their project wasn't the only one that Saint showed an interest in, of course. He would always stroll excitedly around the entire lab making comments about the experiments that were taking place and encouraging those involved. While few people had taken the same route as Nate and Cat – in other words, trying to build something that was to all intents and purposes impossible – the other members of the group were making good progress on a number of practical inventions such as an automated dog walker and an everlasting light bulb.

The person the master inventor always seemed to get most excited about, however, was Travis Heart. The sullen-eyed boy spent every day without fail rooted at his desk making blue-prints. He hadn't touched any of the practical equipment yet, but sat scribbling endless notes and diagrams on to sheets of blue graph paper.

He was always the last person Saint went to on his daily trips to the lab, but the master inventor usually remained there for at least an hour, talking gently with Travis and occasionally slapping his hand against his thigh, exclaiming 'Genius!' in a high-pitched shout. Every now and again they would both turn round and survey the rest of the lab, as if checking for spies, and both Nate and Cat began to joke that there was some form of conspiracy taking place.

It was ludicrous, of course, and as the days passed and the same pattern repeated itself again and again everybody seemed to get used to the long meetings between Travis and Saint. Travis never uttered a word to anybody else anyway, even if they tried to engage him in conversation, and few cared what he did with his time. So long as everybody was working hard, and having fun, things seemed perfect.

'It's going to work,' said Cat. 'Why do I always have to expend so much of my valuable energy to try and convince you? Just bloody wait a minute and see for yourself.'

It had been a little over a month since they had moved into the Saint Solutions complex and Cat had just made the final few adjustments to their invention. Completely by accident they had discovered that by adding a small amount of plasma gas to the water they were boiling, then pressurising it, they could generate a cloud of steam that, while still practically invisible, held together in a consistent blob – one that drifted on a steady path for up to half an hour, rather than simply dissipating into the atmosphere.

Cat had struck upon the ingenious idea of dropping radiation-sensitive sodium iodine crystals into the kettle as it boiled, then monitoring the light that each absorbed as it was suspended in the air. Using a piece of extremely expensive equipment that Saint provided them with, they could check the visual patterns picked up by the tiny particles then translate them into a very rough image. They had already achieved each of these things in separate, controlled experiments, but they had yet to test the invention as a whole.

And that was what they were about to do now.

'Go on then,' said Nate, holding up his hands in resignation. Their obsession over the last few weeks had made them tired and irritable, and they had been snapping at each other since breakfast. For ten days they had been working late into the evening, and the twelve-hour shifts were beginning to take their toll.

'I'm going to!' she replied. 'I'm just waiting for the kettle.'

It amused Nate greatly that while everything else they were using was the cutting edge of technology, they still had to rely on a kettle from Cat's chalet to heat the water. It took for ever.

'Make me a cuppa while you're there,' came a voice behind them, and they turned to see David standing at the doorway to the lab in his pyjamas and slippers. 'Mind if we join you? I hear you're about to make the big breakthrough. Everybody's talking about it.'

Nate was about to ask who 'we' was when a tiny metal figure poked up from behind David's shoulder, scrabbling past his head before dropping into his outstretched hand. 'I found this little guy sneaking around my chalet trying to steal my socks,' he said, smiling.

Nate and Cat laughed and beckoned them forward, happy to have some company – everybody else had retired upstairs, except for Ainsley Stumps, who had fallen asleep with his face in a pile of manure, and Travis, who was sitting where he always sat still making copious notes about something or other.

'Sure thing, Davey,' said Cat as the kettle reached boiling point. David pulled up a chair and sat down, Clint on his knee, as Cat slid a special tube over the kettle spout. Breathless, they watched as the transparent steam rose into a clear glass chamber containing the plasma gas. It was sealed, and Nate turned a small knob to increase the pressure.

'Let it sit,' said Cat, watching it closely with beady eyes. As they waited, the swirling clouds slowed and began to become less wispy, appearing to solidify while still remaining virtually invisible. 'Now, add the sodium iodine.'

Nate pressed a button and a cloud of white crystals was blasted into the steam. Lighter than the water droplets, the particles hung suspended, almost as if floating in outer space.

'Beautiful,' Nate and Cat said together.

'You want me to get the fans?' asked David, but Cat shot him a wicked glance.

'Not on your nelly, David. This has to be perfect.' She walked over to the giant fan that they had set up to one side of the desk and switched it on so that it gave off a gentle breeze. She did the same to two more, which were designed to keep the cloud in a three-metre-square zone inside the lab, and stop it drifting off into oblivion. 'Okay,' she continued when she was happy with the wind speed. 'Turn on the Remote Visualiser.'

'She means the video screen,' whispered Nate to David, ignoring the scowl she threw at him.

'Allow me,' came Clint's metallic voice as he leapt from David's leg. He ran to the giant screen on the table, which was connected to Saint's radiation-sensitive device, and flicked the switch. It gradually came to life to reveal nothing but static and white noise.

'Now,' Cat said. Nate could barely contain his excitement as he twisted off the top of the pressurised container and watched the cloud of steam burst out. It rose effortlessly to head height and sat there for a moment, rotating lazily.

'Pretty,' said Clint.

'What's pretty? Where is it?' answered David, who was, despite denying it, patently short-sighted. They ignored him, watching as the cloud drifted into the path of the first fan, which caught it and blew it into the triangle. Once there, it bobbed softly in a rough circle, caught in the three currents of air.

'Anything?' asked Cat, pointlessly, as she could see as well as Nate that the screen remained devoid of a signal.

'There might be too much background radiation in here,' Nate answered. 'That chamber we used before was hermetically sealed, remember?'

Cat was about to reply when they heard the sound of a chair being scraped backwards along the chrome floor behind them. Turning, they saw Travis get up, tuck his rolled blueprints under his arm and move towards them.

'Wanna come and watch, Travis?' asked David, but his question was ignored, and Travis merely scowled at them as he brushed past, heading for the exit. He nudged the endmost fan as he walked by, knocking it out of place.

'Watch it, you klutz,' Cat shouted, leaping from her chair and lunging for the toppled fan. Without so much as a backward glance, the young inventor disappeared from the room. Cat frantically moved the equipment back in line, but it was too late. The little cloud of steam was bobbing towards the lab door, floating ever higher as it travelled.

'Klutz,' echoed Clint, waving all four arms in the air.

'Goddammit!' Cat shouted, stamping on the floor hard enough for Nate to feel the shockwave travel up the leg of his chair. 'A whole day's work ruined because of that moron!' She began pacing, her cheeks scarlet and her face twisted into a mask of pure rage. Nate knew all too well what she was capable of in this kind of mood, and when she started marching towards the door, rolling up her sleeves, he chased after her.

'Cat!' he called out, knowing it wouldn't do the blindest bit of good. Fortunately, David remained at the table, and just as Cat was about to vanish through the door he called out:

'You guys, hold up! It's working!'

Both Nate and Cat spun round instantly, running back to the desk. On the screen a fuzzy image was appearing, the turbulent static gradually giving way to what looked like a distorted view of the lab. Cat dived under the table and began playing with the radiation-sensitive equipment, twisting the dials with care.

'Any better?' she asked.

'No, worse,' Nate replied as the image vanished back into the hissing snowstorm. 'Try the other way.' She did, and all of a sudden it crystallised, creating a colourless line drawing of the lab. 'Better, much better.'

Cat scrabbled out from under the table so quickly that she bumped her head twice. Cursing, she stood and stared hard at the screen. The sodium iodine crystals were doing their job, absorbing the light from the room. The equipment that Saint had given them was detecting how much light each crystal was absorbing, and translating it into a picture on screen. This image wasn't perfect by any stretch of the imagination, but they could clearly make out the lines of the desks and the rows of scientific tools and equipment. Best of all, they could see four jagged outlines that could only be them. When they waved at the cloud, the moving outlines on screen confirmed this. The only problem was that the cloud was drifting out of the door, caught in the draught created by the air conditioning.

'I'm so annoyed with Travis! I mean who does he think he is?' Cat hissed, but Nate placed a hand on her arm and pointed to the screen, letting the picture speak for him.

As the cloud moved into the main lab they could see the lines of desks and computer consoles, along with the vague shapes of the various plants and animals left in there overnight. There were no people there – for some reason the assistants all deserted the room at half past five on the dot every day, no matter what stage they were at with their experiments – but the general shape and content of the giant room was unmistakably laid out before them.

'I don't believe it!' Cat exclaimed. 'It works!'

'Who's the doubter now?' Nate joked, giving her a hug. She pushed him away, too excited to put up with any of his sentimental rubbish. Seeing his look of rejection, Clint leapt on to Nate's shoulder and hugged his head.

'That's the lift door,' she said, pointing to a distinctive rectangle on screen. 'And that's the shuttle launch console. My God, it really does work. Just wait till Saint gets a load of this in the morning.'

But Nate didn't reply. He was looking at a shape moving across the screen.

'That's Travis,' he pointed out, trying to ignore the sensation of the little robot climbing to the top of his head using his ears as handholds.

'The unpleasant rat is probably going to bed,' added David. But as they watched they could clearly see that he was heading for the hangar, not the lift. Leaning in, the three observers watched as the outline disappeared for a moment before emerging seconds later on an Antigrav. 'The little devil,' said David. 'He's not supposed to be riding one of those alone.'

But, to their amazement, it soon became clear that he wasn't. Another shape emerged from the hangar seconds later, following Travis up.

Up towards the forbidden tunnel.

'Who is that?' said Nate, squinting to try and make sense of the outline past Clint's legs, which were dangling in front of his eyes.

'I think I know,' Cat answered, but the cloud was spinning in the wrong direction, and the two figures were sailing rapidly out of view. Leaving the screen, Cat started sprinting towards the door, Nate, Clint and David close behind. Dashing into the lab and round the first corner, they saw Travis vanish into the tunnel, waving the second figure on.

Nobody could quite believe what they were seeing. From the long, gangly outline, and the mop of untidy hair, it looked just like Ebenezer Saint.

26

David Grows Suspicious

Despite the success of the experiment, neither Nate nor Cat were in good spirits as they made their way back up to the living quarters. When they reached David's chalet he invited them in for a cup of tea, but Cat confessed that she was exhausted and sloped off to her pad, Nate walking her home.

'We did it,' he said as she pressed her thumb against the holographic sensor and stepped through the door. Turning, she gave Nate the best smile she could muster, then pulled Clint from his head and held the little robot to her chest.

'I know, Nate,' she whispered. 'I'm sorry, I know we did it. You and me, against the world, and we did it. I'm just tired.' She paused. 'And homesick.'

He nodded as she pushed the door closed, then went to join David in his kitchen. Although he'd thought about it less during the past few days as they were building up to the climax of their experiment, he missed his mum and dad an awful lot. He spoke to them pretty much every other day (they'd finally managed to work out how to use the canine videophone after two and a half weeks), and although he had said more to them in those calls than he ever had before – except information about inventions, of course, which was strictly forbidden – it still didn't feel the same as actually being with them.

In fact, he was convinced that he was forgetting things about his family and his house. Every time he spoke to his parents he noticed something different about them, tiny things – new clothes, different postcards on the walls, odd mannerisms and phrases – that he would never have spotted if he was still living at home.

They reminded him of what he was missing, and there were times when all he wanted to do was leave the compound and head back to his house, eat dinner with his folks, sleep in his bed, even go to his school and take lessons like the ordinary kid he used to be.

Of course there was more to do at Saint Solutions than there ever had been at home. During their first week in the complex he and Cat had discovered practically every leisure facility imaginable on the same floor as their chalets. Tucked behind one enormous cluster of trees had been a multiplex cinema with screenings of every film ever made – including some that hadn't even been released. They had spent several evenings there selecting their favourite movies from a huge database and consuming the seemingly endless supply of Saint's Strawberry Slurp and popcorn that emerged from special compartments in the chairs.

Tennis courts, crazy golf and a five-a-side football pitch lay concealed in other sections of the floor, while behind a water-fall Nate discovered an arcade complete with bowling, table football, air hockey and about a hundred video game machines. He never forgot what an amazing experience he was being given, what a privilege, but there were times when his heart ached for the old days.

Walking through David's open door, he crossed the spotless lounge and entered the kitchen, collapsing on to one of the metal bar stools.

'Is she okay?' David asked, setting a mug of steaming-hot tea down in front of him. Nate picked it up and took a sip, realis-ing that he hadn't drunk a thing all afternoon. It scalded his lips but the sensation was good, perking him up.

'I think so,' he answered eventually. 'Just tired, I guess. And she misses her mum.' He glanced up at David and, not wanting to appear soft, added, 'But then girls do tend to be a bit soppy.'

David smiled dreamily, stirring his tea with his finger to gauge its temperature.

'I miss mine as well,' he said. 'I don't mind being soppy. We've been away for a long time and it's still a couple of months until Christmas.'

There was a moment of silence.

'I miss my parents as well. I feel so freaked out here sometimes,' Nate finally admitted. His words seemed to strike a chord in David, and the pyjama-clad boy leant forward so that his face was inches from Nate's and began to speak in a slow whisper.

'I've been meaning to bring that up for a while,' he said, looking warily up at the unblinking black eye in the corner of the room that might have been recording his every word. 'I mean, about this place. Don't you think it's just a little too weird?'

'Well, it's been built from the mind of Ebenezer Saint,' Nate answered, 'so it's bound to be like some twisted Disneyland. The guy's nuts.'

'But it isn't just that,' David went on, speaking so low that Nate could barely hear him. 'Have you noticed how it hasn't rained once since we've been here? Outside, that is. And, while I'm on the subject, why we're not allowed outside at all. I thought we were going to get to explore the entire complex, the hills, the lake.'

Nate considered it for a moment. There was so much to do inside the tower that he hadn't given much thought to going outside. Back at home, he did all he could to avoid fresh air anyway.

'It's October, Nathan,' David continued, not waiting for an

answer. 'The weather is never this good in October. I'm telling you, it's not right.'

He gulped down his tea, swallowing noisily before carrying on.

'And those assistants. Haven't you noticed how they all look, well, kind of alike? How many scientists do you know who are in their mid-twenties and gorgeous?'

'Maybe he just likes hiring beautiful people,' Nate replied, shrugging his shoulders. 'He wouldn't be the first and I doubt he'll be the last.'

'But there's more. They are all geniuses. I couldn't find my calculator today so I told an assistant to fetch me another. He just asked me what I needed calculating so I read out the figures and he did them in his head.'

Nate was about to answer that everybody knew their times tables, but David anticipated him.

'They were decimals, Nate, to around fourteen places. And one of them was pi to the fiftieth place. And if you think that's weird, I went to seven other assistants in the lab that day and asked them the same thing, and they all gave me the exact answer. Trust me, that's impossible.'

Nate didn't like what he was hearing. He'd always felt a bit strange here, but David's paranoia seemed a little extreme. There was probably a simple explanation, a Saint-patented brain implant or something else that the world didn't know existed. He decided to change the subject.

'How are your inventions coming along?' he asked. David sighed and leaned back, finishing his tea and gently placing the mug on the counter.

'Not good,' he confessed, 'not good at all. I've been working on a new propulsion system for rockets.' Nate nodded, remembering seeing the plans that his friend had been working on since they had arrived – they had looked fantastic, like a Batmobile that could travel into space. 'But I can't get the bloody thing right. The equations just don't add up, and as it stands it would just end up blowing everybody sky high.'

'You'll work it out,' said Nate. 'You're just about the smartest person here, Saint aside.'

David laughed, but behind it Nate could sense a deep sadness.

'You're the one who invented the Spy Cloud,' he said.

'The Water Activated Light Recording Unit for Sight,' Nate replied, quoting Cat's official title. They both giggled.

'Right, bedtime,' David said, getting up from his stool and ruffling his hair. 'Sorry to chuck you out, old boy, but I'm about to keel over.'

Nate stood up, realising just how tired he was as well.

'Thanks for the tea,' he said, walking towards the door. When no reply came, he turned, and saw David staring mournfully at the floor.

'I just want to feel the wind on my face,' he said, 'to know that there's actually a world out there.'

'Well, ask Saint,' Nate replied. 'I'm sure he'll let you out for an hour or so, on a leash.'

But David's expression said it all – he knew there was no way he was getting outside. They walked through to the main door in silence.

'Just you wait,' he said to Nate, as he closed the door. 'It will be glorious sunshine again tomorrow.'

Nate collapsed into his own bed less than a minute later, trying not to think about what David had been saying. When he woke to his alarm in the morning and looked outside he saw that, for the first time since they had arrived, the giant windows were streaked with rain from the heavy grey clouds above.

It might have been the sudden change in weather – so soon after David's muttered complaints – or possibly the conversation in the kitchen the previous night, but Nate suddenly felt a powerful urge to talk to his parents. Deciding that it wouldn't matter too much if he was late to the lab, especially after their success with the Spy Cloud, he walked back into his lounge and switched on the plasma screen.

'Home,' he said, as he pressed in the large red button.

For a second there was nothing but static, then a blurred picture began to appear on screen. Nate couldn't for the life of him work out what he was looking at – a white background covered in what looked like red hearts. He assumed that there was some fault in the machine, and was about to call one of the assistants when the picture started to move.

'Nate,' came his mum's voice. 'Is that you under there?'

The red hearts suddenly vanished, to be replaced by his mum. Nate pulled a face when he realised that they had been a pair of his dad's pants that were hanging out to dry over the dog Saint had given his parents. On screen, his mum folded the offending item and held it to her chest. It looked as if she was standing in his room, but he was a little miffed to see that the wallpaper had been changed to Spiderman.

'It's so good to see you!' she exclaimed. 'It feels like we haven't heard from you for ages.'

Nate laughed. He had been contacting his parents every other day, although usually for little more than a few seconds to say goodnight. Seeing his mum now, however, Nate's heart lifted, and he wished more than anything that he could give her a hug. But, like always, something was bugging him about the way she was standing. Something subtly different about the way she looked.

'Hi, Mum,' he said, ignoring the feeling. 'How are you and Dad?'

'Good,' came her reply. She turned aside and he heard her calling his dad's name. 'We've been doing some work to the house while you're not here. Your dad's been trying to build an extension to the kitchen.'

Nate whistled, impressed. His dad was usually loath to do anything that involved hard work, and the only time Nate had ever seen him perform DIY was when the plasterwork was ruined by a faulty invention. It had obviously done them a world of good to be left alone in the house together.

'How are things with you?' she asked as Peter Wright strolled in, covered from head to toe in sawdust, paint and, for some reason, mud.

'Okay,' Nate replied, tentatively. 'We've just finished one of our experiments, and Saint's pretty pleased with us.'

His mum smiled, but her expression was one of concern.

'You don't sound too happy about it,' she said.

Nate was about to reply when he realised what it was that was different. His mother's hair, which usually had streaks of grey, was now mousy blonde all over. It made her look younger, but it also made her look strange. He couldn't quite put his finger on why.

'It's just that things are a little odd here,' he went on. 'Some of the kids are getting homesick.'

'Not you though?' said his dad, his brow furrowing. 'You're having fun, aren't you? I mean, you aren't thinking of leaving?'

'No,' Nate said, a little disappointed at his dad's reaction. 'No, I love it here. But I guess I miss you guys.'

'We miss you too, dear,' replied his mum, throwing the pants at Peter. 'And you know you'd be welcome home any time.'

'Thanks, Mum. And I love your hair, by the way.'

There was no response. Nate tapped the screen, thinking that the image had frozen, but his mum and dad were both still moving. He started to repeat his compliment when a band of static flashed across the screen, causing the image to distort as though it was being watched through water. It only lasted for a moment, but when the picture was back to normal Nate could have sworn that his mum's hair was once again marked by subtle streaks of white.

'We'd better run,' said his mum. 'We've got lots to do.'

'Got an extension to build,' added his dad, reaching forward to turn off the videoscreen.

'Okay,' Nate said quietly, watching as the image disappeared. 'See you soon.'

27

Another Invitation

Several minutes later, when Nate strolled into the inventors' lab, he was still thinking about the conversation with his parents. Had he just imagined that his mum's hair was different? Thinking back, he couldn't remember actually studying her head for signs of the white streaks, and he may just have not been paying attention. But there were other things that were niggling him – his dad's newly acquired building skills, the wallpaper, and the way they spoke to him as though he was eight years old again.

His train of thought was broken when he saw that David's mood had deteriorated even further. As Saint praised Nate and Cat for their astounding results, David sat in silence at his desk, solemnly trying to perfect his calculations for the cosmic Batmobile. He didn't even turn up for lunch – his favourite meal of the day – and when Nate and Cat returned downstairs to the lab after stuffing themselves with lobster they found that he had taken off to one of the practical rooms with a case full of welding equipment.

Deciding that they had earned an afternoon off, they wove their way through the various desks and assistants in the main lab and located their friend sitting alone in a small room trying to join two pieces of steel with a weak red flame. Nate noticed that he wasn't wearing his bow tie.

'Hello, Barley,' Nate said, walking in and shielding his eyes from the flame. 'Glad to see you've finally got those plans sorted.

How long do you think it will take you to put that bad-boy space machine together?'

David shrugged and carried on welding, and Nate and Cat looked at each other, unsure whether to leave him alone. Tutting loudly, Cat marched forward and snatched the welding iron from David's hand, turning the dial so that the flame was blue and fierce. She handed it back to him, blinking to get rid of the pinpoints of blue light that danced before her eyes. David held it for a moment before turning it off, raising his mask to look at her.

'Thanks,' he said. 'But give me a few days. I need some peace and quiet to try and get this thing together. I just want to get the ship finished.'

'It's not a competition, Davie,' Nate said, suddenly feeling guilty about their success. 'We're all in this together. Why don't we stay and give you a hand?'

David pulled the faceplate shut and returned to the sheets of metal, firing up the welding iron again. As an afterthought, he pulled up his visor and looked at Nate.

'You know what we were talking about last night,' he said, glancing cagily at Cat before continuing. 'Don't you think it's weird that it's only now started raining?'

'David . . .' Nate started, but the truth was that he did think it was strange.

'And I asked him,' he went on. 'I asked Saint if we could go outside. You know what he said?'

Nate shook his head.

'He said no, plain and simple. That was it, one word, nothing more. No.'

And with that, he went back to his welding.

As they made their way through the lab, Cat grabbed Nate's arm and pulled him to a halt.

'What was all that about?' she asked. 'What stuff were you talking about last night?'

'It's nothing,' Nate answered. 'Just David. I think he's cracking up. Keeps going on about the weather, about the windows or something.'

She paused, chewing her lip.

'Well, maybe he's not cracking up,' she whispered, waiting until a lab assistant had passed them before carrying on. 'I mean, it is pretty freaky here. Nice, but weird. If you know something then you have to tell me, Nate. We're best friends, remember.'

'Come on, Cat,' he said, 'you don't need to remind me. If I thought any of what David said was true I'd let you know, straight away.'

'So what's he been saying?' said a voice behind them, making Nate jump and forcing a short scream from Cat. Spinning around they saw Ebenezer Saint standing inches behind them. Wearing his trademark white suit with golden boots, he seemed taller than usual, more imposing. And it was one of the few times they'd seen him without a smile.

'Nothing,' stuttered Nate, backing away from the figure. 'Well, you know, just about the weather.'

'It's raining, isn't it? Surely he's happy now. And he wants to go outside in it too. What a curious lad he is.'

Without warning, Saint's face suddenly erupted into an enormous grin. 'But what about you two, eh? Champs, that's what you are.' He leaned in, almost having to bend double to lower his head to their level. 'I didn't want to say in front of the others, but I'd like to invite you to my apartments upstairs. You'll like it. I've got a museum up there with pretty much every important invention that's ever seen the light of day.' He winked, his eyes flashing with excitement. 'And some that haven't.'

Standing upright, he fished inside his pocket and pulled out two small rolls of parchment. He handed one to each of them. 'Tonight,' he said. 'Have these with you, or you won't get in. And don't tell a soul!'

Cat wore a giant smile all afternoon, even when she complained that her cheeks were cramping. She seemed to have forgotten all about her uncertainties, in spite of the fact that they'd only just been talking about them. Instead, from the moment they arrived back at their chalets, she spent every moment in the bathroom, worrying about her hair.

'It's not a date, you know,' Nate shouted through the door, holding the cups of tea that he'd made and feeling the old, unpleasant sensations of jealousy return. 'He just wants to show us his museum.'

But Cat wasn't talking to him, and all he heard was the sound of plastic bottles and combs falling into the sink telling him that she was busy. Sighing, he walked through to her kitchen and sat down, taking alternate sips from both cups of tea. He pulled the sheet of parchment from his pocket and unrolled it, looking at the tiny golden text, written in beautiful calligraphy. There was just a single sentence: 'Come at eight and don't be late.'

He twiddled his feet absentmindedly, and puffed out his cheeks several times before realising that he had become extremely nervous. For a moment he wondered if he should put on something smart and brush his hair, but soon abandoned the thought when it seemed too much like hard work.

Instead, he pulled ten packs of Ebenezer's Teasers from the cupboard and set to work building a model bike from the jelly sweets.

It was a good hour later, with the clocks reading ten past seven, when Cat finally emerged from the bathroom. It was the first time in his life that Nate had had to do a double take – looking at her briefly and turning away before his brain informed him that something was different and guided his eyes back towards her.

She stood in the doorway looking slightly bashful. Her hair, although short, had been styled into a beautiful brunette crown, and a subtle combination of blusher, mascara and lipstick gave her face a pre-Renaissance beauty that took his breath away. To top it all off, she was wearing a flowing red velvet dress covered with sequins that sparkled in the soft light.

He'd never seen Cat look anything like this before – she'd always been the tomboy, always shared his clothes, never bothered about her hair or make-up or any of the other things that girls at school seemed concerned with. It took Nate a while to find his tongue, and even when he did he couldn't think of the words he needed.

'Wow, Cat,' he said, feeling himself blush. 'You look . . .'

He couldn't quite bring himself to say it, but Cat knew what he meant and smiled.

'Beautiful? Thanks Nate.' She stepped into the kitchen and sat down, smoothing the dress over her legs. 'Now where's my tea?'

They left Cat's chalet at five minutes to eight and made their way towards the elevator. Before setting off Cat had decided that she needed to spend another fifteen minutes in the bathroom checking her hair and make-up, and when Nate felt they were in danger of being late he had sent Clint in through the outside window with instructions to chase her out of the room as quickly as possible.

Seconds later, after a loud scream and a crash, she'd emerged with a pencil stuck up her nose and a look of barely contained fury. Behind her, Nate could see the poor robot on the floor where Cat had thrown him, his Saint's Strawberry Slurp can shell bent out of shape and all four hands massaging his head.

Taking pity on him, Nate picked Clint up and sat him on his shoulder, feeling the tiny metal fingers grip his shirt as they left Cat's chalet. For a moment the trio walked in silence, looking at the full moon suspended outside the enormous glass panes, brushed lightly by the rain that still fell. Below the vast celestial sphere the lights of the Saint Solutions complex stretched as far as they could see, twinkling faintly through the persistent shower.

The ambient light in the living area, designed to complement the natural world outside, had faded to a soft, orange glow that reminded Nate of the log fire at home. He realised that his nerves had vanished. In fact, he was feeling quite relaxed about their trip upstairs.

'I'm so glad we did this,' Cat said as they rounded the corner, spotting the lift ahead. Nate thought back to the day they'd visited Howard Gardner's grave together, the competition final only hours away and doubts circling both their minds. It would have been so easy not to go, to stay at home in comfort, to never have known.

He nodded when she glanced at him for a response, and in the moonlight she really was beautiful. He wanted to put his hand in hers, the way he'd done so many times before. But something stopped him, a weight in his stomach that kept his arms by his side, a fear that this time it would mean something more.

'I'm glad you did this too,' came a little voice from Nate's shoulder. 'Or I'd still be a bundle of parts and wires in Saint's supply room.'

They both laughed, and Cat reached up to tickle Clint's chin. Behind them, from somewhere inside the indoor jungle came a splash and a laugh as somebody leapt into one of the many pools, followed by a chorus of cheers. The sound gradually faded as they reached the lift. It sensed their presence, as always, and automatically began its swift passage to their floor.

When the doors slid open, they saw the lone figure of David in the massive interior. He seemed shocked to see them, especially when he glanced at Cat and saw her glamorous new look.

'My, my,' he said. 'Don't we look gorgeous.' He was obviously exhausted – giant black bags had sprouted beneath his eyes and he stood in an ungainly slouch that was the complete opposite of his normal rigid stance. 'Off anywhere nice?'

'Upstairs –' said Clint from Nate's shoulder, before Cat lashed out and batted him, hard enough to send him tumbling to the floor.

'Just off to run another batch of tests,' she blurted, her speech quicker than usual, and obviously a lie. 'We wanted to see if the WALRUS worked with different forms of clothes. If velvet was more or less sensitive to the radioactive detectors.'

David looked at her with an eerily expressionless face. He switched his gaze to Nate, who had retrieved the little robot from the floor and placed him back on his shoulder.

'Want a hand?' he asked, to which both Nate and Cat answered 'no' immediately. Realising how it sounded, Nate tried to backtrack.

'What we mean is that you look tired. You should get some rest.'

David didn't take his eyes off Nate for what seemed like an eternity, but eventually dropped them to the floor and shuffled forwards, down the path. Nate turned to him, feeling terrible.

'David,' he said to the boy's back, 'how did it go today? How's the rocket coming along?'

But David didn't answer, eventually disappearing around a row of palm trees. Turning, Nate saw that Cat was already inside the lift, urging him on with an impatient hand.

He followed her in as the holographic panel emerged, showing only the living and lab floors as options. Cat pulled out her parchment, and the panel immediately doubled in size, a third button appearing with nothing but the letter S emblazoned on it. Taking a deep breath, Cat pressed the holographic button, the doors slid shut and the lift shot skywards.

28

A Blast from the Past

Whatever they were expecting to see when the lift reached its destination, this wasn't it. Ahead of them was a wide corridor that stretched, seemingly, to infinity, lined with a red carpet and ornate crystal chandeliers. Hundreds of candles gave the hallway an eerie, unreal feel.

But what was truly remarkable about the corridor was its occupants. It was absolutely packed full of animals. Standing by the lift doors was a beautiful antelope, its dark, oval eyes watching Nate and Cat for any sign of aggression as they stepped, dumbfounded, from the white interior. Hanging over its head, on a chandelier, was a giant sloth, fast asleep. Further down the hall a troupe of four or five monkeys were leaping off the walls, while overshadowing them, and barely able to squeeze its enormous frame into the tight confines of the long room, was an elephant. It flapped its ears lazily but didn't move.

The more they looked, the more they saw. A lion and a cheetah were chasing one another playfully in circles, an anteater was snuffling in the corner searching for dinner, a pair of swans preened themselves in the distance and at one point a squirrel leapt from the wall on to Nate's head in order to get a better look at Clint. The noise in the hall was absolutely deafening. The monkeys shrieked, the lion's roar was so deep that it could be felt through the carpet, and as Nate and Cat stepped forward the elephant let out a fart that sounded like a rocket taking off.

'This is unreal,' Cat shouted, trying to make herself heard above the noise. 'What the hell is going on?'

Nate took a deep breath and started yelling a response, but as he did so the room fell instantly silent. He slammed his mouth shut and listened to his words echo around the walls. Staring down the hallway they saw that the entire menagerie of creatures had frozen. One of the monkeys, halfway between the wall and the chandelier, had fallen flat on its face, while the elephant was stuck in a rather comical pose with its leg held up to avoid a tiny mouse, its face a mask of fear.

'I don't get much company up here,' came a voice from behind a giraffe, 'so I had these guys made.' A series of grunting sounds accompanied the peculiar sight of Saint trying to squeeze himself between the giraffe's left leg and the wall. He appeared to get stuck for a minute before popping out and skidding along the carpet. 'But my God, are they a pain in the butt!'

'You should have made a bigger hallway,' Cat said. Saint laughed as he approached, and ducked down to look at them from beneath the elephant's legs.

'I don't fancy crawling under there,' he said, 'so why don't you come and join me.'

As they navigated their way through the long hallway Saint chatted as if he'd known Nate and Cat for years. He told them how the robotic animals worked, how they fed on specially treated cardboard pellets and how it was actually real animal pelts they were wearing. This last comment earned such a disapproving look from both Nate and Cat that Saint blushed, apologising for his lack of consideration for the animal kingdom.

After five minutes of walking, and no sign of the end of the corridor, Saint suddenly stopped and touched a section of the red wall. A small door slid open, and they walked into a second corridor, much shorter and thankfully free of robotic wildlife.

'I was young when I built Saint Tower,' he continued as they strolled. 'Everyone I worked with tried to take me for a ride, wanting dividends for this, payments for that. Even my parents couldn't say two words to me without one of them being 'money'. So I designed and built my own friends, the animals, like every good inventor should.'

The passage ended in a vast pair of mahogany doors, standing slightly ajar. Walking briskly up to them, Saint gave the left-hand door a hefty kick, causing it to crash against the wall beyond.

'But enough of the sob story.' He spun round with his arms held high and, grinning broadly, announced, 'Welcome to my place!'

Beyond was a reception room the likes of which Nate and Cat had never seen before, not even in the stately homes they'd been forced to visit on school trips. It was vast and round, with two giant, curved staircases in the middle that curled around a fountain shaped like the double helix from a DNA molecule. The stairs led to a balcony high above the ground which circled the entire hall, at just the right level for looking out of the giant windows that curled inwards to form a glorious glass dome. Through it was a flawless view of the moon in its bed of brilliant stars.

'What a pad!' exclaimed Clint, leaping to the floor and scampering off towards the fountain.

'It's a modest place, I know,' Saint said, strutting in with his hands on his hips. 'But it's a little haven I like to call home and it's all I could afford on my salary.'

Nate and Cat followed him into the unbelievable space, watching in awe as the fountain changed colours, from clear to red to blue, then to a dazzling kaleidoscope of different hues.

'And this is just the hall!' Saint exclaimed. He looked at Cat, and took her hand. 'My dear, I forgot to tell you how wonderful you look tonight. It's so nice of you to have made an effort.'

Cat blushed and looked at the floor, and Nate frowned, fighting the jealousy that was playing havoc in his gut. Stepping in between them, Saint looped his arms through both of theirs and began strutting purposefully towards one of the many identical sets of dark double doors that lined the circular walls. Seeing them move, Clint raced back across the floor and bounded on to Nate's leg, hoisting himself up until he was clinging to his pocket.

'Now, I didn't bring you up here to show you my magnificent palace,' he said, his strides so long that both Nate and Cat had to jog to keep up with him. 'I wanted to reward your hard work with a trip to my museum.'

The doors crashed violently inwards as Saint kicked them open. Pulling the stunned duo and their little robot through into a dark room, he spun away and clapped twice. Instantly hundreds of lights embedded in the ceiling twinkled to life, revealing another vast room, this one full of glass cabinets and display items.

'Taa daa!' the master inventor announced, standing frozen to the spot as if waiting for a round of applause. But Nate and Cat were too astounded by the sight before them to oblige. Stepping forwards, they scanned the massive space, open-mouthed and silent, while an awestruck Clint leapt on to a nearby table and jumped up and down in excitement.

'This,' Saint said to Cat when he saw what she was looking at, 'is the first telescope ever invented, crafted by a certain Dutch spectacle maker named Hans Lippershey. Feel free to have a closer look, but if you break it, you pay for it.'

Nate had walked over to a dusty pile of ancient-looking mechanical equipment in the corner near the door. The giant machine was whining slowly through a thick layer of dust.

'That,' Saint said, 'is Babbage's first computer, the great-great-grandfather to the humble PC.'

Clint, meanwhile, had found what looked like a stone knife and was attempting to cut himself out of his can. Saint walked over and picked him up.

'And this, my little friend,' he said, taking the object from Clint and placing it gently back on the table, 'is the oldest known flint arrowhead on the planet. Not a tin opener, thank you very much!'

Every single invention in the room was of the same calibre. From the first sextants used in the eighteenth century to the earliest-known musket. From the original steam-powered locomotive to Henry Ford's Model T car. From Saint's own KleverKar to the enormous bulk of the Saturn V rocket that had carried the first men to the moon, which lay down one side of the room, dwarfing everything else with its immense size.

'The one at the Kennedy Space Centre is a fake,' Saint informed them, smiling proudly.

There was even an early prototype of Harold Gardner's Miracle Machine, the device that Cat's dad had worked on for years before his untimely death. Cat gasped when she saw it, and walked tentatively over to stroke the dials and brush a layer of dust from the smooth surface. It was clear from her expression that she was remembering the times they had worked on it together, but the memories were obviously good ones as she was smiling fondly.

'It's one of the most important inventions here,' Saint said quietly as she rejoined them. 'You should be proud!'

Both Nate and Cat were shaking with excitement as they

made their way around the room, ushered from invention to invention by the beaming master inventor. Clint was also deliriously happy, leaping from table to table, cabinet to cabinet, uttering little squeaks of pleasure with each new sight.

This nearly proved disastrous on several occasions. When Saint showed Nate and Cat the first catapult to have been used in battle on European soil, Clint pounced on to the lever, sending a vast chunk of rock through one wall and out into the hall.

'Well,' said Saint philosophically as he peered through the massive hole, waving plaster dust away from his face, 'at least we know it still works.'

He was less forgiving when Clint attempted to ride a very early version of the spinning top, breaking it in two, then tripped on a clockwork mouse reputedly designed and built by Galileo. By the time they had made their way around the entire hall, the excited robot had almost killed them all by knocking over a rack of ancient Chinese spears, and had also managed to get stuck inside an astronaut's helmet for almost a quarter of an hour while pretending to be Buzz Lightyear.

Eventually, Nate grabbed Clint as he was leaping towards an extremely fragile-looking early version of the television, and switched him off.

'Oh woe is me!' the robot shouted as the light in his eyes faded. Nate tucked him into his pocket and apologised to Saint, who laughed and waved his hands in the air.

'What good is it having toys if you can't play with them?' he said musically.

But it was getting late, and after a few more minutes Saint told them it was time to leave. As they walked back towards the doors, however, the master inventor led them to a small alcove they hadn't seen before. Inside, resplendent on a velvet-covered platform and lit by several different safety lamps, was one of the most beautiful sights Nate had ever seen.

'It's genuine,' said Saint, his voice a whisper. 'Leonardo's hands actually built it.'

It was one of Leonardo da Vinci's gliders, a flying machine that he had designed and built over five hundred years ago. It wasn't the one that Nate had seen in books and on postcards – this seemed more advanced, using two sets of pedals to power an enormous pair of bat-like wings.

The wooden frame looked worn, but still strong, and Nate wanted nothing more than to touch it, to fly it, to see if it really worked. Leonardo was his hero, the man who had come up with the idea for the helicopter, who had mapped the human body, who had designed the first car, the first mechanical calculator, the tank, the machine-gun, the submarine – all centuries before the rest of the world had decided to catch up. Taking a step forward, Nate reached out, but he felt a firm hand on his shoulder.

'I don't think so, young man,' said Saint, pulling him back. 'This one's just for me.'

29

A Turn for the Worse

It was getting late by the time they exited the museum, and although Nate and Cat were both tired Saint asked them to stay for a moment longer.

'I've just got one more room to show you, before you go,' he said, suddenly serious. 'I get a good feeling from you both. You've done great work here, you look out for each other, you have inspiration, talent and a remarkable aptitude for invention, more than most of the competition winners, I feel.'

The two young inventors turned to each other, grinning with pride. Saint began walking towards the next set of doors along the wall, stepping over a massive pile of rubble from the catapult mishap as he went. Instead of opening these doors with his usual aggressive boot, he reached into his pocket and pulled out a golden key on an extendable cord, slotting it in and turning it. The carved mahogany portals swung open into another dark room. Nate and Cat walked tentatively over as Saint entered, clapping to switch on the lights. He turned, looking at them from inside.

'But,' he said, drawing out the word, 'I wonder if you have vision.'

For some reason, Nate wasn't sure he wanted to see inside this new room. It had been such an amazing day. In the space of an evening Nate had been face to face with things he'd never expected to see in a hundred lifetimes. Part of him wanted it to end now, because his gut was telling him that something was about to change. Something profound, irreversible.

By the way Cat gripped his hand, practically digging her nails into his palm, she obviously felt the same, sensing something in Saint's new mood, in his cryptic words, in the silence and strangeness of the room before them.

'Only those with both genius and vision can rightly call themselves inventors,' Saint went on. 'Those who invent simply because they *can* have no claim to the title. Those who invent to make the world a better place, now *they* are true heroes. It's those men and women – like your father, Cat – who deserve to be hailed as the kings and queens of the world, its emperors and empresses . . .'

He paused, then beckoned with his hands. With little choice, the two friends moved forwards, entering the room.

' . . . its gods,' Saint finished.

It took Nate a while to figure out what he was looking at, but when he did it sent a chill down his spine that made him want to curl up beneath a table and hide. His scalp shrivelled, making his hair stand on end, and his legs seemed on the verge of giving out completely.

Practically every inch of space on the wall was covered in pictures of mushroom clouds, the plumes of smoke and fire that were sent a mile high every time an atomic bomb was detonated. Some were tiny black-and-white photographs from the first tests during the 1940s; others were vast colour printouts, the size of a house, that overshadowed everything else in the room. In between the horrendous images were hundreds of sheets of notes, scrawled on parchment, all in Saint's handwriting.

In the centre of the room was an enormous table, easily taking up the same area as one of their chalets downstairs. It was rigged up to a series of small holographic projectors, which displayed what looked like an entire city on the tabletop. But

Nate didn't have time to take a closer look as Saint produced a remote control from his pocket and aimed it at the wall behind his head.

'We were born with these gifts for a reason,' he said, pressing a button. One of the posters on the wall, which turned out to be a video screen, suddenly came to life, the static eruption curling upwards in a demonstration of its incredible force. The image switched, displaying a small tropical island that was obliterated in a second as another atom bomb erupted, creating a blinding flash of light that quickly became a towering column of smoke.

'Oh my God,' he heard Cat whisper to his side, and forgetting any sense of embarrassment he gripped her hand with equal force, pulling her towards him. She drew closer without any struggle, and together they watched in horror as explosion after explosion rocked the giant screen, as bomb after bomb was detonated, as cloud after cloud of radioactive smoke burst forth, as city after city was pummelled into the dust in the blink of an eye.

'We were born to make humankind aware of what it is, of what it can and cannot do.' Saint looked like a man possessed. The screen was directly behind his head, and from Nate's position it seemed as though the explosions were emanating from the master inventor's manic expression. Under any other circumstances the scene would have been ludicrous, hilarious, but right now it terrified Nate more than anything he had ever witnessed.

'We are the ones who will guide the world to a better place, who will bring paradise back to the earth, who will end suffering, end war, end disease, end everything that makes us afraid when we get up in the morning, everything that gives us nightmares.'

He moved forwards with the speed of a snake until he was standing directly above them. In the red, angry light of the room his face was distorted with shadows, his eyes wide, unblinking, wild.

'We are the future,' he went on, hissing the words violently, spraying them both with spit. 'Don't you see? Don't you see why I brought you here, why I wanted you all? You're young, you haven't been brainwashed, you can see what needs to be done.'

He pressed another button and Nate heard something powering up inside the enormous table. Standing out of their way, and giving them an unimpeded view of the holographic city, Saint began to hum – not so much a tune as a nervous, excited moan. Nate looked at the table, still unsure what it was, but Cat soon cleared it up with one terrified, barely audible word.

'Hiroshima,' she said, and Nate immediately saw it. The houses, the buildings, the streets and cars, even the people – tiny, moving images covering every inch of the surface. It was Hiroshima, the Japanese city devastated by the American atomic bomb in 1945.

'Sometimes,' Saint said, 'we all know what needs to be done, even if we can't bring ourselves to think about it.'

With the click of another button the holographic projectors burst into life, carving an image in light that Nate would remember for the rest of his days.

In perfect three dimensions they saw the explosion above the city, the immense shockwaves of energy that carved their way across the landscape like a knife, destroying everything they touched. They saw the expanding cloud, the fire, the force, and they saw the death – every building, car and person reduced to holographic ashes.

What was left was a wasteland.

Saint aimed the remote control at the table and clicked again. The image vanished and the room fell into silence. Nate's ears were ringing with the sound of the explosions, and he realised that tears were falling from his eyes. When Saint next spoke, it was in a whisper.

'The world has to be destroyed before it can be rebuilt,' he said, tucking the remote into his breast pocket. Then, without looking round, 'You can go.'

Neither Nate nor Cat had ever run so fast in their lives.

30

A Cruel Joke?

Nate and Cat made their way back through Saint's quarters to their living area in a stunned silence. But as soon as the chalets came into sight Cat broke into a run, unable to control her sobs. Nate jogged after her, and found her in the bedroom frantically throwing armfuls of clothes into a suitcase that lay open on the bed.

Walking over, he placed a hand on her shoulder. She shrugged it off, but he persisted, and eventually she yielded, collapsing on to the bed and burying her face in the mound of clothes. He held her as she cried uncontrollably for nearly twenty minutes, and kept holding her when she quietened. When he realised she had fallen asleep he let go and got to his feet, pulling a blanket over her before making his way outside.

The lights were off in David's chalet so he returned to his own, sitting on the aerial slide and pushing himself half-heartedly back and forth. The uncomfortable seat made him think about home, and how long it seemed since he had been there. He tried to picture what it was like, to bring some comfort back into his evening, but all he could think about was the image of the bomb exploding over Hiroshima.

In his mind he pictured the same devastation in his own city, his own house being flattened, his own family being scorched alive by the unstoppable radioactive force – so bright that it burned their shadows permanently on to the tarmac. It made him feel sick, and he had to stop swinging for fear of throwing up there and then.

Surely Saint couldn't be serious, he thought to himself. The master inventor had donated billions to saving the planet and its less fortunate species. Why would anyone with such a love of nature, such compassion for people, embrace something that was the complete opposite of life, something that could only ever bring death? It just didn't make sense. Unless it was some kind of trick.

The more he thought about it, the more he started to believe that it was exactly the kind of joke Ebenezer Saint would pull on his young guests. The master inventor had a famously eccentric, and mischievous, sense of humour that could easily have led to tonight's disturbing display. It seemed odd that anyone would devote so much time and energy to a prank, would kit out an entire room in atomic memorabilia for the sole purpose of playing a practical joke. But if anybody had the time, money and space to make it work, it was Saint.

Nate hopped off the aerial slide and began pacing, kicking the tiny stones that lay on the path as he thought about Saint's motives. Several minutes later he found himself laughing about the ease with which he and Cat had fallen for the stunt. He'd probably try it with every one of the competition winners, just because he was Ebenezer Saint, and he could.

'What are you chuckling about?' came a voice from the bushes behind him. Turning, Nate saw David strolling out from the palm trees. He was wearing his swimming costume and was busy drying himself with a towel, shaking water from his ears as he walked.

'Just Saint,' Nate answered without hesitation. 'He's got the strangest sense of humour. I think he's trying to play practical jokes on us all. Probably his way of making us feel less homesick. How are you? Been for a swim?'

'Tried,' David replied, walking to the side of Nate's chalet and leaning on the wall. 'Couldn't really get into it, got too much on my mind.'

'Like?' Nate asked.

'It's the rocket,' David replied, surprising Nate, who had been expecting more conspiracy theories about the windows. 'The proton accelerators, they won't stay in their steel casings. The energy output is too great, and the whole thing just blows.' He sighed, his hands dropping to his side in frustration. 'It's driving me bloody crazy.'

'Give yourself a break, Davie. NASA scientists have been working on new propulsion systems for years – you can't expect to crack it in four weeks.'

'But I need to,' David replied, the same urgency returning to his voice that Nate had heard before. 'I just don't feel right here.' Nate tried to interrupt but David spoke over him. 'I thought this would be the chance of a lifetime, the opportunity to really make something of myself. But I can't stand it here, the whole place creeps me out. The only way I'm going to get home is if I give Saint what he wants, give him his rocket.'

'But it's supposed to be fun, Davie,' said Nate. 'Isn't it?'

Muttering something about needing his sleep, David pushed himself away from the wall and started walking back to his chalet. He turned and spoke to Nate as he went.

'I've scheduled a test date for two days from now,' he said. 'I'm going to have it finished by then, and afterwards I'm going home.'

'But what if it does blow?' asked Nate, concerned.

'Then God help us all.'

Nate woke the next morning to the excruciating pain of something long and pointed being stuck up his nose. Bolting upright, he waved his hands in front of his face to fight off his attacker, unable to see a thing because his eyes were watering from the pain. He realised he was screaming, or at least would have been if his mouth wasn't still full of sleep slobber. Instead, he was making an unpleasant gargling sound that was halfway between a shriek and a death rattle.

Feeling his nose, he soon realised what had caused the pain. As he wiped his eyes clear he saw the end of an HB pencil poking from his left nostril, and with a tug he freed it. Sitting on his chest, watching him with big yellow eyes and uttering a sound that could only be described as a chortle, was Clint.

'Not nice, is it?' said a voice through his bedroom window, and looking up he saw Cat standing there. When she noticed his expression she burst out laughing and disappeared, knocking loudly on the door a few seconds later.

'What was that for?' Nate asked Clint grumpily as he pushed the robot to one side and struggled out of bed. Clint wobbled unsteadily on the crumpled duvet, waddling to the edge and lowering himself carefully to the floor.

'I'm sorry,' he said in his metallic voice. 'I've been reprogrammed. Now I find sticking pencils up your nose utterly irresistible.'

Nate slung a dressing gown over his pyjamas and turned to scowl at the robot as he walked from the room, promptly tripping on a pile of clothes that he could have sworn he didn't leave there the previous night. He fell in such a way that he managed to wedge his shoulders solidly in the right angle between the floor and the wall, and it took him thirty seconds of strenuous, painful activity to get back up.

'And I am also now unable to stop playing pranks on you, I'm most terribly sorry.'

Nate rubbed his neck then made a lunge for the tiny robot. Clint squeaked and tried to bolt under the bed, but Nate managed to wrap his fingers around the dented can and reached inside to flick the power switch.

'Oh woe is me,' said Clint before the lights in his eyes faded, signalling that he was inactive.

Nate walked through the sitting room and opened the door to face Cat, who was still tittering.

'Nice trip?' she asked, stepping past him and lowering herself into one of the leather recliners.

'Very funny,' he answered, collapsing on to the chair next to her. Gradually the events of the night before were returning to him, and he wondered why Cat was in such high spirits, especially given the state she had fallen asleep in.

'So,' he asked, hesitantly, 'you're okay then?'

Cat leant back in the chair, hands behind her head, and looked at him. She had stopped laughing, but there was still humour in her relaxed expression.

'It was a joke,' she said, shrugging. 'It's just his way of breaking the ice. What else could it have been?'

'That's exactly what I thought,' Nate said, relieved. 'I mean this is the guy who invented the car that will stop world pollution: what the hell would he want to do with a bloody nuclear bomb? Bit cruel though, playing a trick like that.'

'Only because we took it so seriously, silly,' Cat said. 'Although it was mean comparing the inventors of the nuclear bomb to Dad. Anyway, it only seems cruel because he probably didn't expect anyone to believe that he'd actually blow stuff up.'

Cat's comment reminded Nate of the night's other disturbing meeting.

'Did you hear about David?' he asked. 'He's planning to test his rocket tomorrow, even if it isn't ready. He told me he wanted to finish it so Saint would let him go home. I just don't understand why he's so desperate to leave.'

'He's just a little homesick,' she said. 'But it is exciting about his rocket. I saw him this morning. He's gone down to the lab already. He's announced it to Saint and everybody, and there's a lot of excitement about it.'

'Well, I hope he knows what he's doing.'

'Relax,' Cat said, getting to her feet as the breakfast chime sounded. 'Of course he does.'

But Nate could remember all too well the look on David's face as he returned home the previous night, and he knew that there could only be disaster when desperation was the motive for an experiment.

31

Laser Specs and Goat Helmets

It was at breakfast that Nate realised he hadn't seen Travis Heart since the night they had successfully tested the Spy Cloud. He wasn't in the hall now, and hadn't been in the lab the previous day.

He asked around as the young inventors gradually made their way down to their workstations and discovered that nobody had seen so much as a trace of the boy for over thirty-six hours – since Nate, Cat and David had witnessed him enter the forbidden tunnel.

It worried Nate that nobody seemed to care what had happened to him. Travis Heart was a nasty piece of work, no doubt about that, but it was still strange that he should have vanished, especially when the competition winners were restricted to a handful of giant rooms.

He made up his mind, as they ambled down to the labs, to ask Saint outright when they saw him that morning. As they walked through the main lab, however, dodging Antigravs and watching a particularly gruesome scene involving the Venus flytrap attempting to swallow one of the assistants, Cat pointed out something to him that made him change his mind.

Although the forbidden tunnel was so high up it was barely visible, there were clearly flashes of purple light coming from inside, tiny strobes of lightning that came and went without a sound. Whatever was going on, Nate was now certain that Travis Heart was involved.

As it turned out, he wouldn't have had much time to talk to Saint anyway. The master inventor only gave them the curtest of nods as he strolled into the lab at a quarter past ten, although he did flick them a golden wink from over his shoulder as he made his way towards David's bench. His blasé manner made Nate and Cat certain that events the night before hadn't been serious, and they smiled at each other in relief. In fact, instead of being afraid of Saint, Nate was surprised to find himself a little disappointed that their mentor had moved on so quickly after their success with the Spy Cloud.

'We've had our glory, you jealous baby,' Cat said, watching him pout. 'Let David bask in Saint's attention for a while.'

'I'm not jealous,' Nate replied, a little too quickly. Trying to change the subject, he sat himself down on the edge of the desk, pulling Clint out from where he'd been rooting around in a box of spare parts under the table. He reached into the little robot's Saint's Strawberry Slurp can and pulled out a sheet of paper that contained his suggestions for their next invention.

'You keep your list in Clint?' Cat asked, frowning.

'He guards it for me,' came Nate's cagey reply as Clint pulled a tough expression and flexed his arms. 'I don't want anybody stealing our ideas.'

'And what ideas are those?'

'X-ray specs,' Nate said, reading off the list and making Cat laugh so loud she almost choked.

'Oh, for Pete's sake,' she said. 'You're not still on about those?'

'Laser specs,' he went on, feigning seriousness.

'No, Nate.'

'Spy specs.'

'Uh uh, not again, Baron von Dingaling.'

'Specs that help you see better,' he said, unable to control his laughter any more and bursting into a fit of giggles. When he had calmed down, Cat snatched the piece of paper from him and read it silently.

'Nate, these are all glasses,' she said, looking up quizzically. 'Why are you so obsessed with specs?'

'I'm not obsessed!' he replied, once again his speed giving away the lie. 'I just like them, that's all.'

'Fine,' Cat said, throwing the paper over her shoulder. 'Let's do it. Let's make some laser specs.'

Nate's jaw dropped.

'Seriously?' he asked. She nodded. 'Right on, sister!'

But despite the fact that Nate had waited his entire life to make a pair of laser specs, he quickly discovered how difficult a task it was. Hiding the equipment for an Optical Detection Device inside a pair of glasses was no problem at all, but attempting to insert a powerful laser, hot enough to melt steel, inside a flimsy plastic framework was nigh on impossible.

Nate started work on the laser while Cat requested a hundred pairs of spectacles from the nearest assistant. Using a set of magnifying glasses – causing Cat to laugh uncontrollably for a good five minutes when she saw his enormous eyes – he began to construct a tiny generator for a gas laser. Clint sat by and watched, every now and then enthusiastically running off to fetch a tool or component for his two creators.

It was one of the trickiest inventions Nate had ever worked on, but it did a great job of keeping his mind off the unpleasant feelings that still lingered from the previous night. Despite the fact that the fiddly components kept slipping from his grip, after a few hours everything had been slotted into place.

Rigging the generator to a temporary power source, he gently slapped Cat, who was rocking back and forth on her chair idly daydreaming.

'Ta daa!' he announced in a booming voice. 'While you've been off in la-la land, I've just built the smallest and most powerful laser known to man!'

Cat burst out laughing at his intense expression and snatched the glasses from his hand.

'Really?' she asked, batting his hands away as he tried to reclaim his invention. 'The most powerful laser known to man?'

Some heads in the lab were turning, and Nate plucked the glasses from her before she embarrassed him further. Placing the modified frames on his head, he hefted a thick steel block from the floor and set it up on the desk, careful to avoid Clint. Several of the young inventors had gathered around to watch.

'Stand back, and don't look directly at the laser,' he said, powering up the glasses and aiming at the steel block. In the hushed silence the high-pitched whine of the generator was deafening, promising to unleash a crimson beam of pure energy.

But when Nate pressed the fire button, all that emerged was a straggly line of weak red light that wobbled around on the surface of the steel block like a laser pointer. In an attempt at humour, Clint ran in front of the beam and clutched at his torso as if he'd been shot by a laser gun, pulling a fake expression of pain before crashing to the desk.

'Okay, it's not quite powerful enough to cut through steel,' Nate admitted, ignoring the robot and the giggles from behind him. He pushed the block to one side before replacing it with a sheet of aluminium foil from his equipment box. 'But it's still one of the most powerful lasers known to man. Just watch!'

The feeble red beam danced around on the surface of the foil but the only things that were burning were Nate's cheeks, which glowed from embarrassment. The laser caused no damage whatsoever to the concrete, wood and rubber blocks that Nate placed in front of it, and after ten minutes he picked up a sheet of paper from the desk and held it right in front of his face.

'It is going to work,' he shouted stubbornly at the young inventors, who had all been rendered helpless by fits of laughter. Pushing the fire button once again he pressed the paper against the generator, willing for the laser to work. To his delight, the thin sheet began turning brown in the centre, a burnt spot that very slowly crept outwards. Then the sheet ignited, causing Nate to whoop with joy.

'I told you!' he shouted, but the unimpressed crowd was drifting away. Nate was about to call out after them when he felt a terrible pain in his fingers, and realised he was still holding the burning paper. He threw it to the floor, quickly followed by the glasses, and turned to Cat, pouting.

'It *was* the most powerful laser,' he mumbled, his brow furrowed in frustration. Clint scurried to the floor and picked up the glasses as Cat slapped Nate on the back.

'It just needs a little more work,' she said.

But by mid-afternoon Nate's laser was no more powerful, and all he had accomplished was a collection of half-burned sheets of paper and a large, steaming mound of melted plastic that had completely ruined the top of his desk.

Cat and Clint had long since abandoned him. Clint was curled up on a spare chair snoring gently, his power cable slotted into a electricity outlet. Cat had moved on to a project of her own involving some of the spare spectacles, and had put together a device that looked oddly like a set of two bicycle helmets with holes in. Throwing the laser specs to one side, Nate peered over her shoulder to get a better look at what she was doing.

'Every time I go into the main lab,' she said slowly, her attention firmly on wiring up a set of electronic cables to the helmet, 'I see that poor two-headed goat trying to kill itself. This should give it a bit of relief!'

'A safety hat for goats?' Nate asked sarcastically. 'Well that's just about the most amazing invention I've ever heard of.'

'Shush, laser boy,' Cat replied. 'It's more than that.'

Nate took a closer look at the invention and saw that the wires were connected to the glasses, which were mounted in the front of the helmets and fitted with a set of lens-size plasma screens instead of glass panels. These screens were linked up to a tiny computer that sat between the helmets.

'Come with me,' Cat said, leaping off her chair and heading for the passageway to the lab. 'Let's see if it works.'

She explained the invention to Nate as they waited for a pair of nervous assistants to open the door to the goat's substantial glass cage. Inside, as usual, the poor animal was butting itself senseless as each of the heads fought it out for control of the body. When it heard the noise of the door it stopped, and four yellow eyes peered at Cat as she stepped into the hay-filled interior.

'The camera on the top of the helmet picks up exactly what the goat is looking at,' she whispered, trying to ignore the expression of suspicion on the animal's two long faces. 'But I've designed some special software so that the image of the other goat is erased. With any luck, they each just won't know that the other is there. Would you mind?'

She held out a handful of pellets, nodding in the direction of the goat, whose expression had turned to one that could only be described as disgruntlement.

'My pleasure,' he lied, taking the pellets and splitting them in two. Stepping forward, he held out his hands and tried to remember whether goats had sharp teeth. Sniffing gently, the two-headed creature shuffled forward and began to suck up the pellets from his palms with a noise resembling a vacuum cleaner in the bath. In seconds his fingers were coated in goat drool.

While it was distracted, Cat walked up to one side of the goat and placed the first helmet on to its left head, slotting it over the horns. It seemed to resist for a second, but as soon as she switched on the monitor it continued eating as though nothing had happened. The second goat head accepted its helmet with nothing more than a quiet bleat, and by the time all the pellets had gone both heads were fashionably dressed in Cat's invention.

For a few seconds the goat's expressions were ones of confusion, and both heads tried to scratch their helmets off at exactly the same time, resulting in the animal gracelessly falling over. When it had clambered back to its feet, however, the heads seemed miraculously content. Instead of butting each other repeatedly, each set about munching away at the loose pellets on the floor as if it was the proud, sole owner of the body.

'And that's another hole in one for the super inventor,' Cat said, making the action of somebody hitting a ball with a golf club. The assistants who had been watching began to clap.

But their celebration was premature. Trotting over to the water trough, the heads began to drink, slurping in a ghastly fashion that sent giant globules of water and slobber flying everywhere.

'Oh, this could be bad,' said Cat, taking a step away from the goats, towards the cage door. 'I didn't have time to make the helmets waterproof.'

'Well how bad can it be?' Nate replied. With the slightest of hisses the left-hand helmet began to smoke, causing the goat to lift its head in consternation. The helmet on the right was

 225

making a whining noise not unlike that of a small child, and sparks started flying upwards from the processor, lighting up the cage like a strobe.

Then, with a worrying series of pops, both helmets short-circuited. The electrical shock they gave out couldn't have been strong, but the goat leapt a good two metres in the air, landing back on the ground in a state of complete panic.

'That bad,' Cat answered, dashing for the exit. Nate turned to follow, but the creature was too quick, galloping as fast as a goat can gallop towards the gate, and what it thought was safety.

Cat had made it to the other side of the cage, and was urging Nate on, but his single head and two legs couldn't compete with the goat's twin brain and four hooves. The animal caught up with him in a flash and, with an excruciating thump, butted him out of its way. Screaming, he hurtled through the air, landing head first in a pile of goat poo.

By the time he had got back to his feet, rubbing manure from his face and nursing his backside, the goat was loose in the lab and causing havoc. He tracked the animal's frantic progress through the glass wall, watching as chairs, test tubes, plant pots and desks were tossed up into the air like bowling pins. Even Ainsley, who had picked that moment to present Cat with a new breed of rose, was sent sprawling across the floor by the rampant beast.

By the time Nate had walked to the cage door it was as if a tornado had struck the enormous room. Experiments lay ruined on the floor, puddles of God-knows-what were dripping from the desks and the assistants unlucky enough to have been in the goat's way were struggling to their feet, still cross-eyed and wobbly.

Meanwhile, the furious goat was leading the most bizarre conga line Nate had ever seen. It ran from desk to desk followed closely by Cat and a dozen white-suited assistants all trying to coax the animal to a standstill.

It was a good twenty minutes later that the goat, utterly exhausted, collapsed by the door of the Antigrav hangar, its two heads snoring noisily as the wary assistants carted it back to the cage.

Looking paler than Nate had ever seen her, Cat sat down on the only intact chair she could find and wiped the sweat from her brow. Fortunately, Saint was nowhere in sight but the lab technicians were all giving her the evil eye as they set about tidying up the scene of unparalleled destruction.

'Don't say a word,' she said to Nate as he opened his mouth to speak. But he could tell she was too exhausted to chase him.

'I think you'd better *goat* to your room,' he said, sniggering, then ducked as the lab's sole remaining chair flew past his ear and exploded on a desk behind him.

32

Things Turn Explosive

The following morning, still nursing his bruises, Nate returned to the lab to find that it had been restored to an immaculate condition. Everything was just as it had been before Cat's disastrous experiment. It was spookily normal, in fact – the assistants were all smiling, the goat was back to butting itself continuously, and if it hadn't been for his extremely painful rear end Nate would not have believed any of it had really happened.

Walking through to the smaller workspace, he discovered David sitting in exactly the same place as he had been for most of the previous day. The young inventor looked terrible, as if he'd been there all night. His skin was pale and waxy, his eyes sunk deep into his face, as though they were afraid of what was coming. He was scribbling notes on some Saint Solutions headed paper, and Nate could see that his hand was shaking.

'Barley,' Nate said. Checking his watch he saw that it wasn't even seven yet. There was nobody else around. David seemed not to hear, so Nate walked closer, peering over his shoulder.

'It's nearly done, I've so nearly nailed it,' David said, slamming his pen down on to the paper and turning to look at Nate. He was smiling, or at least it was something that resembled a smile, but he looked so utterly exhausted that the best he could manage was a slight upturning of the lips.

'Have you had any sleep tonight?' Nate asked, already knowing the answer. 'You should really get some shut-eye, Davie, you look terrible. You can't seriously be thinking about running your experiment in this state.'

'There'll be plenty of time for sleep when it's over, don't you worry,' came David's reply. 'If all goes well Saint's got to let me go. Then I can sleep for a week, a month, in my own bed. Think of it, Nate, *my own bed*!'

'But there's no hurry,' Nate replied. 'Are you really that desperate to leave?'

David was silent as he tucked the notes into his breast pocket. He scraped back his chair and stood, squeezing Nate's shoulder gently as a sign of reassurance before making his way out of the lab.

'Just be in Testing Chamber 3 in an hour,' he said as he walked out. 'Trust me.'

For the next hour Nate did some more work on the laser specs, but his mind wasn't really in it. He was worried for his friend, and although he could see how desperately David wanted to go home, the pressure was causing the poor boy to push himself too far, and too quickly. He was burning the candle at both ends, and in the middle too. And sooner or later the fire was going to get out of hand.

News had spread about the big propulsion test, so not many people made it into the lab that morning. At five to eight Cat walked in, to see Nate rummaging through the large box of lens-free specs, pulling out a black pair and clamping them into the vice on the desk. Beside him was a smoking puddle of melted plastic, all that remained of the seven previous pairs of glasses he'd accidentally burned that morning.

'So, you coming?' she said. Nate turned and nodded, leaving the glasses where they were and joining Cat by the door. Together they walked back into the main lab and through the short hallway that led to the testing rooms.

'I hope this goes okay,' said Nate. 'I'm really nervous for him.'

'Stop being such a doubting Thomas,' Cat replied as they entered the auditorium. 'That boy's a genius, and you know it. The only reason something would go wrong was if Clint was here, which is why I've left the clumsy little robot in my chalet.'

The seating area in Testing Chamber 3 was jam-packed with people. Pretty much everybody from the group was there, excluding Travis, and the remaining seats were taken up by the white-suited assistants from the lab. While the young inventors were chattering away excitedly, the Saint Solutions staff sat in absolute silence, grinning out of the vast reinforced glass window that made up one entire wall of the room.

And it was easy to see why they were speechless. On the other side of the glass, propped up on a framework of thick steel pipes, was a sleek chrome vehicle, roughly the same length as a minibus but the shape of a high-tech car. It was only a prototype, so there was no cockpit, but the steel craft was kitted out with a set of impressive-looking boosters that Nate knew were fully fuelled with highly explosive proton accelerants. He wondered just how much the glass partition had been strengthened.

Nate didn't quite understand the physics behind David's propulsion theories, although he knew the vehicle worked in the same way as conventional rockets, using Newton's laws of motion. But the young inventor had developed a fuel that was much easier to work with, cheaper to make, and practically pollutant free. If it worked, then within a decade everybody could be popping into space for weekend breaks.

Nate took a seat near the front but Cat moved into the row behind to avoid sitting next to Ainsley Stumps, pinching her nose and pointing to the manure stains on his jumper as an explanation. Nate attempted to ignore the smell and turned his attention to the view beyond the safety glass.

David was running around frantically inside the testing booth, making last-minute adjustments to the chassis and double-checking the fuel levels inside the rockets. Several lab technicians were also sprinting back and forth on the other side of the glass, all looking far too young and beautiful to possibly know what they were doing. David was clearly issuing instructions to them, even though no sound could be heard through the transparent wall.

At eight o'clock on the dot Saint charged into the viewing room, marching straight to the front row of seats and leaning intently towards the main attraction. David squinted through the window, breaking into a smile when he saw that the master inventor had arrived. Whatever doubts he had been having about Saint now seemed to have vanished.

David could be seen clapping his hands decisively, at which one of the lab assistants approached him, appearing to say something that David didn't like. Turning away and waving his hands, the young inventor walked up to the small control panel that sat beside the craft, out of the path of its dangerous rockets. The white-suited assistant turned to look at Saint through the window, and although no attempt at communication was made Nate saw Saint tense up, his brow furrowing in concern.

But it was too late to stop David now. Firing up the control panel, he inserted a key and pressed a button, watching closely as a series of spiked graphs appeared on a monitor to his left. Even though the glass was soundproof, the people watching in the viewing hall could feel the rocket's boosters beginning to charge, a steady rumble that started as a tremor then built up to a terrifying crescendo – one so powerful it made the supposedly secure glass rattle in its frame.

From David's serene expression it all seemed to be going to plan. When the rumbling had been steady for a while he pressed several more buttons on the control panel, then pulled on a set of dark safety goggles to shield his eyes from the imminent explosion.

When it came, it was awesome. Instead of the inefficient pillar of fire and smoke emitted by a conventional rocket, the first booster on David's machine punched out a cloud of translucent gas which, Nate saw, had a beautiful lime-green hue to it.

The gas struck the heavy steel plate set beneath the rocket, allowing the machine to push itself forwards. The craft was connected to the frame by two unbreakable diamond tethers, designed to measure the force with which it was being pushed. It was clear from the way the tethers tensed just how powerful the rocket was, and it was still only using one of its three boosters.

Grinning, David pressed another button and the second booster fired up, increasing the sound of thunder in the room and causing Saint to hop up off his seat in wild excitement, shouting, 'You genius! You genius!' through the window. The diamond tethers tensed even more as the rocket strained to break free.

With one booster left, Nate found himself on the edge of his seat rooting for his friend. He suddenly realised that his thighs were extremely painful, and looked down to see that he had dug his nails into his own skin from nervous tension.

Everybody watched as David hit the button to activate the last booster. The rumbling from the rocket increased again, making Nate's chair shake and his teeth chatter. But the booster didn't fire. David could be seen switching off the third rocket then rebooting it, but still no green gas emerged.

'You can do it!' shouted Saint, standing right up against the glass, his words creating patches of condensation that he stooped to see around.

'Cancel it,' Nate whispered to his friend, hoping the message would get to him somehow through the soundproof wall. 'You've proved the bloody thing works, now switch it off.'

'Do it!' shouted Saint. His expression was manic, like it had been in his chamber of atomic horrors, and it chilled Nate to the bone.

'Don't,' Nate answered, trying to ignore his fear, his words inaudible to everyone but himself. 'Don't do it, David.'

But David had tasted success. Twisting a dial on the control panel, he increased the strength of the proton acceleration, causing the vibration to double in intensity. The steel base was now red, and one corner was actually melting, the metal dripping to the ground like butter. The rocket itself was shaking as it fought to be released, the diamond tethers struggling to contain it.

Still nothing had emerged from the third booster. The craft was shaking so much now that it looked as though the steel making up the boosters was starting to tear, glowing from the intensity of the heat within. The assistant who had been arguing with David earlier was approaching him again, gesturing wildly, but David ignored him, turning up the dial even further.

A rivet shot out of the rocket and hurtled across the test chamber, striking the far wall. Seconds later another flew out and struck the glass partition hard enough to create a jagged crack almost a metre long. Everybody in the viewing area jumped, and some of the inventors stood up from their chairs, ready to make a run for it.

Saint, however, continued to shout words of encouragement through the glass, his head a few centimetres away from the impact. David looked up and saw him, twisting the dial even further. The heat being generated by the rocket was so great that it almost made the scene unwatchable, a shifting distorted mirage.

Nate couldn't stand it any longer. Jumping to his feet, he ran over to Saint.

'Stop encouraging him!' he yelled out, standing directly behind the master inventor. 'It's going to explode. You're going to kill him!'

But Saint wasn't listening. He was too busy banging on the glass and shouting at the figure on the far side. Nate, moving beside him, saw his lunatic expression. If the master inventor didn't snap out of his trance then things were going to go seriously wrong.

'He's going to die,' he said, grabbing Saint's arm. This time Saint stared down at him, the madness fading from his eyes as he realised that Nate was right. But it was too late, and they both turned to the window as they heard the sound of the ship's third booster lurching into life.

For an instant Nate thought that David had managed to fix the problem, but he soon saw that things had taken a monumental turn for the worse. Faced with a blockage, the green proton flame had cut a hole in the side of the booster and was firing upwards, pushing the rocket down on to its frame. Unable to cope with the change in directional pressure, the diamond tethers were twisting, threatening to break.

Then, with a deafening crack, the left-hand tether snapped, slashing through the air and striking the window with such force that it shattered inwards, bathing the entire viewing chamber with chunks of glass. With the safety barrier no longer in place, the terrified audience were instantly assaulted by heat and noise from the boosters. The onslaught proved too much for some members of the group, who fled through the door screaming.

Freed from its restraints, the rocket began to tilt sideways. The pillar of lethal green light was descending towards David, but the young scientist was too busy pressing buttons on the control panel to notice it. Nate tried to shout a warning over the deafening roar as the green flame sunk even lower, heading straight for David's head. With a lurch, the rocket threatened to break free from its remaining tether, and the movement caused the flame to suddenly drop, like a guillotine.

David was going to die.

But from nowhere a female white-suited technician burst on to the platform with incredible speed, striking David with enough strength to send him flying out of the path of the flame and into a wall over six metres away. He struck it awkwardly, cracking his head and sliding to the floor, unconscious but alive.

The technician was not so lucky. Before she had a chance to run, the flame descended, striking her in the head and engulfing her in 30,00°C of liquid energy. Nate turned away, feeling the bile rise in his throat. Above the roar he heard the sound of more shouting technicians rushing into the chamber, cutting the rocket's power supply to leave the room in a state of profound silence.

He didn't dare turn around, but something inside of him forced his head up, made him look into the ruined test chamber. The rocket was a mess, the floor had practically melted away and the walls were charred beyond repair. Worst of all, a blackened, unrecognisable shape on the floor was all that remained of the poor technician who had sacrificed her life for David.

A blackened shape which, in front of the remaining members of the audience, slowly struggled to its feet.

33

Send in the Clones

Nobody could quite believe what they were seeing. It was like something from a zombie film. Through the clouds of acrid smoke being given off by the cooling floor, the ruined technician could be seen standing upright in the centre of the room, wobbling unsteadily from side to side. From top to toe she was entirely black, her uniform stripped away. From the viewing booth, it looked as though she had been covered in tar.

Nate raised his hand to his mouth in horror as the shape started to walk towards the chamber door. As it went, enormous chunks of blackened flesh fell from its skinny frame to the floor.

Beside him, Nate heard the sound of Ainsley throwing up, and a series of screams from the teenagers. Strangely, none of the other assistants in the room seemed bothered by what had happened. They were no longer smiling, which was one thing, but they were sitting looking at their fallen comrade with not so much as a glimmer of concern.

'That's impossible,' said Nate, watching as the shape staggered, almost fell, then carried on walking. 'No one could survive that blast.'

Saint, who was still standing next to him, turned to face the room, coughing nervously. He brushed several large pieces of safety glass from his tussled hair before speaking.

'Ah,' he said, 'that was unexpected. I'm very sorry you all

had to see that. What a gruesome sight for such an early hour of the morning.'

The blackened technician stopped when she heard Saint's voice, and changed direction, walking towards the shattered window. As she neared him, Nate saw that almost all the flesh on her arms and legs had dropped off, leaving only bone.

Or was it bone? Squinting to improve his eyesight, Nate saw that what lay underneath the burned flesh looked oddly metallic.

'I guess it's about time I came clean,' Saint said, alternating his stare between the young inventors, who sat transfixed by the terrible scene, and the technician, who stood facing the direction of Saint's voice.

'You see, I don't trust people much. They lie, they cheat, they steal ideas and by God, do they smell – especially when they get older. I mean it's that kind of stench that comes from too much garlic bread, too little exercise – then it becomes old person smell, and I hate that!' He stamped his foot to emphasise the point.

Stepping into the test chamber, Saint approached the blackened remains of the technician and tenderly reached up to her head, which was no longer recognisable. Taking hold of the charcoal-coloured scalp, he tugged, and the woman's entire face fell to the floor. Nate heard the sound of somebody else throwing up, this time behind him. He turned to make sure that it wasn't Cat. Her face was as white as a sheet, her eyes glazed over as though she had retreated inside herself to escape the horrors of the room. The girl next to her was bent double, head between her legs, still being sick. It was beginning to smell very unpleasant.

Nate returned his attention to the assistant, and his heart missed a beat as he saw what lay beneath the human mask. It was another face, but this one was made of metal – a smooth, shiny, steel visage that still glowed faintly from the force of the heat that had struck it at point-blank range. Set into it were two large, golden eyes which, freed from the blackened veil, looked up at Saint in appreciation.

'When my parents tried to get me to sign over Saint Solutions to them and their lawyers – it's a long story, and I won't bore you with the horrible details – I banished every single human from the entire place. Excluding me, of course.' Saint began picking the remaining bits of blackened material from the metal frame, yelping when he touched a particularly hot section. Gradually he revealed a complex robotic torso made up of pistons, plates and wires. 'And I set about making these. They're state of the art, each one programmed to invent, to experiment, to think for itself and learn. They can rebuild themselves, although, as you can see, they are virtually indestructible, and they can also make replacements. Just last week I saw a new model working in the lab, one with significant improvements.'

Nate staggered backwards and fell into a vacant seat. He felt as if he was in a sci-fi movie. The world had never seen anything like this before – it was technology that nobody even knew existed, let alone had harnessed.

'But they do have certain rules, which I picked up from dear old Asimov,' Saint continued, squatting to clean up the robot's long, spindly legs. 'They will always give up their own life to save a human's, as you now know. This isn't always a blessing. Some humans deserve to meet a sticky end, and it's always a shame to see one of my beauties hurt. Not in David's case, though, of course. And those of you at the back, who look like you need clean underwear, will be relieved to know that they cannot harm a living person. Not so far as I know, that is. But they haven't actually met any living people before now, apart from me.'

Saint stood and patted the robot on the head. It cocked its

neck, batting its golden eyes, and seeming to purr at the attention.

'They make great companions,' Saint went on, speaking gently and not taking his eyes from the robot. 'They are my only friends.' He turned to the group. 'Which is terribly sad, don't you think? Hence, you.' He gestured at the seated children, smiling distantly. 'I can trust you – you haven't been corrupted by those stinking, thieving adults yet. You don't want to steal my ideas. All you want to do is invent. Children and robots, now that's the life for me.'

He returned his attention to the assistant.

'Now, since we're all being honest with each other about who we are,' he said, 'I might as well show you everything. This is my darlings in Normal Mode.' He took a deep breath, as if banishing the last doubts from his mind, then said in a firm voice: 'Work Mode.'

The last two words were directed at the robot, who instantly began to change. With the sound of pistons sliding and valves hissing, the legs and arms extended in stages, making the metallic creature a good three metres in size. With a painful-looking lurch, its shoulders punched outwards from its back until they were wider than those of an American football player, while tiny shifting plates inside the head rearranged, causing it to expand to twice its normal size.

With a deep, terrifying growl, not unlike that of a bear, a fearsome jaw began to emerge from the robot's mouth. Glinting teeth sprouted from the metal gums to make the machine look like a cross between the Tin Man and a werewolf, and the friendly round eyes narrowed to demonic slits that viewed the inventors with a look so fierce that Ainsley passed out. With the sound of gears and pistons working at full steam, the robot lurched towards them, as if about to pounce.

'Don't worry,' Saint said, laughing at the young inventors as they pressed themselves back into their chairs. 'They're just designed for optimum efficiency. Big shoulders for carrying equipment, long legs and arms to be able to reach control panels more easily, huge heads to allow more ventilation to their main processors and those jaws . . .' He paused. 'Well, they'd do a great job of scaring away burglars, I reckon. You'll soon get used to them – they're the same golden-eyed assistants you know and love, just in different forms. And do you have any idea how difficult it was to find artificial human skins that fitted? I did that for you young'uns – I didn't want to terrify you.'

Nate stared at one of the technicians to his side. It was impossible to believe that, locked inside that flawless female flesh, there was a giant robot like the one before him.

'Well,' the master inventor went on. 'I guess now you've seen one, you might as well see them all!'

'Oh no,' Nate whispered as Saint took the small remote from his jacket and typed in a sequence of numbers.

'Oh yes,' replied Saint, looking right at him with a sinister smile.

The room erupted into chaos. As one, each of the technicians stood and began trembling, as if it was about to have a seizure. Then shapes began to appear beneath their clothes, as though some kind of creature were running around just under their skin.

With a sickening tearing sound, the technician to Nate's left literally exploded. As the metal skeleton inside her began to expand, her skin split, flying off and slapping lifeless to the floor. Her face blasted open as the skull beneath doubled in size. Lastly, she seemed to step out of her own legs, as though they were pyjama bottoms.

Within seconds, the room was full of enormous, pristine metallic robots whose silver skin glinted in the artificial light. Once again Nate heard the sound of somebody throwing up. Before long, he realised that it was him.

34

Life Goes On

From that moment on, things were very different in Saint Tower. Although the assistants spent most of their time in Normal Mode, they made no attempt to put their human disguises back on. The glistening silver creatures performed their duties as they had before – providing the inventors with everything they needed for their experiments and continuing to offer their vast knowledge of all things scientific. But the children couldn't take their minds off the fact that at any moment the human-sized machines could expand into terrifying beasts, so nobody was keen on using them any more.

The metal assistants tramped noisily around the labs and living quarters, their golden eyes showing no sign of the emotions that their human masks had displayed. Every time one entered the laboratory the inventors would freeze, often huddling together around a single desk and staring in horror as the robot dropped off a palette of test tubes or carried away a waste bin, and only relaxing when it had disappeared.

Saint seemed oblivious to their fear, enjoying the fact that his robots were now unclothed for all to see. From time to time he would command one to enter Work Mode, then charge around on its giant back like a rodeo rider, laughing maniacally until he fell off. He urged the young inventors to do the same, but nobody was willing to so much as step within a two-metre radius of the metal monsters, let alone touch them.

Nate, who until now had been fascinated by robotics, couldn't stand looking at them when they were fully expanded. It was their size – they towered over even Saint himself – and their speed: they were able to cross the lab in three giant strides, like metallic stick insects.

But most of all it was the muzzles that emerged when the machines were in Work Mode. The enormous jaws that stuck out from their heads were like those of a wolf, lined with teeth and continuously dripping a clear lubricant that reminded Nate of drool. Every time a drop landed anywhere near him he'd squirm and back away, disgusted.

In an effort to calm the young inventors Saint encouraged them to call their parents, to talk freely about the robots. 'They're not monsters,' he told them. 'Just ask your mums and dads. They'll be fine!' Nate had spoken to his parents almost immediately afterwards, and had been surprised to discover that Saint was right – they didn't seem concerned at all.

'Saint knows best,' muttered his dad, while his mum simply sat on the sofa and read a book. It didn't seem like them at all not to be concerned, but then it never really seemed like them any more when he spoke to them on the videophone.

Cat attempted to be blasé about the hulking figures, telling Nate not to worry, that they were still harmless and there to protect and help them. But it was painfully obvious that she was bluffing. Nate could see the fear in her eyes when an assistant entered the room, and could tell by the way that she just stared at the floor as the colour drained from her face that she was fighting back her terror.

Even Clint was terrified of the beasts, despite the fact that they were simply bigger, more advanced versions of himself. Whenever one walked by he would scurry up the leg of the closest human inventor and burrow into their clothing. It was becoming a problem – pretty much every one of the children had experienced Clint attempting to climb down their trousers.

Together, Nate and Cat tried to work on their laser specs, just as everybody else in the room attempted to continue as normal on whatever project they were engaged with. But they struggled to get their brains in gear, snapping their heads up as soon as they heard the sound of pistons and heavy metal feet approaching, and taking ages to find their focus again.

This nearly led to disaster on several occasions. One afternoon Nate was performing the delicate task of fitting a new and improved laser generator into the left-hand side of a set of frames. To his annoyance, it was Cat who had finally created a beam powerful enough to burn through more than just paper and still fit inside a pair of spectacles, but he had insisted that he should be the one to install it.

As Nate was nudging the laser into place, an assistant had walked into the room, sending Clint bolting across the floor to safety. The little robot had leapt on to Nate's leg before climbing inside his trousers. Yelping at the sensation of cold metal on his skin, Nate had squeezed too hard on the frame, firing a beam of crimson light at the wall. Despite only lasting for an instant, it cut a penny-sized hole clean through the concrete and within seconds Nate saw Saint's eye peering through it from the other side.

'What is it with you and putting holes in walls?' he asked in a muffled voice as Clint's head emerged from Nate's waistband.

They took to running their experiments in the evenings, when the assistants disappeared – to be recharged, as they discovered – although Saint had taken to leaving a small shift of robots on duty overnight.

During the days they went to visit David Barley in a small side room which had been converted into an infirmary. He had been there for two weeks since his catastrophic experiment, kept in bed by a broken collarbone and severe concussion. He had spent the first few days delirious, believing that he was imagining the giant robots that were administering his healthcare. When he finally came round, and realised that they were real, he had lapsed into fever once again.

Now his condition was stable, but when Nate and Cat walked in to see him one Tuesday afternoon they were shocked to see how much weight he'd lost, and how poorly he still looked.

'Hey, Davie,' said Cat, waiting until an assistant had clunked and clattered its way from the room before sitting down on the edge of his bed. 'How are you feeling?'

'Okay,' the pale, skinny shape answered. Lost in the folds of a giant duvet, he looked like the shadow of the healthy, red-faced boy who had been working furiously on the jetpack on the day of the competition. 'My shoulders and neck are still killing me, but I've only got myself to blame.'

'You did what any good inventor would do,' said Nate, walking to the other side of the bed and sitting down. 'And you so nearly had it, you were so close.'

'It was a faulty weld,' David confessed, sighing. 'I was so tired, I didn't leave enough space for the protons to escape. That was a junior mistake, and now everybody blames me for . . .'

He didn't need to finish. The other students had all accused David of gross stupidity, holding him accountable for the appearance of the robots, and the mood of terror that now hung over the complex. Nate tried to think of some words of comfort but found that he couldn't.

'It will all blow over,' Cat said unconvincingly. 'Nothing has really changed. So the lab technicians are made of metal, not flesh. What does that matter?'

David snorted out of his nose, a sound that wasn't quite a laugh.

'Not for me it won't,' he whispered. He glanced warily up at the wall, where another of the tiny black eyes that Saint used as cameras stared down at them. 'I need to get out of here. I need to get home. I can't stand being like this. I can't take any more of this weirdness, this madness.'

'But you can't leave,' Nate said softly. 'Saint told us, he said we couldn't go home until Christmas. It's only a month or so now, though.'

'It's too long,' David went on. 'And he can't keep us prisoner, it's against the law. We must be free to leave. All he needs is convincing. Anyway, do you really think he's going to let us go home at Christmas?' He looked around to make sure that nobody else was listening, then leant forward in bed, grimacing with the pain and whispering, 'Besides, it's not like he can stop us leaving.'

'David, what are you planning?' Nate asked, lowering his voice even though nobody else was present. 'The only way out is the elevator, and that only lets us go to two floors. Anyway, you're ill. You can't go gallivanting off somewhere.'

But David simply smiled and laid his head back down.

'Trust me,' he said, 'within a week, I'll be gone.'

David was discharged from the infirmary two days later. Saint gathered everybody into the dining area on the night he was due back and they all cheered him as he hobbled in, wearing a neck brace and looking utterly exhausted. Some of the young inventors were glaring at him menacingly, but Saint seemed delighted that his protégé had made a triumphant return.

'Here he is, here he is!' he shouted cheerfully. 'The boy whose face is going to be on the front page of *Time*, the kid who has completely reinvented the art of space travel. Bravo!'

David smiled as he sat down on a bench next to the master inventor, but Nate knew him well enough to see that it was a ruse, and that his heart wasn't in it. For some reason Saint had sent all the assistants out of the living area that night. He had even brought in several bottles of alcohol-free bubbly which he shared between glasses before announcing a toast to David Barley and the magnificent Barleymobile.

Maybe it was the absence of the robots, or perhaps the champagne wasn't as free of alcohol as Saint claimed, but soon Nate began to feel extremely relaxed. In the balmy evening light, with the crimson sun just dipping over the edge of the horizon, everything suddenly seemed incredibly calm and peaceful.

Saint patrolled the room, cracking awful jokes and performing ridiculous acrobatic tricks. Sometimes these worked, like his quadruple backflip over the stones that crossed one of the streams. But at other times his skill couldn't quite match his enthusiasm. At one point, while attempting to climb a tree, his trousers got caught and he dangled helplessly from a branch for a good five minutes before the fabric ripped and he toppled to the floor – the rear of his spotty pink pants visible through the tear.

For a blissful few hours the young inventors seemed to completely forget about the events of the last couple of weeks. Somebody suggested a game of hide and seek, and Nate and Cat dashed off while Saint counted to a hundred. They hid beneath one of the bridges, paddling their feet in the warm water as they waited to be discovered. It turned out that Saint was absolutely useless as a seeker, walking past them several times before he finally stooped down and peered under the wooden panels an hour after the game had begun.

'Oh, there you are,' he said, his brow furrowed. 'You're the first people I've found!'

246

They spent the rest of the evening helping Saint unearth the other inventors, some of whom had picked ingenious places to hide. Lynsey had found a tiny tree hollow and had wedged herself inside – it took all of Saint's strength to pull her free. A girl named Kate Edwards had buried herself under the soil in a grove of trees, using a straw to breathe. Cat had simply put her finger over the top until she had burst upwards from the ground like a zombie, gasping for air.

Soon after the last person had been found, the tired inventors began to drift off to bed, until only Nate, Cat, David and Ebenezer Saint remained. Ainsley Stumps, whom everybody seemed to have forgotten about, had fallen asleep in his hiding place inside one of the litter bins.

'I do mean it, Davie-boy,' said Saint, ruffling the injured kid's hair and making him wince. 'What you've done is absolutely fantastic. It's out of this world. Or it will be very soon.'

He reached into his coat, flashing a golden wink at Nate and Cat before pulling out a piece of parchment. Nate felt himself go pale at the sight of it, and the memories it brought back of his nuclear nightmare.

'I'd like to offer you a very special invitation,' he said, 'to come up and see my museum. It's unbelievable, and there's something amazing up there I know you'll want to see – the Saturn V rocket.'

For a second, the old expression of excitement and enthusiasm returned to David's gaunt features. He looked at Saint quizzically.

'But the Saturn V is at Kennedy,' he said.

'That's a fake,' Nate and Cat answered together, making Saint laugh.

'And that's not all, Barley my little beauty. Ask these guys, they've seen it. You'll be blown away, and not in the same way you nearly were the other day!' He slapped his thigh and laughed even harder. 'Get it? Blown away!'

Jumping to his feet, he did a strange little stretching move, as if about to perform some gymnastics, then started walking backwards away from the table.

'Tomorrow night, David, eight o'clock. Go to the lift and bring that parchment with you or you won't be allowed up.' Saint flashed him a wink, then promptly backed into a pile of ornamental rocks, tripping and falling on his backside with a painful crunch. Leaping upwards, cheeks reddening, he looked at the trio of young inventors, who were trying not to laugh. 'Why does that always happen when I try and look cool?'

He bolted in the direction of the elevator, disappearing behind a cluster of bushes.

'It's worth a look,' said Cat when they heard the lift doors close. Nate detected the slight tremor in her voice and knew she was thinking about Saint's atomic room. She seemed for a moment as if she was going to warn David, but instead her expression softened. 'It really is amazing up there.'

'Just watch out for practical jokes,' added Nate.

But David, without looking at the parchment or saying a word, simply tore it in two.

35

Escape

When Nate emerged from his chalet the next morning he made his way over to Cat's to find that she had already left for the lab. He tried David's, but the boy was obviously back in the mood for inventing as all Nate could hear from inside was the sound of a welding iron at full blast. Deciding not to bother him, Nate headed for the elevator and down to the labs.

The first thing he saw was Clint, who stood under a table on the other side of the room playing cricket by himself with some bolts and a toothbrush. Cat was sitting at her workstation in front of a giant plasma screen which she was fixing into a clear plastic frame, about the same height as her and twice as wide. Puzzled, Nate pulled up a chair and sat next to her.

'We've already got televisions in our rooms,' he joked.

'Y'know, I had the worst dreams of my life last night,' she replied. 'It's those bloody robots – they creep me out so much.'

'I thought they didn't bother you,' said Nate. Her only response was to throw him a look which was supposed to be one of annoyance but instead rang of quiet desperation.

He broke her gaze and looked down at the invention. Cat had fixed a set of tiny fibre-optic cameras to various points on the frame, pointing in the opposite direction from the screen. As always, there was a computer processor attached to the device humming gently, wires leading from it to the laptop on her desk.

'I woke up drenched in sweat and terrified. I couldn't get the image of those hulking metal beasts out of my head. So, I thought, what's the best way to cure my fear? Hide from it.'

'Cat,' said Nate, 'what the hell are you talking about?'

She looked up at Nate, her expression almost one of embarrassment.

'I'm making a panel that will block those robots from my view,' she explained, her voice little more than a whisper. 'I'm going to mount it by my desk, or wherever I'm working. It will record the view and instantly play it back to the screen, but this handy box,' she tapped the computer processor, 'will automatically delete everything that looks like a robot. It's the same piece of software as I used for the goats.'

Nate whistled, impressed. It seemed like a lot of trouble to go to when she could just wear a blindfold, but looking at her feverish stare as she returned to work, he knew that she really, really wanted this.

So he spent the day helping her, allowing her to do most of the work and taking on the role of the assistant, fetching her the equipment and materials she needed while offering occasional pieces of advice about the program. This way, Cat didn't have to rely on the assistants for help, and was able to work with lightning speed in the distraction-free environment.

Clint also popped over after being chased around the room by Adam Watson, head still wedged in a goldfish bowl, who accused the little robot of stealing his toothbrush. After several minutes hiding behind Cat's leg, watching as the boy stomped around menacingly, Clint put himself to good use acting as another assistant.

Working like this, they managed to finish the economically titled Altered Reality Mechanism for Picture and Image Transmogrification in a matter of hours. Shortly after lunch, which they had both skipped in their enthusiasm to finish, Cat clipped the last few wires into place and booted up the central processor. Slowly the two-metre-tall plasma screen came to life, receiving data from the cameras mounted on the other side of the frame to display a picture of the lab.

It was like looking through a window. Cat had managed to align the cameras so that the picture on screen was exactly the same as the view you would have got anyway – the only thing that gave away the presence of the ARMPIT was the thin frame and the fact that the picture would wobble and fizz every now and then.

The picture was so good that in his excitement Clint attempted to run through the frame. He struck the screen with a painful crunch, bouncing off and rolling under a desk.

'It's a pretty pointless invention until a robot comes along,' Cat confessed, lifting Clint up and sitting him on her desk. The dazed robot picked up the picture of Cat's dad, which always sat watching her as she worked, and began to tango with it across the surface.

Minutes later one of the assistants, who had been helping a young inventor lift boxes of gears, started making its way back across the lab. Both Nate and Cat held their breath – partly from fear as the hulking shape got closer, but mainly from excitement as it promised to pass by the Altered Reality Mechanism for Picture and Image Transmogrification.

Incredibly, the robot appeared to vanish as it passed the screen, its shape little more than a fuzzy outline crossing from left to right before emerging again on the other side.

'Bloody hell!' Nate exclaimed, genuinely stunned. 'That's amazing!'

'And that's not the half of it,' Cat replied, swivelling the screen to follow the robot out of the lab. It had stopped to monitor the progress of one of the inventors, and Cat flicked a small switch on the frame's processor. Instantly, the fuzzy outline on the screen blinked before morphing into a visible figure. It was a giant chicken.

Nate sat back, lost for words. Laughing, Cat flicked the switch again and the image of the chicken became one of Saint, dressed in what looked like a fairy outfit. As the robot began walking once more towards the door Cat kept flicking the switch, changing its on-screen image to one of Frankenstein's monster, then to a boy scout, then to a big blob of raspberry jam that wobbled messily before vanishing as the assistant exited through the lab door.

Cat's invention was a work of genius, and Nate could see how much relief it gave her knowing she didn't have to look at the robots if she didn't want to. He was about to give her a hug when he realised something strange was happening.

The shy girl called Bella King, who had still barely said a word to anybody in the last two months, ran into the room and approached Dominic Drake. She whispered something into his ear, and the seated boy shot to his feet and started running for the door, with Bella close behind.

The rest of the group slowly returned to their work, but seconds later the sound of robot feet in the main lab beyond drew their attention. It wasn't just one assistant, they realised as the cacophony grew – a metallic thunder that verged on being deafening – it was all of them.

The curious young inventors started running towards the door. Nate snatched up Clint, who was still holding the photograph, and followed Cat and the crowd through to Saint's main laboratory. Every robot in the room, and there must have been a hundred of them, had abandoned its station and was heading for the lift. They all managed to squeeze into the space – alongside Bella and Dominic, who must have been wishing they'd waited for the next lift – and the doors slid shut.

'What's going on?' asked Nate, spotting Ainsley Stumps

shuffling nervously around outside the lift doors. He ran over to him, followed by Cat and everybody from the lab.

'It's David, I think,' said Ainsley, his small bespectacled face timid, unsure. 'He's gone mad. He's built himself another jet-pack. He's threatening to make a break for it.'

'No,' said Nate, looking at Cat and feeling a chill run up his spine. 'He can't be. I didn't think he was serious.'

The group waited impatiently for the lift to return, piling in when it did and pressing the holographic button to take them up. Seconds later they emerged in the living area, running round the first set of trees to see an incredible sight.

David Barley was standing on the roof of his chalet, wearing a chrome jetpack identical to the one that he'd been building on competition day, only this time it looked as if it had been reinforced with a thick layer of steel and was fully equipped with stabilisers. He was still wearing his neck brace, and looked like he was in agonising pain with the weight of the contraption on his back. But his expression was resolute, determined.

Surrounding him on all sides was a veritable army of robots, all fully extended and tensed as if about to spring. Their muzzles were bared and trembling, and their golden eyes had narrowed to form expressions that resembled utter hatred. They were a terrifying sight, and Nate had to gather his nerves before leading the gaggle of inventors across the floor to get a better view of events. Clint burrowed himself down into Nate's pocket where he trembled gently.

On the roof of the chalet directly opposite David stood Saint, smiling but obviously nervous, his hands outstretched in an attempt to calm the boy down.

Nate pushed his way through the robots, who moved to let him past, and angled himself so he could see both David and Saint clearly. Raised on the flat roofs, they might have been two soapbox politicians about to start a debate.

'David, my dear boy,' said Saint, his words soft, his expression sad. 'What on earth are you doing? You must have hit your head harder than I thought the other day. I think you've gone cuckoo!'

'I can't stay here,' David replied, not taking his eyes off Saint. His finger was pressed against the trigger of his jetpack, ready to fly if the robots showed any sign of movement. 'I just want to go home. Christ, I just want to go outside, get some air, get out of this place for a moment.'

'But this air is piped all the way from Greenland,' Saint cried out, despairing. 'It's better than the slop you'll be breathing out there. Stay here, Davie, you've got all you could possibly want within these fair walls.'

'That's what I used to think,' came the instant reply, 'but I don't have one thing, I don't have the most important thing – freedom! I just want to go. I can't stand it – the work, these robotic monstrosities, the fact that there are cameras in every room watching us all the time. I can't stand you – you're mad.'

'Then why didn't you talk to me?' Saint asked, moving to the edge of the roof. David backed away, tightening his grip on the trigger.

'I did, Saint. I told you how I was feeling, weeks ago. I told you again in the infirmary. I told you I wanted some breathing space.'

'Oh,' Saint muttered. 'Oh yes, so you did. Well we'll sort something out, we'll give you more space. You can have a whole floor to yourself if you like.'

'I don't want a floor!' David screamed. 'I want to go outside! This place is like a prison – no stairs, no fire escapes, no back doors. The lift doesn't go anywhere other than this floor and the lab. I've tried everything and we're stuck here.' He turned to the crowd, addressing the children. 'Listen to me, we're being kept prisoners here. There is no way out. This madman,'

he pointed at Saint, 'is never going to let us leave. I JUST
WANT TO GO OUTSIDE!'

There was a pause. You could have heard a pin drop in the
vast chamber.

'Well, you can't,' said Saint, speaking softly, pronouncing
each syllable with venom. 'You can't leave, David. You are here
until Christmas. No less. That was the deal.'

'And what then?' David shouted back. 'Are you just going to
let us go? Let us leave with everything we know?'

Everybody in the room turned to Saint, awaiting an answer.
When it came, it came quietly, and sent a tremor of fear across
the room.

'No. No, I'm not.'

David's face seemed to twist into a mask of pure loathing.
Nate ran forward, calling out his name but it was too late.
David fired up the jetpack, and with an earth-shaking roar and
a cloud of black smoke he was propelled instantly into the air
above them, circling the room with surprising grace. Saint
turned to the metallic assistants, furious.

'Someone get an Antigrav!' he shouted. 'Get him down
before he kills himself!'

But David had no intention of suicide. Flying round in a
wide loop, he accelerated wildly, speeding towards the giant
windows.

Outside, the vast vista of the Saint Solutions complex was
bathed in glorious winter light, the buildings and rolling hills
picked out in shades of red, brown and orange. Nate wanted to
call out to David to stop, but the sudden terror of being kept
here against his will made him cheer the flying inventor on. He
realised just how much he missed the sun, the wind on his face,
how desperately he wanted to be outside, and he chanted
David's name at the top of his voice. The other members of the
group did likewise, willing him to freedom.

Time seemed to slow down as David shot towards the glass – much faster than he had on the day of the competition. At the last second he rotated his body, so that the reinforced jetpack would hit first and take the brunt of the impact. Nate expected to see a shower of glass, and a triumphant David soaring out over the green rolling hills below, expected a gust of beautiful, real air to come sweeping down across the inventors.

Instead, to their horror, David struck the centre of one of the giant panes and was stopped dead in his tracks. A giant crack resounded around the room, along with a gut-wrenching shout of pain from the airborne boy. The glass didn't so much as crack. It wobbled slightly, strangely distorting the world outside for a second, as though they were looking at it through water.

Then, to their horror, the view of the world outside through that long, vertical pane of glass simply disappeared.

David fell earthwards, his jetpack spluttering, and landed at the base of the window. Above him, instead of the winter scene, there was nothing but a black rectangle, as though somebody had pulled a giant blind down in front of that one pane.

Saint had stopped screaming for an Antigrav, and instead stared with barely contained rage at the damage. As they watched, the black screen flickered, displayed a row of giant numbers, then the scene flashed back into view.

It was a computer image. There was no world outside that window at all.

36

Death of a Friend

For a moment there was silence as the terrible truth sank in – the awful realisation that they were not at the top of Saint Tower at all, that the view over the compound was artificial, a clever illusion. Nate recalled the sinking feeling he had experienced on the first night – in the lift and, later, during the night – and felt a surge of panic as he pictured the entire building sliding beneath the ground, buried under a million tonnes of rock and soil.

But it was a ludicrous thought. Surely nothing the size of a skyscraper could be transported underground without a commotion resembling an earthquake. It was, quite simply, impossible.

Then again, this was Saint's world, and nothing was impossible.

Shaking the thoughts from his head, Nate started to run forward to where David lay in a tangled, motionless heap on the ground, but before he could take more than a couple of steps he heard Saint call out.

'Everybody to your quarters,' the master inventor yelled, the music gone from his voice. 'Right now.'

Nate stopped running and looked around. Nobody moved.

'I mean it, kids. Playtime's over.'

The robots, hearing the seriousness in Saint's voice, all turned to the young inventor nearest them, uttering a noise Nate had never heard before, one that chilled him to the bone.

 257

It was like a dog's growl, only much higher, much faster.

Three of the metallic beasts faced him, dwarfing him with their size. With the sound of pistons firing they stepped closer, their huge metal feet threatening to crush him if he so much as moved. One flexed its arm, the fingers stretching. Nate thought back to the incident in the Testing Chamber, the way the technician had sent David flying through the air with the slightest of nudges. If it wanted, he thought, the robot could crush him like a bug.

He stepped back, raising his hands in submission and trying to ignore his pounding heart. Looking around, he saw Cat standing in the middle of a group of four robots, her face ashen, her eyes locked on to his, uncertain and afraid.

'This doesn't change anything,' Saint said. 'It's just a blip. It will all be okay Just get inside before something terrible happens.'

Gradually, some members of the group started to walk towards their chalets, the robots watching their every move with burning eyes. Cat began to edge away from the metallic monsters surrounding her, and Nate waited until she was near before joining her, linking his arm through hers and gently pulling her along the path.

'Nate,' she said, her voice a tremor, 'tell me this isn't happening.'

He couldn't bring himself to answer, but just watched as the inventors all sprinted through their doors. When they reached theirs, Cat tightened her grip.

'Don't leave me,' she said. He didn't want to, but as he took a step towards her chalet he heard the pounding of footsteps and turned to see a robot striding across the floor in their direction. In three giant steps it had covered twenty metres, and towered above them. No words were uttered from the enormous muzzle as it descended, dripping drool, but the message was clear enough.

'Cat,' he said, but couldn't finish his sentence. Prising her fingers loose he walked to his own door, opening it and casting one final look out at the terrifying scene beyond before pushing it shut.

Behind him, he heard the automatic lock slam into place.

How had it gone so wrong? He thought back to less than a month ago when he and Cat had finished their steam cloud experiment, the truly wonderful feeling of achievement and Saint's proud, almost fatherly approval of their work. He remembered the eccentric inventor's arrival on the day of the competition, his hilarious attempt at riding the space hopper. How could somebody so laid back, so apparently good-natured, have created a world like this? It just didn't make sense.

But then he recalled the room full of atomic bomb memorabilia, the vast model cityscape and the holographic explosion. The manic look in Saint's eyes as he talked of destroying the world in order to rebuild it. It was horribly clear now that Saint's nuclear room was no joke – it was the world as the master inventor saw it, a world that needed to be destroyed. In that light it started to make perfect sense. If you wanted to create a world in your image, a world of fun, of laughter, of genius, then you had to clear a path for it, you had to make a space.

And if there was one man capable of making a space, it was Saint. A billionaire, a genius, a madman.

Nate slid down the door and put his head in his hands, realising that whatever crazy plan the master inventor had, they'd been helping him achieve it for the last two months. It was obvious now why he had invited them there, twenty-five young minds who would create the foundations of a new society. Saint hadn't told them what to invent, but what was to stop him using their work for evil? David's boosters could be attached to nuclear bombs, their spy cloud could be sent to watch over Prime Ministers and Presidents. And God knows what damage Travis Heart's laser could do with Saint's backing. If the master inventor was planning something, then like it or not they were his co-conspirators.

He was distracted from his thoughts by the sound of the huge plasma screen in the room warming up. Looking over, he saw the image of Saint gradually coming into focus. After seeing that face so many times with a beautiful, welcoming smile – on cars, drink cans, clothes, computers and thousands of other products – Nate almost didn't recognise it now. The master inventor stared solemnly out of the television, his mouth tight, his eyes like two twin flames burning right into Nate's soul. He looked, for want of a better description, like a man possessed.

'Okay,' said the face, 'that didn't go as I'd planned. But maybe it's better this way. I mean, it's been a funny few weeks and all kinds of things have been coming to light, so why don't we all just be honest with each other. First things first. What David tried to do just now was very, very naughty. However, he's an inventor, so we'll let him off, and the fact that he managed to build another damn jetpack in a day just goes to show what a genius he is.'

Nate got up off the floor and sat down on one of the recliners as Saint continued.

'I'm sure you'll all want to know that he's okay. Concussed, again, and with an even bigger crack in his collarbone, but okay. You'd think he'd have learned after his last spell in the infirmary that rash decisions can be painful, but he obviously has a very short memory.' He paused, taking a deep breath.

'Now, I'm sure you all have lots of questions, so I'm going to be a little presumptuous and guess what they are. One, the window: no, it isn't a window. We are still in Saint Tower, but believe it or not the entire building has been moved somewhere else, somewhere safe, and somewhere nobody will find us. For those of you who are claustrophobic, I'm sorry to tell you that we are underground. A long way underground. But don't worry, there is plenty of air for your little lungs and, as I said, it is pumped straight from Greenland.

'Two, the robots: no, they wouldn't have hurt you, they can't, they're not allowed to. Not unless they've reprogrammed themselves, which is a possibility, or unless you were coming at me with a chainsaw, in which case they would have pulled you limb from limb. They can think for themselves, which makes them a little unpredictable, but who wants a legion of mindless slaves cluttering up the lab?

'Three, me: no, I'm not mad, I just have an agenda, one that you are all helping me with, and one that you will continue to help me with. You're all very clever, and you're all coming up with such excellent ideas – things that I never would have thought of – and it would be a shame to stop now. Tomorrow, you'll be allowed back in the lab, where you can carry on inventing to your heart's delight. Nothing has changed, remember. I'm still me, you're still you and we all stand together.

'Four, Christmas: as you may just have realised, there's been a slight change of plans. Well, a change of your plans, not mine. To be honest, I didn't actually think any of you would really want to leave. I mean this place has everything you could ever possibly want. I hope you're not too disappointed – and I'll make sure you all get wonderful presents.

'Five, the world: our planet, this lovely place we call home. You'll all be allowed back to it at the end of your year, don't worry.' He paused again, chewing his lip. 'It might look a little different,' he said finally, 'but you will be allowed back out. You're not prisoners here. Just think of it as a boarding school for bright young minds. The world is changing, kids, and you're all a part of it. Embrace this moment!'

And with that he was gone. The screen went dead and the room fell silent. For a second, that was, then Saint's face reappeared.

'Oh, I hope you don't mind staying in tonight – watch a film, calm down, there's food in your cupboards as always – y'know, just chill.'

He vanished again, and this time there was no encore. Nate sat for a moment and tried to think. His fears about Saint had been confirmed – the man was crazy. From what he had seen in the atomic room he couldn't bear to imagine what the master inventor might have meant by the world changing, looking a little different. All he could picture was the force of the atomic bombs Saint had shown them, how they had wiped the land-scape clean.

Trying to banish the mental images, he turned his thoughts to Cat. With no way of getting out of the chalet he couldn't contact her, and he desperately wanted to check she was okay, to talk to her about what was going on.

Spotting a pencil on the floor, he suddenly had an idea. He reached into the large pockets of his overalls, grabbed Clint and pulled. The little robot clutched on to the material, doing his best to stay hidden, but eventually his fingers let go and he popped out.

'Put me back!' he said through all four hands, which were covering his face.

'I'm sorry, little buddy,' Nate said, gently pulling the robot's hands away. 'But I really need you.'

He placed the robot on the floor and snatched up a pencil

and paper, beginning to scribble a note to Cat. He could have used Clint to pass on a verbal message, but for some reason he wanted it to be personal, a message from him. And he knew the last thing she'd want to hear now was the voice of another robot, even if it was one that they'd built.

When he'd finished writing a few lines of comforting words he folded up the paper and stuffed it into Clint's Saint's Strawberry Slurp can suit. As an afterthought he fished around in his pocket until he found the photo of Cat's dad that Clint had left in there, and tucked it gently into the metal alongside the note. The robot muttered a few words of complaint but didn't attempt to remove them.

All of the large windows in the chalet had been sealed shut to avoid escapees, but the smaller ventilation panels were open. Trying to avoid the gaze of the camera embedded into the wall, he lifted Clint up to one and sat him on the ledge. The little robot took one look around then pulled his head back in.

'Nate,' he said, 'there is no way I'm going back out there.'

'You're the only one who can do this, Clint,' Nate answered. 'I need you to get this to Cat's house without those robots catching you.'

'Like a secret mission,' said Clint, gaining confidence in the idea. He began limbering up his arms with excitement. 'Well, when you put it that way.'

'Good luck,' said Nate, nervously eyeing the robots that were stomping around outside the chalets in Work Mode, occasionally stooping down and looking through the windows to check for trouble. He waited until one had crashed past on the other side of the house before giving Clint a nod. Cat's chalet was dead ahead, a ventilation window open.

Clint athletically leapt from the ledge to the aerial cable, sliding down to the middle then swinging his four arms and clambering to the other side. Spinning around like a gymnast, he swung in through the small window, missing his footing slightly and struggling for a hold before finding purchase and pulling himself through.

Nate sat on the recliner and waited, leaping to his feet minutes later when Cat appeared at the opposite window, clutching his note and the photo. Clint sat on her shoulder, offering a thumbs-up to Nate. He returned it, while Cat set about scribbling a reply, and shortly afterwards Clint had made his way back along the wire and into Nate's lounge again. He hurriedly unfolded the note and read:

Great idea sending Clint over. I'm pretty sure they're going to be watching us like hawks from now on, so we have to play his game, we have to pretend we're not bothered, that we want to help. If we don't, we may never get out of here. Lots of love, me. X

Nate beamed at her through the window. He turned the paper over and began scrawling on the back.

'We'll be okay,' he muttered, reading his words aloud as he wrote. 'It's you and me against the world, remember!'

'And me,' Clint added, reading over Nate's shoulder. Nate laughed and scribbled 'and Clint' in brackets at the end. He finished by repeating 'lots of love' and a small kiss, which he quickly changed to six small kisses after a moment's pause. Wrapping the note up, he tucked it inside the robot and sent him out of the window again. Clint made his way back down the wire, this time showing off by running along it like a tightrope walker, all four arms waving to keep his balance.

Nate laughed as he watched his audacious performance, and was so distracted that he failed to notice Cat's frantic waving until it was too late.

From nowhere the vast, terrifying face of a robot appeared, looming in towards the window from where it had been standing out of sight to the left of the chalet. Its golden eyes were inches from Nate's and he saw the lenses spin round, coming into focus to stare at him. For a second he was mesmerised. It was as if the robot had a fire inside its head, one that burned so fiercely it made the eyes glow bright enough for Nate to want to shield his gaze. He staggered backwards, and as he did so the metal giant pulled away, rising to its full height.

Nate ran back to the window, desperately looking for Clint. He spotted him hanging on to the wire from below, looking at the assistant and trying to keep as still as possible to avoid being seen. The colossal robot turned, and seemed on the verge of walking off, but after only a single step it swung back round. Its ferocious muzzle sniffed the air, globules of lubricant dropping to the floor.

It took less than three seconds for the creature to detect the tiny shape of Clint, and without hesitation it reached out with one massive hand and snatched him up.

The little robot tried to cling on to the wire but it didn't stand a chance, and through the window Nate heard a tiny, heart-breaking yelp as Clint was thrown to the ground. The giant raised its foot, and Nate started pounding on the glass in an attempt to distract it. Directly opposite he saw Cat doing the same thing.

But it was no use. Clint looked up at Nate and blinked once, then the metal foot slammed down on top of him, hard enough to crack the rock path.

Nate swung away, feeling numb. What seemed like an eternity later, after he had heard the vile creature's footsteps fade away, he turned back. The first thing he saw was Cat, hands held up to her pale face. Then he stared down at the path. Clint was gone – one small hand, flattened, was all that remained of their robotic friend.

37

Phoning Home

For what seemed like an eternity Nate couldn't move. He could barely even recall how to breathe. All he could do was collapse to the floor and put his head in his hands.

A single image circled his mind, refusing to leave him in peace: Clint's tiny hand on the path. There was no way he could have survived the impact. The battered Saint's Strawberry Slurp can was no match for a tonne of solid steel and a murderous intent. The little robot was gone.

When he could no longer hear the noise of robots outside he struggled to his feet, his legs so wobbly that he thought he was going to crash to the floor again. Looking out of the window, and doing his best not to stare at the path, he saw that Cat had disappeared. He couldn't remember ever feeling so lonely in his life, not even when he had got lost in the woods near his house a few years ago. The thought of facing another six hours alone as night fell over the forest was heaven compared to what was happening right now.

More than anything he wanted to talk with his parents, to hear their voices, to feel like he was at home again. Right now he missed them so much that he thought his stomach was being twisted by an invisible force, that his heart was going to explode. He walked over to the plasma screen and ran his fingers over the button. There was no doubt that Saint would have barred all contact with the outside world after the horrors of the afternoon, but the mere thought of making contact made him feel better.

'Home,' he whispered hoarsely as he pressed in the red button.

For a moment, nothing happened. Then the screen fizzed into life to reveal his sitting room. His heart leapt, and he thought for a minute that he was about to burst into tears at the sight of the familiar lounge. It was empty, but Nate could hear the barks from the robotic dog that doubled as a video screen, and it was only seconds before his mum walked through, drying her hands on a tea towel.

'Mum!' he cried out, pressing his face to the screen. Wendy Wright walked to the sofa and sat down. She was smiling, grinning in fact, and she was wearing a dress that he had never seen before. In fact, as always, there were several things in the room that he didn't recognise, or that looked a little different from how he remembered them. The picture that hung above the sofa wasn't of daffodils any more but of lilies, and the throw that covered his dad's armchair was brown instead of blue. He thought back to the last few times he'd called his parents, and remembered the odd things he'd noticed then.

'Nathan,' replied his mum, before shouting out. 'Peter, get in here, it's Nathan!'

'Mum, something's happened,' Nate blurted out, not caring if Saint was listening in, just desperate for his parents to know the truth. 'We're being kept prisoner here, Saint isn't going to let us leave, not at Christmas, maybe not ever.'

His mum kept on smiling.

'That's nice,' she said, placing the towel over her knee and leaning back against the sofa.

'This isn't a joke,' Nate went on. 'The place is full of robots. And it's underground. Mum, I'm scared.'

At that moment Peter Wright strolled in, his hands covered in grease as though he'd been trying to fix the car – something he had never attempted before.

'Hi, son,' he said, sitting beside Nate's mother and leaning towards the camera. 'You look well.'

Nate pictured his own pale expression, his bloodshot eyes, his look of panic.

'Dad, you have to call the police. Saint's gone mad.'

'He hasn't gone mad,' his dad replied, his voice too calm, too measured. 'He's just doing what's best for you, for all of us.'

'You're a very lucky boy, Nathan,' continued his mum, the tone of her voice equally artificial. 'You should listen to that lovely Saint and make the most of this wonderful experience.'

Nate staggered away from the screen, feeling as though he was about to throw up. His parents sat silently on the sofa, the smiles never leaving their faces. Then it happened again – the band of static that he had noticed last time, the minute flicker that caused the figures of his mum and dad to wobble as though they were sitting underwater. He hadn't given it much thought before, but now he pictured the window outside, the way it had vibrated when the airborne David had struck it, the way the picture had flickered in exactly the same way.

'Saint?' he whispered, a tear rolling from his eye and down his cheek, then dropping softly to the carpet. On screen his mother stood, walking over to the camera and kneeling down so that her face took up the entire television. There were no marks on her skin, no freckles or veins, not even any pores.

'Listen to your mother, Nate,' said the face. It blinked, and when the eyes reopened they were golden. 'She knows best.'

Nate barely slept a wink that night. He lay on his bed, buried beneath his blankets, thinking about the fact that all the times he thought he'd been talking to his parents since he arrived he'd actually been talking to a computer simulation.

How had Saint found out so much about them, about the way they spoke, what they wore, the layout of their house? It terrified him to think about how he had got that information. Had he sent his robots there after the scholarship had begun, or was he using the dogs as spies? For the briefest of seconds he wondered if his parents were okay, but he was fairly certain that the master inventor wouldn't do anything to hurt them – even if only because of the suspicion it would generate.

What scared him more was the thought that for weeks now his parents had probably been talking to a computer-generated version of himself. It made perfect sense – show the parents what they want to see, happy, smiling children talking about how great it was to live at Saint Solutions. They wouldn't suspect a thing – most adults wouldn't even be aware that the technology existed to achieve such a feat.

The implications of this struck him like a hammer in the gut – nobody would know they were in danger, nobody would be coming to help.

During the brief periods of sleep that he managed to snatch Nate saw twisted visions of Clint being squashed, or the little robot's face and the helpless yelp that had been emitted from his voice box seconds before he was ground into dirt. The same nightmare woke him up on several occasions, and by the time the artificial sunlight began to filter in through the window he realised he was more exhausted than he had ever been before.

But it soon became clear that, despite his tragic death, the messages that Clint had carried were not in vain. From the moment Nate made his way out of his unlocked chalet the next morning he and his fellow young inventors were shadowed by the robots. The metal monsters raced around in Normal Mode, which meant they were human sized, but this made them no less terrifying.

In fact, it made things worse because they were able to move more quietly and discreetly, and as Nate and Cat headed for the dining area they had to constantly look round to see where the creatures were. There would be no chance of mentioning anything now without Saint hearing, so they followed the decision made the previous night and played along with the master inventor's plan.

But it wasn't easy. Nate couldn't take his mind off the fact that they weren't at the top of a tower block with nothing but fresh air around them. Now he knew they were deep underground with no air and no oxygen, and about to be buried alive with no hope of ever being found.

Each time the thought entered his head he began to panic, to feel his throat constrict and a terrible sense of claustrophobia set in, and he had to fight to stop himself from running around screaming. Cat, as always, was the one who kept her head screwed on. Ignoring his panic attacks, she made every effort to convince the metal assistants that they were on Saint's side.

'Maybe he's right,' she said as they nibbled on slices of toast that neither of them could really stomach, a robot perched on the bench next to them. 'I mean the world is a pretty awful place sometimes.'

Nate tried to swallow a piece of toast the wrong way, thinking that he'd rather choke than support the madman who'd once been his hero. Unfortunately, it worked, and after thirty seconds of painful coughing and gasping for breath the robot wrenched open Nate's mouth with its cold, hard fingers and plucked out the dripping ball of dough.

'Thanks,' Nate whispered hoarsely, then, after remembering who he was talking to, 'although I could have done that myself.'

It was in the lift, on the way down to the lab, that Cat

revealed she had also tried to contact her mum the previous night.

'She was wearing an apron and scrubbing the carpet,' she whispered, keeping a wary eye on the robot that stood on the far side of the enormous cabin. 'My mum's never worn an apron in her life, and as for cleaning the house . . .'

She didn't say any more for fear of arousing suspicions, but her dark eyes made it clear how upset she'd been. Seeing Cat like this made Nate furious, made him want to run right up to Saint himself and force the master inventor to let them go. But under the watchful golden eyes of Saint's assistants all he could do was squeeze Cat's hand and wait for the lift to reach its destination.

When they arrived at their desks they found a note of instructions taped to the seat of every chair. On each was a line of text from Saint apologising again for the previous night and providing details of a new experiment they were to start working on.

Each person's invention was different. Cat was landed with the complex job of designing and building an electromagnetic amplifier – a device designed to boost the energy of an electronic machine. Nate was bewildered to see that he had been asked to make a drinks machine that actually brewed a good cup of tea.

'You know, that means he thinks I'm cleverer than you,' Cat said, managing a weary smile.

'Are you kidding?' he answered, grinning back. 'Inventing a machine to make the perfect cup of tea is a challenge that has defeated mankind for centuries!'

Nate's grin swiftly vanished as he scanned the room, studying the faces of his fellow inventors. Some, like Ainsley, looked terrified at the thought of not being able to go home, and sat at their desks forlornly, heads in their hands. Others seemed far less bothered about the fact that Saint had lied to them and was keeping them prisoner. Adam was excitedly refilling his goldfish bowl helmet while Lucy was spinning round in her chair singing 'The Yellow Brick Road'. Travis was still nowhere to be seen.

Several of the competition winners met Nate's gaze, and he knew from the silent look that they were thinking exactly the same thing as him: how to get out of Saint Tower. But the children couldn't even take a step without one of the ferocious robots narrowing its fiery gaze in their direction.

Nate sighed and began clearing his desk, throwing the bunch of laser specs he had been building into the odds and ends drawer. After a moment's thought he tucked the most successful pair into his breast pocket so that he could carry on playing with them when he wasn't being watched. After all, what respectable inventor would work on a tea machine?

Cat put the ARMPIT to one side, staring at it mournfully for a moment as though wondering whether to switch it on. Eventually she turned away and, trying not to think about anything other than the task ahead, they set about working.

Midway through the morning they heard somebody singing at the top of their voice and turned to see Saint striding into the room as though nothing out of the ordinary had happened. He skipped lightly to the centre of the lab and spun around, beaming.

'So, how do we like our new experiments?' he asked. 'I know it's not inventing in the traditional sense, because they're all my ideas, but I thought that after *last night*,' he whispered the two words as though they were dirty, 'we could all do with a change of direction. And I do hope nobody feels too bad about the curfew. I mean I built you those chalets and I just thought it was time you made good use of them!'

He laughed, then backed off towards the door.

'I have to go check on things, important things' he said cagily, 'but I'll be back anon!'

But there was no sign of Saint after lunch, nor through the entire afternoon, and by the time the end of the day was approaching nobody had seen a trace of him anywhere.

Nate spent the morning trying not to think about Clint but he couldn't get the image of the robot's face from his mind: his expression of pure terror as the giant metal foot came down.

He kept telling himself that Clint was just a machine, an assortment of wires and circuits and processors, but he knew in his heart that they'd created a living, thinking creature. It wasn't as if they could just build another one – Clint's central processing unit, his brain, had been one of a kind; it had learned and developed just like a child's. He had been as unique as any of the young inventors at Saint Solutions.

Nate could see that Cat had been more successful in losing herself in her work. She told him more than once that the sooner they finished their projects the sooner they'd get to go home, her words echoing David's. By lunchtime she had built the framework for a small electromagnetic amplifier, and a remarkably short while later she had kitted it out with a set of spaghetti-like wires and cables all linked to a powerful generator. The result didn't look like much, but at three-thirty Cat held it aloft and hummed a fanfare tune through pursed lips.

'Don't tell me you've finished already,' said Nate incredulously, realising that all he had accomplished in the last two hours was to twiddle several teabags until they burst.

'Well,' she answered, 'it could do with a snazzier design

and perhaps a nice picture of me on the case, but I think the components are all working as they should.'

'There's one way to find out, I guess,' said Nate, relieved that this was one device she couldn't test on him. The electromagnetic amplifier was designed to work solely on electronic equipment, sending out a stream of charged particles that would give a machine an extra boost of energy – like NOS in a car engine or a cup of coffee in a small child.

In fact, there was really only one thing that Cat could test the gadget on.

'I'm not going near one of those robots,' she said, reading Nate's mind. 'No bloody way. Not even with the ARMPIT.'

But Nate didn't give her a choice. Scanning the room, he spotted one of the assistants in the corner and caught its golden eyes. Clutching at his chest and feigning a heart attack, he staggered around his desk spluttering, waving at the metallic beast. It took the bait, speeding across the lab in record time, its arms extended ready to perform CPR on the struggling inventor.

Before it could, however, Nate leant towards Cat, who was frozen to the spot, and pressed the big red button on the electromagnetic amplifier. With a shrill whistle the device blasted out its charge in the direction of the shocked assistant. Less than two metres away the effect was instant – the robot snapped bolt upright, its eyes opening wider than saucers. It stood like this for a moment, trembling, then with a sudden lurch its top half started spinning.

'Himelly blimmely,' it shouted as it whirled around increasingly quickly, making Nate and Cat dizzy just looking at it. Parts of its body were expanding then contracting as it spun, the muzzle snapping out, then in and the legs stretching then shrinking chaotically. 'Himelly himelly blimelly.'

Coming to a sudden halt, the robot looked directly at Cat,

and Nate could have sworn that its expression was one of fear. Then it bolted off around the lab at high speed, the pistons in its legs straining as it propelled itself forwards at what must have been eighty kilometres an hour.

Fearing for their lives, the young inventors in the lab leapt for cover, diving under their desks or clambering to the top of the equipment shelves. Lynsey especially was devastated as her pristine desk was sent flying by the speeding robot.

'How do you turn it off?' Nate shouted as the assistant did a full circle and came hurtling back towards them like a train.

'You can't,' Cat replied. 'Once you've sent out the charge you can't stop it!'

Nate and Cat threw themselves to the ground as the robot careered past them, tearing clean through Nate's desk and heading straight for the wall. This time it didn't turn in time, and with one more startled 'Himelly blimmely' it ran head first into the concrete, sending dust and debris sailing out over the lab.

By the time it had cleared, Nate and Cat had picked themselves off the floor and walked over to where the robot lay, its head lost in a giant hole and its legs twitching gently.

'At least we know it works,' said Cat.

But Nate wasn't listening. He was looking at the robot's leg. What he had expected to be a solid metal foot looked instead more like a lightweight hoof, with a large hole in the centre. He thought back to the previous night, saw once again the image of Clint disappearing under the giant foot. Or disappearing *into* it.

'Cat,' he said, turning to her and pointing at the twitching foot. 'I think Clint could still be alive.'

38

A Rescue Mission

Nate sped from the lab as a dozen or more assistants rushed in to pull their comrade from the wall. Cat followed him, demanding to know where he was going.

'The feet,' he shouted as he ran. 'They're hollow. Saint must have designed them so they wouldn't be too heavy, so they wouldn't slow the machines down when they were running.'

'But we saw his arm, Nate,' Cat replied. 'He was squashed, pulverised.'

Nate ducked into a quiet corner of the lab, behind a giant pot plant, and pulled Cat in with him. After checking to see that they were alone he raised his watch and pressed the button twice until the data from Clint's homing beacon was displayed. In the horror and confusion of the previous night he hadn't thought to check to see if it was still working, but although the signal was extremely faint, it was there.

'Exactly,' he replied, trying to make sense of the numbers on the digital screen. 'We only saw his arm. Where did the rest of him go? If he'd been properly squashed there would have been flattened bits of little robot everywhere.'

Cat paused to think for a moment, then her face suddenly came alive.

'Well, where is he?' she demanded, grabbing Nate's arm and twisting it so that she could look at his watch. 'We have to go and get him.'

Nate yelped, the pain in his tendons enough to make him think Cat was literally pulling his arm off. Snatching it back, he scowled at her and then returned his attention to the homing signal.

'I'm not sure what it's telling me,' he said. 'There's barely any signal at all, and it appears to be coming from below us.'

'Where below us?' Cat replied. 'We don't know how much of this bloody tower is even here any more, or where *here* is.' Nate shuddered, thinking once again about being buried underground. 'And the lift only lets us go to two floors.'

Nate shook the watch and looked at the data once again. The numbers were definitely telling him that Clint was somewhere under their feet, a long way down.

'Well Saint did say that the whole tower has been moved underground,' he said. 'Which means that there must still be dozens of floors. But I think I might know where Clint is.'

He pulled back the plant and peered out at the lab, watching as a number of robotic assistants carried their fallen colleague towards the elevator. The malfunctioning machine looked okay but it was still muttering 'Himelly blimelly' and there were wisps of smoke rising from its dented head.

'We just need your ARMPIT,' he whispered smiling despite the situation. Before Cat could open her mouth he added, 'And we need to make some changes to it.'

Nate waited until the robots had passed them and entered the lift, then he sneaked out from behind the pot plant, heading back to the lab. Before he had taken a few steps, however, he felt Cat's hand on his arm. Turning, he saw her staring at him nervously, chewing her fingernail.

'Tell me you're not thinking what I think you're thinking,' she said.

'You know I am,' he replied, managing a grin before taking her hand and leading her back to their desks.

The changes they needed to make to the Altered Reality Mechanism for Picture and Image Transmogrification weren't complicated, but they had less than half an hour to complete them. Already it was coming up to the time of day when the robots changed shift, leaving the lab to charge, and Nate had every intention of being in the lift with them as they descended to the floor below.

'Hold still, Nate,' Cat shouted and he realised that his left leg was bouncing up and down in nervous excitement. Pressing his feet firmly on the ground, and his bum squarely on the stool, he sat and waited patiently while Cat scanned his face and body into the computer.

'How long does this take?' he asked, earning another glare.

'I said stop moving,' she snapped, waiting for the handheld scanner to beep before continuing. 'The software is already in place on the processor. I designed it so that whenever the cameras recorded a robot, the program would automatically delete it and replace it with a simulated background.'

'So it would look like the robot wasn't even there,' Nate said. 'And in theory if we just tell the computer to delete anything that looks like me or you from the image, and replace it with a background –'

'Then we should be invisible so long as we stand behind the screen.' Cat finished transferring the 360-degree scan of Nate to the small black box attached to the frame then began to alter the code using her laptop. 'Of course, Saint has most likely programmed his robots with extremely sharp senses of smell and hearing, not forgetting that they probably all have radars and X-ray vision anyway.'

'It's going to work,' Nate replied, ignoring her remarks. 'All we need to do is get down there, find Clint, and get back up again.'

'Avoiding Saint and his army of robots,' Cat continued, going pale at the thought.

'It's Clint,' Nate said softly.

Cat nodded. Unplugging the cables that linked the ARMPIT to the laptop, she patted the device gently and smiled. Turning the lightweight frame so that the cameras pointed directly at her, she switched on the giant screen and waited for it to warm up.

'Fingers crossed,' she said. Nate leant forward, watching as a crystal-clear picture of Cat and the lab appeared on the plasma display. It was just like looking through glass.

'I can see you as clear as day,' Nate replied.

'Good,' said Cat, taking a deep breath as she flicked the switch on the processor. Almost instantaneously the image of her flickered then vanished, leaving a picture-perfect view of the lab in her place.

'Bingo,' Nate said, grinning. 'You've completely vanished!'

He reached up and flicked the switch again, barely holding back his laughter as Cat reappeared but in the shape of a giant chicken.

'What do you want to do about these other image changes?' he asked, sniggering as the chicken slapped its forehead with a wing.

'I'd forgotten about them,' came Cat's words from the chicken's beak. 'There's no time to delete them now, so we'd just better not touch the switch when we're down there.'

'Well then, clucky,' Nate said, hopping to his feet and flicking the switch repeatedly until Cat had become invisible again, 'let's go see if we can fool the most sophisticated artificial intelligence on earth.'

By half past five Nate and Cat had made it all the way around the main lab twice without being spotted. The first time they had taken it extremely slowly, shuffling at a painful speed with their backs against the wall and their noses pressed firmly against the lightweight screen, poking their heads around at regular intervals to see where they were going.

But none of the robots seemed to have any inkling that they were there. In fact, the only thing that threatened to give them away was the sound of Cat's knees knocking together in fear as they made their way past the first of the giant sentries.

Once they had got that under control, however, they began racing round the room, even walking right up to a robot as it was working on an experiment and stealing a test tube from under its muzzle. The hulking beast looked extremely confused for a moment before staring right at the screen, scratching its head in puzzlement and eventually walking off to find some new equipment. Nate and Cat had laughed at this all the way back round the lab. It was only when they reached the lift that they both fell silent.

'It's five-thirty,' Cat said, looking at her watch as they manoeuvred themselves and the screen in such a way that they were just outside the lift but invisible against the wall. Sure enough, the robots on day duty were starting to filter towards them, the noise of metal feet on the floor deafening as they moved in unison. With any luck, Nate thought, they were heading downstairs to be charged.

The lift emitted a slight hum as it rose to the lab level, the doors opening to reveal the enormous white interior. As one, the robots marched in, and resisting every urge to scream and run off, Nate and Cat shuffled round into the lift cabin, holding the screen between them and the ferocious assistants.

'This is a very bad idea, Nate,' Cat whispered, her words almost lost behind the sound of marching metal. Nate looked at her with what he hoped was a reassuring expression, but he knew that his face mirrored her mask of fear.

'How bad can it be?' he replied softly as the doors closed and the lift began to descend, so fast that Nate thought his stomach was being sucked up into his brain. 'It's probably just a bunch of robots sitting around plugged into the wall and dreaming about robot holidays and cyber pensions. I bet they've even got little chalets like ours, only metal.'

Cat glared at him. The lift was still hurtling downwards at full speed – thirty seconds, forty – wherever they were going it was a long, long way beneath the lab. Nate felt his ears pop from the change in pressure, and wondered if he was being pulled to the bottom of a giant grave where he'd be buried for all eternity. He was on the verge of throwing away the screen and running around in a state of complete and utter panic when he felt the lift begin to slow down.

A few seconds later it came to a halt, and Nate and Cat waited in complete silence as the robots marched out. When the sound of their feet had died down the two inventors moved slowly to the lift doors, still hidden behind the plasma screen.

'Little chalets,' Nate repeated optimistically, not quite able to bring himself to look at the view on the other side of Cat's invention. 'And a cute garden with metal flowers.'

But when they finally steeled themselves enough to poke their heads out from behind the screen nothing could have been further from the truth.

Cat was so shocked at the sight in front of her that she let out a cry – half fear and half awe. Nate, on the other hand, felt his entire body turn to something not unlike a big bowl of jelly, and let his grip on the screen slip. The ARMPIT toppled forward, threatening to crash, but he managed to shake the paralysis from his limbs in time to grab it.

'This is a *really* bad idea,' Cat hissed as they ducked back down behind the screen, shuffling forward and to one side, and keeping their backs to the wall as they exited the lift. Hearing the familiar hum of the doors, they turned to see them slide shut.

'Well, it's too late now,' Nate replied, taking another peek from behind the screen. 'Besides,' he said, attempting to reassure himself as much as Cat, 'it isn't as bad as it looks.'

But that was a lie. In front of them, stretching so far into the distance that the far wall was invisible, and towering so high that the ceiling was lost in smoke and shadow, was a vast chamber. It was easily large enough to contain three or four of the giant labs, perhaps more, but while the labs contained a visual feast of scientific equipment and ongoing projects, colourful screens and charts, this room contained only one thing: robots.

Each of the room's giant walls was literally covered in Saint's metallic assistants. They were mounted on platforms and apparently fixed in place by a series of cables, some of which were obviously transferring energy to the machines in order to charge them up for the following day. Like some kind of nightmarish wallpaper, the robots – all fully extended with their muzzles bared – were stacked head to toe, and arm to arm, for as far as he could see. There must have been a hundred thousand of them, maybe more.

Thankfully, though, they all appeared to be asleep, their eyes closed and their heavy limbs motionless.

The only things moving in the room were a series of enormous metal cranes, embedded in tracks on the floor, which slid along the walls like vast, black spider legs. As Nate and Cat watched in awe the cranes descended towards the group of assistants that had just left the lift and began snatching them up as though they were weightless, lifting them towards vacant slots in the wall.

With the deafening sound of pistons screaming, the cranes had fitted every single robot into place in the space of a few seconds, and started pulling charged assistants out of their positions and dropping them gently to the floor. The refreshed troops began marching back towards the lift, ready to take on the evening shift. Nate and Cat cowered behind the screen until the lift doors had closed once again.

'I just can't believe my eyes,' Cat whispered, her face pale and her hands shaking. 'There are millions of them. What on earth does he want with all of these assistants?'

'They're just for lab work, surely,' Nate replied, uncertainly. 'I mean what else would you need an army of killer robots for?'

Again he found himself thinking about Saint's room of atomic madness, his words the previous night as he talked about their planet. *It might look a little different.* Was this his plan? Robots on every street corner, golden eyes watching every move, muzzles bared and ready to chew dissenters to pieces at their master's command. The thought made him feel sick, and he turned his attention back to his watch.

'Clint's up there,' he said, pointing to the left-hand wall. 'As far as I can tell he's about a quarter of the way up, a hundred and twenty-eight metres.'

'That's great, Nate,' Cat replied sarcastically. 'Did you put your climbing shoes on?'

Nate didn't reply, and instead watched as one of the spider-leg cranes descended to ground level. At the tip of the crane was a large claw, used for lifting the robots, as well as a number of other pieces of equipment – what looked like a scanner, a welding iron and a delicate series of fingers presumably used to make repairs to the robots' circuitry. The crane appeared to be scanning a robot on ground level, its welding iron firing up and sealing a loose joint with a firework-display of sparks.

'Just wait here,' Nate said, 'and stay behind the screen.'

Then, before Cat could protest, and before he could listen to the sensible side of his brain, he started running.

39

The Chase is On

The room was huge, bigger than he had first thought, and it took him almost thirty seconds to sprint to the left-hand wall. Fortunately, the area wasn't guarded, presumably because Saint believed that none of the young inventors even knew it existed, and because even if they did nobody would be crazy enough to break into a barracks full of robots.

Reaching the first of the unconscious assistants, Nate paused, gasping for breath. The metal crane was still working on the robot on ground level but it looked as though its task was nearly complete, the scanner disappearing into a slot in the metal. Ignoring the burning sensation in his legs, Nate started running again, almost falling into one of the enormous tracks in the floor.

From a distance the crane had looked relatively small, but as he ran the contraption grew until it towered above him, its spindly body bent double and its claw the size of a van. The welding iron was being folded back inside and Nate heard the sound of pistons hissing as the crane prepared to move.

Trying not to think about what he was doing, he charged forwards and leapt.

He almost didn't make it, his fingers slipping as he clutched at one of the crane's delicate probes. But he managed to tighten his grip just as the vast spider leg began to ascend, pulling away from the ground with sickening speed. Nate felt his stomach churn and his head spin as the floor was snatched away, and heard the wind thumping in his ears as he passed row after row of robots.

Seconds later the crane shuddered to a halt midway up the wall. Glancing down, Nate realised that he could barely see the ground, and as he struggled to hold on to the smooth metal he wished he'd thought the plan out a little more carefully.

Clint couldn't be far away. Nate began to scan the feet of the robots above him to see if he could make out the trampled mess of their little friend wedged inside. But before he could even focus he felt the crane begin to tremble, and without warning a hole opened up in the metal in front of Nate's face and the scanner shot out, nudging his arm and almost knocking him off.

Fighting to keep his grip, Nate grabbed at the scanner, but almost as soon as it had appeared it was sucked back into the tip. Nate snatched out and managed to wrap his fingers around the cold metal, but seconds later he heard the sound of a welding iron, and to his horror another compartment opened in the crane and a flaming torch shot out, heading straight for his head.

He had no choice but to jump. Yelping, he threw himself off the crane towards the wall. For a second he thought he hadn't made it, and saw two lines of robots fly past as he hurtled towards the floor. But he stretched out a hand and made contact with one of the metallic beasts, crashing into its leg. The impact knocked the wind out of him, and he let go again, sliding down another two rows before finally managing to find purchase.

Gasping for breath, Nate wedged his foot on the shoulder of the robot and gripped the cold leg of the one above. He waited until the feeling of nausea had passed before looking at his watch.

Clint was twenty-four metres above him and seventeen metres across. He stared up and tried to work out roughly where on the wall that would be, but the sparks from the claw above him prevented him from seeing, and the sheer number of robots made him feel dizzy.

Taking one more look at the ground a hundred or so metres below, Nate swung his arm round and gripped the leg of the next robot along, moving his foot so it was resting on the metallic head to his left. With growing confidence he made his way along the wall, moving from robot to robot until he was directly under the homing signal coming from Clint.

Now all he had to do was climb. Digging his fingers into the waist of the robot above him, he pushed up with his legs, grunting with the effort. Moving painfully slowly, he eased his way up robot by robot, trying to ignore the vast, lethal muzzles that he found himself face to face with and thankful that the eyes were closed.

With each agonising effort his watch told him he was getting closer and closer to their little friend until, barely able to suppress a whoop of joy, he crested one metal assistant to see a very familiar face wedged into a giant foot above him. He scrabbled up the final couple of metres, his heart pounding.

Clint was in bad shape. His tiny frame was crammed inside the space, his arm missing, his can ripped and dented beyond repair. The gears and circuits inside were exposed, the damage illuminated by the sparks that shot out from every joint. Reaching up, Nate gripped Clint's tiny frame and pulled gently until the little robot slid free. One leg detached immediately, striking the ground several seconds later, and his head hung limp and lifeless.

Had they made the journey for nothing? Turning Clint around in his hands Nate saw that the side of his head had been crushed by the blow, and through a tear in the steel casing his central processor could be seen, the wires that linked it to Clint's central nervous system either disconnected or torn in two.

Halfway up a wall full of killer robots wasn't the best place to perform an emergency operation. But Nate was so desperate to see if Clint was okay that he couldn't wait until he was back on solid ground. Wedging his feet into the nearest robot to stop himself tumbling, he reached inside Clint to see if he could bring him back to life. Carefully, he slotted the most important wires into their sockets, then flicked off Clint's main power switch, preparing to reboot him.

Taking a deep breath, he pressed the switch again and willed the robot to respond. Inside, he heard the processor gently whirr, then shudder to a halt, before once more starting up. Then, with the weakest of movements, Clint's left eye slid open.

'Clint!' Nate exclaimed as quietly as he could, so excited that he almost dropped him. 'I can't believe you're still alive.'

Clint strained to lift his head, peering at Nate for a moment without seeming to recognise him. But after a few seconds his processor had warmed up, and his vocal synthesiser kicked into action.

'You took your time,' the robot said, his voice so distorted that it was barely recognisable. Laughing out loud, Nate tucked Clint into his baggy pocket and prepared to make his way back down to ground level.

'We're not out of the woods yet, little buddy,' he replied quietly as he carefully positioned his foot on a metallic head beneath him. 'It's a long way down.'

Clint attempted a reply, but his voice was so weak Nate couldn't tell what he was saying. Deciding that if he made it out of here in one piece he'd give their little friend the sexiest new suit and voice he could find, Nate continued downwards. It was when he was face to face with the terrifying muzzle of one of Saint's assistants that Clint spoke again, his voice louder in an attempt to be heard.

Nate looked down at the little robot and put his finger to his lips, then looked back to find himself staring directly into a pair of burning golden eyes. The assistant was awake.

Both Nate and the giant robot were frozen for the space of time it took to realise what they were looking at. Then, with a blood-curdling scream that almost caused Nate to lose his grip, the machine bared its muzzle, its silver teeth glinting in the soft light of the room, and globules of lubricant flying out into Nate's face.

He ducked just as the creature's jaws snapped shut, its furious gaze tracking his movement. With lightning-quick speed the robot lashed out with its muzzle, each time coming within inches of taking Nate's head clean off. Screaming again, the metallic beast flexed its arm, ripping it from the cables that held it in place and snatching at Nate with its long fingers.

The commotion had alerted the robots on either side, and to Nate's horror he saw a dozen pairs of golden eyes opening, narrowing instantly into expressions of pure hatred as they saw what was happening. Straining against their power cables, they began to tear free.

Nate was in their territory, one that they had obviously been programmed to defend at all cost. *They think for themselves,* Saint had said, and Nate knew that it would be instant death if they caught him, even if the master inventor himself was to stand in their way. Looking down, he saw the crane beneath him preparing to move. It was his only chance of escape, but it was too far away.

The robot he was standing on lurched forward and its muzzle snapped shut again, the razor-sharp teeth this time slicing through Nate's overalls. Pressing Clint as deep into his pocket as he would go, Nate leapt from his perch just as the assistant tried to grab him.

Dropping rapidly, he snatched out just in time to grab the

leg of another assistant, and looked up to see the robot directly above him breaking free of the cables and reaching down. With nothing to support it, the hulking beast slipped from the small platform, letting out a wail of rage as it flew past Nate's ear and crashed to the ground below.

Moving as quickly as he could, Nate hopped from robot to robot until the crane was below him. It was a long drop but the wall was literally exploding into life as the assistants woke to help with the chase.

Looking to his left he saw that one of the beasts was vaulting towards him with terrifying speed, gripping the arms and legs of its comrades for support. The sound of thunder to his right told him that another of the robots was doing the same thing. He had seconds in which to act.

The hulking robots reached him just as he propelled himself from the wall. They hurtled into each other with a deafening crash that sent them flying outwards, screaming towards the ground in flames.

For a few seconds Nate thought he was going to meet the same fate, but his legs hadn't failed him. With an agonising crunch he flew into the crane just as it was pulling away from the wall. It dipped downwards with breakneck speed, passing row after row of golden-eyed robots who were waking in order to join the hunt.

Nate leapt from the crane before it reached the ground, landing painfully and stumbling before righting himself. Looking behind him he saw each of the room's giant cranes lifting robots from the wall and depositing them on the ground where they immediately began the chase. Fully extended, they could cover the length of the giant chamber in seconds and they could crush him as easily as they had Clint.

'Cat!' Nate shouted as he approached the lift. He could see nothing up ahead against the grey wall, and for a moment he thought she might have moved to get a better view of what was going on. But to his relief Cat's bodiless head emerged as if by magic and ushered him on.

'What have you done?' she shouted as he dashed behind the screen, taking one last look at the room as he did so to see a veritable army of robots in pursuit. 'They're going to find us here.'

'Only if you keep talking,' he snapped back, tucking his legs beneath him and trying to make himself as small as possible. Together they pushed themselves back against the wall and held the screen up, tilted so that the robots couldn't see over the top. Silently they prayed that it would work as well as it had in the lab above.

The thunderous sound of metal on metal grew to a nerve-shattering crescendo as the robots approached, but the silence that followed terrified Nate and Cat far more. It meant that the robots had reached the wall and were searching for them. Neither of the young inventors dared look to see what was happening, but they could imagine the scene – the giant beasts scouring the area for any sign of them, eyes burning, teeth bared, massive arms flexed and ready to deliver the killer blow.

Cat had buried her face in Nate's arm and he held her. Feeling the touch, she looked up, the fear in her eyes worse than he had ever seen it. But there was still determination there, and strength.

'We have to get back in the lift,' she whispered, barely audible. 'It's the only way we're going to get out of here.'

In the corner of his eye Nate could see the robots standing beside the lift doors, some part of their internal programming informing them that if their quarry couldn't be found on this level then it must have headed up to the labs or living quarters.

Seconds later, the doors opened. All they needed to do was get inside.

'Let's move,' Nate said, getting very slowly to his feet and making sure that the screen was still between them and the robots. Barely breathing, they began making their way to the open doors, knowing from the sound of pounding feet that the army of assistants was marching inside. There were only a few metres left, and the robots were still flooding in, a seemingly endless parade of metallic fury.

Luck was on their side. The sound of the robots marching easily covered their entry into the lift, and the ferocious assistants seemed too distracted by events to consider checking its interior. Nate and Cat made their way round the cabin, past giant legs the size of tree trunks, before huddling right at the back. After forty-five seconds of unbearable silence, the lift reached the lab and the robots stormed out.

It was only when the doors closed again that they dared peek from behind the screen. The lift was empty.

Nate realised that he'd been holding his breath for what felt like minutes, and let out a loud, shuddering sigh. Both his body and his mind were utterly exhausted, and taking Clint from his pocket he passed him to Cat before practically collapsing against the white wall.

The lift reached the accommodation level and Nate and Cat made their way out, Cat talking gently to Clint and dragging the screen along behind her.

'We almost lost you,' she said to the little robot. Then, dropping the screen to the floor, she leapt on Nate, hugging him with more strength than ever before. 'And I almost lost *you*!' she said. 'Don't ever, *ever* do anything that stupid again, Nate, or I'll kill you myself.'

Trying not to think about how close they'd both come to dying, and indeed what still might happen when Saint found out about their unauthorised tour of the lower level, the two inventors staggered back to Nate's chalet.

'I'll make the tea,' Cat said as Nate lay down on one of the leather recliners. But when she returned from the kitchen moments later she found Nate fast asleep, Clint curled on his chest and clutching at his overalls with his broken fingers as though frightened to ever again let go.

40

A Recovery, Of Sorts

When Nate awoke the following morning the first thing he noticed was that his entire body ached. It wasn't just his legs, but his arms, stomach, back and even his ears all throbbed painfully as though connected to some kind of electric torture machine. Sitting up and rubbing his temples he found himself in his bed, and saw with a shock that it was coming up for midday. Clint was nowhere to be seen, and Nate's watch appeared to be missing as well so he couldn't track him down.

As he eased himself from under the blankets, the memories of the previous day came flooding back and he shook his head, almost unable to believe that any of it had happened. Taking off his overalls, which Cat had thankfully left on when she put him to bed, he looked in amazement at the patchwork of cuts, scrapes and bruises that marked his skin. He wondered how he'd managed to survive.

After a quick shower, Nate slung on some clean clothes and walked gingerly outside. The living quarters were deserted, and he had a sudden fear that Saint had found out about the rescue mission, and had sent his robots in to finish off the young inventors once and for all. Walking over to Cat's chalet, however, he peered through the window to find her sitting at her desk, her expression of concentration illuminated by the light from her soldering iron.

He knocked gently on the glass and was met by an enormous

grin. Moments later Cat sped through and opened the door.

'Morning, you,' she said, giving him another hug that sent waves of pain through his chest. 'How are you feeling?'

'All I'm feeling is pain,' he said, following her into the kitchen and slumping down on one of the stools. Cat laughed as she put on the kettle. While they waited for it to boil Nate scanned the room, stopping when he noticed something unusual about the tiny black camera embedded in the wall. It had been dug out, and the wires had been connected to a small, black box that Cat had fastened to the plaster.

'You're lucky you can feel anything at all,' she said, hopping up on to the counter and swinging her legs, 'the way you were carrying on yesterday.'

'What's happened to the video camera?' he asked, ignoring her comment. She followed his gaze to the wall and shrugged.

'I just like my privacy,' she answered. 'I rigged up a video loop of me pottering about the chalet and have been feeding it into the cameras in every room. Instead of seeing what I'm really up to, whoever is observing on the other end of that camera will have to watch me doing the most boring things imaginable – cleaning the kitchen, counting grains of rice and picking my nose. It blocks out the sound too so we can say what we want in here.'

Nate whistled, impressed.

'I've made one for you, too,' she said, 'and for David.'

'Oh, and where's Clint?' Nate asked. 'He hasn't run off again, has he?'

'I took him back with me last night,' Cat replied. 'I figured that if Saint or any of the robots saw him they might work out what happened. I'm giving him a new body, of sorts, so that we'll never lose him again.'

Nate waited until Cat had finished making the tea before asking the question that was really bugging him.

'What about Saint? Has he said anything? I thought the assistants would have come to take us away by now.'

'Me too,' she said, passing Nate a mug of tea. 'But there's been nothing. Nobody's seen Saint this morning, and as far as I can tell the robots did a quick search of the lab then disappeared back downstairs. It looks like the whole thing's been forgotten.'

'Weird,' said Nate, still expecting the master inventor to burst in at any moment and toss them to his assistants. 'Well, show me Clint's new outfit then. I was planning to jazz him up a bit myself. I should have known you'd beat me to it.'

Cat led Nate through to the lab area. The little robot's ruined shell lay on her desk, the metal buckled beyond repair, his three remaining arms and single leg hanging off the side like strands of spaghetti. His head had been split in two and the processor inside was missing. Scanning the room Nate expected the little robot to appear dressed in a three-piece suit and bowler hat or, more likely knowing Cat, a ball gown or miniskirt. But their metal friend was nowhere to be seen.

'You're sure he hasn't run off again?' Nate asked, but Cat simply tutted and pointed at the desk.

'He's right there, silly,' she said, laughing as Nate scanned the surface, his brow creased in confusion. Maybe she had found a way to make Clint invisible. 'You didn't think I'd dress him in a three-piece suit, did you?'

'Of course not,' Nate answered, blushing. His roving eyes suddenly landed on his watch, which was lying to one side. It took him a while to notice that it looked a little different from how he remembered it. 'He's not in there, is he?'

'Bingo,' she answered, walking forward and lifting the watch from the desk, holding it out for Nate to inspect. Taking it from her, he saw that the digital screen had been replaced with a minuscule holographic projector, and that Clint's main

296

processor had been welded to the back. A tiny optical camera had been mounted to the watch face and even his vocal synthesiser had been fixed to the strap.

Cat reached over and pressed the watch's single button, and the projector warmed up. Seconds later a computer-generated three-dimensional image of Clint rose up from the watch face. He was only ten centimetres tall, and semi-transparent, but every detail of his body and face had been lovingly recreated.

'Ta da,' the robot said as he performed a clumsy tap dance, his squeaky voice back to its full strength. 'This isn't quite what I was expecting when you said you'd give me a makeover.'

'You look better than you did yesterday, though,' Cat interrupted. 'And at least nobody will find you in there. We'll give you a new body as soon as we're back home.'

'Yeah,' Nate said to the on-screen Clint. 'By the time we're finished you'll look like C3PO.'

'That sounds like a brand of toilet cleaner,' Clint said.

They all laughed and Nate strapped the watch to his wrist. It was much heavier than before, but it was still comfortable. As he waved his arm around Clint pretended to hang on for dear life, before eventually sliding inside the watch face.

'Oh woe is me!' he said as he disappeared.

'Smart move,' Nate said.

'Of course it is,' came Cat's smug reply.

For the next few hours Nate and Cat worked on the watch, tightening up the seals and improving the computer-generated version of Clint, giving him all the expressions and habits he had possessed when solid. In no time Clint was blinking, scratching, performing acrobatics and even belching like a trooper. The little digital robot even farted loud enough to make the watch vibrate, but this time Cat simply laughed.

'I thought we were trying to keep him hidden,' she said as Clint apologised, twiddling his four thumbs nervously.

As dinnertime approached, the young inventors from downstairs began making their way up to the chalets, all shadowed by the robotic assistants. Still fearing punishment from the master inventor, Nate checked with them to see if anybody had seen Saint. But apparently he had entered the forbidden tunnel that morning and hadn't reappeared all day.

David, of course, was still not up and about and, ready for a break, Nate and Cat downed their tools and left for the infirmary. Clint was allowed to come as long as he kept himself hidden, but the curious robot kept popping his holographic head out of the watch face to see what was going on.

As soon as they left Cat's chalet they were approached by a robotic assistant, but after narrowing its eyes suspiciously at Nate all it seemed to want to do was trail them through the living quarters. They thought their robot chaperone would stop them visiting David, but it seemed to have no problem with the idea, and simply stood to one side of the room as they walked up to the bruised figure in the bed.

'What on earth were you thinking?' asked Nate, recalling David's jetpack ride. 'That was the craziest stunt I've ever seen anyone pull. You could have killed yourself!'

'It would have been better than staying in here,' David answered tersely, but he soon broke out into a bashful smile. 'It was crazy though, wasn't it? And a bloody good laugh as well, until the crash. Is that Clint?'

Nate looked down to see that the little robot had popped his head out to flash David a wink.

'Long story,' Cat said, raising an eyebrow.

'You were right about the windows,' Nate admitted, prodding the image of Clint until it sank back down into the watch. 'About them being fake.'

'Well that's the funny part,' David laughed dryly. 'At first I thought they were fakes because of the weather, but then I convinced myself that was rubbish and that Saint was bluffing – I mean who has the ability to move an entire building underground? That's why I decided to try and break free. I thought I had it for a while – I could taste that freedom.'

They all glanced nervously at the metallic figure in the corner of the room but it appeared to be ignoring them. David shuffled under the duvet to try and get comfortable and invited Nate and Cat to sit down on the bed. Nate went to do so but David grasped his hand, steering him so that he was sitting in a way that directly blocked David's lap from the robot's line of vision. What now? Nate thought, frowning.

'So, I take it you guys have decided to join Saint on his quest for world domination,' he said, cheerfully, but neither Nate nor Cat was listening – they were watching intently as he began spelling something out on the duvet with his finger. Using large, unmistakable movements he inscribed letter after letter on to the soft fabric.

'Yes,' said Cat, trying to keep the conversation moving so that the robot guard wouldn't get suspicious. 'He sounds okay, really.'

I, spelled David, *KNOW*

'I mean,' continued Nate, not really paying attention to the words coming out of his mouth, 'he's all right. Nice guy and all. Good lips.'

A WAY OUT

Cat flashed Nate a worried look.

'Er . . . good lips, good hair, good ideas,' she continued.

NEED AN ALIBI

'Great ideas, love the robots,' added Nate.

A DISTRACTION

'Beautiful aren't they? Just beautiful.'

TONIGHT, AT 10

'David,' said Nate as he realised what had just been spelled out, 'it's not worth it.'

But David flashed him a look that made him instantly close his mouth. Alerted to something, the robot stepped forward, its cold grey feet tapping against the hard floor. It walked up to the trio on the bed and stood there in silence. Nate tried to cover up his tracks.

'No, it's not worth it,' he repeated hesitantly. 'The bathroom's so far away, it's not worth the walk. Just pee in the bed.'

All three faces turned up and grinned nervously at the robot. It flashed its golden eyes at them for a moment as if considering the validity of what it was hearing, then marched slowly back to the wall.

'It's *really* not worth it,' said Nate, turning back to David, but the injured inventor's pale face was unmoved, and his only response was to carve out in the duvet two huge numbers: *10*.

The robot that had accompanied them into the infirmary remained with David, but another was waiting outside to follow them back to the lift.

'Are you going to do it?' Cat asked, trying not to give anything away. Nate entered the lift's open doors and waited for Cat and the machine to join him before pressing the holographic button to take them up.

'No,' he answered, then, shaking his head in frustration, 'I mean yes, what else can we do? We can't abandon him. And what if he's telling the truth?'

'We?!' was Cat's answer, eyebrow raised.

'Oh yeah, sister,' Nate replied. 'We're in this together. We've both got everything to lose.' He made the sound of an explosion, softly, and imitated an expanding mushroom cloud as best he could with his hands. Clint had appeared again, and he made the same motion with his four arms. Cat sighed deeply and stared at the floor.

When the lift reached its destination they shuffled out and made their way back to the chalets, the robotic assistant never leaving their side. Cat invited Nate back to hers where she handed him five small black boxes complete with wires – the machines she'd designed to fool Saint's video cameras.

'They're easy as pie to rig up,' she said. 'I don't suppose the fact that I've lovingly made these for you means I can avoid coming out tonight, does it?'

'Just meet me outside five minutes before the time,' Nate replied as he opened her door and stepped outside, closing it before Cat could reply.

41

A Distraction

The next few hours were painfully drawn out. First Nate made himself a cup of tea, and sat in the kitchen trying to think what David could possibly have meant by a distraction. It wasn't as simple as setting off the fire alarms – the warning system in the building was far too advanced for a smoky sock held under the sprinkler. Maybe a small explosive, he thought, before instantly dismissing the idea as way too dangerous.

Several equally ludicrous ideas later – which included unleashing the angry two-headed goat on the lab again – he gave up, throwing his mug into the sink and marching through to the sitting room. He spent an hour rigging up Cat's machines to the video cameras in the wall, recording an image of himself in every room then feeding it into the cameras as a continuous loop – in such a way that he never appeared in different rooms at the same time. Whoever was watching would see Nate walking around the house like a zombie doing nothing of any interest.

When he was finished he flicked on the television, selecting a light-hearted musical from the list of movies on Saint's database and sitting down on one of the massaging recliners to watch it. Despite the film, the seconds still managed to tick by relentlessly slowly. Nate's mind drifted back to David's plan. It was crazy to think he had a chance. Even if he had found a way out, he hadn't a hope in hell of reaching it without being detected. Especially with the number of injuries he had sustained in recent weeks. There were only so many times that Saint would be lenient, Nate thought, only a certain number of times he would let his patience be tested. Then it would be goodbye David, and nobody in the outside world would ever know.

Half of *Mary Poppins* and *The Pirates of the Caribbean* later and it was coming up for the hour. Peering out of his sitting room window, he saw Cat emerge from her house, a human-sized robot bounding over to her as she walked hesitantly across to Nate's chalet. Still not sure what he was planning to do, Nate tightened his watch, took a deep, shuddering breath and opened his door, stepping out into the cool, climate-controlled air. Cat was waiting outside, and he took her hand as they began to walk.

Fortunately, only the one metallic assistant followed them towards the lift. Nate wondered where the rest of Saint's troops had gone, but soon noticed a dozen golden eyes burning in the dense vegetation, following their every step.

'So,' said Cat as they reached the doors. They were closed, but as always the lift sensed their presence and began its journey to that floor. 'Do you know how this experiment is going to work?'

'Nope,' Nate answered, following the ruse. 'I think we're just going to have to wing it, and hope the results are what we expected.'

'Great,' came a sarcastic voice from Nate's watch, although Clint was obviously too nervous to emerge.

The lift doors opened to reveal an empty white interior. Stepping in, Nate had a sudden moment of doubt, a terror that almost rooted him to the spot. All he wanted to do now was return to his chalet, curl up and go to sleep, then stick out the rest of his time at Saint Solutions, just going with the flow, whatever that was.

But there was no turning back. As the robot stepped into the lift, and the doors started to close, Nate found himself doing the stupidest thing he had ever done in his entire life.

It was almost as if his body acted without his permission, his brain passing electric signals down into his muscles without being commanded to by his conscious self, the part of him he once thought was responsible for making decisions. The robot was halfway through the doors, moving quickly to step through them before they slid shut. As it was in the process of bringing its back leg into the lift, Nate charged.

He threw himself forward with all his might, every ounce of his strength, catching the metal machine off balance. The impact was agonising – the robot was huge, and felt as though it weighed the same as a small car, and if both of its feet had been planted on the ground Nate would have probably broken his shoulder without moving the creature an inch.

But with only one leg down, the unexpected blow sent it careering backwards, arms circling, eventually toppling and crashing to the path. Seconds later the doors closed, but not before Nate saw three of its identical comrades bounding from the bushes, expanding to their full size, their muzzles bared and screaming.

It was truly terrifying, but he had no time to think about it as he turned to Cat. She was staring at him, horrified.

'That was your plan?' she said. 'Oh God, they're going to kill us.'

'We're going to die!' exclaimed Clint from Nate's wrist.

'Listen,' he snapped, ignoring them both. 'We've got seconds till this lift stops. We're going to run to the hangar, we're going to get on some Antigravs, and we're going to make a break for the tunnel.'

'Nate . . .' she said, shaking her head, but he didn't let her finish.

'Cat, it's the only way we're going to cause a big enough distraction. It's the tunnel or nothing. Think about it. Saint will assume we're just trying to see what he's up to – he'll think we're there to help him. We can do this.'

'But what if he doesn't believe us?' she replied, wide-eyed. 'What if he realises we're helping David escape? Nate, he could kill us.'

'What if he takes my batteries out?!' squealed Clint, jumping up and down on the watch screen. 'Oh woe is me!'

'We have to do it.' Nate reached out and squeezed Cat's hand. 'You and me. It has to be you and me now. There's nobody else.'

As the last word left his lips, the lift slowed to a halt and the doors slid open.

Beyond, at the far end of the lab, were two robot sentries. They were in Normal Mode but as soon as they saw Nate and Cat step out of the lift they began to move forwards, their silver limbs extending to monstrous proportions, their expanding muzzles releasing the same fearsome, high-pitched call as before.

'Run!' yelled Clint, his holographic legs pumping furiously as he tried to sprint.

Nate started running, grabbing Cat who was frozen to the spot.

'Cat!' he shouted, pulling her along with him. 'Come on!'

She wrenched her eyes away from the robots, who had broken into a run. The hangar was only seconds away – the main bay door locked tight for the night but the smaller door ajar. Yet Nate knew the metal beasts could cover the distance between them in just as quick a time. Behind them he heard the relentless pounding of steel feet on the chrome floor, the crash of glass and the splintering of wood as they pulverised the desks in their path.

Nate and Cat ran as fast as their legs could carry them, hurtling through the door as the first of the robots reached them. It snatched out with one of its elongated arms, narrowly missing Cat as she launched herself through the small gap. She hit the ground screaming, as Nate slammed the door closed and pulled an Antigrav in front of it as a barricade.

But it wasn't enough to stop their pursuers. One of the robots threw itself at the large bay gate hard enough to make the entire room shake, and leaving a massive dent in the metal. The other joined in, hurling its entire weight into the steel and causing the top of the door to tear away from its casing.

'They're going to kill us!' Cat shrieked. Nate couldn't believe that this was the second time in twenty-four hours that he was being pursued by giant robots wanting to tear him limb from limb.

'Now fly!' came Clint's metallic voice again.

Nate jumped on to an Antigrav and fired it up with his palm as the robots continued to batter the door from outside. Each impact ripped it further from the wall, until they could see the demonic eyes through the hole.

The sight was enough to inspire Cat into action. She jumped on to the machine next to Nate's and started it.

'I can barely steer these!' she said. 'Nate, this isn't going to work.'

Another two deafening crashes rocked the room, causing waves of dust to drift down from the ceiling. Nate doubted that the door could stand up to much more. He suddenly had an idea.

'Saint!' he said. 'Everybody said he was in the tunnel. We can use the homing function.'

'But –'

'It's our only hope,' Nate said. 'He won't hurt us if he thinks we're just curious about what's on the other side of that wall.'

He hit the white button on the dashboard, saying Saint's name. Cat did the same. Almost immediately the Antigravs shot towards the battered bay doors.

'Oh lordy,' Nate said. But seconds before impact the massive robots charged at the door together, crashing into it with such force that it literally exploded out of its casing. The huge metal gate sliced through the air and passed between the two airborne Antigravs, its razor-sharp edges missing the riders by inches.

Speeding up, the two hovering frames boosted through the newly created hole, firing past the stunned robots and accelerating upwards with such force that Nate felt as if his stomach was being ripped away.

Within seconds they were soaring through the lab, high above the ground, heading straight for the tunnel.

'We did it!' Nate shouted, looking back to see Cat clinging on to her handlebar for dear life. She had her eyes closed, but she was smiling bravely. Clint was curled up into a ball on the watch face, his tiny body shaking.

The distraction had worked. Looking down Nate saw that the ground below was seething with metallic forms, heading for the hangar. Already the two robots that had beaten down the doors had reduced to human size and mounted Antigravs, and were in hot pursuit. As he watched, a dozen or more followed, blasting from the hangar in a trail of blue light.

But as they rounded the corner Nate saw the tunnel come into view, its entrance a giant black maw in the grey wall. He couldn't believe he was doing this, couldn't believe he was actually going to see what was inside the forbidden tunnel.

Pressing the handlebar forwards until it clicked against the frame, he made the Antigrav double its speed, hurtling into the tunnel so fast that he lost control for a second, almost decapitating himself on the ceiling.

Checking to make sure Cat was still with him, he pulled on the bar to slow the craft down a little. The robots were hot on their heels but Nate was suddenly nervous about what he might find up ahead. The tunnel stretched on endlessly, its walls ribbed with black columns, its floor and ceiling the same obsidian material they had seen at the base of the tower. They shot along it, the Antigravs still homing in on Saint's own vehicle.

A light appeared ahead of them at exactly the same time as the robots burst in through the end of the tunnel. Cat, who now had her eyes open, looked over her shoulder, shouting a warning. They both punched their handlebars, accelerating again towards the exit.

They flew from the tunnel like cannonballs, the Antigravs dropping almost instantly to the ground, creating yet another rollercoaster-like effect on Nate's gut. It wasn't enough to distract him from the sight ahead, however. Even Clint uncurled himself in order to take in the unbelievable view.

Before them, stretching as far as their eyes could see, was a city. Not a model, or a holographic imitation like in Saint's private chambers, but a real one built into an immense cavern in the ground. Everywhere Nate looked he could see life-size, red-brick houses, concrete tower blocks and cars in their thousands sitting on tarmac roads. Grey churches rose from the streets, their spires visible above the tiled rooftops, while in the distance skyscrapers reached to the black ceiling half a kilometre above.

If there had been any doubts about Saint's claim to have moved the entire building underground, they were banished by this miracle of engineering. If this vast city was on the same level as the lab, then Saint Tower must have descended hundreds of metres below the surface of the planet. It was an operation of unimaginable scale – carving out a chamber large enough for a city then filling it with buildings of every shape and size.

Nate's thoughts scattered as the Antigravs ducked down to ground level. They boosted through the empty streets at what must have been over two hundred and fifty kilometres an hour, dodging the cars and turning the rows and rows of houses into a blur. Nate held on as best he could, almost losing his grip as his machine swerved to avoid a red double-decker parked in the middle of one street, then rising to pass over a bridge that spanned a slow-moving river.

Behind them, the robot sentries were closing in, their Antigravs powering along exactly the same route. Nate wanted to go faster but didn't dare, terrified that either he or Cat would tumble to the ground below, or steer their machines into a wall. Either would mean instant death at this speed.

They reached the skyscrapers in less than half a minute, bolting over a large plaza and flying so close to the glass wall of one vast tower that Nate could have reached out and touched it. From there, the Antigravs flew out over a body of water, eventually slowing as they approached a small island, dropping down to land between a cluster of warehouses.

'This is bad,' said Clint unnecessarily, pointing a holographic finger at the group that stood there, waiting for them. Seven of the nine were robots – huge, fierce and looking ready for confrontation. But it was the two other figures that Nate and Cat looked at most fearfully as they stepped from the machines. One of them was Saint. The other was Travis Heart.

42

Sick 'em, Boy

Saint stepped forward, his face blank, his expression unreadable, but before he could say anything the air was filled once again with the deep throbbing of more Antigravs. The pursuing robots landed in the open space between the warehouses, climbing off instantly and making their way over to where Nate and Cat were standing.

Nate hadn't realised how many had been chasing them – fourteen had landed and another twenty or so appeared to be hovering above the scene, waiting for further developments. With a single wave of his hand Saint brought the robots that had landed to a halt.

'Well, they're nothing if not thorough,' he said, walking towards the two young inventors, who were trying to catch their breath after the terrifying flight. 'Forty robots needed to chase down two novice fliers, and they can't even catch you! I think I need to beef up my security.'

He stopped close enough to Nate and Cat for them to be able to smell his aftershave, a sickly vanilla scent that made them both feel nauseous.

'But well done for having the guts to have a peek,' he added. Nate's sigh of relief was almost deafening in the silence. Saint had fallen for it, he thought they'd been so desperate to know what was through the tunnel that they'd risked life and limb to find out. That was a good sign – it meant that David hadn't been caught. 'The only other one of you to make the trip was this young man, dear old Travis, and that was on the second night!'

They looked at Travis, who glared back at them with an expression of barely disguised loathing. Clint stuck out his tongue and blew a massive raspberry at the boy, but nobody paid him any attention. Saint was about to continue speaking when one of the robots closest to him approached, bending down so that its muzzle was practically touching the master inventor's ear and whispering something.

Saint looked at Nate and Cat, his humorous expression turning to one of suspicion. Nate felt his heart drop.

'Really,' Saint said, drawing the word out. 'Why doesn't that surprise me? And I suppose that neither of you know anything about Mr David Barley's attempted escape from the infirmary?'

They both stood in defiant silence, devastated. Saint moved to one of the Antigravs and fired it up.

'Well, it's neither here nor there now,' he said as he rose into the air. 'Davie-boy has gone too far. I can't be doing with his irritating, destructive behaviour any more. It's time he realised just how serious this is.'

'Don't hurt him,' said Nate. He meant it as a threat but it came out more like a plea. 'Just don't hurt him.'

Saint began to accelerate, the airborne robots swooping round automatically to act as a protective convoy.

'Oh don't worry, David won't be harmed,' he shouted as he flew off in the direction of the city. 'But I wouldn't want to say the same for his family. Take them inside, they need to see this.'

The warehouses on the island didn't look like much from the outside, but they contained some of the most high-tech equipment Nate and Cat had seen since arriving at the Saint Solutions complex.

Without uttering a single word, Travis led them through a small corridor into the large interior. Surrounding them were the robot guards, who had shrunk down to normal size in order to fit through the door and stayed that way, obviously not considering the two inventors a threat. Clint was bouncing around on the watch, throwing punches at the guards, but dived back into the screen when Nate glanced down at him, finger on lips.

When Nate looked back up he gazed around the large room in awe, marvelling at the computer banks, the vast screens that displayed the city from every angle, the holographic projectors running simulators that seemed to bathe the room in purple light.

'Travis,' said Cat, equally impressed, 'why is there an underground city in here?'

The boy didn't answer, moving over to a desk and tapping some code into a laptop. The screen mounted on the wall above his head, easily the size of a barn door, suddenly switched from a view of the city's skyscrapers to one of Saint.

He had made the journey back to their living quarters in seemingly record time, and now stood once again on the roof of a chalet holding David by the scruff of the neck, shouting wildly. He was obviously being filmed by one of the robots, which panned around gently to show the young inventors gradually making their way from their chalets, most in their pyjamas, some rubbing their eyes as if having just been woken.

'I had hoped it wouldn't come to this,' Saint bellowed, his voice crystal clear on the screen. Nate noticed that at the master inventor's feet sat one of the tiny dogs that had been given away to the parents on the day of the competition. It sat panting happily, watching calmly as the crowd gathered in front of it.

'I truly did. I mean, I'm no monster. I thought you'd all want to be here, to help me change the course of history. But some of you' – to Nate's horror, he slapped David round the face, causing the boy to wince in pain – 'weren't happy, some of you didn't want to stay, some of you ungrateful wretches just won't give up your pointless and, quite frankly, illogical attempts at escape.'

David struggled against Saint's iron grip, the boy's eyes manic, murderous.

'We just want to go home,' he shouted. Several members of the crowd murmured their agreement, one girl even repeating David's words at the top of her voice. Saint pulled an expression of disgust.

'Then you're all crazy,' he said, 'and craziness is wrong, and needs to be punished.' He threw David to the flat roof of the chalet and bent down to pick up the dog. 'You'll all remember these adorable little fellows,' he said gleefully, stroking the dog's neck. It wagged its little electronic tail in response. 'These cute little mutts that all your loved ones have been using to speak to you. Well I'd like to introduce to you the real little doggy inside – the beast within, you might like to call it. It's not quite as lovable.'

Nate and Cat drew closer to the screen, unable to comprehend what was going on. They watched as Saint threw the dog to the ground and muttered something, a code word that made the small canine's eyes suddenly light up with fire. Then, in a mechanical process similar to that of the robot assistants, the dog began to change shape.

Its back legs grew first, raising the creature's rear end and causing it to growl with discomfort. The front legs extended next, raising it to the height of a Great Dane, and the metal plates of its body began to swell, sliding apart so that the animal doubled in size. The head was the last thing to change – the small, toothless jaw began to stretch, generating the sound of squealing metal as it was forced outwards, razor-sharp teeth cutting through the tough gums and creating a drooling maw of deadly steel.

Those children closest to the beast staggered back as it snarled at them. It uttered harsh, deafening barks and bared its enormous teeth. David had got to his knees, every trace of colour gone from his face. He obviously thought he was going to die.

But Saint had something else in mind, something far worse. He clapped twice, and the dog froze as the video screen began to slide out of its back.

'Like I said before, you're all here for the duration,' he whispered menacingly. 'There are no more chances, no more Mr Goody Goody Nice Saint, especially for you.' He looked down at David. 'So why don't we give your folks a call.'

Nate felt sick to his stomach. Surely this couldn't be happening. Not this. But, as they watched, the screen on the dog flashed to life and David's mum and dad appeared, looking tired but happy. Unlike the computer-generated images of parents that had been shown to the children in recent weeks, this was real. There was nothing artificial about the way that Mr and Mrs Barley sat bolt upright in bed when they saw their son, on his knees and covered in bruises. Nothing fake about the way David's mum reached out a hand to her only child, so thin and frail compared to the rosy-cheeked, digital version that she had been speaking to on the videophone.

'David?' his dad said. He looked the spitting image of his son – even, remarkably, wearing a bow tie with his striped pyjamas – but with a messy comb-over that hung down by one ear. 'What in –'

But he couldn't finish. Both he and his wife looked in horror at the sight before them – the giant robots, their terrified child, the manic Saint. The rather dumpy woman on screen let loose a whimper.

'David?' she shouted, panicking. 'What's going on? Mr Saint, what are you doing?'

'Mum,' David called back, holding out his hand. 'Run!'

But it was too late. Saint leant forward, a twisted smile on his face, and muttered the words again. This time Nate heard what he said, and the relish with which he said it.

'Sick 'em, boy.'

Cat buried her head into Nate's chest, sobbing uncontrollably as she realised what was about to happen. Nate watched for a moment longer, as the image of the Barleys started shaking, as their faces morphed into expressions of utter terror, as David started beating the top of the chalet in frustration. Then he could bear it no longer, pressing his face against the top of Cat's head, holding her as tightly as he could.

But that couldn't protect him from the sounds. The awful noises of ripping, tearing and screaming that filled the room, the gradual fading of the shrieks, the sobbing of the young inventors and, worst of all, a soft, musical laugh from the chalet roof that continued long after everything else had fallen silent.

43

The End of the World

Saint was still chuckling to himself when he returned to the warehouse in the artificial city a few minutes later. He strolled in through the doors, slinging his white coat on the back of a chair and rolling up his shirt sleeves.

'My, my – what a busy day it's turning out to be,' he said, walking over to Travis and patting him on the head in a fatherly fashion. He turned to look at Nate and Cat, who hadn't moved since witnessing the horror on screen. Cat still had her head buried in Nate's chest, where she had soaked his overalls with tears that still flowed. Nate gently stroked her hair, and stared at Saint with a look of pure hatred.

'I'm sorry you had to see that,' Saint said, looking, for a second, remorseful. But his expression soon returned to the trademark smile. 'It was necessary, however. Events have moved on much more quickly than I could ever have imagined, thanks in no small part to the incredible progress made by all you young inventors. Now is not the time for wastage and distraction. David will recover, eventually. He'll get his priorities straight as soon as he sees what we're about to accomplish.'

Saint walked to the control panel beneath the huge screen, adjusting the image so that it once again showed the towering skyscrapers.

'Which brings me on to today's experiment,' he continued. 'Quite an exciting one, if you ask me.'

'You didn't have to do that,' Nate hissed, feeling the anger seething inside him, a fury that he wanted to let loose. 'Not his parents.' He wanted to erupt and kill Saint there and then to avenge his friend, to wipe that smug grin off his face, to pound him into the floorboards. But the robots were everywhere, watching him like hawks, and he knew he would be cut down before he'd even taken his first step.

Saint turned and held a finger to his lips.

'Shhhh,' he whispered. 'You two are on thin ice as it is. I'm going to give you the benefit of the doubt and assume that you were both so eager to find out what I was up to in here, to help out with my experiment, that you broke the rules and flew through the tunnel. I'm going to assume that you had no part to play in David's pathetic escape attempt, that you were not indeed planning a distraction, that I don't need to introduce your parents to my real little four-legged friends. Especially you, Cat. I mean you wouldn't want to lose another parent because of a dangerous invention.'

Nate felt Cat's head jerk up, her body tense as though about to fly at the master inventor, but he held her tight, refusing to let her loose. He tried not to think about his parents being chewed to pieces, his mother's screams, his father putting up a useless fight, but the images circled his head relentlessly. They had to go along with whatever Saint wanted. Now there was simply no other choice.

'I'm also going to assume that you had nothing to do with the rescue mission that took place in the barracks last night,' Saint went on, 'which resulted in a very expensive repair bill for damaged assistants.'

Nate looked at his watch, saying nothing, as Clint curled into a tiny ball and disappeared back into the screen. Travis looked up at Saint in confusion, and for a second Nate and Cat relished the knowledge that there were some things the master inventor was keeping even from his most trusted protégé.

'So relax, find a seat. You have a front-row view of the beginning of a brand-new world,' Saint continued.

'Why the city?' Nate asked, not moving, trying to keep Saint talking.

'I'm glad you asked,' he replied, dashing swiftly between keyboards and control panels, carefully studying a series of codes on a monitor before resuming. 'I had my assistants build it, brick by brick, tower by tower. It took them five years and it's been sitting there gathering dust for weeks.'

He switched on another vast monitor further down the wall, one that revealed a small purple car on a roadside. It looked like a Beetle.

'And do you know how hard it is to have built a city and not be allowed to blow it up?' he asked. 'It's like making a sand-castle at the beach – it's just no damn fun unless you can pelt it with stones afterwards.' He stretched out his arms, dashing around the room making the noise of a fighter jet and its machine-gun. 'Pretend that you're bombing it from up high.

'At first, all I wanted to do was detonate an atomic bomb over it, one of my own design, to see how much damage I could cause. But then I began thinking. I want to rebuild the world, see, start from scratch, make it fun and safe and wonderful. But the problem with nuclear warheads is that they make so much mess. You can't set foot in the detonation zone for years, animals have a funny habit of mutating into freakishly strange beasts – you're familiar with our friends the two-headed goat and the killer flytrap – and it's just a waste of time and energy.

'I couldn't find a way of making an atomic bomb "safe", if you'll excuse the paradox, so I began experimenting with different methods of destruction. But none of them worked. They were all too small, too weak. I'd have needed an army of millions and a thousand years to get my *tabula rasa*, to clean the canvas ready for my masterpiece.'

He paused, flicking open a small case on a control panel to reveal two large red buttons. As he pressed the first, they saw the walls of the warehouse gradually disappear behind a glowing band of pulsating blue light.

'Shields are up,' Nate heard Travis say, turning his head to see the young inventor carefully monitoring a series of spiked graphs onscreen.

'Good job too,' Saint replied, his eyes twinkling. 'We're going to need them.' He looked once again at Nate and Cat. 'I got so close so finding a way but it kept on eluding me. Until, that is, I hit upon the idea of inviting you lot to stay.'

He dangled his finger above the second button.

'I knew that some of you would be young enough to understand my dream, to know that the world is not a nice place and want to change it. I knew you'd all have new ideas, things I'd never even dreamed of contemplating, let alone making. Even I have lost some of my creative energy as I've got older – and I'm older than you think.'

He began circling his finger over the button.

'It wasn't that I needed you to help me with my inventions,' he went on. 'I needed you here because children think about things in a way that adults never do – so much creative freedom! I knew that most of you probably wouldn't want to create weapons, but I was fairly sure that the things you came up with would probably have other uses. I also knew that a few of you would want to create things that go bang, and that sooner or later you'd work out a way of cleansing this planet without the need to live in a radioactive shelter for a century.'

He flashed a wink at Travis, and Nate saw the boy smile for the first time. It was a grimace, twisted and dark.

'Travis nailed that conundrum right on the head the

moment he blasted a giant hole in my conference room on the day of the final. Between us we've finally managed to create the weapon that will change the face of the earth.'

Nate couldn't believe what he was hearing. He wanted to tell Saint he was a madman, to implore him to think again, to stop what he was doing, but he couldn't quite remember how to speak.

'Of course, a weapon of such destructive force is pointless unless you've got what it takes to rebuild,' Saint went on, 'and that is what I've spent a lifetime doing. Think of Saint Tower as one giant seed, a Noah's Ark if you like. I have the technology to recreate every plant, every animal, and even a master race of people. It will be a perfect world, children.'

He sighed as he thought about his twisted paradise.

'Your timing is actually quite remarkable,' he continued. Nate lifted his eyes to the screens that showed the deserted artificial city beyond, and imagined it full of people, of children, of animals. He couldn't bring himself to watch what was about to happen, but neither could he tear his eyes away.

'I have become death, the destroyer of worlds,' Saint whispered, then his finger dropped. 'Kaboom.'

Both Nate and Cat flinched as the button clicked, expecting to hear the sound of a catastrophic explosion, to feel the ground shake, to feel the air sucked from the room as the weapon did its terrible work. But there was no noise at all.

Something was happening, though. The screen showing the Beetle was instantly filled with a blinding purple light. Nate wrenched his gaze away to the next monitor, which showed a section of the city from above as it was gradually swallowed by a fast-moving ball of colour. Each of the enormous screens

showed the same sight – a city vanishing beneath a wave of purple – until the room and everything in it was bathed in the eerie
hue.

Saint switched the video displays off with a flick of a single
switch, and stood for a moment by the console, breathing hard.

'Did it work?' Travis asked, walking to a desk in the middle
of the warehouse and frantically scanning a series of printouts
that were being hurled from a laserjet. 'What happened?'

'I have no idea,' Saint said finally, turning. 'I can't see
through walls, Travis.'

He pressed one of the red buttons again to disengage the
shields, causing the blue haze against the walls to fade away.
Then he walked to a robot and whispered something to it,
watching impatiently as the hulking beast picked up a Geiger
counter from a nearby desk and stomped through the door. It
returned seconds later and handed it back to Saint. The master
inventor grinned.

'Well,' he said, 'at least we know we don't have radiation
poisoning.'

Sliding on his jacket, Saint sprinted towards the warehouse
door, ushering the rest of the group out. Two of the robots
went to give Nate and Cat a shove but they found themselves
walking swiftly of their own free will. Although neither wanted
to admit it, they were desperate to see what kind of damage the
weapon had inflicted on the world outside.

'That purple light you saw was an evolved version of Travis's
laser gun,' Saint explained to them as they walked, 'only with
the force contained inside a suitcase-sized vessel, and powered
not with batteries, but with proton accelerants – we have our
pesky friend David to thank for that.'

They walked through the door, but their view of the city was
blocked by the warehouse. There was a fine, purple dew in the
air that caught in their hair and stained their clothes as they

made their way around the large building.

'Interesting,' said Saint, watching his suit slowly change colour. 'I was getting a little bored with white anyway. And purple is quite a regal colour.'

With only metres to go until they rounded the warehouse, Saint stopped and turned, a sheepish look on his face.

'Now, don't be too disappointed if this isn't what you expected,' he said, addressing them all. 'I mean, it is my first time and all.'

But as they made the short trip to the edge of the warehouse and looked out over the water to the land beyond, they realised that the experiment had been a total, and catastrophic, success.

Where there had once been a city of bricks and mortar and stone and concrete, of houses and shops and churches and tower blocks, there was now nothing but a mound of dust. Everything had been reduced to a vast heap of purple ashes that danced in the artificial wind, creating swirling shapes in the air as they drifted lazily down to the ground.

Absolutely nothing recognisable remained – the shifting, undulating dunes of powder stretched to the horizon, right to the entrance of the tunnel which was visible in the distance. A lifeless purple desert.

For a while nobody spoke, and they stood rooted to the spot watching the clouds of ash billow over the water, turning everything purple. It would have been a beautiful scene, thought Nate, tasting the bitter dust in his mouth, had it not heralded the end of the world.

To his side, he heard Saint begin to laugh, a sinister, low chuckle that rapidly grew into a howl of delight. The master inventor ran over to Travis and grabbed him, lifting the boy off his feet and spinning him around.

'Blow me down and knock me sideways!' he shouted at Travis's shocked expression. 'We did it, we absolutely, positively did it! Saint and Heart – what a heavenly combination! I'd kiss you, if nobody else was watching!'

He suddenly let go, sending the young inventor crashing to the ground. Getting to his feet, Travis brushed the purple dust from his overalls and looked out over the wasteland, his own swelling laughter imitating Saint's. And like two hyenas howling at the night, they marched and danced and laughed and sang against the apocalyptic backdrop – a vision of madness and destruction that Nate knew would never, ever leave his head.

44

Saint and Sinners

Neither Nate nor Cat managed to say a word as they waited for the two delighted inventors to finish dancing. They remained silent as they were ushered back to the warehouse, and stood numbly while a fleet of replacement Antigravs was brought out to the island – the ones standing outside had been obliterated by the explosion, much to Saint's irritation.

It was almost impossible to believe that the world could be on the verge of complete and utter annihilation, that something as small as a suitcase could harness enough destructive power to obliterate an entire city in seconds. For all they knew, Saint could already have sent his weapons out into the world. There could be cars sitting in New York, in London, in Beijing, looking apparently harmless but ready to detonate at Saint's command.

Nate tried to imagine the devastation that could be caused in a city full of life, and shuddered.

They were given Antigravs and told to fly straight back to their chalets, Saint putting any thought of escape out of their minds by baring his teeth and growling in imitation of the killer robotic dogs. Cat didn't look as if she was in any state to fly, so Nate clambered on to her Antigrav, standing behind her and firing it up. Together, they sailed over the desert of purple sand, high enough above it to avoid the thick ashes that had once been buildings and cars.

Back at the chalets there was nobody in sight, but from the chilling sound of crying and screaming audible from behind the walls it was clear that the young inventors were inside, still reeling from the incident with David's parents. The lights were off in David's chalet, and nobody answered the door when Nate knocked, so he and Cat walked slowly to their own living quarters.

There were no robots in the area at all. There didn't need to be now – nobody in their right mind would be willing to step out of line, knowing the consequences.

Nate walked into Cat's chalet and they both sat down in the kitchen, still unable to think of anything to say. After a minute Cat looked down and saw the purple ash that covered their overalls and skin, and ran off to the bathroom. Nate heard the sound of water running, and he suddenly realised that he was just as filthy. Returning to his chalet, he stripped and jumped into the shower, relishing the feeling of the warm water on his skin.

When the bathroom was so steamy that he could no longer see the door he got out, drying himself, then slinging on some fresh clothes. He strapped his watch back on, looking at the image of Clint sitting forlornly on the screen. Unable to think of anything to say to the little robot, Nate walked through to his lounge. Cat was sitting on one of the recliners, looking clean but exhausted. She was clutching the photo of her dad.

'Are you okay?' he asked, realising how ridiculous the question sounded as soon as he had said it. She smiled weakly as he collapsed next to her.

'Oh, fine,' she replied. 'I've just seen a good friend's parents chewed to death by a robot dog, had my family threatened with the same death, and witnessed the planet's destruction in progress. I've never been better.'

'Yeah,' Nate answered, 'it's been just like Christmas.'

 325

'More like Halloween,' said Clint from the watch.

Nate and Cat both laughed but it was short-lived, and once again they fell into silence as they thought about what they had witnessed in the last few hours.

When Cat did finally speak again, her words shocked Nate.

'Maybe he's right,' she said. He glanced at her, thinking that this was another ruse, another deception to fool any hidden microphones in the room. But her face was deadly serious. 'I mean, Dad used to say that the world would be a better place if we could start from scratch, knowing what we know now. What if Saint can create a world where there is no war, no suffering? Maybe we do need to destroy before we can rebuild.'

Cat's words were an almost perfect imitation of Saint's, and Nate leant forward, grabbing her hand and squeezing it.

'Cat,' he whispered, but she carried on, her eyes wide, determined, lost.

'Think about it, Nate. You saw the power of that weapon. If it was used to cleanse the world then we could have a paradise, we could live in peace.'

He didn't reply. She was delusional, her will shattered by the events of the day, her mind confused. Nate's wasn't much clearer. He couldn't deny the sense of power he'd felt when he saw the purple bomb explode, saw the city in ruins. It was the power of a god, one that could make the entire world bow down before him if he chose to harness it. But, unlike Saint, he knew what the cost would be in terms of life, the billions of deaths, the eradication of species after species.

'But your dad knew that starting from scratch would mean the death of almost everybody on the planet,' he said quietly, holding Cat's hand until she came round. She blinked, shaking the thoughts from her head, and seemed to find a new resolve.

'Saint's counting on his threats keeping us in line,' she said finally. 'But we have to stop him, Nate. We have to try.'

He looked at her, shaking his head. Once again he pictured his parents meeting a horrific death at the jaws of one of Saint's vicious beasts.

'We can't risk it, Cat. The army has to do it. Somebody like Saint can't have planned something like this without somebody telling the government,' he answered. 'What about your mum? They'll kill her.'

'They're all going to die anyway,' she said. 'Think of the power of that thing. You think Saint's going to get them out of the way when he detonates it, that he's going to make an effort to save our folks?'

Nate knew she was right. But it seemed so much easier not to get involved, to put his head down and let what was going to happen just happen. Better that than actually be responsible for his parents' deaths.

'It's you and me, Nate,' Cat said.

'And me,' shouted Clint, his holographic body hopping up and down.

'It's you, me and Clint,' she corrected herself. 'But not against the world this time, *for* the world. If we don't do something, then there won't be a world for us to be against.'

'But what can we do?' he asked, feeling powerless, feeble. 'Saint has an army, we can't even sneeze without a robot saying "bless you", and if we slip up once, Cat, just once, then it's the end, it's over. We could die. We don't even know if David is still alive.'

'We'll think of something,' she answered, getting up and making her way towards the front door. 'We always do.'

Nate had expected another night of bad dreams, visions of the end of the world, of dead parents and chaos, but when he woke the next morning he couldn't remember having a single nightmare. Sleep had been a black void, a blissful state in which he could forget about everything that had happened the previous day, the rapidly worsening scenario of the last few weeks.

He wanted nothing more than to be able to crawl back under the duvet, to return to that dreamless state, but Clint wasn't prepared to let him.

'It's twenty to eleven,' the robot shouted, stretching out a tiny transparent arm and pretending to poke Nate in the cheek. 'I didn't think you were ever going to wake up!'

Nate started to grumble a response, but stopped when Clint's words had sunk in and he realised he was three hours late for the lab. Throwing on a clean pair of overalls, he dashed out of the chalet, and running across the path to Cat's he pounded on her door. There was nobody home, so he made his way swiftly to the lift and down to the floor below. The main lab was a hive of activity, the robotic assistants furiously working on a seemingly infinite number of experiments.

Nate saw, to his horror, that they all appeared to be constructing the same kind of object – a suitcase-sized bundle of wires, steel plates and purple crystals. Scanning the room, he made out hundreds of them. The forbidden tunnel had been sealed off, the ruined city beyond having served its purpose.

Picking up his pace, and watched closely by the lines of robots that stood along the walls, he sprinted into the lab to see the competition winners sitting at their desks in silence, all hard at work with spanners, saws, welding irons and a multitude of other tools. Cat was tightening the screws in a handheld electromagnetic amplifier, oblivious to his entry, while in the far corner even David was engrossed in his work, putting together a bundle of small boosters that looked like proton accelerators.

It was towards David that Nate walked first, jogging across the lab floor and noticing that nobody was even looking up to acknowledge his presence. It was as if overnight the bunch of vibrant, enthusiastic inventors had been turned into zombies, terrified of even the slightest movement.

'Hey,' he said softly when he reached David, resting a hand on the boy's shoulder. 'Are you okay?'

David jumped at the touch, turning to stare at Nate. He looked like a completely different person – still pale, still gaunt, but now all the fire had gone from his eyes, all the fight, all the sense of rebellion. He was a shell.

'Fine,' he said, then turned back to his work. Nate backed away, shocked, and made his way over to Cat. She saw him coming and put down the device she was working on, arching her back.

'Nice of you to join us,' she said, picking up a screwdriver and scratching her nose with it. 'Just what time of day do you call this?'

'Brunch time,' Nate answered, trying to make a joke. He pulled up his chair and sat facing Cat, marvelling at how refreshed she looked compared to the night before. She had this incredible ability to cure herself of pretty much anything with a good cry. After a healthy downpour she was ready to get on with her life despite any disaster or setback. He needed to cry more, he thought.

'Poor David,' he said, looking over at the boy. 'He looks like death.'

'I know, but anybody would after what he went through last night.' Cat slotted the screwdriver into her overalls. 'I went over to his chalet this morning to set up those image alteration devices for his cameras, to give him a bit of privacy. It was like he didn't even notice I was there.'

Nate frowned and turned his attention to the rest of the room.

'What's going on?' he asked, nodding at the hard-working inventors.

'What do you think?' was Cat's answer. 'They're terrified that if they don't do as Saint asks then their parents will be the next on his hit list. Some of them have been here since five o'clock this morning, trying to get in his good books.'

'We need to tell them,' Nate said, getting to his feet. 'We need to let them know what they're doing, what they're helping Saint accomplish.'

'It won't make the slightest bit of difference,' she replied, shaking her head. 'They already know.' Nate crashed back into his chair, confused. 'Saint came in this morning, made an announcement, told them he was planning to change history, make the world a better place blah-de-blah-de-blah. They know what he's up to, but they're too scared to do anything about it – he told them he'd only save their loved ones if they did as he said.'

'And you?' Nate asked, looking at the project she was working on, wondering if she'd considered whether Saint was going to use the electromagnetic amplifier to increase the power of his bomb, or to give extra strength to his legions of robots that would scourge the rubble afterwards looking for survivors.

'I'm scared too,' she replied, looking at her shoes, ashamed. 'But I'd rather be on this side of the wall, Nate, I'd rather be responsible for destroying the world than be destroyed alongside it. And I want my mum to be here too.'

He looked at her with a strange mixture of shock and disgust, then turned to his desk, trying to make sense of things. He felt a hand on his arm, turned to see Cat looking at him.

'But I'd still rather look for a third option,' she added, and winked.

Saint made several appearances over the course of the day, Travis always at his side. The relationship between the two would have been comical if it hadn't been so disturbing. Saint seemed to have reverted to his old self – playful, articulate and enthusiastic, walking between the benches and desks offering words of encouragement to the young inventors, telling them what a good job they'd done, helping fix wires correctly or patch up loose ends.

Travis was the opposite, making his way around the room like a dictator, criticising sloppy design and continuously telling Saint to calm down, to stop cooing, to stand still. For some reason, Saint always obeyed him, standing bashfully to one side each time he was scolded.

Travis saved his most merciless criticism for David, who for some reason he had developed an intense hatred for. On his first visit of the morning he picked up one of the proton accelerators that David had been working carefully on and threw it to the floor, shouting something about it being too big.

David, who at one time would have picked up the rude boy with his large hands, held him upside down and shaken him until puke ran out of his nose, merely cowered by his desk. Nate was longing to step in, to help out his old friend, but he was scared of Travis, of the influence he seemed to hold over Saint, and of his furious temper.

After lunch it started again, with Travis swiping a mountain of components from David's desk, then actually slapping him round the back of the head for not working fast enough. This time both Nate and Cat rose to their feet, ready to charge. But thankfully Saint leapt in, jumping between the boys like an anxious parent and pushing Travis gently away.

David simply got down on his knees and began picking up transistors, circuit boards and other pieces of equipment. It was a heartbreaking sight, but Nate was powerless to do anything about it.

 331

Saint himself seemed to be ignoring them. According to Cat, he had walked right past her desk on his first visit that morning, without even a glance in her direction. During the next three visits of the day he only talked to them once, and that was to ask Nate how his tea machine was coming on.

'You mean you still want it?' Nate said, aghast. 'I mean, with everything else, I assumed you'd want me to work on something more important.'

'If it's going to be a perfect world, Nate,' Saint had replied, leaning forward, 'then it needs a perfect cup of tea. Trust me, son – this is important.'

And so for the entire afternoon he worked on the tea machine, even managing to lose himself in the task so completely that he forgot about Saint and his crazy ideas for the better part of an hour. It was Cat who stirred him from his trance-like state, shaking his shoulder gently and pointing to David, who was slouching from the room carrying a box full of parts. Looking at his watch, Nate saw that it was nearly half past five.

'David,' he said, 'are you off? Leave all that, do it in the morning.'

David stopped shuffling for long enough to turn and look at Nate, his expression vacant, dead.

'I need to finish these,' he said in a slow, slurred voice. 'Saint says I'm the only one who can mix the proton propellants well enough. I'm taking them upstairs.'

'You look like you need a break,' Cat called after him as he started walking again, but there was no response. 'He looks terrible,' she said to Nate, sitting back down.

'Well, wouldn't you?' was all Nate could think of to say.

45

A Date for the Diary

In a way, the relentless work made the next few days bearable. Each morning the inventors would head to the lab and become immersed in their projects, unwilling to even think bad thoughts about Saint for fear of what it might lead to.

After a while, it was as if they all started trusting him again – telling themselves so many times that nothing strange was happening that they actually started believing it. Besides, Saint seemed to be in no hurry to put his terrifying weapon to use. The robots in the main lab worked steadily on the numerous devices, spending hours at a time checking each cable, working with the same precision as a brain surgeon to ensure that everything was perfect.

David managed to provide two or three proton accelerators a day – an amazing feat given the complexity of the invention – and he would stand and watch as each was checked by Travis then passed on to the assistants to be fitted.

Whenever Nate woke at night and glanced at David's chalet he would see the flash of a welding iron through the window, and the lack of sleep and hideous pressure seemed to be getting to the boy, who grew thinner and paler every day. On the few occasions Nate saw him when he wasn't working, he sat alone in the dining area, deep in thought. Nate hated to imagine what was going on inside his head.

He only managed to talk to David twice during the next two

days, the first time to ask him if he knew where the key was to the lab's only particle accelerator (he'd had a theory about splitting the atoms of tea leaves to try and create a supertea, but had almost created an artificial black hole that would have destroyed the world much more swiftly than Saint's bombs). The second time was when he followed him to the dining area at lunchtime to see if he was okay.

'You don't look well,' he said tenderly as they sat down together. Nate had ordered a huge, steaming plateful of sausage and mash, but David was content with a large black coffee. 'You should eat something.'

'Strangely, I haven't had an appetite for a while,' he replied without malice. 'I don't think I'll ever want to eat again.'

David took a sip of his coffee and stared dead ahead, his blue eyes watery and expressionless. Suddenly, Nate found himself angry with the figure before him, the once carefree and energetic David Barley now reduced to a self-sorry husk. Slamming his fist down on to the table, he leant towards him, his words hissed rather than spoken.

'Are you just going to let Saint get away with this? He's going to destroy the world.'

'What does it matter if he destroys the world?' came the reply, spoken without any hint of emotion. 'He's already destroyed mine. Why would I care if the rest of it disappears?'

'But why help him? Why not try and kill him?' Nate realised just how loud he was speaking, his words now almost a shout. A golden-eyed assistant on the far end of the dining terrace was watching them eagerly. He continued in a whisper. 'You should be furious, David. He killed your family.'

But it didn't seem to work. David simply drank the rest of his coffee and stood up. He turned to Nate as he was leaving.

'I know he did, Nate, and if I try anything else then he'll kill your family too, and Cat's, and everybody else's. If we behave, they might be saved. If we don't, they'll die at the hands of his dogs or his bombs. Face it, he's won.'

'He hasn't!' Nate retaliated, not caring if he was shouting. 'He hasn't won, not until the last of those bombs explodes, not until there's no world left to fight for. There's still time. I thought you found a way out – I thought you were a fighter.'

'I did find a way out,' came the mild reply as David walked away. 'But it's too late. It's over.'

Furious, Nate swiped his untouched plate of lunch from the table, sending an arc of sausage and mash and china sailing through the air and crashing to the ground.

He hasn't won, he thought as he watched his old friend disappear behind the trees. But right now he wasn't sure how much he believed it.

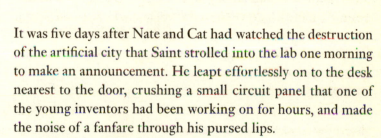

It was five days after Nate and Cat had watched the destruction of the artificial city that Saint strolled into the lab one morning to make an announcement. He leapt effortlessly on to the desk nearest to the door, crushing a small circuit panel that one of the young inventors had been working on for hours, and made the noise of a fanfare through his pursed lips.

'Ladies and gentlemen, or should I just say boys and girls,' he sang in an excited voice. 'All your wonderful hard work has paid off, all those hours, those tired and bleeding fingers, your poor, beleaguered eyeballs, your beautiful, bountiful brains – it's all been worth it.'

Nate felt his heart sink, predicting what was coming. He knew how quickly the days were passing, how their time was running out, but he hadn't expected the deadline to have rushed up on them so quickly.

'I think that we're ready to rock, ready to roll, ready to change the world, baby, make it our own, clean out the trash, burn our bridges, napalm the jungle, dredge the riverbed . . .' he paused. 'Come on, help me out here, I can't come up with all the analogies myself.'

'Begin the genocide?' Nate thought he'd said the words under his breath but Saint heard them. The master inventor leapt off the desk and sprinted to Nate's side, skidding to a halt on his knees, arms outstretched.

'Oh Nathan, always the drama queen!' he shouted. 'Yes, if you like, begin the genocide, though I do hate that word. It seems so stale, so lifeless. Ha! Lifeless! No irony intended there – that one just popped out!'

He bounced athletically to his feet and started dancing a jig in the middle of the lab, speaking as he waved his arms in the air and jabbed his feet out from side to side.

'It's gonna be tomorrow, it's gonna be tomorrow,' he chanted time and time again. When he was out of breath, he froze, looking around the room by moving just his eyeballs. 'Tomorrow at midday, we load up, we plant, we detonate. Just think, by the evening you'll be able to name your country. Bagsy England's purple and pleasant land! Then just take your pick of plants, animals and people and we'll clone 'em and set them free – it will be just like Saint's Sims.'

Saint laughed maniacally, then flipped himself backwards, doing a full loop and landing nimbly on his toes. Then he turned and ran from the room, arms waving excitedly, long blonde hair trailing behind.

'Tomorrow?' Nate said, taking Cat's hand. 'What the hell are we going to do?'

She stared at her desk, her eyes flicking back and forth as though she was deep in thought. Eventually she looked up, checked that there were no robots within hearing distance, and whispered softly to him.

'Whatever we can, Nate, whatever we can.'

David hadn't been in the lab to hear Saint's announcement, so later that afternoon Nate decided to go and pass on the message. He didn't hold out much hope of inspiring him into action, but he thought that if David knew just how long they had left to try and destroy Saint's plans he might somehow come out of his trance.

Making his way upstairs, he saw that the dining area was empty except for a couple of young inventors solemnly prodding bowls of porridge with their spoons, so he walked over to David's chalet and knocked firmly on the door.

There was no answer, so Nate headed for the nearest window and peered in, only to be greeted by a sheet blocking his view. Completing a full circle of the building he saw that all of the windows had been covered with sheets or patchworks made from David's clothes, but they couldn't muffle the noise of the welding iron within.

Nate thought about the sheer amount of steel, proton accelerants and other components that David had been carting up to his chalet every night after leaving work. He thought about the number of drives that were being checked in the main lab, all of which had been built by the young inventor. He must have been working twenty-four hours a day.

Nate knocked on the glass and shouted David's name. The roar of the iron stopped and seconds later the sheet was pulled back, revealing a ghost-like face.

'Can I come in?' Nate asked when David didn't say anything. 'I've got important news.'

'Just so long as you're not going to give me another lecture, Nathan.' David's face disappeared, and seconds later he could be heard opening the door. Nate trotted back round and dashed inside, closing it behind him.

David's chalet looked as though one of his proton accelerators had exploded inside, at least the part that Nate could see did, anyway. Directly ahead, blocking most of the sitting room and the door to the hallway, hung even more sheets, and with no natural light he found it almost impossible to see past the end of his nose. Even the small patch of visible floor wasn't strictly visible – it was covered in parts of proton drives, oil and grease.

'Well, I'm glad you're looking after the place well,' Nate said, smiling, but the gesture wasn't returned. David just stood and stared at him, glancing at his watch twice in five seconds and shifting impatiently from foot to foot.

'What do you want, Nate?' he asked.

'Well, a cup of tea would be nice,' Nate replied. To be honest, he was sick to the back teeth of tasting cups of tea, but he wanted the chance to talk properly to David, so anything that would lengthen their meeting had to be good.

'I really don't have time. I've got to get three more proton accelerators to Travis this afternoon. He's mad enough as it is that I only managed two yesterday.'

'Saint's planning his attack tomorrow,' Nate blurted out. 'Tomorrow at noon.'

David looked directly at Nate, his expression unchanged. His eyes seemed even greyer than they had the other day, his face thinner, deader. Nate shook his head and started turning back to the door, suddenly convinced that talking to David was pointless, that the poor broken boy was beyond hope. But as he did so he saw David raise his finger to his lips, then usher Nate forward with a movement of his hand.

'Then maybe you can help me finish up,' he said, winking. 'I could do with somebody to double-check the seals on the propellant, while I weld shut the casings.'

He peeled back one of the sheets and stepped through. Nate followed. What he saw when he emerged on the other side nearly made his heart stop. Clint, who had been standing on the watch face, swooned, disappearing into the screen.

Nate looked at David in awe, overjoyed, tears suddenly running from his eyes. He had to fight to stop himself from breaking down right there, from grabbing David and kissing him repeatedly.

Where there had once been walls inside the chalet there was now one giant room. Everything had been pushed to one side, or ripped up and plastered over the windows and the telescreens, while equipment and parts littered the floor. The cameras fixed into the walls had all been fitted with Cat's image-alteration devices, no doubt feeding images of David pottering around the house to whoever was keeping an eye on him. Two finished proton accelerators sat by the kitchen sink, ready to be carried downstairs, but it wasn't these that Nate was staring at, his heart pounding.

It was the vast, glittering body of chrome that sat in the middle of the giant space, the hulking shape of a craft, of a vehicle complete with cockpit and boosters. It was David's ship, only bigger, only more spectacular, only finished.

Nate reached out and touched it, feeling the heat where the last of the steel panels had been welded only seconds before. He investigated the engine hatch, where the genius inventor had set two of his proton accelerators in place ready to blast the ship out of the building. To freedom.

'Tomorrow, you say?' asked David, closing the hatch and scratching his head. He picked up one of the heavy accelerators from the floor and handed it to Nate, speaking in code. 'I think I can finish by then. If you can take this one to Travis I'll work on the rest. Just make sure you let everybody know what's going on by first thing tomorrow, say, seven o'clock. I can't do this alone.'

He pointed to the cockpit, and Nate saw that the interior of the ship was empty, and easily large enough for twenty-three passengers.

'If we all get together we can make the deadline, Nate,' he continued. 'We can all make the grade. Saint will be proud of us.'

Nate grinned and strained to hold the accelerator with one arm as he grasped David's hand with the other. Shaking it fiercely he saw the fire return to the young inventor's eyes, saw that his defeat had only been a ruse, that he had never given up the fight. He had fooled Saint, fooled Travis and he was going to get them out of there.

But as he made his way out of the door, struggling to hold the sensitive equipment in his arms, he realised that David's ship only solved half of the problem.

Saint was still going to try and destroy the planet, and somebody would have to stay behind to stop him.

46

Spreading the Word

Either the robot assistants had caught wind of something strange in the air, or Saint had tightened his security with the date of his attack less than twenty-four hours away. When Nate returned to the lab after leaving David's proton accelerator on Travis's desk he saw three of the enormous sentries, in their hulking Work Mode, standing watching the inventors at work.

As soon as he hurtled through the door, desperately trying to think of a way to arrange the mass evacuation without giving the game away too soon, one of the robots lurched forward, blocking his path. Nate tried to stop, skidding across the smooth floor into the creature's leg and finding himself face to face with the snarling mouth.

'Sorry,' he shouted as he backed away, hands up to show that he wasn't planning an attack. 'No running in the corridors, I know.'

Fortunately the robot sensed no threat, and backed away, leaving Nate to walk slowly and carefully to his desk. Cat glanced up at him as he sat, noticing his shaking fingers, his sweaty face.

'Been for a run?' she asked. He so desperately wanted to tell her about the ship, about the escape planned for the next morning, but he couldn't risk the robots overhearing. Instead, he shook his head and pulled the prototype tea machine towards him.

The previous day he'd managed to install a tiny computer chip that analysed tea molecules as they were being heated by the hot water. He'd also fitted a microscopic laser, similar to the one used in the laser specs but much smaller, which was designed to zap any inferior tea particles, leaving what was, scientifically speaking, the ultimate cuppa. It had taken hours, but without thinking he ripped half of the mechanism out and threw it into the bin.

'Er, Nate,' said Cat, looking at him with a single cocked eyebrow. 'What are you doing?'

'You'll see,' he said, fiddling around in his parts drawer for a fresh computer chip and slotting it into the data entry point of the laptop. 'Just give me a moment.'

Taking a quick peek behind him to make sure the robots weren't looking in his direction, Nate started typing in the code for a fresh program. Instead of giving the laser instructions to target tea molecules, he gave it specific coordinates, ones that would hit the bottom of the standard-size Saint Solutions tea cup hard enough to leave a permanent mark.

Taking his time, and triple-checking to make sure the laser would strike the right place, he wrenched out the processor and jammed it into the tea machine so hard that it almost snapped in two.

Cat didn't take her eyes off him as he wired up the new card to the laser, sloppily soldering the joints and then slamming the front panel closed. He span round to the nearest robot.

'Tea cups,' he shouted. 'Twenty-two of them, now.'

The robots had been appointed as sentries but, thankfully, they were still programmed to help out the young inventors as they carried on with their experiments. With what sounded like a sigh, the hulking beast stomped off in the direction of the kitchens.

Trembling with anticipation, Nate climbed on to his chair

and coughed loudly several times until everyone in the room was looking at him.

'I've cracked it,' he said, looking at each of the tired, scared faces in turn. 'Prepare to taste the best cup of tea in the world!'

Cat glanced at the machine, which was dripping metal from the soldering iron and which now looked about as clean and appetising as the underside of a bus. Nate threw her a look that told her to stay quiet, and she recognised it straight away, returning to her own work.

Five minutes later and the robot walked daintily back into the room, twenty-two tea cups hanging off its elongated fingers by their handles. Nate couldn't help but laugh at the ridiculous sight before sliding them off in twos, and slamming them on the desk. He hit the button to warm up the tea machine, stuffed a handful of fresh leaves in the special compartment at the top and slid a mug under the spout, in the direct path of the laser.

'I hope your taste buds are in good working order,' he shouted over his shoulder, 'because this is going to be heavenly, and you are going to love me for it.'

Jabbing a finger at the activation button, Nate heard the laser firing up. He watched as the tea was dropped into the cup inside a special strainer, and the steaming water started to pour in. Sensing the rising heat, the laser began to fire minuscule points of light designed to eradicate unwanted molecules.

Thirty seconds later the machine pinged like a microwave, signalling that the brew was finished. Nate removed the first cup and handed it to Cat.

'I guarantee that this is the best cuppa you've ever had,' he said, grinning at her.

Cat took a sip, pulled an expression that looked as though she'd just eaten a dog turd and spat a mouthful of tea back in Nate's direction. It hit him square in the face, drenching him.

He wiped off the tea and spit with the back of his hand and turned around nervously to see the robots stepping closer, sensing that something was up.

'Nate, what the hell is –' Cat started, but he interrupted.

'Cat,' he said, speaking very slowly and ignoring the sensation of cooling tea dripping off his nose. 'This *is* the best cup of tea you have ever tasted in your whole life.'

She looked at him for a second before it sunk in. Grimacing, she downed the rest of the vile drink, which tasted like burning china. As she took the last sip she peered into the mug, spotting the brown, uneven pockmarks in the white base.

The tiny dots spelled out four words: D'S 2MORO 07.30. ESCAPE.

Wiping her mouth with the back of her hand, Cat made appreciative sounds and rubbed her stomach, watching out of the corner of her eye as the robot backed away.

'That is fantastic,' she said, breaking into a grin. 'Nate, you're a genius.'

Getting everybody else in the room to drink their tea proved to be a nightmare. While some of the young inventors got the hint straight away, slurping down the horrible liquid with a forced smile and quickly scanning the message at the bottom of the mug, others didn't have a clue what was going on.

Little Ainsley took one sip and turned green, ranting for a good five minutes about how the country was famous for its tea, and how Nate's creation was a travesty. Eventually Cat marched up to him, held back his head and practically poured the hot liquid down his gob, waving the empty mug before him until he nodded.

Lucy, meanwhile, who claimed she was allergic to tea, drank it anyway, sensing that something was going on. She read the message then promptly broke out in huge red spots and started foaming at the mouth.

It was only when the entire group had read and understood the code that Nate realised he hadn't thought about what to do with the evidence. As they all stood there trying to think of compliments for the drink to keep the robots' suspicions at bay, he considered what would happen if one of the guards discovered the secret instructions, or if, worse still, Saint went to make himself a cup of tea later that day only to find those words at the bottom of his mug. The game would be over, and it would almost definitely mean the end of twenty-three pairs of parents.

It was Cat who thought of the solution, pulling out her bin and slamming the cup down inside, so hard that it shattered into pieces. When the robots glared at her, golden eyes raging, ready to pounce, she explained that it was Greek tradition to smash crockery at times of celebration. Cat wasn't Greek, and had made the fact up based on a book she had once read, but it seemed to put the metallic sentries at rest, and with the deafening sound of smashing china the entire group slam-dunked their mugs into their waste bins until all that remained were splinters and dust.

The commotion was loud enough to cause Saint to come running into the room from where he had been working in the main lab.

'Celebrations, eh?' he asked, obviously delighted. 'I knew you'd all come round! Keep it up, you little monkeys!'

And with that he dashed back out.

Nate couldn't believe how easy the secret communication had been, how simply they had fooled the robot guards. But then, they were inventors, he thought, smiling proudly as he sat back down. Working out clever ways to make life easier was what they did best.

In fact, the hardest part of the entire operation was returning to work. There was a noticeable shift in the mood of the room as the group realised escape was possible. Of course, everybody had seen what had happened to David previously when he had tried to make a break for it, but this time something was different. It wasn't that they stood a better chance, it was that they were desperate to escape. And once they were out, they could alert the authorities to Saint's demonic plan. It was now or never, everything or bust. And they wanted to go out fighting for survival, not begging for their lives.

Nobody could focus on what they were doing. Glasses were knocked off tables, absentminded inventors leaning back on their chairs fell painfully to the floor, potions exploded creating black clouds that hovered in the air for ages, even Clint was so excited that his holographic image spent the day dancing around on the watch screen, humming the same tune again and again.

Thankfully, however, nobody made any mistake that would give the game away. Despite the thought of escape being on everybody's minds, it left nobody's mouth.

At half past five on the dot the competition winners began to filter out of the lab, making their way back to the living quarters. Nate stood up to follow the crowd, stretching and holding out his hand to pull Cat up from her chair, but she stayed put, still working on the electromagnetic amplifier. She had completely remodelled it after they'd tested the last one with disastrous results, and Nate couldn't make out what she'd done with it. But then, she was the clever one.

'It's okay,' Nate said, dropping his hand to his side. 'You don't have to do that now.'

'It's nearly finished,' she said. 'Might as well go out on a

 346

good note, stop Saint getting suspicious. Give me another hour. I'll meet you upstairs.'

Nate nodded and headed out, leaving Cat alone in the lab save for a sole remaining robot. He walked to the lift, noting that Saint was still running round the lab barking orders and screaming with excitement. When the lift doors opened out on to the living quarters he strolled back to the chalet but stopped when he rounded the corner, looking at the paradise before him.

A myriad of different emotions fought for control inside him. He thought back to the day they had found out about the competition – a day that felt like years ago – to the moment they arrived, and the realisation that they had won, to their first glimpse of the place where they thought they'd be spending the next year of their lives, to their first one-on-one conversation with a hero, a saint.

Although the vast screens that they had believed to be windows had been switched off since the day David flew into one, the ambient late afternoon lighting was on. It was the same colour as a winter sunset, making the entire chamber glow as if it was made up of orange, flickering embers.

Above him the birds still chased one another playfully, oblivious to the events taking place around them. The sound of trickling water from the brook beside the path made him realise how tired he was, how much he just wanted to collapse.

Only one more night, he told himself. Whatever happened, for good or for bad, he knew in the pit of his stomach that this would be the last night he would spend inside Saint's headquarters. He didn't know if he'd ever see his own bed again, if he'd ever have breakfast with his parents, or see his dad's face covered in porridge, or hear their angry shouts as they discovered his latest assault on the plasterwork. But he swore, then and there on the terracotta path, that he'd die escaping rather than remain here another day.

He briefly checked out David's place from a distance to make sure he hadn't been found out, but the sound of welding irons blazing from within let him know things were still okay. David had carried the second proton accelerator down himself that afternoon, telling Travis that he'd have to work through the night to get the last couple done in time for the attack and demanding no interruptions. It looked like his request was being honoured.

Nate was terrified that the robots would discover what David was really working on, or that Saint would pay him a visit and uncover the Barleymobile. But nobody seemed interested in the boy; everybody assumed that he had been broken, that he no longer had the will to escape. If he could just keep up the ruse for one more night . . .

Nate was swinging to and fro on the aerial slide an hour and a half later when he saw Cat approaching him from the lift. She looked tired but happy, and held in her hands two identical copies of the device she'd been working on for Saint. Nate hopped off and offered Cat the suspended seat, which she took gratefully.

'So, you finished it then,' Nate said as Cat pushed herself lazily along to his wall, kicking out and whizzing back towards her own chalet. She bounced and came to a halt in the centre.

'Done and done,' she said, holding it out. 'I even made two for good luck. I just hope we never have to see him use them.'

From one of the chalets nearby they could hear music, and laughter, and they realised it was the first time in weeks that their fellow inventors had been celebrating. Even though a dozen of Saint's assistants guarded the living area, their muzzles bared as they patrolled the paths, it was as if a weight had been lifted. They listened to the sound, relishing it.

'I hope they've got good reason to be cheerful,' said Cat.

'Well,' Nate replied, hesitantly, 'it's either going to be home free, or the end of the world. Either way, they might as well have fun.'

They both laughed.

'We should do the same, I guess,' said Cat, quietly. Nate looked down at her, stared deep into her eyes and saw an expression in them he'd never noticed before, one that threatened to melt every bone in his body, and made his heart swell. He didn't have a word for it, couldn't explain it, but he seemed to know it. He took her hand and they entered his chalet, taking a seat on a reclining chair in the main room. Nate wrapped his arms around her and she curled into him, and they sat like that for what seemed like a wonderful eternity.

Eventually Nate felt Cat drift off in his grip and held her even more tightly. It could well be their last day on earth tomorrow, but he didn't care. At this precise moment in time he was sitting with the best friend anyone could ask for, somebody he trusted with his life, somebody he wanted to spend every waking second with from now until oblivion. Nobody could ever take that away from him.

Beaming, Nate rested his head on Cat's hair, feeling the gentle touch of sleep. He didn't resist, and with a deep, shuddering sigh he closed his eyes and drifted away.

47

Judgement Day

Morning came around far too quickly. Waking to feel a painful crick in his neck from sleeping practically upright in the chair, Nate wiped the sleep from his eyes to see that he was alone in the room. Terrified for a moment in case he had slept in again, he glanced at his watch. Clint was sitting on the edge of the screen, dangling his feet over the edge and resting his head in all four of his hands.

'What time is it?' he asked the little robot, but Clint simply stared back up at him.

'Time you got me out of this watch and into a new body,' he said, irritated. 'Do you think I want to spend eight hours every night staring at you slobbering on your pillow.'

'Clint!' Nate snapped, still afraid that he'd missed the escape attempt and that everyone had left without him. Muttering something that Nate couldn't make out, Clint vanished for a second to be replaced by the time. He saw to his relief that it was only six-thirty.

'And where's Cat?'

'What am I, a concierge?' asked Clint, but when he saw Nate's furious look he answered, 'She said she had work to do. She's gone down to the lab.'

He had a shower to try and wake himself up, setting the temperature to cool and forcing himself to stand in the powerful blast of water for a good ten minutes in order to clear the fog from his mind. He would have to have his wits about him today; his brain had to be sharp, clear, if they were to stand any chance of defeating Saint.

While drinking tea in the kitchen he thought long and hard about what he needed to do. If David's plan worked, and he managed to carry them all to safety, it still left Saint free to send his bombs out into the world. They might well be able to alert the authorities to the diabolical plan once they were out in the open, but Nate doubted whether they'd be quick enough to stop it. The bombs were so small that once they had left the compound they could ride to their destination in even the smallest of cars. They would never be found.

The thought forced him to confront what he had been doing his best to ignore – the fact that somebody had to find a way to destroy the bombs. Somebody had to stay behind. With David flying the ship, he knew that the only people who would even be willing to consider the idea were himself and Cat. Up until now he had tried his best to believe that somebody else would stop the master inventor, that the army would turn up at the last minute and abseil in through the roof, that tanks would crash through the walls and arrest Saint like in some James Bond movie. But it wasn't going to happen. The fate of the world lay in their hands.

At seven o'clock he peered out of his window to see several young inventors strolling over to the dining area, as they did every morning. Gradually, more and more followed. Nate made his way out of the door, joining them and sitting on a bench, looking out for Cat. She was nowhere to be seen.

Nate was relieved to see that the hall was apparently free of robots, apart from two that were taking breakfast orders as usual. He wasn't hungry, but asked for an omelette and a glass of milk when the metal monster approached him. It stomped off, and Nate glanced through the trees in the direction of

David's chalet, praying that he had managed to finish their escape vehicle.

At ten past seven Nate saw Cat emerge, looking flustered, from the direction of the lift. She crashed down on the bench panting, slamming one of the electromagnetic amplifiers in front of him.

'Where the hell have you been?' he asked. She drew a deep breath and started talking, trying to be as quiet as possible.

'Downstairs,' she said. 'Saint's got all his bombs in the lab. There's hundreds of them, Nate. There's enough there to wipe out every major city in the world.'

He felt a chill run up his spine, and tried not to think about the damage, the billions dead.

'Saint was down there, he looked delirious,' she continued. 'He's really going to do this. He's going to kill everyone.' She paused, holding up the remaining amplifier. Nate noticed that it was beeping softly. 'I gave him one of these, told him to leave it next to the bombs, that it would help charge them up. He was so excited that he barely even noticed I was there, and he didn't even look at what I'd made. He just left it where I told him.'

Nate looked down at the device she was holding. He recognised the electromagnetic components, the small dial showing EM activity, the pulse reader. But there was something wrong with it, something he couldn't quite put his finger on.

'Cat,' he asked slowly, looking around to make sure there were no robots in earshot. 'What have you made?'

She smiled nervously and tapped the small box against the table, using her other hand to imitate what looked like an explosion. He realised straight away what she was indicating, knew instantly that the box wasn't designed to amplify electromagnetic rays: it was designed to disrupt them. It was an EMP, an electromagnetic pulse, and the quiet beeps meant that it was on a timer.

'Oh God,' he said. 'How long?'

'Forty minutes,' she replied. 'We've got forty minutes to get out of here.'

Nate thought about the bombs, thought about the electrical mechanisms that were used for detonation, the proton accelerators that were sensitive to the slightest variation in electromagnetic activity. He could picture the small, devastating purple cases stacked up downstairs, ready for dispersal around the globe, and knew exactly what would happen when Cat's device fired off its electromagnetic shockwave in forty minutes' time. Invisible, undetectable, the pulse would travel through the bombs at the speed of light, disrupting the sensors, setting them off and reducing the entire building to purple ashes within seconds. He hoped that they really were a long way underground, otherwise Cat would be also responsible for destroying most of the city.

And if David's flying machine wasn't ready, they'd all be incinerated as well.

But Nate trusted his best friend, and knew that she'd pull through. So long as there were no disruptions in the next ten minutes, they'd be okay.

Seconds later, Ebenezer Saint walked in.

It took a while for the chatter in the dining area to fade away as the young inventors noticed Saint standing there. The mood instantly changed from one of nervous excitement to one of fear. He was accompanied by seven robots, all normal size but all looking ferocious. Nobody so much as breathed. Had he found out? Was he about to unleash his hordes on them and their loved ones?

Saint stood for a moment, looking at the terrified expressions before him, then burst out laughing.

'If looks could kill,' he shouted, 'then I'd be as dead as a doornail right now.'

He began stumbling around across the terrace, holding his neck as if he was choking, eventually collapsing on to a table and sending dishes flying.

'I don't know what could possibly be wrong with you all,' he continued, lying on his back on the surface and staring at the ceiling. 'You're about to be a part of the biggest thing to happen to this planet since, well, since it formed 4.6 billion years ago. What I wouldn't have given to have had a chance like this at your age.'

He flipped himself off the table and strolled back to his escorts.

'Come on,' he shouted. 'Get your groove on, give me a smile, let's get this party started!'

There were a few nervous chuckles and Saint pulled an expression of disgust.

'Fine, be like that. I'll enjoy this bash by myself. I can have fun as Mister Ebenezer-no-mates. You just wait – when I'm the only person left to talk to, you'll soon come a-running.' He started walking back to the lift. 'I'm going to make some final preparations, relax, have a drink. We're going to roll out this afternoon, and you'll all be there to help. But I still want to see you at your desks this morning – there are things we need to finish.'

There was an audible release of breath as Saint disappeared around a grove of trees, his robots clanking after him. Seconds later, however, his head popped out from behind a bush, grinning.

'Oh wait,' he shouted to them down the path. 'I've got a good one.' He paused, coughing, then said dramatically, 'I don't know why you all look so down, it's not the end of the world!'

And with a deranged howl of laughter he vanished. The sound of the lift doors closing let them know that this time he really had gone.

'I thought he was going to stay,' said Nate, realising that all the blood had drained from his face. 'That would have been the end of that.'

'But he didn't,' answered Cat, checking her watch to see that it was twenty-five minutes past seven. 'And it's time to go.'

Slowly, several of the young inventors got to their feet, including Nate and Cat. Others stayed where they were, not wanted to desert the dining area too quickly for fear of alerting the two robots who were busy collecting dishes.

Trying not to look behind them, Nate and Cat led the small crowd towards the lift, turning at the last minute and taking the path that led back to the chalets. There was no robotic cry of surprise from the terrace, no sound of pounding metal feet. Ducking behind the first of the small houses Nate ushered the inventors forwards with his hand, sending them scampering across the grass to David's chalet. He stood at the door, looking exhausted but eager, raising a thumb at Nate.

When the first batch of inventors had made it through the door, Nate peered around the side of the chalet, watching a string of teenagers make their way towards him, stretching and yawning and trying to look as blasé as possible. Scanning the distant dining terrace through the trees, he saw that there were only two or three people left at the tables, and he willed them to hurry up before the robots realised what was happening.

The second group filed past him and into the chalet. David hissed at Nate, mouthing the words 'how many more' when he turned around. Nate held up three fingers then returned his gaze to the terrace. The last inventors had started making their

355

way along the path. It looked as if they were going to make it.

But as they reached the junction and turned towards the chalets, Nate saw the robot look up from the table, its golden eyes following their path. For a second it looked as though it might just let them go, but then some clause in its internal programming kicked in, and with terrifying speed it expanded to full size and practically leapt across the ground, crunching to a halt in front of the three terrified inventors.

For a moment there was silence, then one of the three, Lynsey, stepped towards the robot, a resolute expression on her face.

'We just need to get some equipment from our chalet,' she said. Her tone was firm, but even from where Nate was standing he could hear a tremor in her voice. 'We've got to help Saint get ready for the attack. He needs us to finish the clean-up device we've been working on or there will be a delay. And there can't be any delays.'

The robot didn't move, silently considering the words, her expression, assessing whether or not the girl was telling the truth. After what seemed like forever it turned away, convinced, and stomped back to the terrace. It took the three inventors every drop of willpower in their bodies not to run towards the chalet, and with painful slowness they eventually made their way through David's door.

'Come on,' David said, waving frantically at Nate and Cat. Smiling at each other, they sped through into the chalet.

The sheets had all been pulled down, and the floor cleared to allow for a smooth take-off. The gleaming ship sat proudly in the middle of the giant room, tilted up on a small framework of steel so that its two boosters were pointing down at the ground at a slight angle. Inside, cramped together in the tiny space, were twenty-one delighted faces. David held open the door for Cat, whose expression was one of shock at seeing the Barleymobile.

'I can't believe you did it!' she said to David, kissing him on the cheek as she raised her foot and placed it on the frame, ready to haul herself onboard. Nate noticed that she was still holding the photo of her dad, and he hoped that it would bring them good luck. 'Do you really think you can fly this thing?'

'I hope so,' answered Clint from Nate's watch. The little holographic robot was straining his four arms out to try and touch the ship's glittering body.

'I'm going to give it my best shot,' David replied. 'It's not going to be a comfortable ride, I'm afraid. It will get hot in there, and bumpy, and we may all die before we even get out of this chamber, but that's better than staying here, right?'

'Right!' said Nate and Cat together. Nate placed a hand on David's shoulder, speaking softly. 'But you do know a way out?'

'I found it, Nate,' David said just as quietly. 'I found the air vents. I knew they had to be somewhere. If this place is underground then it needs air from outside, and there are giant pipes designed to pump it in. They're in the lift shaft. You can hear them when you're travelling up and down. We're going to have to crash through the wall pretty hard, but my lady's made of reinforced steel so I think she can take it.'

He slapped the ship twice on the booster nearest to him. From the rattle it gave off it didn't sound terribly robust, but David seemed not to notice.

'Now,' he said, 'are we going to stand here talking all day, or are we going to blow this joint?'

But no sooner had he stopped talking than a vast explosion rang out behind them, so loud and bright that Nate thought his head was being crushed. The force of the blast blew him forwards, slamming him into the side of the ship. Falling to a heap, he wrenched open his eyes, ignoring the agonising pain, and saw Cat beside him, bloodied and still but groaning. David was buried beneath a mountain of brick and plaster. From the hatch

357

in the ship he could hear the sound of screaming, and he soon saw why.

Where the front of the chalet had once been there was now a giant hole. And through it, staring at them with a look of pure, terrifying malice, was Saint.

48

Game Over

He stood in front of an army of robots, their hulking bodies blocking the light from outside the chalet. In his hands he held Travis's laser gun, the tip smoking gently from the force of the blast that had all but demolished one side of the building. Travis, his face expressionless as always, stood by his side.

'Well, why am I not surprised?' he hissed. He was so angry that his whole body shook, his eyes enormous, unblinking, insane. 'I guess this is what you get when you recruit a bunch of *inventors*.' He shouted the last word, spit flying from his mouth. 'Constant trouble.'

He raised his head to the ceiling and let loose a cry of rage, one that chilled Nate to the bone and made him cower back against the side of the ship, which had survived the blast with little more than a large dent. It was over. The master inventor was going to kill them.

Saint passed the gun to Travis and strode forwards into the chalet. The first thing he did was pluck one of Cat's image-alteration devices from the rubble, where it was still attached to the camera.

'And this,' he said, crushing the device with his long fingers and throwing the pieces to the floor. 'I was building these when I was still in nappies. How dare you try and fool me in my own home.'

He darted across the chalet. Nate tried to move away but the ship blocked his path, and he was powerless as the giant man grabbed him by the throat and wrenched him out of the rubble. Saint's arms may have been scrawny, but he lifted Nate as though he was a rag doll, his fingers like iron around the boy's throat.

'And I am very, very disappointed in you,' he said, raising Nate up so that he was staring straight into his eyes. Nate couldn't breathe. He slapped his hands against Saint's arms, his head, but to no avail. The master inventor seemed not even to feel the blows. His eyes bored into Nate's, a vision of hatred. Trying to draw in breath, he realised that Saint's ferocious expression was going to be the last thing he ever saw.

But just as the world started to go black Saint released his grip, throwing Nate effortlessly out of the chalet to one of the robots that stood several metres behind him. He managed to suck in a glorious lungful of air before crashing into the steel body, feeling its long fingers grip his rib cage, squeezing.

He shouted in pain, trying to prise the fingers loose, but he couldn't move them so much as a millimetre. Clint was standing on the watch face, trying to pound the robot with his four fists, but his holographic arms were powerless. The pressure on Nate's ribs was agonising; he felt like he was being crushed alive, and something hard and sharp was pressing into his chest. Held like this, high above the ground, Nate saw Saint step forward and pull Cat from the wreckage in the same barbaric fashion.

'Don't you hurt her,' Nate tried to shout, but his constricted chest couldn't find the strength to make the words anything more than a whisper.

'Oh and what a shock,' Saint said, dangling Cat in front of him, ignoring the kicks that she fired in his direction, the defiant gob of spit that struck him in the cheek. 'The two little peas in a pod, working together, trying to upset my plans. Oh lah-de-dah-de-dah.'

He prised open Cat's fingers and snatched the photo of her

dad, using his teeth to shred it into pieces.

'And don't think Daddy's gonna come and help his little darling daughter,' he said, spitting the flakes of paper to the ground. 'He's *dead*!'

Cat started to scream with rage but stopped when Saint threw her out of the chalet with the same casual disregard. Nate saw a robot snatch out its arm and grab her from the air, wrapping its steel digits around her stomach and squeezing tightly. She groaned in agony, making the same futile efforts to pull the fingers loose.

'And the rest of you,' he shouted, peering in through the ship's hatch, banging his hand on the steel and seeming to relish the screams from within. 'You're pathetic, like sheep. Not a spine among the lot of you. I give you the world and look at how you repay me. You get the chance to change the course of history and what do you do? Cram yourselves into a coop and bury your heads in the hope of escape. You make me SICK. Only one inventor with any guts among you,' he threw a glance at Travis, his expression softening for a moment. 'Only one.'

Nate saw Saint turn away and scan the chalet, looking for something.

'Oh Davie-boy,' he called out. 'Where are you, you little worm? Killing your parents not enough, was it? Well how about you show your fat little face and we'll let you watch as everybody else's mumsies and dadsies get their heads chewed off. How would you like that?'

Nate saw a pile of rubble inside the chalet, inches away from Saint's left foot, start to move. It was only the slightest of shifts, but he realised that David was underneath, alive. There was still a chance that the inventors in the ship might make it to safety, but not if Saint detected the figure coming round beneath him.

His head was pounding from the explosion, he could still barely breathe because of the grip around his chest, and he found it almost impossible to get his thoughts in order, but he struggled to think of a distraction. Saint was livid, stomping around the rubble trying to locate David, his eyes wild, his mouth foaming.

Nate suddenly recalled an incident many years ago at Cat's house, when she had flown into a rage after not being able to finish an extremely complicated wind-up toy. She had picked it up and thrown it to the ground, stamping on the pieces until they were dust. Her dad had quietly held her until she had calmed, before explaining that anger could never be anything but harmful, that rage could only ever be destructive.

If anything was going to be Saint's undoing, it was his temper.

'Did you think any of us were actually going to help you?' Nate shouted, struggling for breath and once again trying to wrench himself from the iron grip. Saint turned around and stared at him. 'Help a madman like you, help destroy everything we've ever loved? You're crazy, Saint.'

The master inventor began walking out of the chalet towards Nate. His look was enough to make the young inventor cower against the robot, his entire body shaking uncontrollably, but he kept going, trying not to look as David's bruised face appeared from the rubble.

'You're alone, Saint,' Nate continued. 'That's why there's nobody here, that's why you replaced every single living thing in your life with machines, nobody else could possibly agree with you, nobody would go along with this insane plan.'

All eyes were on Nate as he continued his tirade, even Cat's. She looked at him as Saint approached, shaking her head, willing him to stop before he was killed. The robots were also staring at him, their muzzles dripping as though awaiting the order to bite off his head. Travis Heart was the only person who was still gazing at the chalet, at the pile of bricks and glass that was gradually crumbling away to reveal a person.

 362

'Even Travis,' Nate blurted out, the robot's grip like rods of steel against his ribcage. Hearing his name, Travis snapped up his head from the chalet and turned to face Nate, scowling. 'Even good old Travis Heart here doesn't want to help you. We've all heard him boasting, telling us he's using you for your weapons, for your wealth, that eventually he's going to get rid of you, become the next master inventor.'

Saint, his eyes practically bulging from their sockets, glared down at Travis. The boy had never said anything of the sort, not to Nate's knowledge anyway, but in his current state Saint looked as though he'd have killed him even for the idea being suggested.

'That's a lie!' Travis shouted, stuttering, his gaze swinging back and forth from Nate to Saint. 'That's a damn lie. I've never said anything like that.'

It was the first time Nate had seen Travis look scared, and it made him want to laugh. But he tried to remain focused, looking past Saint's shoulder to see David getting slowly to his feet, shaking his head and wiping the blood from his eyes. He looked stunned, but when he saw the confrontation going on outside he knew exactly what to do. Quietly closing the ship's hatch, and still unseen by the crowd outside the chalet, he crept round to the far side, climbing into the cockpit.

'Don't be bashful, Travis,' Nate went on. 'Saint likes people with a bit of guts, a bit of ambition, remember. I'm sure he won't object to your plans.'

Travis was gripping the laser gun so hard his knuckles had gone white. He hoisted it to his shoulder and pointed it at Nate. It was terrifying, but Nate knew he had to distract them for only a moment longer. Cat was calling his name but he ignored her, watching as Saint bounded over to stand above Travis.

'This true?' he asked. 'You better tell me, Heart. I don't want to wake up one morning and find a knife in my back and you running my show.'

Travis didn't take his eyes off Nate, didn't move the gun an inch.

'You know it isn't,' came his cool reply. 'He's lying.'

Nate suddenly realised what it was that was digging into his chest. He moved his fingers to the breast pocket of his overalls and tugged at the plastic frame inside, all the while keeping eye contact with the enraged Travis. The laser specs were a little bent, but they still looked in good working order. He placed them nervously on his head.

'You wouldn't shoot a kid with glasses?' he said weakly, forcing a bark of laughter from Travis.

'Believe me, Wright,' he hissed, 'I would. But I'd take them off if I were you. You're not going to want to see this coming.'

Saint looked as if he was prepared to give his protégé the benefit of the doubt, and turned his attention back to Nate. Fortunately, both crazed inventors were too furious to remember that he didn't wear glasses. Pretending to scratch his head, he pressed the button to turn on the generator.

Inside the chalet, David had shut the cockpit's glass screen. He looked at Nate sadly, knew that he couldn't do a thing for him or Cat. It didn't matter, Nate thought, staring into the barrel of the gun as it charged, watching the colourful clouds as they all gradually turned purple. He wondered if being shot with a laser would hurt, or if it would be over before he even knew what was happening.

What came next did so with such speed that Nate couldn't follow it. David fired up the proton accelerators inside the ship. At exactly the same moment, Travis pressed the trigger of the laser gun, and with a sickening hum the purple clouds inside shot forwards, ready to be unleashed.

Trying not to scream in sheer terror, Nate pressed the button on his glasses and fired out a minuscule crimson ray. It impacted with the end of Travis's gun just as a beam of purple light blasted out of the end.

The shot from the laser specs did just enough, nudging down the tip of the gun so that the devastating beam missed its target and instead struck the robot that was holding Nate. He felt the world erupt, felt himself flying through the air, and for a moment everything went black.

Gradually the sounds of chaos dragged him back to reality. Shaking the drowsiness from his head, he opened his eyes and saw Saint screaming in rage, saw the robots running forward, saw Travis frantically trying to recharge the gun, saw Cat fighting to free herself and looking desperately in Nate's direction.

He had been blown backwards a good twenty metres by the blast, and lay on his front pinned down by the bulk of the robot, which straddled him, motionless. Looking round he saw that the creature's legs had been obliterated by the laser, and that, incredibly, his own body seemed intact.

The laser specs hadn't been so lucky, and the broken pieces were scattered across the ground between him and the chalet. His watch was also in a bad shape. The holographic Clint was sprawled over the ground, flickering on and off as the projector struggled to cope. The little robot managed to look up, one arm waving at Nate and the other three rubbing his head as he crawled sluggishly back inside the screen.

Ahead of Nate, David's ship was powering up – the proton accelerators making the ground tremble violently – but one of the robots had the craft in its vice-like grip, its long fingers bending the metal as if it was paper.

'Stop them!' he heard Saint cry. 'Do not let that ship off the ground. And Travis, shoot them for God's sake!'

But Travis's gun was still charging, and only one of the robots could fit inside the chalet. Another was busy smashing through the side wall, trying to get to the chrome craft inside. With nothing to support it, the roof was threatening to crum-

365

ble. Through the cockpit window, Nate saw David slamming his fist down on the ignition switch.

Nothing happened. The ship still rumbled but no green flame emerged from the boosters. The second robot had almost demolished the side wall, seeming not to feel the bricks and mortar that crashed down on to it. Once it was inside, there would be no hope.

David reset the ship's ignition system then raised his hand again, looking out of the window at Nate. Tears streamed down his face, but Nate nodded at him to go. David saluted, then slammed down his hand.

This time, the ship's boosters erupted. A vivid green cloud blasted out of both rockets, instantly incinerating the side wall and sending the second robot hurtling backwards through three chalets behind it, tearing them to shreds.

The ship lurched forward, but stopped as the first of the metal beasts tensed its arm, holding it back. There was the awful sound of rending metal as the ship fought to free itself, rivets flying from the chrome body. The boosters fired a relentless pillar of light, the sound deafening, the green flames setting alight to everything behind, leaving a trail of fire that stretched out of the chalet for over a hundred metres.

Then, with a sound halfway between a crunch and a pop, the robot's arm was wrenched from its socket. Released from the grip, the ship lurched forwards through the chalet's other wall, the bricks and plaster exploding with the impact and the roof collapsing on to the metallic assistant inside. David lost control for an instant and the ship skidded along the floor, the sheer force of the boosters sending it crashing through two more chalets. But then he pulled up on the controls, sending the Barleymobile careering skywards.

'Shoot him shoot him shoot him!' Saint screamed. 'They're getting away!'

But it was too late. The silver craft did one loop high above the enormous room, building up speed, then descended with terrifying force towards the group of people and robots below it. Through the windscreen, David's face was twisted into a mask of concentration as he guided the shining vessel straight at Saint and Travis. Nate knew the look in his eye, and knew that David wasn't planning to leave without avenging the death of his parents.

Seeing what was happening, Saint leapt athletically out of the way, jumping like a cat until he was hidden behind the wall of a chalet. But Travis wasn't so quick. He was glaring at his laser gun, shaking it impatiently as he waited for it to charge.

It was only when the ship was metres away that he sensed it, and looked up to see the vehicle dropping towards him. He froze, helpless, as the chrome shape passed over his head with inches to spare. Then David pulled up sharply, and Travis was lost in the green light of the boosters. When the ship had risen, nothing remained of the boy except ashes.

David swung the craft around and headed for the lift shaft. With an enormous crash it burst straight through the double doors, bending the metal inwards, then performed an impossibly sharp upward turn, ripping through the top of the lift car and blasting upwards into the dark tunnel.

All but one of the lift cables snapped and the car hung for a moment, groaning as it tried to hold up its own weight, then the last cord gave and it crashed downwards, the sound gradually fading into echoes, then disappearing.

The only noise in the living area was the roar of the fires that raged around the chalets. The ship had made it, out of the room at least, and David knew where he was going, knew the escape route.

But it left Nate and Cat alone and trapped.

49

The Only Way Is Up

Saint walked slowly out from behind the chalet, his pale, expressionless face much older than Nate had ever seen it. He staggered to where Travis had been standing, crouching down beside the scorched ground and running his fingers through the green ashes. He lifted them to his face and watched as they drifted gently back to earth.

Nate tried to squirm free of the robot that was pinning him to the floor. The pain in his chest was agonising, and he wondered if he'd broken a rib. Ignoring it, he continued pulling, eventually managing to free his torso. But one of his legs was stuck fast, and he had no time to pull it free as Saint stood up and looked his way.

'Well,' the master inventor said, his voice a whisper. 'That's the end of him.' He stood and walked towards Nate, three of the robots hot on his heels, their golden eyes furious at having seen their mechanical comrades destroyed. 'And those other wimps have all flown the coop on that ridiculous machine, which I guess leaves you and your little girlfriend there.'

Saint loomed over Nate, bending down and grabbing him by his hair, pulling up his head so that he could look him in the eye.

'Since everybody else has deserted me, you two may as well do the same. By which I mean dying, of course.' Nate felt the heavy steel weight on his legs lifted as a robot grabbed its dead comrade and hurled its body effortlessly across the chamber. It wrapped its other fist around Nate's chest and lifted him into the air, making him scream with pain.

Reaching into his jacket, Saint pulled out a long, golden knife and held it to Nate's throat.

'You know, the knife is one of the oldest inventions on the planet,' he hissed. 'We've been using it to kill each other for millions of years. So I guess it's quite fitting that one inventor should use it to dispatch another. Yes?'

Nate began to struggle but it was no use. The robot held him tight. He looked up at Cat, ready to say goodbye, only to see her stretching her hand around the arm of the robot that held her, reaching for something in her pocket. She was staring back at him, scared but in control.

'I'd love to say that it has been a pleasure meeting you,' Saint continued, pressing the cold, sharp blade against Nate's throat hard enough to draw blood. 'But that would make me a liar.'

'Saint!' came Cat's cry as he began to draw the knife across Nate's skin. He stopped, looked around.

'Don't you worry, sweet pea, your turn's a-coming.'

But Cat had managed to retrieve the object from her pocket. It was the second EMP device. Nate had forgotten all about it. She held it up in the air, finger on the pulse button.

'You know what this is?' she asked, wincing as the robot tightened its grip. Saint studied it for a moment then snatched the knife away, moving swiftly across to where Cat was being held. He stopped in front of her, staring at the device with a nonplussed expression.

'Of course I do. It's the electromagnetic amplifier you've been working on,' he sneered. 'It's not going to do you much good now, unless you're planning to give an extra boost to my assistants here, and help them kill you a little more quickly. Of course you could probably throw it at me – it might give me a nasty old bruise on the noggin.'

But Cat ignored him. She pressed the button to warm up the device, and a shrill electronic whistle cut through the air.

'Look again,' she said. 'This doesn't amplify electronic equipment. It's a pulse, Saint. It destroys it.'

'You're bluffing, little girl,' Saint said, squinting as he took a second look at the device. But the expression on his face said it all. He recognised the design, he knew she was telling the truth. 'Well boo-hoo,' he said. 'That thing's got a range of fifty metres at most. It might knock out these guys here, but there's an army of robots downstairs ready to leap on their Antigravs and come and skin you alive.'

'True,' she answered, smiling. 'But then there's the little matter of the second one that I gave you earlier. Now where did you leave that? It wasn't downstairs was it? Not on the bombs? Oh my, that was stupid.'

Saint's face contorted into an expression of rage once again, and he raised the knife in her direction. But she simply grinned at him. Nate knew that it couldn't be long until the device downstairs emitted its charge, fifteen minutes at most. It might take them with it, but at least the world would be free of Ebenezer Saint – would be safe.

'Handy things, timers,' she said.

Saint whirled around to the nearest robot and started to bark instructions at it, but before he could say two words Cat pressed her thumb down on the button. The tiny machine whined, then beeped once as the electromagnetic pulse shot out.

It was invisible, but the immediate effect it had on the robots wasn't. They froze, the joints between their limbs sparking aggressively, the fire fading from their eyes, leaving empty black sockets. Nate felt the grip on his chest loosen and he tumbled to the floor, seeing Cat do the same.

Everything electrical in the room instantly short-circuited.

The lights in the chamber flickered brightly for a second before exploding, raining a shower of glass down on to the floor below. The huge room was pitch black except for the orange glow of the fires still raging in the chalets.

Nate grasped his ribs with one hand and scrabbled forwards, making out Cat's outline in the orange half-light ahead. She had returned to the chalet and was picking something up from the ground. Saint was between them, but he was stamping around furiously, slashing out with his knife, too angry to control his actions. Nate made his way around the demented master inventor in a wide arc, grabbing Cat by the arm. He saw that she had recovered a tiny shred of the photograph of her dad.

'You're both going to pay for this,' Saint bellowed, sweeping the golden knife through the air, screaming at the ceiling and stamping his feet. 'I'm going to kill you both. You're so dead and you don't even know it yet!'

Nate and Cat began to back away, but before they could find the path Saint's eyes had adjusted to the light. Spotting them, he lunged forwards, carving the air between them with his knife and slicing a hole in Cat's overalls. Screaming, she clutched at her side.

They ran, sprinting over the smouldering rubble as best they could. Nate held on to Cat's arm, ignoring the pain in his ribs, fighting to keep from passing out as they rounded the path that led to the ruined elevator. Saint was only metres behind, but he was struggling to stay upright on the wreckage-strewn floor, his long legs buckling several times as he sprinted carelessly after them. He was yelling commands, shouting for reinforcements, but whatever device he used to talk to his robots had been destroyed by the pulse.

'Where are we going?' Cat cried out as they reached the lift doors. They had been bent and buckled out of shape, a vast

 371

hole in the centre where David's ship had passed through. Nate wasn't sure what he was doing, but he knew there was an air shaft in there somewhere, one that could lead to freedom.

Saint gave them no time to think, sliding around the corner behind them and charging forwards again. Nate climbed through the ruined doors into the shaft, trying not to look at the black abyss that stretched out below him. He thought about how far the lift had descended to get to the robot level, and knew for sure that if he fell it would be instant death.

'Nate?!' Cat hissed. 'Not in there!'

'It's the only way, Cat,' he shouted back from inside. 'This whole place is going to blow. We have to try.'

He heard her scrabbling in behind him, standing on the tiny ledge and gripping the buckled doors. Saint had almost reached them – all he had to do was slash at their fingers and they'd fall. They had seconds to act.

It was dark in the shaft, but Nate could make out the shape of a maintenance ladder on the wall to the left of the doors. It looked as if it had been loosened by the force of the falling lift car, and the section that led to the floor below had completely disappeared – ragged holes in the concrete showing where it had been wrenched from the wall. The section that led to the upper floor was still intact, but didn't look like it would hold them both for long.

'He's right behind us,' Cat yelled, trying to edge away from the hole in the door. Nate swallowed deeply, took a deep breath and jumped.

For a second, there was nothing between him and the ground far below except air. He soared over the abyss, his heart pounding so loudly that he could barely hear anything else. He began to fall sooner than he had expected, feeling his stomach rise into his throat as he began to descend. He wasn't going to make it.

But throwing out his arms he managed to grasp hold of one of the rungs, the impact seeming to dislocate his shoulder, making his ribs burn. The ladder shook when he landed, but he held tight, scrabbling until he had a foothold, climbing up so that he was level with Cat. She shook her head, terrified.

'I can't,' she said.

'Pounce,' he told her. 'You can make it, it's not far. You've jumped three times this distance in PE.'

Closing her eyes, Cat pushed herself away from the ledge just as Saint appeared through the hole, slashing the air where she had been standing with his blade. Cat's leap was stronger than Nate's, and she practically landed on him, clutching at his arms as she fought to find a secure footing. She managed to grip a rung with one hand but the ladder rocked unsteadily, causing her foot to slip on the cold metal. For an instant, she hung above the black void.

'Oh God,' she said, looking down and scrabbling for a foothold in the dark. Her fingers were sliding from the rung. 'Nate, I can't hang on!'

'Just don't look down!' he shouted, grabbing her overalls with his free hand and pulling her towards him. Her right foot found purchase on the metal ladder and she tightened her grip, pressing her shaking body against his for a second before urging him onwards.

There was no time to congratulate her. Saint had started clambering through the hole, screaming curses at them. Nate set off up the ladder, climbing as fast as his injuries would let him, with Cat close on his heels. It was a long way up, but they had to try and find the ventilation shafts.

They made good progress, Nate only slipping once when he tried to climb two rungs at a time. Saint was furious, but it seemed to take him a while to work up the courage to make the leap, and they had a good head start by the time they felt the ladder shake as he landed on it. He couldn't descend to the lab, couldn't save his bombs. And Nate knew that even if the ladder had been intact Saint was too angry to think, too incensed to do anything other than chase them. With frightening speed, the master inventor began to climb.

Somewhere close above them Nate could hear the sound of machinery, and glancing up he saw two vast circular tunnels in the side of the shaft. One had a fan that was lazily rotating. The other had only a hole where David's ship had wrenched its way through. The circular vents were the way out, their escape route.

They were on the opposite side of the shaft.

50

You and Me Against the World

Nate stopped climbing and stared forlornly at the tunnels. The vents were too far away, and there wasn't even a ledge in this part of the elevator shaft that they could use to make their way round. It was over.

Below them, Saint was closing in, his lanky limbs hauling him up the ladder with frightening ease. Exhausted, Nate wondered if they should just jump. Rather die by their own hand, and that of gravity, than let Saint have his satisfaction.

But Cat had other ideas. She yanked Nate's trousers and pointed up ahead, where the doors to the next level were visible twenty metres or so above them, a faint glow spilling out into the lift shaft.

'Keep going,' she said, casting a nervous look down to where Saint was emerging from the darkness, his knife held between his teeth. 'I've got a plan.'

They carried on desperately, ignoring their aching limbs, fighting against the pain, until they reached the level of Saint's quarters. Stepping off the ladder and on to the ledge, they shuffled round carefully, clinging to the dirty wall for safety. Cat's EMP blast had been more powerful than they thought – short-circuiting everything on this floor – but thankfully the lift doors were open.

Clambering out into the long hallway beyond, they ran as fast as they were able, using the candlelight to avoid the lifeless animals. It was as they were scaling the enormous bulk of the elephant, which had collapsed on to the ground, that they saw Saint climbing from the shaft, his suit torn and filthy, his hair matted, his eyes those of a madman. Seeing them, he began to run.

'Hurry!' Nate said, pulling Cat over the side of the elephant, leading her past the last of the mechanical creatures to the part of the corridor they had walked to before. He slapped the wall furiously, the hidden door opened and they ran through into the smaller hallway beyond.

'I hope you know where we're going,' Nate said. He had no idea what the time was, but by his best estimation the second EMP was due to detonate in less than five minutes, and then they'd all be nothing but shadows and dust.

Cat ran past him, slamming into the double doors at the end of the corridor and almost tripping into the main hall. The giant room was silent, the fountain off, the screens that they had once thought were the curved windows of the dome black and viewless. She bolted to her left, kicking open the doors to the museum and running to the booth in the corner.

'You have to be joking,' Nate said as she turned to face him, flushed and panting.

But she was deadly serious. Pulling the velvet rope to one side she climbed on board the rickety wooden flying machine, Leonardo's masterpiece, and put her feet on the ancient pedals.

'It will never work,' Nate said, rooted to the spot. 'It's five hundred years old!'

Cat pushed down on the pedals and the machine moved slowly forward with a tired groan.

'It's this or nothing, Nate,' she said. 'And I know just how badly you want to see if this beauty will fly.'

He looked at her, bemused, but leapt on to the wooden glid-er when he heard the hall doors fly open and Saint's voice outside, demanding to know where they were. Sitting behind her, he held on to the worn wooden handles and placed his feet in the second set of pedals, pumping as hard as he was able. The flying machine began to pick up speed, its wings flapping absurdly.

'Did this ever actually fly?' Nate asked as they hurtled towards the large double doors, the rickety frame shaking so hard he thought his bones were knocking together.

'I have no idea,' came her nervous reply. 'But I doubt it!'

Barely squeezing through the double doors, the machine burst out into the main hallway. Saint, who was standing by the staircase, whirled around to see it crash across the floor, making for the corridor beyond. Livid, he bolted towards them.

The sight of the madman hot on their heels made them pedal even faster, and Cat steered the craft round the corner so sharply that it almost toppled, the wooden wheels straining against the axles. As they pedalled down the corridor the craft lifted off the ground, its large wings flapping like a giant bird's and occasionally scraping chunks from the red walls.

But they weren't going fast enough. Saint was hurtling after them, his long legs covering the ground with remarkable speed. They bolted through the door that led to the main corridor, which Saint fortunately had left open, skidding round the tight bend to find themselves staring at a gauntlet of lifeless animals ahead.

'Keep going,' Cat shouted. 'Just pedal with everything you have.'

They did, hearts pounding, lungs burning, muscles screaming out with pain. The wheeled craft sped down the corridor, rising up and soaring over a group of birds, knocking the head off a swan, before crashing back down and skidding along the floor.

It rose again almost instantly, so high this time that it

smashed into a chandelier, showering them with glass. Nate yelped as he found himself face to face with a robotic monkey, and threw it to the floor.

The flying machine dipped again, falling with such force that one of the three wheels snapped. The wooden frame threatened to grind to a halt but they kept pedalling, barely making it over the frame of the elephant. This time, they stayed airborne.

But when Nate looked back to check on Saint's progress he saw that the master inventor had sprung on to the elephant, launched himself from its back and was now hurtling through the air towards them. He impacted with the back of the flying machine, instantly pulling it down.

The open doors of the lift were only metres away. If they could just hang on. But Saint's weight was too much, and with a crunch the plane's rear end smashed into the ground, carving its way through the carpet and slicing the mechanical antelope in two.

Saint dug his heels in, holding on to the tail with all his strength, trying to slow them down, his eyes blazing.

'You're mine,' he hissed through the knife held in his teeth.

With a lurch the flying machine burst through the lift doors and out into the shaft. It began to drop immediately, whirling around out of control. It was too heavy, there were too many people. Nate swung around, and saw Saint's frantic attempts to hang on.

'We were never yours,' he said. Then, with one swift motion, he pulled the knife from Saint's lips and jabbed it at the fingers of the crazed inventor's left hand. With a scream, Saint let go, and almost immediately Cat managed to right the craft, bringing it round in a tight circle and directing it at the air vent below them.

Nate stared down as the shape of Saint vanished into the

black abyss of the shaft, the sight bringing him an incredible sense of relief.

But the sensation didn't last. From far below, on the floor where the lab was, came a sudden blinding purple light. It began to climb the shaft, swallowing Saint's body before it could hit the floor, and rising up towards them with devastating speed, tearing the very walls of the lift to pieces and making the building shake and groan.

'Er, Cat,' Nate said, mesmerised as the wall of colour charged towards them, destroying everything in its path. But she'd seen it, and guided the flying machine through the tunnel with no fan, speeding past the entrance and bouncing off one wall before managing to find a steady course. Borne on the wind that was being pushed out of the compound, the glider sped along the metal shaft.

Behind them, the light reached the entrance to the vent and began pouring down it, the very metal exploding into dust as soon as it was touched. The tunnel arced gently skywards, and they pedalled as fast as they could, the wings beating furiously as Leonardo's flying machine carried them up, Cat using the eerie purple light to see where she was going.

They weren't moving fast enough. The light was catching up, travelling at a crazy speed, less than thirty metres behind them and gaining fast. Nate tried not to look at it, tried to concentrate on pedalling, but he couldn't drag his eyes away, couldn't stop thinking about what it had done to the artificial city.

A cry from Cat dragged his gaze forwards again, and looking ahead he saw a light. It was only a pinprick, but as they sped onwards it grew, expanding until they saw a cavernous exit ahead. Beyond was the most glorious sight Nate had seen in his entire life: daylight – clean, bright, and real. He doubled his speed, and the craft accelerated towards the end of the tunnel, away from the purple glow.

Then, with a whoop of joy, Nate and Cat flew out of the pipe and into the cold, fresh air beyond. The machine started to drop, crashing to the ground and sending them both flying, rolling across a hard surface until they came to a painful halt against a rock.

Dragging his head up, Nate saw the purple light burst from the shaft and shoot off at an angle. With nothing but air to greet it, the destructive beam soon sputtered and faded, leaving a giant crater in the rock.

Inside, nothing remained of Saint Tower but purple dust.

Nate picked himself up and ran over to Cat, who had been thrown across the ground and was now lying in a motionless heap. He sat down next to her and gently lifted her off the cold earth so that her body was leaning against his. He could hear breathing, and sat for a moment, holding her tight. Eventually she opened her eyes, her face covered in blood, and smiled at him. In her hands she held a tiny scrap of photograph, a shred of glossy paper from which her dad's eye twinkled up at them.

'Did we make it, or is this just heaven?' she asked as Nate brushed a strand of hair from her eyes.

They looked around, shocked at the sight that greeted them. The city was nowhere in sight, and instead there stretched a vista of snow-covered peaks, dotted with rocky outcrops and sparse patches of vegetation. There was not another soul to be seen. Nate was about to answer when a tiny voice called up from his wrist.

'If this was heaven, then I wouldn't still be stuck in this watch.'

'Clint!' exclaimed Nate, lifting his arm so that Cat could see the tiny robot on the cracked screen. The image was weak, and flickering, but there was no doubt that Clint was in good working order.

'In the flesh,' the robot answered. 'Well, sort of.'

Laughing, Nate and Cat picked themselves up and stood in silence for a moment, assessing their injuries and taking a closer look at the view. There wasn't a single building in sight, but the sound of birdsong and the various creatures that scuttled nervously in front of them made it clear that the world hadn't come to an end.

'Saint Tower must have travelled here underground,' whispered Cat in awe. 'He must have dug tunnels.'

There was a pause as Nate thought about Saint, and his screaming face as it disappeared down the lift shaft.

'But where is here?' he asked, taking a deep breath and relishing the feeling of the cold, clean air entering his lungs.

It didn't matter. They'd escaped with their lives. They'd managed to stop Saint in his tracks, to kill him before he destroyed the planet.

'So,' said Cat eventually, 'we've saved the world then.'

'Yup,' Nate replied, wondering how they were ever going to find their way home. 'Does this mean we can still be against it?'

Cat turned to look at him and laughed, slotting her arm through his and leading him off down the rocky slope.

'Of course it does,' she said with a smile. 'It's always you and me, Nate, you and me against the world.'

Epilogue

Far below the ground, in a tiny section of the Saint Solutions compound that was always protected by shields and that not even the robotic assistants had known about, a red light began to blink on a control panel.

Gradually, the sound of machinery filled the air and lines of code began to emerge on the various computer monitors set into the walls. On one, a digitally generated profile of Ebenezer Saint appeared, the monitor zooming in to the smiling face.

A computer program began inputting code in small green letters on the screen:

Ebenezer Saint:

// Memories accessed //
// Personality downloaded //
// Personal data recovered //

The noise of the machinery increased as streams of data were processed before being fed into a small, quiet figure in the corner of the room. After a minute the data streaming stopped, and with the sound of pistons the human-shaped figure slowly raised its head. It had no face as such, but a pair of golden eyes stared out at the room.

'So,' it said to nobody in particular, its mechanical voice hesitant, shaky, 'I'm dead.'

The robot froze for a moment as it accessed the memories that had been transmitted seconds before it died. The golden eyes narrowed, burned. Then the creature got to its feet and made its way to the door. Beyond was a long tunnel leading upwards. Displayed on the screen in flashing green letters, were five words:

Ebenezer Lucian Saint reincarnation: successful.

Acknowledgements

The invention of this book was inspired by too many people to list here, but Gordon and Jamie would like to offer extra special thanks to the following: Lizzie Loukes and all the staff at Waterstone's in Norwich Arcade, who set the ball rolling, and everybody who helped us get to the shortlist of the Wow Factor competition – especially those judges who voted for *The Inventors*! Also everybody who kept us sane while writing (the Mario Kart Boys especially, you know who you are), everybody who helped shape our original manuscript into something presentable (Lynsey and Uncle Frank and their grammar machines), respective dads George Smith, who inspired Gordon with a love of storytelling and mystery when he was just a wee bairn, and Christopher Webb, who did the same for Jamie, Take Five for being the most relaxing place in the world, Lucie Ewin, Mandy Norman and Sue Mason for making the book look so gorgeous, plus the Faber team, who have made us both feel so welcome. The biggest thanks of all go to our wonderful editor Julia Wells – who turned our story into a real-life book and who, in doing so, made our wildest and longest-held dreams come true.

We love you all!